ΛUGMENT

Red Fever Book I

C R MacFarlane

To my sister
Wanda.
Love you
always.

ISBN 978-1-7753564-0-0

www.blueponypress.com

For Avery, who never gives up.

THE GIRL SAT ON THE cold, white floor, fluorescent lighting shining off the slick surface. Ropes of permanently matted hair hung over her face. Electric burn marks blistered across her arms and legs, visible around the tears in her stained jumpsuit. The wounds would heal by nighttime, ready to start fresh again in the morning.

If she closed her eyes, she felt the memory of straps running across her forehead and chest and legs, and the strange pulling sensation of being caught in a gravity trap, so she kept them open. Scratching a spot on her shoulder, she leaned into the feel of fingers against skin. Her hand felt nothing, dead and senseless where the nerves had been stripped away.

A solid bench functioned as a bed in the opposite corner, an open latrine the only other furniture in her small cell. The monitoring station was clearly visible through the fortified, full-length permaglass wall, and she observed them as much as the soldiers observed her.

The researchers didn't know what she was, not really, so they tried to bring it out, while she fought to keep it in.

She made a list of things she knew to be true: Name: Sarrin.

ID code: 005478F. Female. Born on Earth. Nineteen or twenty years old (as well as she could count, there were lapses of time gone from her mind). She was a prisoner of war — a forgotten remnant of a darker time.

Each day was the same: guards woke her, only to fill her small cell with sedative gas which she simply gave in to now. When she woke again, she would be strapped to a cold metal table, held down by a small-range artificial gravity well for extra security. They would run the day's experiment protocol, sometimes talking into a little microphone. She would distract herself with figures or facts until they gave up, inject sedative and return her to her cell. Later, they would bring her a meal — too little and the minerals artificial — and prepare for the next day.

She counted now the numbers of things: Guards: eleven. Cameras: twelve. Prisoners: one. Objects that could be used as lethal weapons: in here, zero, but in the observation room, thirty-eight. Possible escape routes: three.

But where would she go?

She had escaped once, early on. Through the ceiling, across the roof, the lawns, and over the nine-metre barrier wall. But there was nothing beyond.

The planet — identification unknown — was barren. Its red-purple, dusty surface blended into the hazy atmosphere, the horizon invisible and unchanging. She had run for hours without so much as a hill or crater. Even hardy brome grasses could not grow. There was nowhere to hide, no way to survive.

Eventually, the soldiers in their hovercrafts had dropped enough gas bombs that she had succumbed and awoken in her cell, as though nothing had happened. The routine resumed, day-in day-out, the only differences the dose of sedative and the meals which became less and less.

Her stomach rumbled. After three years, her body had become finely tuned to their schedule, and the United Earth Central Army soldiers ran like clockwork. The meal was never late.

A minute passed, then five, then ten. The seconds ticked off in her head.

She started to shake. Sweat beaded on her back.

In the monitoring station, all but one guard had disappeared. Her breathing quivered. Something had gone astray.

Her pulse pounded in her veins, each thump shaking her core. The beats came further apart, slowing.

No, that wasn't right. She looked at the single guard — he had slowed too. She was speeding up.

The trance, the monster she fought to keep caged within, called to her. A change in routine was unusual, dangerous. Darkness clouded around the edges of her vision threatening to take control.

She shut her eyes and started to count, reciting Fibonacci sequences to distract her brain. *1-1-2-3-5-8…* She couldn't let it take hold, not after all these years. Not for a late meal. *233-277-610-987—.* She lost count and her breath came in rags. Her finely tuned instincts screamed at her to stand and run. To fight.

She refused. She had to keep making them believe they had been wrong all these years; if they thought she was normal, maybe they'd let her go. But normal people couldn't do the things she could, she was certain. What would it be like to be normal? To live without the trance? To be somewhere not here? What would she do? Would they leave her alone?

Her eyes squeezed harder. She would read. Yes. About engines. She liked engines. They spoke to her, purred and hummed, soothed her mind.

Impulse thrusters were driven by controlled fusion reactions.

The FTL drive worked based on gravity mechanics.

Gravity was a particle easily controlled. Grav-wells could be used to control her.

Her eyes flashed open. A man stared back across the permaglass, stroking his finger along the scar that ran across his right eye and curled wickedly down to his mouth. A scar she had given him.

Luis Guitteriez. He ran his tongue over his lips, the corners turning up in a grotesque imitation of a smile. He leaned forward, resting on the ornate walking stick he always carried with him, as though he were about to come through the permaglass barrier.

Her feet pushed against the floor, scrambling, but her back met the cold, hard, white wall of her cell.

Trapped.

He grinned, a predator toying with its prey, his eyes beady and dark like the demons in her dreams.

She swallowed down her scream and hoped irrationally to demolecularize and disappear into the solid steel behind her. Why now? Why after all this time?

There had been no doubt in her mind that Guitteriez orchestrated this series of experiments. But after three years of the same tedious work, so had let herself hope, even believe, that he had lost interest. Foolish hope.

The head researcher joined him at the permaglass wall, standing crisply in his grey dress uniform. She barely noticed him, fixed instead to Guiterriez's dark hair and leathery scowl and gleaming white medical coat. Her every sense finely tuned to the doctor.

Without shifting his gaze, he spoke to the researcher beside him. The permaglass deadened all sound, but she had a perfect view to read every word from their lips. "No response?" Guitteriez asked. "Even with the increased protocols?"

"Nothing, Doctor."

Guitteriez rubbed his chin, cracking his jaw side to side.

"Perhaps if you told us more definitively what you're looking for…," tried the researcher.

"You would know it if you saw it." His eyes drilled into her, hunting for the thing he had never been able to discover.

Even she didn't fully know what they had opened in her mind. She didn't want to know. Didn't want any part of it. She pressed herself deeper in to the corner against the wall.

"I'm just saying, it would be easier —."

Guitteriez turned abruptly to the researcher. "It is not for you," he frowned. "We will have to push harder."

The researcher paled. "Are you sure? She's just a girl, Doctor, less than a hundred pounds. We did 30,000 volts today."

"I am sure." He clenched his fist and turned his gaze back to her. "She is the answer. She is the Gods' gift and our Path to salvation." But it was in his eyes: he no longer saw her as a mission for the Gods; this was personal. He hunted her and would not relent until he had taken the thing he wanted. He wiped the stray saliva that had pooled where the scar left a jagged hitch in the corner of his mouth, and his eyes gleamed with deadly certainty. "She will change everything. We just need to break her open first."

Sarrin pulled her legs in tight to her chest. Possible escape routes: zero. Probability of survival: zero.

ONE

GALIANT IDIM HATED SPACE. HE hated waiting. He hated the cold. And he hated never having a newsfeed.

And yet here he was, stuck in a tin can hundred of lightyears from the fields and forests of his home. The old freightship, Ishash'tor, floated in the middle of celestial nowhere, on their way back from a freight run to the outer planets in the Deep Black.

In his hand he held a portrait. Not a picture, not a digital rendition in a screen, but a real, honest-to-the-Gods sketch. Made with charcoal on a handmade pulpy sheet with a frame of sticks and dried flowers. Aaron stared back at him from the drawing, remarkably lifelike. Gal reached out to touch the face, but stopped himself, afraid to upset the coloured dyes.

Only a cracked fool would keep such an item, its very non-digital existence treason, let alone the subject matter. Aaron had been dead for six years, and Gal still couldn't let it go.

Besides, if they were gong to arrest him, it would be for something far worse.

In the background, the thruster engines hummed, sending their subtle vibrations through the floor. He swirled his cup of

Jin-Jiu in front of him, savouring the warm aroma and the release from the memories that haunted him.

The room was dark, the only illumination coming from the bright array of stars outside his porthole. He liked it dark, it hid the soul-gutting decor. Everything on the ship — on every United Earth Central Army ship — had been painted the same dull, dejected, desperate grey. It was meant to crush Hope.

Sure, you could have little-h hope out here. The kind where you 'hoped' there would still be a can of one of the more edible rations in the mess hall when you went to fix your meal, or 'hoped' that the fresh water tanks had a few drops in them when you wanted a drink because the ship-recycled water had a funny taste and you couldn't stop your mind from guessing what that particular flavour was.

But big-letter-capital-H *Hope* was hard to come by. Hope that somehow you could hide from your past out in the crushing confines of deep space long enough to make a ripe old age and die. If you wanted Hope, you had to get it from the Gods, and Gal was getting none.

The old tin mug fit comfortably in his hand. A gift from his father, it too was both a cherished and hated souvenir that he couldn't bear to part with. It had been through the academy, the rebellion, the war, and it hung on, tied to his pack, as he escaped the crushed and dying Earth.

With another sip, he checked the standard date. Four years ago, almost to the day, the war had ended when the planet imploded on itself, killing millions. All that remained was a fiery ball of rock and molten atmosphere.

And the Speakers themselves, of course. Five men and women directly descended from the Gods. Of course they had been evacuated first. Of course they said it was meant to be; it was the Will of the Gods.

At least they gave the folk Hope, in exchange for all they had taken away.

The door chimed, startling Gal. He grunted, and the door took it as permission and slid wide open with a mechanical clunk.

Commander Rayne Nairu took two long strides and snapped to a precise military stance in front of his desk.

He slammed the picture down, sliding it surreptitiously closer to hide it against his body.

"Good news, Captain." A subtle smile appeared on her usually placid features. A lock of her dark, curly hair bounced free of its neat military knot.

He wanted to stand to tuck it away but stopped himself. "Report, Commander?"

"Maths and Navigation are ready. We'll be back at Etar in less than six hours."

"One jump?" He frowned, leaning his elbows on the desk as he gripped his mug. "It should be at least two."

"The senior mathematician says so. 'Fortuitous Field Drift,' he called it."

"Oh." It really wasn't fortuitous at all.

One more interstellar jump and they would be back within communications range of the central planet. The weeks they spent out in the Black between planets on their freight runs were peaceful — as close as Gal could get anyway. But there was no telling what would be waiting for them when they returned to Etar. Every time the old freightship approached the station, he wondered if the Central Army might have an armed escort waiting for him. If they had finally figured out who he really was and what he had done.

Gal shut his eyes and swirled the warm liquid around in his

mug, inhaling.

"Are you drinking again?"

When he opened his eyes, she was glaring at him. "It's okay, Rayne," Gal smiled, hoping he could charm her, "just a taste, a little warm-me-up — it's always cold here."

She folded her arms and leaned back against the wall. Sighing, she said, "We've known each other a long time, Galiant. Tell me what's going on."

"It's fine, Rayne, I promise."

"I haven't said anything to Central Army Command, but I'm worried about you. You weren't like this before, it just keeps getting worse. I want to help —."

He slammed the mug on the desk, it's tinny echo dampening on the grey walls. "I just —," but how could he explain it? "Some days it's too much. You're not stuck out here with me. I would leave this Gods-awful assignment too if I could, but I can't."

"I don't want to leave," she snapped. Pausing, she clenched her hands, picking her words. "I know you've seen terrible things, but you have to stop. You're an officer with the United Earth Central Army. And that stuff is illegal, it's a sin. The Gods will Provide — they'll provide you salvation if you want it — but you have to let them in."

The last thing he wanted was a lecture on the sanctity of the Gods. He left the mug on the desk, at the same time shuffling the picture to the ground with his knees. He stood and pulled back from the drink with his hands up. "It's not a problem. See, I can just leave it when I want to." He waited, but she made no argument. "I suppose we're on our way to the bridge to oversee the jump?" He started toward the door.

"Gal." She reached out, hand pausing halfway between

them.

"What?"

She pressed her lips together and, here in the privacy of his quarters, placed a comforting hand on the side of his face, making his heart leap. "For two years, we've been out here, running the cargo that no one wants, to the places no one wants to go. I know it's not glamorous. I know you're more than this. They almost made you an admiral." She started to shake her head. "And then the demotion…. I don't even know why we're stuck out here, running freight in the Deep Black. After all we've been through, you won't tell me. Maybe I can help you, talk to my dad or put in a commendation. Did you think of that?"

He took her hand and placed a kiss against the palm before pushing it away.

They were stuck in the Black because he couldn't get into too much trouble out there working for Freight, not like when he'd been in Exploration. But how could he say that, tell her all the things he'd done? She would never speak to him again if she knew even half the truth.

"Let's go to the bridge."

She sighed. "Yessir."

Rayne waited for him to pass and then kept pace a precise stride-length behind him. He'd tried to break her of the habit for years, but she insisted on showing the proper reverence of a commander to her captain. She did everything by the UEC handbook.

They walked in silence through the grey on grey corridors, distance marked only by the uniform repeating bulkheads every ten strides. Rayne held a large data tablet, studying and tapping at it as they walked.

"How much of the crew are we turning over this time?"

She sighed. "Eighteen of twenty."

"I guess that's not as bad as some trips." He shrugged. His ship was nothing but a filter, taking the new graduates from the Central Army Academy, getting their ears wet, and weeding out the worst of the cadets before they passed on to real assignments. Three-month tours of the most desolate planets under the stars, delivering freight with the disgraced Captain Galiant Idim. No one chose that. No one stayed. Not if they could help it. "Who's staying?"

"Lieutenant Wood and —."

"Wood? Oh no."

"Come on, Gal. He's a good engineer."

"That's the problem. Why is he here?" Kieran Wood had graduated top of his class and actually requested a posting on the Ishash'tor. It didn't make any sense. "He's weird as anything. I don't trust him."

"Be grateful," she chided. "He agreed to stay one last tour to make sure the new chief is up to speed. Then he's moving on."

"Fine. Who else?"

"Ensign Ramirez."

"Did you sign off on his request for leave?"

She bit her lip again. "No. We're trading ninety-percent of the crew — we need all the experienced hands we can get. He can take leave after the next tour."

Gal glanced back. "Grant him the leave, Commander."

"He's barely done one three-month tour, I can't in good conscience grant him a holiday."

"His father's sick. He needs the time."

She paused, fingers hovering over her tablet. "How do you know that?"

He shrugged. He wasn't about to tell her the crewman stole

six auto-syringes filled with analgesic. Or that Gal had secretly signed off on them so the Central Army's count stayed even.

His mind flashed an image of Aaron. It wasn't nice what they did to traitors.

"I didn't realize," said Rayne, her fingers in a flurry. "I'll draw up the papers before we dock."

"Thank you."

They continued to the upper deck, turning to the grand corridor that led to the command bridge, fancy doors and entrance looming ahead.

"One more thing, Gal." Rayne paused, stepping to the side of the grey corridor.

Curious, Gal followed, leaning against the wall so they were nose to nose, nearly lip to lip. He studied her lovely features, painting them into his mind.

"Permission to speak freely?"

He cast a grin back at her. "Always."

Her lip slid out from between her teeth as she stared at the ground. "We'll be returning a day ahead of schedule."

"Yeah."

"With the extra time, I thought we might visit the General."

He jumped. General Oleander Nairu: Rayne's father. He turned away, shaking. "I —." She wanted to ask the General, as an official, to sign his consent to their union — they had talked about it often enough — but Gal couldn't. "We work together," he said weakly. It sounded pathetic even to his ears, but he couldn't tell her the real reason. He started again towards the bridge.

"It's not fraternization if we're married, Gal," she called after him.

He stopped, not daring to turn around. Rayne, whom he

loved and could not hope to love, who lived her life by the UEC
handbook, was suggesting a loophole. But it was too dangerous.
Bad enough that she had stayed on his ship for three years,
turning down multiple promotions to stay. "I'm sorry, Rayne. I
truly am." He put a foot on the first of the two stairs that marked
the entrance to the bridge.

"Is there nothing between us?"

Pain seared through his heart and he clutched the handrail to
stop himself from rushing back and wrapping her in his arms. A
distant memory, a threat, played in his minds ear: *He may not know
what you've done, but I do. And I will pick at every person you ever care
about until I am satisfied you have paid for your crimes.*

"Of course I love you." He forced his legs up the stairs,
triggering the automatic door to hiss open. "But you deserve a
better life than I can offer." He loved her so much he had no
choice but to push her away.

* * *

Gal steeled himself, staring at the grey carpeted floor as he walked
directly ahead to the padded captain's chair in the middle of the
deck.

The crew — seated or standing at the glossy control panels
that wrapped around the bridge — had already dropped their
salutes and turned back to their work by the time Gal looked up.
If they had bothered with the formality at all. A side effect of
Gal's constant effort to avoid direct contact with any of them. It
was important he not get too close. He could give them that
much, at least.

Kieran Wood, the chief engineer, peeked up from the blocky
Engineering console, studying the captain. He caught Gal's gaze
and flashed him a wide-mouthed, idiotic grin.

Footsteps treaded softly onto the bridge, staying behind Gal and out of sight. The other crewmen turned, and his jaw clenched as he twisted to see.

Rayne's expression stayed rigid as she took her position at the Tactical console to his right. And where the crew barely acknowledged their run-down captain, they flashed adoring smiles in her direction.

He couldn't blame them. Rayne — a fierce tactitian — had once confided her intense desire for children. Until that time came, she put all her mothering efforts into the cadets. Each of them had arrived young, green, and too incompetent to earn a posting on a more respectable ship. Now an efficient crew surrounded him, thanks entirely to her.

"Have you completed your final checks?" she asked.

The mathematicians nodded at each other and confirmed their final report. They fed the calculations to Navigation where the pilot entered the jump into the computer.

"Gravity drive reads full capacity," reported Kieran. "No issues on the engine readings neither." This was the most important piece to Gal — he didn't care if the calculations were off and they ended up on the wrong side of the galaxy, but considering they would be travelling via a gravity pulse literally strong enough to bend space, he wanted to know the engines and graviton generator were working properly.

Begrudgingly he admitted Kieran was a decent engineer, and he at least felt confident the gravity drive wouldn't explode around them. Small miracle.

The large viewscreen that occupied the fore of the command bridge currently showed nothing but vast expanse of empty space.

"All systems report ready, Captain," said Rayne.

Gal grunted his assent.

"Preparing to jump," said the pilot.

"Jump."

Gravity tugged and pulled, and Gal felt weightless for an instant, his spine jarring as they landed back in normal space. The viewscreen showed familiar system, a single star at the centre.

"Confirm position," sighed Gal, although he already knew.

"Back at Etar," confirmed the navigator.

"Set a course for Etar 1."

"Aye, sir."

"I've got normal reports from the Engine Room," said Kieran.

"Good." Gal let out a breath and stood from his chair. All routine. He could hide in his ready room until they reached the orbital station.

A computer chime sounded, causing the crew to pause in their work, glancing surreptitiously to the Tactical console which currently doubled as Communications.

"We are receiving transmissions," said Rayne.

Spontaneous clapping erupted around the bridge. Gal gripped the back of his chair and steeled himself.

"Quiet now," said Rayne, and the crew obeyed. "Your personal messages will be sent to your quarters where you can read them later. Central Army business first."

They bent their heads to their work, but the bridge buzzed with renewed excitement. He envied them.

"There's a high priority transmission," she said, studying the display in front of her. "My Gods!" She looked up at Gal, eyes wide with wonder.

"What?" His fingers dug into the grey fabric.

Her hand came up to her open mouth.

"What is it?" Gal needed to know.

"A request from the Speakers."

"The Speakers?" His knees nearly collapsed under him.

She nodded, eyes bright. "We've been requisitioned to transport the Poet Laureate, Halud DeGazo. He's coming here. Aboard our ship. Gal, do you know what this means?"

His lungs seized and left him gasping for air. He didn't know what it meant at all. The Poet was the sixth most powerful man under the stars. He reported directly to the Five Speakers, who purported to be the direct descendants of the Gods. They spoke the Words of the Gods, the human race following along on the Path.

But the Poet… on the their run-down freightship… on Gal's ship — there was no reason.

"Hey, isn't that somethin'?" said Kieran, his lazy drawl filling the deadly silence in Gal's head. "Geez. The Poet Laureate…. Could be a real boon for the ship, I would think, Cap'n." He grinned like an idiot again.

Gal stared. Kieran Wood was a lunatic, he was sure of it.

Rayne continued to read to transmission, giddiness dripping into her voice. "It says he's making the journey to report on the conditions of the new colonies."

"Really? That's it?" Kieran scrunched up his face. "There must be some happening for the Poet himself to go. He's been quiet for months."

"It just says he's going to report on the colonies." Rayne shrugged, but her grin only grew.

"Or maybe there's some special something goin' on."

Gal, for the first time, agreed with the engineer. But it wouldn't be a good special something. They knew, and the Poet was coming to report on him.

"Gal? Are you alright?"

"Huh?" He spun to see Rayne watching him. "What else is

in the manifold? What else are we taking on?"

She glanced down, scanning quickly. "The usual — supplies, rations, medicine. Oh —," her eyes lit up with surprise, "and a group of colonists going to Selousa."

It hit him like a physical blow. "Colonists? To Selousa? The colony is dead."

"Maybe that's why the Poet is coming," said Kieran.

"Of course," Rayne said. "They must be trying again, now that there's been more time for the terra-forming to take hold. If the Gods say it's time, that's wonderful."

It was not wonderful. "I need full background checks on all the new crewmen," ordered Gal, springing for the door and moving faster than he had moved in a long time.

"What? Gal, what's going on?"

The doors slid open in front of him, and he leaned into the doorframe, suddenly dizzy. "Do it, Rayne." He stumbled away.

He heard the last strains of Kieran's drawl behind him as the doors shut. "I'm not sure he's really feelin' better, Raynie."

He gripped blindly at the wall, finding his way to his cabin by rote.

They knew. They had to.

It was a message: the Poet, the colonists.

Maybe it was just meant to shake him up. Test him.

He scrubbed his hand across his eyes as a vision of Aaron flashed over him. His mind played a memory, clear as the day it happened:

Aaron's hand gripped the iron bars. "How did you get in here?"

"It wasn't hard to sneak in."

"This is the most guarded place on the planet."

"Are you alright? I didn't believe there were prisons, not the way Hap tells it."

"I'm okay. Gal, promise me, you'll keep going. I told them I'm you, so you have a head start to get somewhere safe. But don't give up the fight. Never give up the fight."

"Aaron, we'll get you out of here."

He shook his head. "I'm slated for dispatch tomorrow."

"Dispatch?"

"To one of the colonies."

Gal reached into his closet, to the far back of the highest shelf. He pulled out a long, slender bottle, half-full of amber liquid. Jin-Jiu. The only thing that helped him forget. He pulled the warmer from the drawer in his desk and dropped the bottle inside. He stared, waiting for it to heat up.

His mind looped the scene with Aaron endlessly.

"The colonies?"

Aaron nodded carefully. "'A chance,' they call it, 'a new start where my independence will be an asset'."

"Let me help you." Gal pulled on the bars uselessly.

"I'm done, Gal."

Two months later, the reports came in that the colony had failed. Starvation. No one survived. It was the Will of the Gods.

Despite the promise Aaron had drawn, Gal did give up.

He reached for the bottle, a new threat echoing in his head. *"We know what you have done. Your life has been spared as your disappearance would cause too many questions, but should you ever show your face on the Central Planets again, we can destroy everyone you have ever cared about."*

The threat and the loss of Aaron had been enough. He'd stopped, shutting down huge operations. He'd agreed to the freight run in the Deep Black. And he'd turned away everyone who ever tried to get close to him.

Except the one person he could not stay away from: Rayne.

What would they do to her?

He'd destroyed Earth. He'd started a war. His fate was sealed. He was only kidding himself to think he'd survived this long.

The Poet was coming. Six hours until they docked with the station.

He gauged the Jin-Jiu — a handbreadth filled the bottom of the bottle, enough to keep him sedated for most of the trip. Then he wouldn't have to endure the waiting.

He poured and took his first sip, the sweet, warm drink soothing his frayed nerves. The endless loop settled to a dull roar at the back of his brain.

Rayne still had a chance, he realized. He could save her, maybe, as the last thing he ever did. She'd be heartbroken, but he could save her career and save her relationship with her father.

With his last ounce of strength, he pushed the banged and beaten mug away. He would need all his wits about him to have any type of chance.

* * *

Gal stood by the airlock, staring down the spaceway that connected the ship to the station. He had not left the ship, even to visit his regular Jin-Jiu smuggler — what was the point, after today?

Rayne had been dispatched to handle the new crew orientation and check that the cargo had been loaded and secured properly. She'd not been quiet about her desire to be there to greet the Poet, but Gal had insisted.

He didn't want her there when it happened.

His grey dress uniform blended in with the grey paint as he stood, waiting. His mind drifted in and out of focus, a not terribly light dose of Jin-Jiu floating through his veins to silence the memories and let him think.

The sharp rasp of a throat clearing cough punched through the Jin-Jiu haze. Gal looked up to see a single man in a long grey cloak standing in front of him, a small valise tucked under his arm.

No squadron of elite soldiers stood waiting. No media recorders. Not even a tactician present to arrest him.

Piercing blue eyes scanned him, a bemused smile turning up the thin line of stylized facial hair and grey eyebrows. "Captain Idim, I presume?" The Poet let out a soft chuckle.

Confused, Gal snapped to attention and saluted, five fingers pressed to a spot directly over his heart. "Master Poet, please forgive my inattention."

"At ease." The Poet waved his hand good naturedly. "Many people expect a large entourage, but I much prefer to travel without one, it allows me to examine the fabric of life more clearly."

Gal's tongue suddenly seemed too large in his dry mouth. This was not like any of the scenarios he imagined. What was the Poet doing? Surely, they must have known. Surely, the Poet wouldn't actually be taking passage on the old Ishash'tor.

But he waited alone. And he was not, it seemed, arresting Gal.

"Captain?"

Gal started. No knowing what else to do, he saluted again. "Sorry, sir. I'm feeling a bit overwhelmed."

"Oh? And why is that?"

He gripped the wall for support. Maybe they didn't know. It would be a fool's blunder to tell them outright. "It's an honour to be in the presence of such grace as yourself, Master Poet."

The Poet held up his hand, shaking his head modestly.

"Please call me Halud." He waited, watching Gal intently. "Perhaps you could show me to my quarters?"

"Right." He squeezed his fist, digging nails into his palm while his mind desperately tried to work through it. "Follow me." His pulse hammered in his ears as they moved through the corridors. There was something else, some bigger plan, he concluded, there had to be.

Rounding a corner, Gal froze, the corridor suddenly filled by a gaggle of crewmen leaving the mess hall. The kids were fresh-faced, eager, and laughing. He glanced at the Poet — he couldn't punish the kids just for looking at their captain, could he?

Halud strode forward, the crewmen gawking, the ones in back running into the ones in front. He smiled broadly. "How marvellous! Welcome to Service." He shook each of their hands.

Gal slunk into the shadow of a bulkhead.

"Commander Nairu!" the Poet exclaimed, pushing forward as Rayne came out of the mess hall behind the others.

"Oh Gods," moaned Gal, earning him glares from the closest crewmen.

Rayne beamed as the Poet shook her hand and then she saluted, pressing five fingertips into her chest, head bowed.

The Poet returned the gesture, and then used a finger to tilt her chin up again. "You have been out here a long time, Commander. The Gods smile upon your loyalty and dedication to serving the good of your fellow man."

Rayne blushed, and Gal watched in horror, trying desperately to make sense of the situation.

The Poet kept hold of Rayne, but addressed the crew again. "None of you is to give the Commander a hard time, you understand. I am told she is both a devout and fierce tactician, so it's in your best interest to stay on her good side." He chuckled and whispered something private into her ear.

The Poet made his way to the front of the group, eyes fixed on Gal, a decided unreadable ferocity in them.

Gal prepared himself for chaos.

But Halud turned, again addressing the crew and leaving Gal to wither against the wall.

"You must all be very excited for your first assignment, for this opportunity to serve your Gods."

The group nodded zealously, hanging on the Poet's every word. Gal wondered if the Poet would direct them to attack, but that was hardly the way of the Speakers.

"Know this: the Gods work in their own special way through each of you. Sometimes the Path is not the thing that we choose, nor is it the route that seems the easiest to follow, but the Path is always where you end up. Even in the darkest of situations, know that you — even in that moment — follow the Path. The Gods we Serve. In the Gods we Trust."

The crewmen repeated the litany.

The Poet nodded reverently and addressed them again. "Mark my words here today. Captain Galiant Idim is one of the Gods' finest officers. I would trust him with my life, as you now trust him with yours. Godspeed to you all."

The crewmen turned like a horde staring at Gal, their eyes holding a mix of surprise, curiosity and disdain.

The Poet took him by the arm and lead him away. "So eager, aren't they?" he shook his head, laughing softly to himself.

Gal stumbled until his stride steadied under him. "Yes, sir." His head started to pound as the warmth of the Jin-Jiu left him.

"I feel badly for them, now that must leave the hallowed halls of the Gods and the Speakers and their Academy. Real life is never so black and white as we would like, is it, Galiant?" The

Poet's crystal blue eyes sliced into him like laz-fire.

Gal stopped short, heart thumping in his ears. Irrationally, he envisioned the Poet pulling open his chest and ripping free the lungs and heart.

"Which way, Galiant?"

* * *

Gal keyed in the authorization code to program the lock mechanism to the Poet's quarters, still trying to sort out what was happening. "I'm afraid it's not much," he said. "We don't normally transport dignitaries."

The Poet pressed his thumb to the digital scanner with a smile, imprinting the lock to his biometric signature. "No concern, Captain. I am pleased you could take me on such short notice. It is a fine ship, and I am happy to be on board. It will do very nicely for our needs."

Gal tapped his five fingers to his chest in a quick, customary thank you, wishing he was already retreating down the corridor. He rubbed his hands nervously on his sleeves. "Dinner is served in the mess at nineteen-hundred. The commander planned a special meal."

"My thanks to you and your officer. Sadly, I am afraid I will have to decline — there is some work to finalize before we are out of range. Is it possible to use your communications array?"

Gal nodded, suppressing his instant sigh of relief. "I'll send Lieutenant Wood to set it up for you."

"Much appreciated. My apologies for missing the meal."

Gal turned on his heel to leave, but the Poet stopped him: "Ah, I almost forgot — I have a gift for you, Galiant. You don't mind if I call you Galiant, do you?"

He shook his head dumbly, feet planted. What else could he say? One wrong move and there was no telling how the strange and unusual meeting would end.

The Poet reached into a compartment on his luggage and pulled out a long, slender parcel. "I have heard it is your favourite."

Gal didn't need to unwrap the package to recognize the bottle. He stared at the Jin-Jiu. But how had the Poet gotten it? How had he known?

"Go on. Take it."

Gingerly he reached out, his fingers wrapping around the neck of the bottle.

"Tell me about yourself, Galiant." The Poet leaned casually against the door frame. "Where is it you were born? You don't look like Old Earth stock."

Still gazing at the wrapped bottle in his hands and wondering what the proper protocol was when given a gift of illegal drink by a dignitary, Gal replied without thinking, "No — Indaer."

"Oh," the Poet chuckled softly, "It's been a long time since I've heard it called that. One of the first planets colonized when humanity began its reach into space from Earth. Rich mineral deposits and excellent crop yields."

Also the place the Central Army landed when they were forced off the Earth. They had set up their headquarters there, and changed the name to Etar — something about a new hope. The Poet had delivered the address.

Gal scrambled to cover his misstep. "I lived on Indaer. When it was forest and farmland. But that planet's gone. Nothing but a small forest preserve now. They paved over the farms to build the central city. I only said I'm from Indaer because that's what I remember. I haven't lived there since it became Etar"

"Understandable. There have been a number of changes." The Poet scanned him with his laser eyes before his features melted back into a friendly smile. "You fought in the war, did you not, Gal?"

Gal slumped into the door frame for support. "Yeah."

"I read your personnel file," the Poet continued. "Quite a decorated career you had: the Shining Compass, the Nations' Cross, and the Ruby Star."

And a host of other medals that didn't mean much more now than they did then. "Sure." His hands clenched on the bottle, as memories of platoons and laz-cannons assaulted him. Things he only wanted to forget. "What about you, where did you grow up, Poet?"

"Fighting is an awful thing," said the Poet, blatantly ignoring the turn in conversation. "But it is also great for the changes it brings."

Gal shook his head, screams and explosions already flashing through his memory, dragging him out of the present and into the past.

"'The only way to move forward is to change. Sometimes the change is not what we want it to be, but it can set things in motion that we would not have dreamed otherwise.' Do you not agree?"

His legs gave out, only the wall keeping Gal upright. They weren't the Poet's words, they were Gal's, said too many years ago. What kind of torture had they planned for him?

His mouth said something — maybe rude, maybe incoherent. White light shone across his retinas, and an unnamed buzz rang in his ears. He turned and stormed down the corridor, the bottle clutched firmly to his chest.

* * *

Gal collapsed into his chair, picking up the overturned photo frame from the floor beneath his desk. Aaron's face stared out at him — youthful, rugged, hopeful. Dead.

He slammed it back down.

Memories surfaced: *In the dark of night, calls came through their old-fashioned radios — Gal on this side called to Aaron on the other. Stars shone bright overhead, and their breath came out in cold puffs.*

His pack pressed into his back and he kept low, footsteps crunching on the cold ground.

Two weeks away from graduation, the Central Army Academy had taught him only half the things he knew, but he still happily used their vision enhancement tech. Through the engineered contact lenses, the walls looked dirty yellow, but he knew they were still the same grey as when they'd scoped the place in the daytime.

Explosions sounded off, progressing precisely down the long sides of the building, dust and con-plas flying into the air. There were desperate shouts, and then sirens. Laz-fire blazed across the lawns.

And somewhere in all that mess, Augments escaped. A war that had long been silent began in earnest. A planet died.

Gal pulled his warmer from the drawer, dropping the bottle of Jin-Jiu inside.

Xenoralia nervosa — the Red Fever. That was how it all began.

The story felt unusual, unexpected. It started with a virus that affected less than ten-percent of the population, and would end with the loss of an entire planet. Absurd, but that was exactly what had happened.

Twelve years before that night of explosions and laz-fights, the Red Fever had claimed its first victim. The next day, twenty. The following day, a hundred. Only pockets of the population were affected, but it decimated those regions like wildfire. It affected men and women of all ages — but strangely, not the children, not at first.

In the adults, it caused tumours, erratic mitosis and whole body neoplasia until they were so disfigured they became unrecognizable. In the best cases, debilitating lumps and boils covered the whole body. A couple of people even survived it — though they envied the ones who didn't.

Researchers learned what it was: a transgene, a retrovirus. It inserted into the DNA and changed the growth of cells — some proteins were gained, some were lost, entirely new products started showing up.

Once they identified the virus, they started to recognize the effect it had on children. It didn't just insert into their genome, it changed it in ways no one could predict. The children became — for lack of a better word — augmented, genetically enhanced. They became something else: Augments.

It acted like nothing seen before. Its origin remained a complete mystery. Was it natural or designed? And why?

The infected children — their bodies still growing, their cells still dividing and moving — became stronger, their dexterity increased to almost incomprehensible levels. They were smarter too. They never forgot, and even when no one told them a thing, they could know it. The younger they were when infected, the more profound the result.

The Central Army and their researchers offered to help the infected adults and children, and they submitted willingly. The medical trials weren't always successful, but no one blamed the government — they were doing more than anyone else. A couple people were 'cured,' but more by chance than anything else. Thousands died in the hospitals.

The disease ran its course and receded, but the children, orphans now, were still being treated in the Central Army compound at Evangecore.

They weren't sick. They had been strong and healthy before they went in, so why the children were still being held, no one knew. It was the Will of the Gods, said the Speakers. And there they stayed for the next twelve years.

A rumour started that the Augment children were being experimented on. They were being trained. A couple of people went so far as to say the army was trying to figure out how to strengthen its soldiers without subjecting them to the disease.

That night when Evangecore was bombed, the children fled. Most of them were teens by that time. They blinked in the light, but they were fit, and they ran. They escaped into the woods and shot down an elite platoon with a single, measly 64V laz-pistol.

Gal saw it in his mind's eye: *screams and explosions, trees silhouetted against the dark night, lit up by the light of hovercrafts dropping soldiers by the dozens into the battle. Periodically a single laz-pulse would strike out from the forest, and slowly all of the Central Army's men and machines lay crumpled on the ground.*

He poured his mug full of Jin-Jiu, eager to drown the memories and the demons they brought with them.

The war lasted three years, jumping from continent to continent as the Augments fled. They were careful though, and Gal respected that, keeping away from the inhabited areas and cities as much as possible.

The government continued developing new weapons, up to the manic 200MV laz-cannon. By that point, Gal had made commander and worked to get his regiment to the North where they would deploy the cannon. The Army had discovered their stronghold and said the Augments had accessed the Earth's core and they were using its energy to fuel a weapon that would destroy the Gods. So the Army went to destroy them. And Gal tagged along to see if there was anything he could do.

Soldiers worked their way across the frozen ground, Gal panting with the extra effort needed to move through the waist-deep snow. Far ahead, alpha regiment moved the cannon into position. He encouraged his men to move faster, but they were not fast enough.

The laz-cannon fired. A bright beam of red shot through the air, aimed at a small grouping of hills whose rocky peaks just poked through the snow. A boy sat as sentry, too far away to make out clearly, but no doubt he was just a kid.

Gal stopped, shocked. He watched and waited for the boy's imminent demise.

But something in the air flickered and caught the laz-fire — a kind of forceshield. It rippled with colour. The cannon's laz-stream poured into it, undulating the shield like water flowing into a pond.

Gal left his men and ran wildly to the alpha commander, but she wouldn't stop, wouldn't decrease the voltage.

He slammed the cannon with the butt of his rifle. It wavered but kept firing its stream of intense energy.

The forceshield buckled. Rapidly, it changed through red and orange and yellow to bright white. And then it went black.

Gal stood, staring at it, deaf to the terrified shouts around him.

Stored up energy in the forceshield dissipated like a thousand lightning storms. Bright, hot light shot out the top and bottom. It burned a hole straight to the very core of the planet, turning the hills and the Augments inside to vapour. The ground under them shook and lurched, crumbling down into the magma below.

He downed the mug in one long series of gulps, sucking on it like he was drowning and it was the only thing that could keep him afloat.

He'd managed to move his regiment back to the transport which took them to an airfield where he'd boarded a ship and left the planet for the last time. Thousands were left behind when the Earth collapsed and imploded on itself. And the war was suddenly, definitively over.

TWO

KIERAN WOOD RAN A HAND through his freshly buzzed hair, enjoying the prickly sensation as he rubbed his hand back and forth.

Around him, twelve new crewmen buzzed anxiously, darting from console to console in the open engineering bay. They tugged at their new grey coveralls, scratching the collars and the heavy padded shoulders.

"Is this alignment sufficient?" asked the man who was supposed to be his replacement as chief engineer, gesturing to the computer panel over the open access port.

Kieran glanced at the output and raised an eyebrow good naturedly. "We're going to hurtle ourselves through the very fabric of space-time."

The engineer — Ensign Cade Textile — shrugged. "The handbook says 95% is sufficient, and this is reading 96-point-3."

Kieran reached down to adjust the filaments himself. "If there's one thing you're going to learn about me over the next three months, it's that I like to aim a little higher than sufficient." He finished his tweaking and punched in the codes for the computer to run another diagnostic. "The Ishash'tor here is twenty-five years old — ready to be retired. And yet, we've not had a single engine malfunction in the last year."

The ensign turned an unusual shade of puce, and Kieran quickly analyzed his expression for anger or resentment. Fortunately, he only detected embarrassment.

"No worries though, hey." Kieran slapped him on the shoulder. The last thing he wanted to do was tell the man how to do his job — on the one hand it wasn't the way he liked to operate, on the other he'd signed a mission briefing specifically stating that he wouldn't influence the outcome of events. "When I go, you can do what you want, Ensign. It's just my job to show you the ropes."

He left the engineer, taking a quick stroll around the bay to check on the others before retreating to the little alcove he called an office. It had a computer terminal and was out of the way enough. The last message he'd sent home had been a few days ago, and if he didn't keep in regular contact, they would get worried and come for him.

His fingers stretched across the input screen, accessing the subroutines that would let him send an encrypted message, but when it came to actually write the note, he paused. There was nothing to say. Had been nothing to say for months.

He'd come here to explore the newly terra-formed planets in the Deep Black, thinking the freightship would be a perfect excuse to visit as many places as possible. And the captain was rumoured to have once been the foremost officer in New Planetary Exploration. It should have been a recipe for intrigue. Something at least. But all he'd done for a year was frog-jump back and forth across the galaxy.

A quiet chime sounded from his terminal — a service request.

He tapped on the icon, the details expanding across the screen: the Poet needed communications access. And Kieran knew just the engineer for the job.

He picked up a mobile service kit from the storage lockers, waved at his team, and nearly skipped out the door.

The Poet's guest quarters were three decks below, and Kieran took the time to remind himself of his training. He had a list of questions carefully prepared by the time he arrived at the door and pressed the request chime.

The door slid open a moment later, a tall man with peppered hair and long-grey robes greeted him.

"Howdy-there, Poet." Kieran spread his hand on his chest. "I'm Lieutenant Wood. Here to connect your communications port to our array." At the last moment, he remembered to salute — five fingers coned together, the point pressed into the middle of the chest. The same weird way that they prayed.

The Poet returned the gesture. "Thank you for coming."

Kieran grinned, carefully projecting an air of slight incompetence. People liked to open up if they didn't feel threatened, if they didn't think someone was carefully filing away everything they heard and saw. "Sure thing."

He followed the Poet to the fold-down desk and the wall terminal hidden behind it. He used the desk to hold his toolkit — not that he needed more tools than a computer access code, but he could buy a little more interview time if he made a show.

"Have you — have you been an engineer for very long?"

"Oh yeah." He selected the hand-spanner and a flashy little laz-torch. "It's not that hard really, you push this button, you push that button. Computer does most of it." He popped the panel, letting the screen swing open to expose the inner wiring.

The Poet frowned, pressing his lips into a tight line. "Do you feel it's necessary to take apart the console?"

All the intel Kieran had on the Poet suggested he was nothing more than a figurehead. He gave speeches that the folk lapped up — the same blah blah about the Path of the Gods.

But the man currently watched him with a single raised eyebrow and a deadly patient smile. "Close the panel."

The words echoed strangely, and Kieran found himself closing the panel before his mind registered the order. He gulped uncomfortably, mind racing to integrate this new information and rewrite the assumptions he had made.

He pushed out a laugh, adding a tinge of nervousness and a hint of embarrassment. "Busted. You know your way around a communications port."

"That I do."

"Sorry. I'm a big fan and we don't often get a chance to see the non-mandatory broadcasts. Forgive me for trying to use my opportunity to speak with you a little more." He gestured at the now shut panel. "I thought I'd stabilize the connections and put you on a lower-frequency transmission. The signal goes farther that way before it degrades too much."

For the first time, the Poet's grey-blue eyes lit up in appreciation. "That is understandable then. I thought all the broadcasts were mandatory."

"Yeah. We don't spend too many hours at Etar, so they get prioritized a little."

"Do you have a favourite?"

He gulped — the recent propaganda was all pretty gaudy. "Uh. The one where you talk about Etar and the forest preserve and the progress that's been made."

"Oh really?"

"Yeah." But probably not for the same reasons as everyone

else. "'Definitive Might of the Gods, for they know all and see all and bend the world to their good,'" he quoted. A bead of sweat collected at his temple.

The Poet eyed him skeptically.

He jabbed his fingers into his chest again for good measure, grinning.

"Yes, yes. Well remembered," said the Poet with a reassuring smile, but his voice sounded empty.

"Truth be told," Kieran said quickly. "I liked your poems more than anything." And it was the truth.

The Poet's blue eyes lit up, the low-light in the room twinkling off them. "Not many people care for the poems, so now I favour more direct prose. And the needs of the Speakers and the Gods, of course."

"Of course." He turned to the panel. "I'll have this sorted in a jiffy, here, Poet."

"Would it be possible to set the transmission to a specific frequency?"

Kieran frowned. "Narrow band?"

"For classified communique."

"Yeah, but —."

"New security measures. It's alright, I can program them in the console. I have an algorithm."

"No, it's fine. Good thing I brought my toolkit." Kieran swung the screen open again, revealing the connections inside. "Besides, I don't like people loading programs onto my ship — even if it's just local code — without my knowing. Safety risks, you know."

"Of course." The Poet placed a small data tablet on the desktop with the specified frequency.

Kieran adjusting the wiring, switching connections until he

had the system configured to the Poet's specifications. The Poet appeared relaxed, and Kieran chanced digging for more information. "I heard there's rebels afoot on the planet, whispers of John P. Are you having security issues at the Speakers' Compound?"

The Poet flinched, colour draining from his cheeks, eyes suddenly hard and unreadable. "Thank you, Lieutenant."

Kieran bowed his head, pausing for a final salute as the Poet shepherded him out the door.

He grinned as the door closed behind him. The Poet's reaction couldn't have been more clear: there was something happening on the central planet. Something with John P.

Kieran had read the words of the famous rebel, his counter-broadcasts against the Gods disappearing almost as quickly as they arrived. Kieran had saved every one from the last ten years up until three years ago when John P had suddenly disappeared without a trace. But the crewmen brought whispers of a resurgence, and the Poet had all but confirmed it.

* * *

Eight hours after departing from the orbital station at Etar, Rayne felt like she might be catching up. She made her way to the Cargo Bay to check the last few items on her list before they made their first jump into the Black.

The Cargo Bay took up the entire lower three floors of the ship. The space was designed to be malleable depending on what they were hauling, and they currently had the scaffolding configured with a half-deck on each of the upper two levels. The lower floor housed the heavy cargo — building supplies mostly — and the hover carts and lifts they used to move it. The upper floors held smaller containers: food rations, medicines, clothes. And the colonists.

Descending the stairs to the second level, she scanned the deck quickly. The Central Army technicians at the orbital station had installed an approved living area for the colonists. It was spacious and set out with comfortable looking cots and benches, even a vid-screen. A thick fence surrounded them, stretching all the way to the floor above.

"Hello," Rayne called.

There were twelve colonists, and they sat in a rough circle, heads bent in prayer. At the call, glances turned her way. A middle-aged woman with wavy auburn hair slowly rose to her feet and came to the barrier.

"How are you and the others doing?" Rayne smiled, suddenly nervous. "We're preparing to jump out of Etar's system."

The woman stared at her, face slightly obscured by the mesh.

"I'm sorry about the fence," said Rayne. "Central Army regulations — we can't let civilians wander around an Army ship, you understand."

"We're not criminals."

"Of course not. To leave your home for a new colony is incredibly brave and righteous. I am Commander Nairu. Please let me know if there is anything you need to make your journey more comfortable."

The woman glanced behind her, looking to the group still on the floor. Each of them watched the interaction with interest. She stared at them, and then turned to stare at the floor, deciding. "I'd like to speak to Captain Idim."

Rayne stepped back. At a loss, her mouth flapped open and closed.

The woman stepped forward, grabbing the fence and rattling it like a cage. "Please, take me to see the captain."

Shaking her head, Rayne regained her senses. "I'm afraid I cannot. You're civilians on a Central Army ship, you must stay in your approved area."

"You don't understand," she cried.

Rayne bit her lip. "I can ask the captain if he has the time available to visit you here. That's all I can do."

"Please, please tell Galiant I need to speak with him." The woman clung to the fence, her features drawn tight as her eyes searched over Rayne.

"How do you know his name?"

"Please tell him it's Minerva."

Rayne frowned.

The colonist rattled the fence with her hands. "Will you?"

Eyes wide, Rayne pressed a hand against her chest. "Yes, of course. I said I would let him know, and I speak truth. We are all servants of the Gods."

"Okay." The woman sighed and pushed away from the barrier. "Thank you."

"I pray to Gods for your safety," Rayne called after the woman. She turned, taking the stairs two at a time.

"Don't bother," a voice floated after her. "No one's listening."

Shaking the icy chill that crept over her, Rayne pressed her five fingers to her chest and prayed, as she had promised, for the colonists' safety. She shut her eyes as she walked and sent the prayer to the stars.

Gal would be hiding in his quarters, and she took the most direct route to see him. Biting back the memory of her last visit to his quarters and the failed proposition that had followed, she pressed the chime.

One day, Gal would get over his irrational fear of her father, and her father would agree — because he always said yes to his

Rayne —, and they would be married, a True Union under the eyes of the Gods.

The door did not immediately slide open like usual, and she pressed the chime again. Still no answer. Banging her fist on the actual metal of the door, she called out, "Gal, it's Rayne. I need to speak with you."

He could be somewhere else — the mess, or even the bridge — but she knew him too well. He avoided the crew at all costs. Abusing her power as senior tactician, she overrode the lock and forced the door.

"Gal?" She said into the dim lighting of his small room.

Her eyes fell upon his form, curled up on the bed.

Maybe he was just sleeping. He'd been frantic since they'd gotten their orders to transport the Poet, and probably hadn't slept the entire two days they rested at Etar station.

She crept across the room, sitting carefully on the edge of his bed. "Gal?" she said softly, shaking his arm.

He groaned, remaining as immobile as a stone.

She shook a little harder. "It's time for our FTL jump out of the system. The captain should oversee it, yeah?"

He groaned again, flopping over and leaving a thick line of drool on the pillow. And under him, curled in his arm, laid a half-full bottle of Jin-Jiu.

Rayne bolted off the bed. She paced in the little room, palms pressed against her cheeks. She tried shaking him again, hard, but his eyes only fluttered and he fell back into his stupor.

He had promised. He said he would be better. And stupidly, she had believed him.

"Oh Gal," she muttered, propping the pillows around him. She pulled the Jin-Jiu out of his hand and tucked it deep in the back of the nightstand, promising herself she would come back to dispose of it properly as soon as she could.

The trip to the command bridge was short, barely long enough to dry her eyes and recollect herself, but she bounded up the landing with determination. New faces greeted her, and she made a point of acknowledging each of them.

She took a seat in the captain's chair, and she wiped the sweat from her palms across the grey armrests. It had been a while since she'd had to occupy it in Gal's absence — another stark reminder that he was not improving as much as she had thought. Foolish, wishful thinking.

Clearing her throat, she announced, "The captain is occupied. Have you finalized your calculations?"

The new junior mathematician wrinkled his brow and turned his gaze from her to his senior.

Fortunately, the senior mathematician — who had been the previous junior mathematician — did not appear terribly shaken by the change. "Yes, ma'am."

"Engineering?"

"Ready to rock and roll," said Kieran absently, his fingers dancing over the console in front of him.

She turned at the odd turn of phrase. "What?"

Kieran shook his head, a bashful grin creeping ear to ear. "All systems are go."

"Thank you. Navigation?"

The pilot turned around. "We're meant to have the captain here. No disrespect, ma'am. Only it's our first jump as a new crew, and the captain should be present for all major ship functions."

She sighed, pressing his palms into her thighs. "In the absence of the captain, I am your commanding officer and will oversee the jump."

"Where is he?" continued the pilot. "According to subsection thirteen-dash-A, the captain should be on the bridge for all gravity jumps."

Rayne ground her teeth together. She knew the rulebook backwards and forwards, probably better than this crewman. And normally she stuck to it. But if they waited to Gal to wake up, they could be floating at the edge of the solar system for hours. And Central Command would definitely notice, and definitely investigate the reason for the delay. "The captain will not be joining us."

A snicker from the back of the room drew her attention. The crewman whispered to the man next to him. "Told you he was a drunk."

Rayne shot to her feet. "He is your captain. He is occupied with ship's business. And you will show him his due respect."

"Sorry, ma'am. It's just, he has a reputation."

She straightened her uniform, flattening out an imperceptible crease, and glared at the crewman until his eyes dropped shamefully to the floor.

"Anyone else? No? Then are we ready to jump?"

There were no arguments and the pilot put her hands on the controls.

"Jump," Rayne ordered.

The ship hurtled across the galaxy, accompanied by the standard sucking and squishing feeling that still made her insides churn.

"Everyone alright?" Rayne asked.

Half the crew clutched their heads or steadied themselves against the wall, but they seemed okay. No one vomited at least.

"Good. Next jump is in nine hours. Get some rest."

* * *

Gal groaned as the door chime sounded, pulling him from his drugged quasi-sleep. The pillows had been piled around him, and his bottle had gone missing.

The traitorous door slid open, and Rayne stood in the corridor. "I didn't expect you'd open the door."

"I didn't mean to." He tore up the sheets, looking for his missing drink.

"We made the first jump." Her cold expression told him he was in trouble.

He stopped fumbling. "Sorry."

She sighed. "I thought about being mad at you, but we have a long trip ahead of us."

He became suddenly hyper-aware of his twisted sheets and rumpled dress uniform and the dried drool that caked across his cheek. "It was just one time — the Poet and the colonists, it was too much."

She held her hand out to stop him.

He waited for her to speak, but she looked lost. "Rayne?"

She sighed, then pulled on his wrist and tugged him out of bed. "Come on."

Of all the times he'd imagined her in his room late at night, this was not how it was supposed to go.

He tugged down the rumpled uniform with one hand while she dragged him by the other. "Where are we going?"

"You missed dinner."

"So?"

She scowled at him.

Anyone else, and he would have turned back, but Rayne, and especially an annoyed Rayne, he obeyed, following her through the corridors like a child.

A handful of crew sat around a table playing some game on a

tablet, but otherwise the room was quiet. The lights were dimmed except over the tiny kitchen.

Rayne chose a small table at the far side of the room and gestured for him to sit.

"What time is it?" he asked, taking a chair.

"Oh-three-hundred. We've got about three hours left until the engines are ready for the next jump."

He stared down at his hands neatly folding in his lap, unable to look her in the eye. "Thanks."

"Sure." She paused and he could feel her trying to catch his gaze. "What happened?" she asked.

Gal shrugged. "Just tired." He made an effort to look alert, even though the Jin-Jiu haze still surrounded him like a fuzzy bubble. He molded his lips into what he hoped was a sober smile.

She looked away, watching the crewmen that cawed with laughter — the game must be getting good. When she turned back, her expression sagged with resignation. "Come on, I'll fix you something. What do you want? We've got a full stock of rations."

"I'm not hungry."

"We have protein noodles, if the crewmen haven't eaten them all already."

He shook his head again. "I'm really not hungry."

Her smile fell, cooled into an impatient frown. She walked away without saying a word.

He heard the familiar opening of a vacuum pack, the hum of the kitchen's warmer, and then a bright ding. Rayne returned with two steaming ration bowls. She plopped one in front of Gal unceremoniously.

Questionable contents in a paper bowl. Rayne had been raised on the stuff and loved it. But he had grown up on a farm and tasted real food.

"Now tell me what's wrong," she ordered him. "You were supposed to be cutting back."

He'd known her long enough, and there would be no evasive maneuvering when she was in this mood. "The Poet asked about the war," he said. That was true, after all.

She sat back, her face twisting as she picked at her words carefully, "I know you don't think kindly on the war, Gal, but many people are proud. Even if we lost our planet, humanity is still here, still strong — who knows what could have happened. You defended us. No one knew what was going to happen. As much as you don't think you did, you saved us."

If she only knew the half of it. What if there had never been a war in the first place?

"We have a planet. It's not the original one, but the crewmen tell me people are starting to think of it as home. Warmer too. And there aren't any supercharged killing machine-children on it."

Gal poked at the semi-solid mystery-food mass before him. "Do you really think the kids were that bad?"

"The Augments? If they were half as dangerous as the government told us they were, they would have killed us all. It was the virus, it made them hyper-aggressive. You know that as well as anyone."

That's what the researchers had reported.

"The Poet's job is to report on all facets of humankind. You fought in the war, it makes sense he would want to ask you about it. The anniversary is coming up. Don't let it get to you, yeah."

At that moment, Kieran Wood, previously unnoticed, popped out of the shadows and swivelled around in his chair. He shifted it noisily towards their table. With an unrefined plop, he dropped his own ration container on the table, gobs of gravy spilling out. "Hey, guys," he grinned.

"Gods," muttered Gal, dropping this head down. He hadn't even seen him tucked away at the little corner table. The chief engineer made a point of showing up at the worst times.

Rayne smiled politely and set her hands in her lap. "Hello, Lieutenant."

Kieran grinned, eyes lighting up like some idiot child, and he started spooning some of the glop past his lips. "So, whaddya know about the Poet?" he said, mouth half-full with the resequenced protein they were calling potatoes. He leaned back in his chair, throwing his feet onto the table.

Gal shuddered at the drawling accent — he never had bothered to ask where Kieran came from. And the manners — oh why, if he was stuck out here, did he have to be stuck with Kieran Wood? A whacko, a real spread-mad individual, who actually requested a posting on the freightship, so he could 'explore the planets in the Deep Black'.

Gal shoved some of the food-glop into his own mouth, making a point to chew it all the way down, staring laz-bolts at the engineer. It was true they weren't the strictest on protocol this far out, but Gal could be a real stickler when the mood struck. "Get your cracked feet off the table, Kieran."

The engineer jumped, but the size-ten, UEC-issue, grey boots stayed on the table.

Gal tried a different tactic to get his point across: "I know the Poet annoys me only half as much as you do, Wood."

The boots slipped down and Kieran shrugged.

"I know he's getting off at Selousa, and that's all I need to know," said Gal.

"We have orders to transport him, it's not up to us to know

why." Rayne spoke softly, her voice carrying warning.

Kieran seemed to take a moment's pause, and Gal let himself hope that would be the end of it. But his eyes got bright again, and he said, "He's kinda an odd fella, wouldn't you say?"

"Lieutenant!" Rayne's voice pitched half an octave higher than normal. "You're directing your scans where they don't belong."

"Nah, I was in there fixin' his computer for communications. Weird guy. Why do you think he chose the Ishash'tor. I mean, she's a great ship, but the messenger ships can get to Selousa in half the time. Nicer fixins too."

"Kieran," Rayne warned.

But Gal had had enough. Enough of the day. Enough of the Poet. Enough of the engineer. "Quit trying to make something out of nothing. Not everything is a secret plot, there's not something to explore on every uncharted moon. Life isn't that interesting. And the Poet definitely doesn't care about anything that happens on this ship." He took a heaving breath, forcing his seizing heart to calm down. "The commander and I were talking. We were having a private conversation, and that's what we would like it to be."

Kieran froze, and the laughter from the far side of the room stopped.

Gal recoiled from his own sudden outburst, realizing he was standing up, fists on the table with his food spilled all over the deck — the Poet must have shaken him more than he thought.

"Why don't you go check on the engines, Kieran," Rayne said at last.

"Sorry," muttered Gal.

Kieran waved him off as he left, his half-full ration bowl still on the table.

"Gal," Rayne admonished, "I know you don't like him, but he's watching you all the time because he wants to learn from you — not because he has some spread agenda. He's doing his time here like all the others. He's already been reassigned — one last trip to get the new chief up to speed and then he'll be out of here the next time we're at Etar. Try to be civil until then, yeah?"

"I know, I know." He scrubbed his face with his hands.

Rayne scooped up a spoon full of purple-orange stew, eating in silence.

Gal took a hesitant poke at his rubbery-looking noodles.

"Speaking of odd," said Rayne, tapping the corner of her mouth with a napkin, "the colonists have asked to speak with you."

"Tell them no."

"I did — well, I told them I'd ask you but that you were busy. That wasn't the strange part."

His heart started to crash around again, and he dropped his fork.

"I thought they would be excited, but they looked ... worried — I don't know, it was strange. One of them told me her name was Minerva, and she asked to see you."

Gal collapsed into the back of his chair. He must have had too much to drink, but usually it worked the other way — he used the Jin-Jiu to chase away the memories. "Minerva?" It couldn't be the same one.

"Yeah. Do you know her?"

"Absolutely not!" He pushed away from the table, chair crashing across the floor as he stood. "I can't see them."

"Gal?" Rayne called out.

His feet carried him to the door as fast as they could. The Poet, the colonists, and now Minerva. It had to be someone else, some different Minerva.

He sprinted through the ship's corridors, taking the most direct route to his quarters. He rounded a corner and stopped short.

"Oh hello, Galiant." The Poet's terrifying blue-eyes bore into him from the far end of the corridor.

Gal made an abrupt turn. "Not now, Poet!"

He ran his hands through his hair. The Poet was watching him, the Speakers were tempting him. And yet Minerva — if it was the same Minerva, and of course it must be — had been one of his most trusted allies.

Once, he had seen into the barren wastelands beyond the UEC compound walls at Selousa. He'd seen how the colonists had starved, their bodies growing weaker and weaker as they had run out of minerals. He'd watched them turn on each other, rip flesh from limb. Wasted frames and wasted minds.

Maybe it would be better, maybe the conditions had improved. Maybe what happened to Aaron really had been an accident. Maybe there was some other woman called Minerva in the cargo hold. All of it simply an unfortunate coincidence.

He leaned against the wall, panting. The hard black screen of a locking mechanism caught his eyes. The storage locker called to him.

But the Poet would be watching Gal and he would be watching the colonists. It was too dangerous. Minerva was strong, smart. She'd have to make it on her own.

And yet.

As though Aaron stood in the corridor beside him, a voice whispered in Gal's head, reminding him that he could not stand by and do nothing.

The consequences of getting caught were dire, and his

sensible mind played him an image of Rayne, reminding him of what he had to lose. It was too much, too risky.

He walked away, but the voice stopped him, a ghost hand tugging his shoulder and turning him to stare at the locker once again. Heart thrumming, he knew he couldn't leave them to die, no matter the consequence.

THREE

GAL SET A HESITANT FOOT at the edge of the upper cargo deck, peering over the railing. The lower half the cargo door laid open, forming a ramp. The hold filled with the muted sunlight and dry, dusty air of Selousa, casting a red-purple haze over the usually grey place.

Rayne stood tapping at her data tablet by the open door, presumably overseeing the cargo transfer. She marked as each colonist passed by in a single file line, flanked on all sides by UEC soldiers.

The cargo lift whirred, making the trip to the second level and descending again, loaded with cargo containers. Crewmen loaded the containers on hover-carts and floated them down the ramp.

Gal bit his lip and started down the clanking metal stairs. His footsteps fell heavy under the weight of the container he carried in his arms. He gritted his teeth with each stomp, but Rayne — thankfully engrossed in conversation with one of the new crew — never turned to the noise.

He descended to the second level, feet slipping on the slick surface of the rearrangeable plastic panels that made up the floor. The panels were set up in a standard half-deck configuration, and the stacks of cargo hid him from view of the deck below.

Crewmen grunted, shuffling containers and calling out row numbers as they collected containers meant for the colonists. Gal clutched the container in his arms, pleased he had guessed right and his container was the same size as the ones they were loading.

There was no way he could deliver the package to the colonists directly. Someone would see, and someone — maybe the soldiers at the base, maybe even Rayne — would take a look inside. Would they charge him with stealing or insubordination? It didn't matter, it would all be blasphemy.

He pressed himself against the stacks of containers, keeping out of view as he shut his eyes and breathed. He thought immediately of Rayne, and the shock-confusion-disappointment that would register on her face. He thought of the Poet's terrifying blue eyes drilling into him. Then, he thought of Aaron. And he thought of Minerva and her cold corpse buried under wind and sand.

He pushed himself upright, and slipped in to the loading area. "Here," he said, thrusting his cargo container in the arms of a surprised crewman. "Don't forget this one."

The crewman nearly dropped the container, his knees buckling. "Sir?"

"What?" he snapped. It was all he could manage, the breath nearly knocked out of him

"For the colonists?" The crewman frowned and stared at the box in his hands.

Gal raised an impatient eyebrow to cover his thumping heart. "Yes. You left it over there."

The crewman shifted, struggling with the weight. "It's

heavier than the others."

Gal shrugged. "And?" He couldn't help but wonder what — if anything — was in the other containers.

"Just wondering what was in it, sir."

His legs nearly gave out, but Gal growled and pushed on. "At the Academy, did they teach you to question your superior officer?"

The crewman paled. "No, sir."

"Or the Army? Your Gods?"

Eyes wide, the crewman took the container and scrambled toward the lift.

Gal retreated. Back in the safety of the stacks, he took a deep breath, and another. His hands shook and he pressed them into the stacks to steady himself.

The cargo lift whirred as it made another descent.

He scrambled for the stairs. The container might be the right design, but it didn't have an ID tag, and Rayne would surely notice that.

His hands slid along the worn railings as he leapt down the stairs. He had to make it to Rayne before the container.

"Gal?" She glanced up and down, scanning his entire body.

He passed a hand through his hair casually, wiping away beads of sweat. He forced himself to shuffle towards her. "Hi."

"How are you feeling?" Her data tablet tilted down, and she graced him with a smile. "I saw quite a lot of injury reports coming from the medical bay. Nothing too serious, I hope."

He placed himself on her far side, leaning against the frame of the cargo hatch. "All minor. I didn't want to bother you, I know you have your hands full our first trip out."

She turned towards him, and Gal relaxed, nearly melting into her warm, brown eyes. "Same as you didn't want to bother me about the malfunction in the weapons locker?"

"I could handle it. You always say I should be doing more. It is my ship after all."

"I'm your senior tactician. You wrote off half a dozen laz-rifles."

"Nothing you could have done. Freak malfunction."

"Maybe not, but I would have liked to assess them. If nothing else, it would make my report easier."

He glanced at the floor. "Sorry. Trust me when I say there was nothing you could have done. One of the battery cells imploded and set off a chain reaction. When I got there, the whole locker was smoking and they had melted together into a big gob of plastic."

"Really? I've never heard of that happening."

Gal shook his head, eyes still riveted to the floor. "Me neither. I was concerned the whole mess would explode, so I got rid of the them as fast as possible. It's all in the report. I had to visit the med bay a few times for the burns on my arms."

"Oh, Gal." She reached out, grabbing his forearm.

His heart leapt into his throat, both from the unexpected touch, and the knowing that if she lifted the fabric, she would see pale, healthy, entirely unburned skin.

The hover-cart saved him. "Oh look." He stepped back, pulling his arm from her grip.

The data tablet snapped back into Rayne's hands as she took stock.

Gal found it difficult to breathe.

"What do you have there, Jameson?"

"B-thirty-six through B-forty one."

She tapped on her tablet. A frown slid over her eyes.

"Uh, Rayne." He tugged on her coveralls. "I need to talk to

you."

She glanced over her shoulder. "Give me a minute."

"It's urgent," said Gal.

She sighed. Then miraculously waved her hand. "Thank you, crewman. Bring it down with the others."

The hover-cart slipped by and down the ramp, sliding easily across the black tarmac dusted with red. The crewman unloaded it with the others in a pile next to the group of colonists who were flanked on all sides by tacticians from the UEC base.

Did no one else think it odd that they carried heavy weapons, capable of killing a man with one well-placed shot, just to ensure the civilian colonists did not interfere with Central Army business?

"So, what is it?"

"Huh?"

Rayne stared at him intently. "You said you had something urgent."

"Oh, yes."

His eyes roamed across the hazy tarmac, following the tall grey wall that surrounded the landing zone on all sides. One heavy door led to the base itself: grey walkways and grey buildings with grey rooms and grey furniture.

The other door, the one to which the colonists were being led, opened to the barren landscape beyond the walls.

He hoped Minerva would understand. That she would somehow see the container and understand that the rations and medical supplies and weapons were all he could do.

And he hoped it would be enough. Little-h hope.

* * *

Halud DeGazo stepped off the open cargo ramp, leaving the UECAS Ishash'tor behind. A chill ran through him despite the warm and sticky air. He paused at the fortress gate separating the

UEC base from the landing tarmac to consider the weight of it. He had visited several bases over the years, but none like this one. None with such an important secret.

Officially, he came to observe the colonists, report on conditions and talk about hardships — Poet Laureate type work. It had taken years of careful cultivation to reach his position. And when he suggested the report to Hap Lansford, First Speaker of the United Earth Central Army, there had been no hesitation.

But it wasn't the Speakers he was loyal to, and he hadn't come to Selousa on government business.

Years of looking, months of planning, and suddenly all the pieces had fallen into place. The only part still uncertain was the captain himself. Halud's efforts to become friendly with the man had failed miserably, and while Halud had his suspicions, he had no way to know if Gal was truly the man he thought. After all, the rebel had been in hiding so long, most of his followers assumed he was dead.

Halud found an empty bench in the courtyard. Several of the freightship's crew wandered the small green space around him, marvelling at the automatic water and UV lights. The Central Army always made grass grow, even in the most desolate of places.

He touched his five fingers to his chest, bringing the tips together in one place directly over his heart: Faith, Knowledge, Prudence, Strength, and Fortitude. He would need all five of the Gods. He prayed, touching his fingers to his forehead and tossing the prayer to the stars, where hopefully the Gods would hear it and smile favourably upon them.

He repeated the whole process again, just for good measure.

Six weeks before, he had made contact with someone on Selousa. Someone sympathetic, someone who had also lost a

friend. By necessity, he didn't know the contact's name or even
what he looked like. But the contact had told Halud to come, that
everything would be set, and so he had trusted.

A small, flashing light caught his attention. He looked down
at the newstablet attached to the end of his bench, and dragged
his finger across to open it.

The new newsbloid had been uploaded. Selousa sat too far
out of the way for most ships, including the messengers, so the
news was never current. The newsbloid had been sent three
weeks ago from Etar onboard the freightship, brand new here in
the Deep Black.

On the front page, a poem he had written sat next to a picture
of the First Speaker, Hap Lansford. Halud read an article on the
terra-forming of a half dozen new planets. And an article about
gene splicing in lilies to make them more adaptable to new
conditions.

Then in fine print, at the very bottom of the sixth page,
buried beneath an advertisement for rejuvenation ozone therapy:
Far side. C-5. Don't be followed.

He blinked twice to be sure his nervous imagination wasn't
playing tricks. His knees nearly gave way as he stood, but he
could do this. For her.

Picking his way through the compound, he pretended to
examine it, run his hand across the grey walls, make notes in his
tablet. With one last check, Halud slipped unseen behind the far
wall of the compound.

The door marked C-5 hung open a fraction of an inch.

He pushed it open, wincing at the hollow creak, and entered a
standard, dull-grey hallway.

All the UEC compounds had the same layout — it made it
easier for soldiers to transfer back and forth — so he walked until

he came to a door he did not recognize, an extra door. It too had been left slightly ajar, and he slipped through.

A UEC soldier stood in the shadow. His uniform hung partly undone and his voice echoed darkly, "Master Poet."

Halud shivered. "Yes."

"Are you sure about this?"

"I am."

The soldier raised a single eyebrow.

"It isn't right what they've done to her. We both know that."

"You weren't followed?"

"No."

"Good. This would be hard to forgive, even for someone like yourself, Master Poet." The soldier's voice cut into him, shooting down his spine like ice. "You want to continue?"

Halud nodded. "Thank you for helping."

The soldier turned and descended a dark staircase. Halud followed. Light from the hallway faded, leaving him groping in the dark. They passed through a heavy door, the soldier bypassing its handprint scanner with a keycard.

The door shut behind them, the echo shuddering down the spit-shined black metal corridor they had entered. Halud flinched with each clack-clack their shoes made on the floor. "Will there be guards?" Certainly they would hear if they continued like this.

"I've taken care of them," the soldier answered.

Another heavy door opened. The walls turned from black to clinical white. Disinfectant burned his nose and eyes. But it wasn't clean. The smell covered something dirtier, darker.

"What is your purpose here, Mister DeGazo?" the soldier asked.

For the first time, Halud caught a clear look at his face: beady eyes in a heavy brow. "What?"

"I have to be clear of your intent, Poet. Did anyone send you?"

He stepped back. "What? No. I'm here for my sister."

"You've come entirely of your own volition?"

"Yes, of course. You know that. Why are you asking all these questions?"

The soldier nodded, his narrow mouth turning up sharply. Halud heard the click of a recording device as the soldier's hand flashed a signal.

A set up.

Soldiers sprung from the ceiling. Sharp clatters and shuffling sounded from the intersecting hallway. The soldier he thought was his ally pulled out a laz-gun, and the others piled onto him.

But if it was a set up, why send him all this way?

She was here. She had to be.

He pushed forward with all his strength, even as the soldiers pinned him down.

He screamed her name: "Sarrin! Sarrin!"

* * *

Sarrin woke with a start, her mind already racing. A dull, unplaceable sound reached her ears, even through the permaglass.

The monitoring station in front of her cell sat unmanned, completely.

Her mind screamed a single thought: *something is very wrong*. She had to get out. Now.

Three possible escape routes: the ceiling, the door, the floor. Floor would be fastest.

She had seen these types of cell constructions before, knew the seemingly solid chamber would be bolted on all sides to titanium I-beams, knew there was always a weak seal in the corner. The other corners were clearly visible; it had to be under the cot.

Throwing the flat mattress to the floor, she drove her thin fingers in the minute space between the solid cot and the wall. Her teeth gritted, and the metal bed bent under the force, letting her slide her hand through, grab and pull. Its metal fasteners bent like hinges, and the cot ripped back, revealing the corner seal.

A muffled shout came from the main room.

No matter, she only had to pull up the floor enough to slide through.

Gas hissed from the air vent above her head: sedative. She held her breath and started to count — she had four minutes at a full run, twelve if she stayed still.

Behind her, dead bolts clunked out of place on the cell door and the magnetic seal released. Surprised, she turned, watching the door swing inwards. For a moment she stilled, confused by the sight of the door that she had never seen open before.

Someone out of sight yelled, "Sedate the prisoner." Then, "Subdue him, he's pushing forward."

Through the open door, a panicked looking tactician shot off three dart-injectors in rapid succession.

They hit the wall — Sarrin already spinning to the side, her movements automatic.

She leapt to the door, pushing it closed. It would be too dangerous if they came in, too dangerous if she went out. She would escape through the floor.

The guard pushed back, his eyes wide as he stared at her through the three-inch thick permaglass.

Shouts and grunts came from the hallway. The guards came into view, a single man in the centre of them, fighting against their grip as he staggered forward.

She gasped, sedative gas burning her throat. Her nearly photographic memory remembered him perfectly, even though she had last seen him age 4-standard. Halud. Brother.

For a minute she felt the sedative — not enough to fall, but enough to pause — before her rapid metabolism chewed it up. Adrenaline rushed through her tight veins. Time slowed, her perception speeding up.

Halud struggled. His eyes caught on her, and he started shouting.

No no no. Everything felt too far away, too dark. She couldn't lose her grip on the world. Couldn't let the monster out. Was this the experiment Guitteriez had planned?

A laz-gun fired in the hall.

A black curtain dropped across her vision, and she pushed it back, struggling to keep control.

"Sarrin!" Halud screamed.

She opened her eyes. Guards: fourteen. Prisoners: two. Weapons: eighteen. Objects as deadly weapons: forty-two.

No, no weapons, she shouted to herself. Even she didn't know what she was capable of, didn't want to know. But if this was Guitteriez's experiment, it was working. The laser bolts and the shouting and the fear threatened to push her over, to put her somewhere she wouldn't be in control.

The terrified guard still pressing on the opposite side of the door, seemingly frozen. In the hall, Halud struggled, and another round of lax-fire bounced around the glossy white corridor.

There had to be a way out, there always was. They taught her that. She shut her eyes and forced her memory to recall the first non-combat thing she could: old engine schematics. She focussed, painting the image in detail until everything else fell away. Only then did she trust her eyes to open.

In the ceiling above the guard's head was a light — a recessed light. Escape routes: one.

She stepped back from the door, the guard falling in as the door opened under his weight. She leapt over his head, reaching for the light fixture and punching through it. The shattered fixture rained around her, leaving a trail of micro-cuts. Her other hand caught the edge of the ceiling, and she pulled herself through the hole.

A laz-bolt exploded behind her.

Scrabbling in the space above the ceiling, she made her way around the structural supports. Her mental map found the fixture closest to Halud, and she smashed with her fists, sending it crashing down. She peered through the hole, throwing herself back as a guard fired into the ceiling. The bolt bounced off the support, tearing through the metal construction with a dangerous scent of ozone.

Her reflexes, fast as they were, were untrained and sloppy after suppressing them for years in the cell. Panic surged through her.

The darkness clouded into the edge of her vision, tempting her. There was a way she could win, ensure her own survival. It reminded her of the speed and precision she could achieve if she just trusted it.

A tactician grunted as he heaved himself into the ceiling through the hole behind her. His laz-rifle fired, bolts bouncing off of every surface.

Gods.

She dove headfirst towards Halud.

The chaos below threw her senses into overdrive. She stepped on someone, falling as her feet unexpectedly slipped out from under her. She tucked into a roll, and her legs caught another guard, automatically toppling him over.

Yet another guard reached out, brushing her arm — the first person she'd touched skin-to-skin in years. His fear and anger transferred, zapping her like lightning, and she shrieked, pushing away.

She panted against the wall. A laz-rifle buzzed in her hands. And a taser prong stuck in her arm, its long coils spilling out. She didn't remember acquiring either one. A mini black-out, the monster was getting closer.

There'd been time for the monster to rip out the rifle's biosensor and reset it too. It hummed at her, waiting.

No no no. The rifle clattered to the ground.

She pulled the taser prong from her arm, it's 100mV charge still active. Her heart raced nearly as fast as her head, the world swimming around her. Escape routes: unknown.

She inhaled raggedly. Guards moved slower and slower.

Her brother struggled a mere two strides away. His blue eyes met her own. Time had weathered him, pushed his features into grim adulthood, far from the boy she used to know.

They were both quite far from what they used to know.

Halud spun to throw off his captors, a guard flying into the wall. He jumped out of their reach and grabbed the laz-gun from the floor. "Run!"

Her legs obeyed.

Behind her, Halud's laz-rifle fired in quick succession.

Her head swam. The darkness threatened, but she couldn't let it. Wouldn't let it. Still, every ping, and zing, every shout drew her closer.

"Here!" Halud shouted, pointing to a door. They passed through together. Grey robes billowed behind him as they climbed the dark hallways. They were running, just the two of them, like kids. The trance slipped a little farther away. They raced up the dark stairs, through the grey corridor, and broke out into the dull, outdoor light behind the compound.

She blinked, overwhelmed by the scent of cold dust and dying grass from the planetary compound.

Laz-fire rained down from the roof above, and Sarrin slammed herself into the cold, grey wall of the building, pressing flat. She touched her five fingers to her chest.

Halud pulled at the door, trying to go back in, but it held closed, locked. "No retreat, only what lies ahead," he said — an old litany. He cast her an apologetic look, then squeezed his eyes shut and stepped out, firing at the guards hidden on the roof. He let out an inhuman howl, a death roar as he sprayed laz-bolts wildly. Uselessly.

But they weren't done. She'd survived far worse. If the world would just stop spinning, if the blackness would leave her alone long enough to just think.

She turned to the door, sparks flying as she ripped open the electric panel. She crossed three wires, holding them until the simple mechanism overloaded, and the door sprung open.

Halud's face lit with surprise, and he darted through the opening.

No one waited for them inside, and Halud leaned against the wall to catch his breath. "Well, that was surprisingly convenient," he panted. He flashed a smile, a peek of boyhood shining through. "I didn't know you could do that."

She was tempted to ask what he thought they had been teaching her all these years, to snark at him like she had when they were kids in the wide open fields of their home, but her voice had forgotten how.

The sound of footsteps spurred them on.

They ran through the facility, the mental maps coming to her easily. The main entrance lay straight ahead, but the blackness sensed two guards and told her to go round. Halud kept straight.

With a shout, he came upon them. He shot one in the chest, burning through the pericardium into the heart, blood pouring from the wound. Halud's next shot only grazed the second on the arm, but he kept running and slammed the guard into the wall.

She gasped. Her overly sensitive and finely tuned body felt the empty, rushing, hollow feeling of a man dying. For all the violence she'd seen in her life, it still made her sick.

"Come on, Sarrin." Halud strapped another rifle over his shoulder and pressed two laz-guns into her hands.

Her fingers tightened around them reflexively.

"You just point and pull the trigger," he yelled at her, as if she didn't know. As if she hadn't spent her entire life being trained. He stepped over the bodies, through the front foyer of the UEC compound, and paused at the last set of doors leading to the outside.

She stared at the bodies, cold and empty.

"Come on, Sarrin. There won't be much time."

She nodded and followed. The subtle pulse of the laz-guns felt too familiar, too dangerous. They were a part of her, merely an extension of her being. And she was something else entirely.

He pushed through the door first. Nearly a dozen laz-bolts exploded into the ground, sending Halud jumping back.

Ten laz-bolts. She had seen each of them, measured their trajectory and speed. Six independent shooters, slightly spaced apart on the roof above, but still standing foolishly close together.

The darkness showed her the movement map, actions rippling through her muscles. She saw how to leap into the air, fire five shots, and kill them all. It was possible. Easy, even.

Her hand gripped the M250 laz-gun in preparation.

No!

She stumbled to the ground.

"It's not over until it's over, Sarrin. Don't give up." Halud took a deep breath, his voice shaking. "We just need to make the tarmac. I didn't come all this way…." Fear rolled off of him, waves of it crashing around her.

His blue eyes met hers, glossy with unshed tears. "I'm sorry, Sarrin."

Why? she wanted to say, he'd come all this way, given her more hope than she'd had in years. But her throat got confused and words just jumbled around in her mouth.

She couldn't let him die. The trance tempted her, but it showed her only an escape route for herself, not for Halud. And there was no telling what it, what she, would do, or if she would be able to stop.

She pushed the darkness aside, scanning the scene. There was always a logical solution. Her own map came, this one born of memory, the same way that engineering specs and engine schematics did.

But Halud took off running before she could signal her plan. He launched forward, his arm over his head as though that would stop the high frequency laser bolts.

She threw herself after him. The sound of laz-rifles charging buzzed in her ear. But the guards weren't half as fast as the simulators, and their laz-bolts dug into the ground at her feet.

Halud ran straight for the gate, firing laz-bolts over his shoulder. Foolishly straight. A bolt flew at his head, and Sarrin fired her own laz-gun, intercepting the shot, both of the bolts fizzing out harmlessly.

She jumped in front of another, catching it with the side of her thigh. The smell of charred flesh greeted her, but the bolt disappeared all the same.

"Come on, Sarrin." Halud ran ahead, oblivious of how close he'd come.

She dug her feet into the ground and ran, ignoring the fire that radiated from her burned muscle.

Halud raced toward the gate — the only opening in the perimeter wall. Guards poured from either side of the opening, filling it. More shouts and laz-rifles sounded in the courtyard.

A solid wall of guards blocked them. She grunted, the only thing she could do to catch Halud's attention. And she leapt onto the wall itself, climbing, the same as Halud had taught her to do so many years ago.

* * *

Gal sat on a cargo container, gripping the edge until his knuckles turned white, as he stared out the open cargo bay door into the red-purple haze. The crewmen had disembarked for shore leave an hour ago, excited to explore the UEC base. Luckily, the Poet had gone with them, and Gal was free to wallow in his memories for a few hours until they returned.

Next to him, Rayne sat working a cloth over an already polished M700 laz-rifle. "What are you thinking about?" she asked without looking up.

He sighed, and tore his gaze away from the wall, the heavy gate to the barren wasteland long-since shut. "Do you think those settlers will make it?"

Her hand slowed, pausing in her polishing for just a millisecond. "You tell me, sir."

The way she said 'sir' reminded him that Gods and their Speakers frowned on blasphemy, and the question was too close.

"If the Speakers say it is time to try, then it is so," she said. "They know the Gods' Plan and their reasons." She reached over and squeezed his leg. "I'm sure they'll be alright."

Gal nodded, blowing out a heavy breath. Maybe this would be the time, maybe Minerva and the others would make it after all. Little-h hope.

She returned to polishing her rifle, moving the cloth by rote. "Can I ask you something," she asked in a small voice.

"Anything."

"Why didn't you want to visit the General with me when we were at Etar?"

His heart crumpled inside of him, and he slumped forward. After a minute, he'd regained enough strength to speak. "Rayne, I'm sorry. I —."

"I accepted a transfer request before we left Etar," she said bluntly, fixing her gaze straight ahead.

"What? I don't understand. We've been out here together for years. What changed?"

"Nothing. And nothing will, that's why I have to go." She glanced at him, eyes glazed with unshed tears.

His heart shattered. "Rayne."

"I don't think this is the Path the Gods intended for me. When the Poet came on board, he said —."

"The Poet?" Gal jumped in his seat. "You can't trust anything he says!"

She clucked her tongue once, annoyed. "Well, he said some things that spoke to me, and helped me make a decision I'd been thinking of for a long time. He told me that we all have a part to play. That the Path may not be comfortable or easy, that it can require sudden changes, shifts we might not choose for ourselves. We should not be disheartened, and instead should continue to focus on our Service to the Gods, because that is what will always play through in the end."

Gal's mind reeled. "He said that?"

"Yes. I've gotten too comfortable here, I've been afraid to change. But I'm not meant to be out here ferrying freight, Gal." She sighed. "Neither are you, but that's a different story."

It made sense, it did. But the sentiments, if not the exact words, Rayne had quoted had a terrifying familiarity. "I want you to stay," he blurted.

"I'm sorry, Gal."

He said the only words that came to him: "I love you. If anything —." If anything happened to her, it would be his fault.

A hint of red crept into her fine features and her mouth worked as though looking for the thing to say.

A little of the big-H hope crawled into him. "I can do better. Please stay."

"I've already signed the transfer."

"No. I need you with me." He knew he sounded desperate, but this felt like the end. A terrible tightness squeezed all the air from his chest. "Our Path is together." If she was close, at least he could protect her; at least he would know she was safe.

She blinked at him, her lips pressed together in pity. He felt his heart shatter, taking the last semblance of life out of him.

Rayne sprang to her feet suddenly, laz-rifle braced against her shoulder and aimed through the open cargo door. "Gal! Get down." She rolled behind the cargo box, rifle set over the top of it.

From beyond the hatch came the unfamiliar, unmistakable sound of laz-fire. High-pitched zings grew louder, closer, before Gal could react. He stood and took a curious step forward. "What in the Deep is happening?" A laz-bolt reflected off the gangway at his feet. Burning ozone filled his nostrils.

A voice from the tarmac: "Here! The ship!"

Rayne's rifle charged.

A man in billowing grey robes sprinted up the ramp. Gods, it was the Poet.

Gal stood dumbfounded.

The blast from Rayne's rifle shot high and to the left, flashing off the cargo bay wall behind the Poet.

A girl came up beside, laz-guns in both hands. She stopped, her eyes wide. One hand quickly aimed a laz-gun at Gal's head. The other jerked to the side, shooting the control panel.

Halud doubled over, panting to catch his breath. "We made it."

The cargo door groaned as the hydraulics moved; the heads of UEC soldiers disappeared behind the closing hatch.

The girl turned her second laz-gun at Rayne.

Rayne had her rifle pointed right back.

The Poet flopped onto his side, still breathing hard. A cracked smile spread on his features.

Gal stood there, his mouth hanging open as his mind struggled to comprehend all the erratic and dangerous thoughts that came into his head.

The hatch sealed with a hermetic hiss, leaving the cargo bay silent except for the quiet pings of laz-bolts bouncing off the hull.

The Poet picked himself up from the floor.

"What in the Deep is going on?" Gal shouted.

"We have to go," said the Poet, waving his arm as he took a step towards the stairs.

"Go?" Gal planted his feet. "Where? What do you think you're doing?"

"Off this planet." The Poet came to him, resting his hand on

Gal's arm, forehead bent inches from his own. "I sense the call for great changes."

Gal stumbled backwards.

"Is this what you were talking about, Poet?" Rayne asked. She slung the laz-rifle over her shoulder.

Gal wished she was a million galaxies away.

The Poet frowned at Rayne.

"We're here for the peaceful haul. That's all." Gal threw his arm in front of Rayne, grabbing the Poet and turning him away from her.

The Poet bit his lip, and glanced back at the girl.

Gal's gaze followed. Filthy, hollow-boned, every finely conditioned muscle ripping under her skin — Gal felt the fear of ending when he looked at her. "No," he whispered.

"I need you, Gal. I came to your ship for a reason. Don't you understand?"

He did understand. And it terrified him to his very bones.

"What do you need from us, Master Poet?"

The Poet's gaze turned back to Rayne.

"Rayne, no!"

But it happened anyhow. Gal watched Rayne's ever-reverent face set with determination. He watched the Poet's eyes narrow with shrewd understanding.

"We need to leave the planet."

"Our crew!" shouted Gal. "We're here to run freight."

Rayne stepped in front of him. "We're here to serve the Gods. However we can."

"Rayne," he gasped. Dear, sweet Rayne who had never questioned the Gods or the Speakers once in her life.

She turned on him.

Gal clenched his fists, shouting, "I serve my Gods by running freight. That's all I want."

"I know who you are, Galiant," said the Poet.

"I'm a freight captain."

"Hardly. This is a mission you can't afford to pass on."

"You're going to get us all killed —."

Rayne slapped him, actually hit him. "This is the Poet Laureate of the United Earth Central Army," she hissed. "His words are Truth, he speaks for the Speakers of the Gods."

Wide eyed, he tried to plead with her.

"Don't be a fool," she whispered back at him. "This is your chance. Whatever failures of the past, the Gods have given you an opportunity to make it right."

"This isn't —."

Sparks flew from the light fixtures overhead — circuit overload. The pinging on the hull escalated, dozens of separate law-guns firing repeatedly. Gal recoiled, reaching for the flask in his pocket, gasping when his hand found nothing but emptiness.

Ghosts of memory whipped by him, but twisted, terrible. A firing squad and certain death outside. Certain death inside. And Rayne, standing there beside him.

"Hey, what's goin' on?" Kieran Wood leaned over the railing of the upper level, shouting down at them. "There's laz-bolts tearin' up my hull."

Gal groaned, clutching his straining chest. Why? Why was the engineer here? Why was any of this happening? For a minute, he thought he would be better off in the wasteland with Minerva. He would probably live longer, at least.

Rayne sprinted towards the stairs, shouting orders: "Prep the engines. Raise the shields. Prepare to break atmo."

"No!" screamed Gal. He fell to his knees. The girl — the thing — was gone. The Poet stood over him. And screams of long-dead demons sliced across him like physical blows.

Rayne stopped, turned. "This is what the Poet meant, Gal. Whatever demons have possessed you…. I serve the Gods, fully and wholeheartedly. Here is my chance to prove it."

He reached his hand out to her meekly. "Rayne, he's —."

"If you take this away from me…."

Gal pressed his lips together. "This is a bad idea."

"You're stuck, Gal. You can't even see a life beyond this freightship. But you deserve more. You are more."

Another shower of sparks rained down, the lights in the cargo bay flickering.

"We have to go, now," the Poet said — he turned to Rayne, addressing her directly. "That's an order, Commander."

Kieran still hung over the railing, watching.

"Lieutenant, the Poet Laureate's given us an order!" Rayne shouted.

Kieran stayed for a moment, staring down, and Gal felt a twinge of hope, mixed with dangerous curiosity as he felt the engineer study him. Then Kieran cracked his jaw, and pushed away. "Yes, ma'am."

And Gal sat alone in the cargo bay, trying to comprehend what had just happened. The lights flickered a final few times and finally gave out, casting him into darkness.

* * *

The half-finished diagnostic screamed in protest as Kieran ripped the sensor wires from the engine. "Sorry, no time for that," he said to the machine. He checked the data chip in the main console, and set it to record — now, there might finally be something worth sending home.

His fingers flew over the complex start-up sequence. Ion injectors hissed and the rotors clunked to life. In the background, laz-bolts hit the hull, pinging off the reflective metal.

"Engines on," he shouted into the comm screen. "Take 'er —."

The ship lurched off the ground, casting forward.

He slammed his fist into the comm. "Take 'er easy. Engines are cold."

In the wide open and entirely empty engineering bay, the row of work screens set into the walls flashed in unison: engine warning. "Great," he muttered.

He turned to the central console — a large round bench, and turned on the 3D display. A hologram of the ship flickered to life. Pinprick red dots highlighted the damage — superficial only.

He turned on the comm again. "Who's flying this thing?"

"*It's auto,*" Rayne's voice filtered down.

"Autopilot?"

"*We don't have a pilot.*"

"Oh."

Autopilot explained why the floor kept pitching back and forth. It took feel to move a ship the size of a warehouse through a gravity field with dense atmosphere.

"*We'll need the FTL,*" came a smooth voice — the Poet.

"Can't," said Kieran. "Regulations say I can't spool the plasma until we leave the planetary boundaries." Most regulations he didn't agree with, but that one seemed smart.

The pings of laz-bolts moved lower on the hull, shifting around the ship. At least this time they've gone away from the fragile gravity drive. He glanced at the 3D display and the little flashes of red, trying to figure out what they were aiming for, but they still hadn't caused any serious damage.

The ship jerked out from under him, and his head slammed into the console. "Jesus," he gasped. *Damn autopilot.*

Bright red lit up the fore-starboard thruster.

"*What happened?*"

"We've been hit." He manipulated the controls on the bench in front of him, zooming in on the area. "A few of the thrusters have been taken out."

"*Fix it!*"

The floor tilted wildly, and the 3D display showed the ship spinning over the starboard side, no longer held up by the weakened thruster bank. The ship's artificial gravity failed to compensate for the spin in the planet's competing field, and Kieran fell, his feet slamming into the wall.

Drawers spilled open and tools crashed across the bay. *Stupid autopilot.*

He bent down, his feet on the wall beside a work screen, tapping rapidly through the controls. The steering algorithms needed to be adjusted, or they'd slam into the ground in exactly the same place they'd started, only upside down. Of all the things not to leave home without, pilot sat top of the list.

"Come on, come on," he shouted at the computer. A slow progress bar creeped across the screen as it checked his calculations. They were right, he'd been doing them for years without any kind of computer, he should've just bypassed the checks. Instead, he scratched at his arm and pounded on the wall.

On the other side of the bay, something dropped. The girl from the cargo bay crouched on the wall the same as he did, squinted at the screen. As if the day couldn't get any weirder.

Ding — the computer finished. His finger flew so fast at the 'Implement' icon that it hurt.

The swirling gravity evened out and the ship righted itself. On the 3D view, the ship breached the atmosphere and the planet receded.

He let out a breath he didn't know he'd been holding, scanning across his ruined engineering bay. The girl had disappeared. "Hey," he called out.

The comm buzzed again, "*Kieran, the FTL.*"

"Yeah, yeah. One thing at a time." He kicked through the debris on the floor and went to the engine room.

The girl in his engine room surprised him, her hands flitting around the internal portion of the massive gravity drive.

"Hey," he snapped. "That's my engine."

Her eyes flicked up, fixing him with a steady stare. Her hand darted out and touched the control pad.

"Don't!" He rushed in and grabbed her shoulder.

She grabbed his hand with alarming ferocity and twisted it off.

Kieran gasped and stared down at his hand to be sure it wasn't broken.

Silently, she pointed to the screen, opening and closing her mouth, her eyebrows knitting together.

The plasma had started to heat up and spin, she had turned on the FTL gravity drive. "You're supposed to wait until we leave planetary space."

"*Where's our FTL?*"

He punched the nearest workscreen to return the comm. "Plasma's spooling. Another two minutes maybe."

The girl tapped at the engine, features drawn into a scowl.

"What?" He shouted at her. The computer buzzed at him from the other room. "Not now!"

The 3D display flashed in the other room, and the work screens showed another alert. He peered into the main room and gulped, hitting the console in the engine room. "Rayne, have you seen the warship behind us?"

The girl had disappeared from sight. *Jesus.*

"*Plot a jump!*" shouted the Poet.

He checked. "Three minutes left for the plasma to spool."

"*Three? I thought it was two.*"

"It's an old ship. I shut down the drive for maintenance on Selousa. The plasma's cold."

"*I don't think they've seen us.*"

"Why is the Comrade all the way out here?" he asked. They were supposed to be doing training maneuvers.

A clank sounded in the gravity drive. The girl's bare feet were hanging out of the access port.

Jesus. He passed his hand rapidly over his head, navel, and both shoulders. "Get outta there! Plasma stream's live."

Another clank.

She slipped out, moving so fast he didn't see her slither by. The data screen blinked as she tapped rapidly through the screens.

"What are you —."

The FTL bypassed it's checks. For a second, everything paused, and then they were pulled and compressed, squeezing through an artificial gravity well powerful enough to fold the fabric of space. Instantly, they arrived at their new destination halfway across the galaxy.

Wherever that was.

FOUR

"AMELIA, MY HUNTER." GUITTERIEZ SMILED, brushing his hand over her arm. "You're upset aren't you?"

Commandant Amelia Mallor bit down on the inside of her cheek, suppressing the illogical shudder that coursed through her from his touch.

The bridge of the UECAS Comrade hummed around them, the quiet murmurs of a dozen elite soldiers in crisp uniforms as they worked at gleaming white consoles. They were watching, she knew, as they always did, waiting for her next move.

Her warship hovered in geosynchronous orbit above Selousa.

Her head ached. "Far be it from me to doubt you, Doctor, but I find the plan difficult to understand."

He tilted his head. "How so?"

"You call me your hunter, and yet" — she growled involuntarily — "you have ordered me to stay while my prey escapes."

"Anger does not become you, Amelia." The doctor closed the last of the space between them, gripping both her shoulders and pressing his thumbs into the joint until she squirmed in pain. He relaxed the hold. "Is this not your task, Commandant, to help me in my work?"

Warmth flooded through her, anger forgotten. "I am sorry, Doctor. It's just, usually you ask me to detain them, not set them free."

"Not free," he said, shaking his head. "The laboratory has just gotten a little bigger."

"Should we not go after her?"

"Not yet." He grinned wickedly, scar curling across his cheek.

The wickedness in her leaped in anticipation. This hunt would be special, she was sure of it. Together, she and the Doctor were an unstoppable team: cunning, deadly, ruthless.

"You have confirmed our agents are in play?" Guitteriez asked.

"Yes. The message has been spread in the circle of influence on Contyna. An hour ago, I received word from our agent that the code had been uploaded into the freightship."

He nodded. "Good."

"What of the freightship? How will we find it and the girl again?"

"You think the thief on Contyna will hear these rumours?"

"It is certain."

"When he comes, he will bring her."

Amelia grinned. "And I will capture her for you."

"No."

"What?" She struggled to soften the sharpness that came into her voice, lest the doctor feel the need for another correction. "I fail to understand."

"It is a rouse." Guitteriez stepped close to her again, but did not reach his arms out. "There is a signal chip embedded in her skull that we need to activate. Then we will be able to monitor her every move."

"She will be free. Dangerous."

His hand came up to her shoulder, resting gently: a warning. "You will have your hunt, my dear. We will catch up to them when the virus takes hold and the freightship is floating in the dead of space."

The commandant's eyes flew open. "The plan is foolish. She has skill with engineering. What if she is able to escape? We should destroy her now."

Guitteriez's thumb pressed into her shoulder. "Relax, Amelia. Do not me regret my decision to involve you in the mission."

The warm sensation warred with her agitated heart.

"The technicians assure me there is no fix for the computer program. Every move has been plotted, checked, and pre-determined. She will not escape."

He pulled her against his chest, wrapped his arms across her back, and slowly her racing heart started to calm.

"I love you," he said.

She nodded against his embrace. "One more thing. Why the farce of drawing them to the warship? Why not activate the implant while on Selousa?"

"She would have seen you coming."

"Me?"

"This one is smart, wary. Everything must seem as though it has happened without interference for our experiment to be successful."

* * *

The pain radiating from Sarrin's upper thigh rated minor concern at most, even though the laz-bolt had torn through the skin and into the superficial muscle. Rarely did she allow herself to be hit, but she had calculated its effects on her to be significantly less than if the bolt had continued on its path and hit Halud.

She chewed a leaf of Yunnan she had found in the galley, turning it into a thick paste. She waited for her brother to look away before pressing the salve into the charred hole — he had always hated the sight of blood.

Every few steps, Halud would look back, checking to see that she followed him through the ship's corridors. His furtive smiles made her uncomfortable.

Instead, she focussed on analyzing her surroundings. Ship: Sycia Class, a freightship ten years out of manufacture. It had the inefficient layout of an early model, and that, combined with the stale musty odour and grimy brown staining on the walls, told her it was at least thirty years old. Standard crew size of twenty. Maximum jump distance 6,270 parsecs.

Halud stopped and pressed his thumb against a biometric door mechanism. The door opened and he stepped aside. "You'll stay here with me."

Her finely tuned reflexes vibrated as she scanned the room. Bed: one. Table: one. Weapons — *no!* She sat stiffly in the single chair Halud offered.

Cautiously, he sat on the bed, rubbing his palms across his grey trousers, robe spilling out around him. His body hummed with energy, his smile shining with exuberance. "Sarrin," he breathed.

He rushed across the room, arms around her, hugging her, before she could scream out and tell him to stop. She felt him shaking, felt the tears falling onto her worn jumpsuit. It burned like fire in the torn patches where skin met skin.

No way for him to know the danger he was in.

Her body tensed, became like a stone in his arms, but he continued, "I thought I'd never see you again. I've been searching for you all this time, and I couldn't believe when I found out you were alive... and now you're here, with me. Thank the Gods for being so good." He pulled back. "Sarrin?"

The grey-on-grey pattern on the carpet repeated twelve times across the room, and ten along its length. Thirteen escape routes and thirty-five objects that could be used as deadly weapons, not considering the latrine or wardrobe.

"Sarrin? Look at me." His hand reached out.

She forced herself to look up, look into the blue orbs spilling with moisture. She appreciated the difficulty Halud had overcome to find her and extract her. Certainly, he had gone to great lengths to be together again — but the last time she saw those eyes they peered out from his hiding place high in the apple tree as the soldiers captured her and beat her and took her away.

His eyes tightened with concern, and he studied her now at arms length. "Can you speak?"

Truthfully, she didn't know. Earlier had been the first she had tried in three years.

What would she say, even if she could?

Halud's face drew tighter. "What did they do to you?"

She flinched as he reached to touch her leg.

"Oh, Sarrin" He stared into her eyes, searching as though the answer could be gleaned from a simple retinal scan. "Do you — do you want something to eat?" he asked finally, "Or, or maybe a shower?"

Her condition must be abhorrent. Hygiene had scarcely ever had time to be a priority, but she had been educated on the general basics. She pulled at her sleeves, covering the burns and the tattoos running down each arm, and nodded.

"You must be hungry," he resolved, turning away. "I can find some food and proper clothes, while you clean up."

He was almost to the door. Her brother, the one who had taught her to climb trees and played for hours in the forests. Who had run away and taken care of her after their parents fell sick and died. She had to say something.

She worked her mouth, trying to get the vowels to sound. "Wait," she said, although it came out as a garbled cough.

The door opened automatically, Halud pausing in its silhouette.

There weren't words. They'd all escaped her head.

He smiled sadly. "It's going to be okay now. I'm going to keep you safe this time."

The door sealed behind him, Sarrin staring wide-eyed at the spot where he had stood. The edges of her vision grew fuzzy again, as an unfamiliar conglomeration of thoughts coursed through her head. Above them all: worry. It wasn't her that needed to be kept safe.

* * *

Gal fell into his chair. His pulse whooshed in his veins, thready and uncertain. His back ached. On his desk laid the overturned photo frame, facedown so Aaron couldn't see him, not like this.

The scene in the cargo bay played over and over like a bad vid.

It was a minute before he had the strength to reach down and slide the Jin-Jiu from the drawer. The half-full bottle slid into the warmer with a satisfying plop.

The old tin mug fit in his hand, so familiar it felt a part of him. His face reflected, warped and twisted in the dented metal. The image changed as the cup spun, but it was never right.

He shut his eyes and convinced himself none of it was happening before he pulled the bottle from the warmer.

The door buzzed. The cracked old ship didn't even wait for

him to grunt before it opened.

"Did you override my door?"

"No, I…," said Rayne. She huffed nervously — overriding a superior's door was a major offence to, unless, o course, you were commanded by the Gods. "I knew you wouldn't open it."

He slid down in his chair.

She pulled the bottle from his hand. "This is hardly the time." It went out of sight, tucked behind the desk as she sat. "This is our chance to prove ourselves in the eyes of the Gods, Gal." A smile — a real smile — played across her features, and his heart softened in her radiance. It was the most animated he had seen her in a long time. Youthful almost, vibrant.

He had thought it was just time, age that had made her change, but maybe she had been losing hope too. But now he could see the hope, big-H Hope, in her eyes. The corner of his mouth tugged up.

"The Poet —."

His heart seized, throwing him back. "No, not the Poet!" The blue eyes, the long grey cloak flapping the cargo bay haunted him, tearing apart whatever hopefulness his mind had managed to conjure.

"He's humanity's greatest asset. His path is the God's Path. Our part is easy. We just have to —."

"Rayne!"

"What?"

He threw his head back, shaking out the swimming feeling. "Give me my bottle. You can't keep it from me."

"We're on a mission for the Gods."

"No we're not." He knew it, plain as day.

"Gal!"

"Rayne." He rubbed his temples, his sigh turning into a

shout.

"You're a United Central Army captain."

"Not anymore."

"What's gotten into you?"

"The Poet." He shut his eyes as whispers rocketed around his head, coming from the desk — from the photo frame. "Please, Rayne, I don't want to do this. I need that bottle."

"The Poet came here for you. He needs your help."

"I won't." The girl had made Gal's blood run cold, but he was wrong. Had to be. "Maybe there's still a way out of this."

"Then you don't have to do anything to help him. I will. Until you're ready." She leaned forward. "Whatever happened before, it's in the past. The only thing we can do is look to the future. The Gods say it is so."

He groaned. "Enough about the Gods."

"The Gods are good. Why won't you take this chance?"

"Hap Lansford didn't send the Poet. And if he did, we're in worse trouble than I thought."

She stilled.

"Think, Rayne. We don't know anything about the Poet's mission."

"It's not for us to know. Faith allows us to trust as we follow the Path."

He loved her, but the way she regurgitated litanies at hime made his skin crawl, and he scratched at his arms. "No one sent the Poet! He's out here on his own."

"You don't know that. You told me you went to school with the First Speaker, that he was a friend. He knows you the way I do: a good and honourable man. If there was ever a mission of this importance, I would send you. Every time."

The whispers started again. "I'm not good."

"Yes, you are."

"I'm not honourable."

She leaned forward, eyes burning. "Yes."

"Stop it, Rayne."

"Gal! Let me help you."

"Hap Lansford spared my life once. He promised not to do it again. The Gods have left me, the same as they've left the Poet. I'm sorry, Rayne, but the Poet's on a cracked mission. That's the truth."

"It isn't. One day you'll see."

"What happened to the peaceful haul? We could do it, just you and me. We'd be together, no hassle, no worry. Just freight. From Etar to Selousa and back. Please. I'll stop drinking."

She bit her bottom lip, eyes soft. But her face hardened as she dismissed the idea. "Gal, we can't. This is our Path. The Poet has come here for us. For you. Don't you see it? You're not meant to be ferrying freight."

But he was. It was so much safer. That's what he was meant for, it couldn't be more clear.

A single, little brown hand waved from behind the desk. "Gal?"

His eyes grew wide, staring at the hand, and he blinked rapidly.

Another hand appeared, and another. Too small to be human.

He stood, leaning over the desk, too perplexed to look away.

The hands continued down to bodies. Shrivelled and grey-brown. Their faces featureless, eyes hollow. Hundreds of them. They cheered when they saw him.

He rubbed his fists into his eyes. The vision didn't clear. Instead, they rubbed their eyes too and cheered.

He fell back into his chair, hand over his gaping mouth.

"Gal?" Rayne repeated, her voice turning shrill.

Apparitions stood behind her.

"I know you've lost your way." Wide eyed, she pleaded with him. "I know things have been hard, but believe me when I say you deserve more. You are more."

The demons climbed the desk, standing atop it, waving. They too placed their hands over their mouths in perfect mimicry.

"Stop it," he grumbled.

"It's true, Gal. Why else would I stay out here this long?"

More climbed the desk.

"I see now that it was my Path. I chose to stay for you."

"Stop!" His hand swept across the desk. It passed through the grey-brown figures, knocking the photo frame across the room.

Rayne jumped back. "Gal!" A creature stood on her shoulder, its little hands dug into her perfectly neat hair.

"Where is the Jin-Jiu?" he demanded. There had to be a way to make this stop.

"You don't need it."

Long drowned memories were surfacing. He couldn't let them. "Yes, I do." He tried to clear the desk again, the visions jumping over his arms as it passed.

"Gal, calm down."

He roared as he tried to catch one, slamming his fists into the desk.

Rayne gasped. "Whatever demons have possessed you. Galiant!"

"No, no, no," he screamed. He caught one of them in his hand.

It had scraggly clumps of hair, its skin melting from it's bones.

The eyes and mouth were nothing but dark, hollow holes.

A demon.

It grabbed him and shook his hand, talons digging into the flesh.

He threw it across the room. It crumpled against the wall, lifeless.

Rayne looked back at him, eyes wide. The demon standing on her shoulder clutched where his heart might have been and fell, limp, smacking on the grey carpet floor.

The others, one by one, all crumpled and died, falling on each other in a wave.

Dead bodies. Dead bodies everywhere.

He had killed them.

And they were multiplying. Bodies on top of bodies. They were endless. Soon he would be drowned.

Bodies. Bodies. Bodies.

He waded, knee-deep, and then waist-deep, through the wreckage, trying to get out from around his desk, but it was no use. He stared at Rayne, unable to reach her as the bodies piled up around them.

Hundreds of faceless men and women.

From across the room, Aaron stared at him from the charcoal drawing.

They had all followed him and he had turned them into demons and killed them.

Rayne had followed him. She thought she was out here for good, for the Gods.

He met her eyes again, terrified, shaking. He had to make sure she was safe, whatever it took. That was all he could do now.

* * *

"The commander found these for you."

Sarrin took the pile of folded jumpsuits from Halud. The fabric was dark grey and worn in the knees — the uniforms had belonged to somebody, but there weren't any holes and the sleeves were long.

He set two steaming bowls on the little desk in the corner of the room. It was not normal meal-time, but her stomach rumbled the same.

Her muscles tensed as she felt his eyes following her.

"It's okay, Sarrin." He smiled at her again. "Standard rations."

She took the chair, her mind turning. It flipped back, to a place she knew but didn't recognize: *An extraordinarily tall man stared down at her, and she craned her neck to look back at him. The man's usually jovial expression was drawn with worry, and it made her want to weep. He turned his attention to a boy: Halud.*

"Your mother isn't well," said the man. "You have to go."

The boy whined.

"Promise me you will run. Trust no one but each other. Stay hidden. There's no telling what will happen." The man glanced up, a hovercraft working its way silently through the sky. "Go! Go now!" The man pushed Halud away, then took Sarrin by the shoulders and spun her around.

Halud raced across the open field, beckoning for her to follow him into the cover of trees.

"Sarrin! Sarrin!"

She gasped as Halud's touch in the little cabin brought her back to the present. He was yelling, gesturing wildly. "It's too hot! Sarrin! Sarrin!"

Her hands were clenched around the bowl of steaming soup, an odd sizzle-sound and accompanying the smell of melting flesh. She pulled her hands away quickly and assessed: second degree burns. It didn't hurt, it never did. She flexed her left hand, watching with mild curiosity. The burns were already blistering.

Halud peered at her hands, quickly turning away. He stifled a sick groan.

She clenched her hands, hiding them from him. The burns would be gone in a matter of hours.

"What were you thinking?" He stood, reaching for her. "We have to get you to the infirmary."

Sarrin shook her head — it would bring up too many questions, and it was entirely unnecessary. Hesitantly, she held out her hand, holding it so he would have to look.

His sickness turned to fascination. "It's already healing. How?" He reached to touch her hand, but she snatched it away.

He sat back in his chair. "I don't understand, did you not feel the burning?"

She turned away. Her heart raced, and she felt herself slipping, darkness clouding in. She grabbed the table, clinging to something real, tangible.

Halud finished talking as she came back to herself. He paused and looked at her expectantly.

She stared intently at the soup. She could feel Halud looking at her. Every noise and variance in the light threatened to overwhelm her — too much stimulus, too much new information. The distant sound of the engines, slightly misaligned, almost threw her into the trance.

She forced the soup into her belly as fast as possible.

After the meal, she showered as best as she remembered how, and changed into the borrowed coveralls. The grey uniform was too big but at least it was clean. There were an additional thirty-four items in the bathroom that could be used as lethal weapons. A terrifying prospect.

Halud beckoned for her to sleep on the bed. It wasn't very

big, but he intended to share. Maybe they had done that once, when they were small, but she couldn't remember. She curled on the floor, assuming the standard sleeping position taught to her before she could even remember.

She felt him looking, waited tensely for him to roll back over, and his breathing to slow.

He fell asleep almost immediately.

Sarrin, however, laid awake, forcing her body to be still.

Her mind started to sort through the jumble. She assessed her tactical situation, which she noted was the best it had been in a long time: she was free; her brother was here; they were on a ship; someone was going to hide them; and maybe, just maybe, she could escape it.

She glanced at her hands in the darkened room — shiny new skin where blisters were an hour before.

The Gods would guide her. She touched her fingers to her chest and then her head. *I believe in the power of Faith, and Knowledge, Prudence, Strength, and Fortitude. I want this to end. Please let it end.*

She opened her fingers and imagined the words floating up to the stars.

Sleep would not come tonight.

Sighing, she swung her legs under her, and slipped soundlessly from the room.

* * *

Kieran stood in Engineering, staring at the displays. He plugged the diagnostic probes into the engine and started another deep scan. His gut told him to be worried, something felt off and he couldn't figure out what.

The ship sat in the middle of empty space. He pulled up a star chart on the 3D display, and started studying it, hoping he might recognize the system and be able to determine their location. Lord knew he'd seen enough star systems.

The Poet had ordered him to take them to Contyna. But with the navigator and the mathematician left behind at Selousa, it was up to him to figure out where they were before he plotted their course.

The jump coils in the gravity drive generated a pulse of gravitons, strong enough to bend the fabric of space. A tunnel formed and the ship moved through it almost instantaneously. The stronger the coil and the longer the pulse, the farther they went with each jump. Simple.

What was not simple was aiming the tunnel, folding together the right sections of space. The mathematicians had a complex set of formulas to figure it out. But the girl had jumped them without any plotted course, and working the calculations in reverse for the untrackable jump....

He sighed, rubbing his palms into his eyes. They couldn't have gone more than 6,270 parsecs — because that was the ship's max. Problem was, it could be 6,270 parsecs in any direction from Selousa. They could be anywhere on the probability sphere he drew on the holographic display, and there wasn't so much as a debris cluster on the sensors to help mark their position.

It would be a long night.

Not that he'd give it up for anything. Finally something interesting for his research.

The engineering bay felt unnaturally quiet. Standard crew complement included a staff of eight, but they had been on planet with the navigator and mathematician. Only by sheer coincidence had he still been on the ship, trying to figure out a benign rattle that had come up in the engine part-way between Etar and Selousa.

He missed home something fierce, especially his Mama and his brother Andy. And his dad who taught him everything he knew about engines. His mission away from home had been nearly worthless, until the Poet and that girl showed up.

It didn't matter if they really were on some secret mission for the Speakers like they said, or running, or planning to take down the entire organization. At least it was something to do. What could they possibly be doing? Running from? How had they ended up on the old freightship? And what was the warship Comrade doing all the way out at Selousa when it was scheduled for training drills halfway across the sector?

The girl walked in. He nearly missed her, bare feet floating silently across the floor. Borrowed coveralls hung off her like an ill-fitting sack, but his keen eyes still picked up a subtle favouring of the left leg. Her wrists rubbed together and across her forearms, hands held out strangely.

He held his breath, observing, trying to glean as much information about her as possible before she saw him. People were only themselves when they were alone. And he considered it his mission now, more than anything, to figure out who she was.

She padded along the far wall, sticking to shadows as she moved towards the engine room. Her face looked tired, eyes sunk in and cheekbones hollow. She also looked mostly starved to death.

What had happened before she came running aboard their ship?

He crept towards the engine room so he could continue to observe her.

Her entire forearm trailed along the engine casing, caressing. She leaned into the humming machine, her features softening.

At once, her frame went rigid, lips tightening. She pressed her ear to the engine. Her eyes opened and looked straight at him.

He gasped involuntarily, caught and frozen in her glare.

Her eyes raked him up and down, as he held his breath. She tapped once at the engine, and tapped again, impatient.

"What?" he gasped.

Opening and closing her mouth, she knitted her eyebrows together. She pointed to the engine again.

He waited for her to say something, but she didn't. "You think there's something wrong with the engine?"

A single eyebrow raised, and she nodded.

"Yeah, me too," he said. "I've got the scans running on 'er now."

She pressed both arms against the casing, shoulders coming up and down as she breathed deeply.

His training reasserted itself, and he remembered she was a person just like any other subject. No reason to be so nervous, except his heart felt ready to beat out of his chest. "Hey-there," he put on his best friendly tone, and extended a hand, "I'm Kieran. We didn't get to meet properly —."

Her eyes snapped towards him, and he jumped back.

Wiping sweaty palms on his coveralls, he fought the sudden instinct to flee. "The Poet said yer name is Sarrin?"

She glanced at his upper arm, frowning as though the answer could be buried in the cloth of his uniform. A shake of her head a moment later, and she turned away, walking and tapping and listening to the engine. A terrible coughing, rasping whisper came from her lips. It took him a minute to work out.

"Kepheus?" he repeated.

She nodded once.

"Yeah. I've been getting weird readings, nothing serious, just a little funny since we left Etar."

Faster than he could blink, she disappeared from his sight. He caught just her feet slipping into an open access hatch. He tried to catch her leg, but it moved too fast. "What are you doing?" he yelled, concern overwhelming his fear. At least the plasma wasn't superheating this time.

The computer dinged, the scans done.

Her feet were too far in to see.

Sighing, he went to the nearest work screen. "Hey," he called out to her, "you're right. The Kepheus alignment is off, but by point-oh-three-one. I'll get the aligner."

Quickly finding the tools, he squeezed himself into the narrow tube, bracing against the heat. The engine block was a single T-shaped crawlspace nearly as long as the ship was wide. Kieran's shoulders took up the entire width of the access tube.

Sarrin had the panel off the Kepheus drive — the massive chamber where the plasma rose and made its superheated current that powered the graviton generator. He touched her leg, tugging on the baggy, grey coveralls.

She froze, leg jerking out of his grip. Her palm rested on the metal chamber.

"Careful. You'll burn your fool hand off!" His own hand grazed the Kepheus drive with a sizzle, as he tried to grab hers to pull it away.

Faster than he could see, her entire body spun around, curled in the blind-end of the access tube.

"I'm just tryin'...." He clutched his own hand. "You can't touch it, it gets too hot."

She blinked back at him.

Jesus, what was happening? He slumped back against the wall. "I didn't mean to scare you." What did the Poet want with this girl? He gritted his teeth and reminded himself to be more friendly. Friendliness lead to trust. Trust lead to information. He put on his best smile. "Here, I'll show you." He scooted forward.

She coiled back again.

He scooted back. "I'm not going to hurt you. I just didn't want you to burn yourself. I'm sorry I yelled."

Tremors running through her body, she blinked rapidly. Her eyes, wide and vibrant blue, refocussed, and she inched forward, reaching again for the Kepheus.

Kieran stopped himself from reaching out again. She was bright, if the ship's narrow escape told him anything, maybe he was telling her too many things she already knew.

"Calibration 99.8." Her voice came out broken. "Flow-through gasket is loose."

He looked where she pointed, and when he turned back, she had skittered into the opposite side of the T junction. She pointed again to the Kepheus drive.

He scanned it with his handheld. "Aligned within 3 one-thousandths. That's better than I can do with the instruments."

She snuck silently down the tube, nearly to the open access hatch.

"Wait. How did you —?"

She was gone.

He tripped coming out of the tube and fell on the floor. What exactly had he landed in?

She stood over him, the nine-eights spanner held out.

His hand took it reflexively.

"Flow through." She pointed.

"What?"

Before he knew what was happening, she climbed over him and into the access port, the spanner once again in her hands. She had said the gasket was loose, he remembered suddenly.

"Oh, hey!" Kieran reached for her leg again, but it had already disappeared. He banged on the side of the hatch. "No, no, no. I'd better do it. It can't be too tight or the whole thing will jam."

She flew out of the small opening, moving so fast he couldn't be sure if he'd actually seen her climb out or if she had simply appeared hovering over him again. The spanner rested in his hand.

Somehow, he realized his mouth hung open and closed it.

He picked himself off the floor, and flopped into the access tube, but there was no need — when he checked, the gasket was tightened perfectly, exactly as he would have done

The engine room was empty by the time he pulled himself out of the engine.

In the main engineering bay, the 3D display had changed, a new area highlighted on the star chart. He checked against the scans three times, but his work had been done for him.

He ran through the calculation to plot the jumps only paying half-attention. Despite all his training, his preparing and hoping and waiting, Kieran couldn't help the worry that this was far more than he'd bargained for.

FIVE

SARRIN BRACED, CLINGING TO A support in the ship's cargo bay, as the auto-pilot jolted them down on a landing tower. Planet: Contyna. Population: 10,097. UEC presence: minor. Location: twelve-hundred light years from the central planet, far in the Deep Black, the middle of nowhere. According to the database, Contyna had been terra-formed ten years ago. The settlement recently became viable, supported by iron mining in the vast sand dunes that covered the mostly barren planet.

The darkness clawed at her mind, and she squeezed the support beam with her hand until she felt its alloy start to bend.

Halud had become increasingly paranoid in the few days they took to travel to Contyna. A mysterious contact waited on the planet, someone who could hide them, but Halud feared they would be set up again as they were on Selousa. She wanted to tell him not to worry, all would be fine, there were few traps she couldn't get out of, but when he talked in circles late into the night, all she could hear were Guitteriez's words echoing around her own head: *We just need to break her open first.*

"Here you go." The first officer held out a laz-gun. "The

Poet wanted you to have one in case you need to protect yourself."

The weapon was small, only 64V, single pulse — the kind that fit entirely in your hand and kids played with. It made Sarrin's heart accelerate and the edges of her vision blur.

Did normal children play with the weapons? She tried to recall, so far back it barely seemed real. Memories layered on top of other memories: Halud playing with a similar gun, chasing her through the gardens until the tall man who must have been their father had yelled. The gun was a toy, but it sent a shiver up her spine, even then.

She had parents. Her beating heart stopped. A single memory: *A woman laid in bed with long dark hair spread out over a pillow, death on her face. And then Halud running far ahead, her short legs pumping to keep up in the long grass.*

Halud went over his plan one more time. He spoke to the captain, but it was the first officer who listened intently. "I'm sorry to say that this will be the most dangerous part of the mission. We must not be detected by the Central Army patrols on our way to or from the facility," he said.

"Right," said Rayne. "Because this is a covert mission for the Gods, and they are not yet ready to know."

"Uh, yes. We have set the ship down on a nearby landing tower, instead of flying to the hanger as our contact intended. I believe it is important that we fully assess the situation before we enter ourselves into it. We will make our way on foot, and enter the compound here," — he pointed to a grainy, out-of-date satellite image — "at the back door. We can assess the situation in the compound before deciding if it is safe to make contact."

Sarrin squeezed the support beam again. There were too many variables, but she couldn't find the words to suggest hacking the video surveillance, or taking a multi-pronged approach to the facility, or utilizing underground conduits instead of walking through the open streets — no way to share the hours of tactical theory that had been drilled into her head.

And so, the darkness clawed at her, showed her all the places the plan could go wrong, and reached dangerous tendrils over her vision.

"Whatever you say, Poet," Gal shrugged. "We drop you and the girl off at the hangar and we leave, right? That's our job done. Maybe we can still make our freight route and pretend none of this ever happened."

Halud bristled.

Rayne pushed in front of Gal. "We serve the Gods. We will be with you to the end." She saluted with her five fingers.

Halud's eyes widened in surprise, making him look incredibly young. Incredibly like the boy Sarrin had known. Incredibly like the last twenty years had never happened. But when he spoke, his voice came out hard and adult: "The engineer and first officer will stay with the ship."

The engineer made an odd noise. "The way I see it, Poet, you're gonna want a few more people on your side here if you don't know what we're walkin' into." He picked up one of the laz-guns and looked it over, inspecting it clumsily. Sarrin doubted the engineer had handled many firearms, still he'd been nothing but keen to help at every opportunity since they'd left Selousa, and she couldn't deny a pang of gratitude. He nodded towards the first officer. "And Raynie here's the best shot on the ship."

Rayne stood calmly, waiting for instruction. Her laz-rifle, slick and polished, hung precisely over her shoulder: 300V, fast-pulse, 150-metre range.

Halud paused, considering.

"This is a fool plan," slurred Gal, far from sober. The outline of a small drinking flask bulged in his pocket. "Why am I coming with you?"

Colour and hope drained from Halud's face. He turned to Rayne, "Yes, alright, we'll all go. But we need to start moving if we want to maintain the element of surprise."

"The Gods we Serve, in the Gods we Trust." Rayne prayed, tapping her fingers to her chest fervently.

Sarrin prayed too — prayed that the miniature laz-gun resting in its holster on her thigh would stay there. That her hand wouldn't inexplicably reach for it and start firing.

As though the situation they were walking into wasn't dangerous enough, the simple possibility of losing control threatened to overwhelm her. Time slowed and her head started to spin. Somehow she found herself placing one foot in front of the other, travelling down the ramp behind the others and off the landing tower.

Their UEC coveralls blended in with the dust stained uniforms of the iron miners as they walked through the streets. Dry heat and bright sunshine assaulted her senses, the spinning dust clouds tasting of iron, of blood. The folk kept their eyes to the ground, quickly shuffling past on their thin, wiry frames, but their emotions bounced around like crashing surf, making Sarrin dysphoric with the sensations.

A voice wafted into her consciousness: "Sarrin, you okay?" The engineer's furrowed brow and bright eyes and teeth sharpened into focus in front of her.

"Fine." Her voice sounded far away from her.

The sloshing and clinking of the captain's flask suggested he'd taken yet another drink.

She forced herself to exhale, pushing herself closer to reality.

Kieran knelt down, connecting his handheld to the

warehouse's back door. It flashed once, the security system bypassed, and they entered.

Halud's plan had not been specific beyond breaching the warehouse, but the service lift opened straight ahead and they all climbed in together. An enclosed space with a single door in and out. Her breath came in short gasps against her pounding heart. She tapped against her leg while she distracted herself, estimating the length and width of the box, calculating its volume, standard gas-weight, and the litres of water it would take to drown them all. *Stop*, she told herself.

Rayne checked her laz-rifle, preparing in case there was need to fire.

The miniature laz-gun rested heavily against Sarrin's thigh.

Elevator doors opened. Too slowly. Halud said something, but she couldn't hear it amidst the pounding in her ears.

She forced herself to breathe.

The maintenance corridor was long, straight, and narrow — if they were ambushed here, there would be nowhere to take cover. Extreme tactical error. Her inner ear burned, adrenaline making all of her senses incredibly sensitive as she hunted for sound. There were faint footsteps below: eleven sets, male, moving quickly.

Halud tested the few doors in the hall but they were all locked. He led them to the far end, stopping where the corridor opened into a rough stairwell. He turned and looked nervously at Gal.

Desperate for distraction, Sarrin pinched her arm, hoping the sensation would give her something tangible to ground against.

"We'll try the next floor," said Halud.

They followed him up flight after flight, ragged breathing echoing around the barren staircase. They stopped at the uppermost floor of the twelve-story warehouse.

"Should we go in?" Halud nodded at the corridor that opened in front of them.

"You keep looking at me like I know something," said Gal, "but we shouldn't even be here. We should have left Selousa and disappeared beyond the Deep Black. That's the only way to survive whatever fool errand you've put us on." The captain took a drink from his flask.

Halud shook his head. "I have to see this through."

Gal groaned and leaned against the wall, sliding down until he sprawled across a set of stairs.

"What's wrong with you?" Halud snapped. "I came all this way —."

Rayne stepped forward, craning her neck. "Sirs, I see an access hatch part-way down the corridor," she said. "Kieran could open it and we could have a look through into the main hangar."

Halud huffed, his normally silken voice shaking. "Yes, excellent. Thank you, Commander. Excellent idea."

Kieran moved into action, sliding up the stairway past the group and into the corridor. The others followed, crowding around to watch. It took the engineer less than a standard minute to open the panel. "Big freight bay," he said when he pulled his head back into the corridor, "lots of cargo boxes and a small shuttle. No one down there though." He waved for Rayne to join him.

Sarrin pressed her ear against the wall. Despite Kieran's assurance, she could hear the men in the hangar shuffling now, twisting and setting something. Some kind of machine, not a laz-gun she thought, but something else familiar — if only her wrecked mind could think.

The first officer slipped back into the corridor. "My tactical assessment shows there are suitable sources of cover spread around the room. I recommend the rest of us infiltrate the area and provide protection while you meet your contact, Master Poet."

Halud shifted his weight. "It's too exposed, I won't put Sarrin in that position."

Gal frowned, the parts of his expression shifting too slow. "You're going to have to meet this contact some time or come up with another plan."

"I have a bad feeling," whined Halud.

The corridor was too narrow, far and close at the same time. Gal said something, and Halud something else — all lost to Sarrin, her mind drifting too far away. A hand reached out, her body instinctively flinching away. Rayne herded her towards the service lift. Halud and the captain moved in the opposite direction.

The elevator doors opened and the closed, swallowing her and Rayne and Kieran, trapping them. Her body vibrated in anticipation. Definitely a trap.

She listened for signs of the men below, but they had gone still and silent. Her eyes searched the elevator box frantically for an escape route — a hidden service door or panel that would open — but the walls were smooth, bare except the single button control panel.

Kieran reached a hand for her shoulder. "Your brother and the cap'n will be just fine."

His touch bolted through her. She stopped herself from breaking his arm, twisting away instead. She found no door, no exit from their cage. The elevator finished its descent. A sound of quiet shuffling reached her from the corridor beyond.

She pushed Kieran to the side with her elbow, muscles coiling and preparing to spring.

Rayne frowned opposite them, gripping her rifle, and mirrored their move to cover beside the door.

The doors swooshed open, the entryway empty in front of them.

Sarrin blinked. Perhaps she had been wrong, her mind so badly fractured it was just plain making things up now. She took a single steady breath.

She heard a rapid flurry outside, followed by the click of a mechanized trigger and a hollow-sounding explosion of air. An improvised smoke grenade landed on the floor and started spewing white gas.

Demons. She stared at it. The white-grey colour and sudden odour of ammonia identified the fast-acting neuro gas — they would all be unconscious in 5.4 seconds. Sooner if they panicked.

Darkness crowded around her vision, black clouds rolling over the white.

"Looks like there was no one in there, Boss," said a disembodied voice in the entry.

"Be patient," came the reply. Somewhere in the back of her brain, Sarrin recognized the deep voice. "We need to be careful with this one," he said.

Kieran started to claw his eyes.

The monster whispered to her; it painted the scene in her head — eight men crouched against the wall — it showed her a movement diagram: maximum casualties with minimum effort. Escape was possible, always possible. But the others....

The boss spoke again, deep and clear and concise. Familiar. A friend.

She used the voice to pull herself back to the surface. Putting her hands on her head, she stepped into the doorway. The neuro-gas filled the hallway, only glimpses of the men showed through as they started to move towards the elevator, wearing goggles and breathing filters to protect themselves. Their leader — Hoepe Fallows — smiled behind his mask, and motioned for her to lie down.

Kieran copied her, mimicking the hands-on-head submissive posture as he laid on the floor beside her. Mentally, she thanked the Gods as the darkness receded, and she cursed herself for being so wrecked. She used to have far better control.

Behind, a laz-rifle clicked and charged. Rayne stepped into the open doorway, and a laz-bolt seared above Sarrin's head. An instant later, Rayne slumped, succumbing to the neuro-gas. Two of Hoepe's men rushed in, catching her and binding her hands as she lost consciousness.

Kieran started to cough and wheeze on the floor beside Sarrin. Feet rushed all around them, and Kieran was lifted up and carried away.

A gentle hand hovered over her arm, keeping a space between them as he pressed a breathing mask to her face. Hoepe leaned in, "It's good to see you, Sarrin."

*   *   *

Kieran let himself be pushed into the dark room. His vision blurred from the stinging tears and the scratched faceplate of the breathing mask they'd put on him before binding his hands.

His heart hammered in his chest, and his breath came in gasps. He searched frantically for Rayne, but the men had taken her in the opposite direction when they led him and Sarrin across the wide-open hangar.

He blinked, trying to replay the scene, the whole thing still a blur in his mind. He suspected Sarrin had known they would be there, even before the gas started pouring from the grenade. How? How did she know to surrender? That they would be friendly? Were they friendly?

He took a deep breath, as the hand gripping him tightened and directed him into a dark, narrow corridor. He couldn't afford to panic. He had to observe.

Kieran stumbled over a half-step, the guard spinning him against a wall and pushing him down. The ropes dug into his wrists as he jerked and landed hard on the ground. "Who are you?" he asked, caution warring with panic. The man pulled the mask off, and he repeated the question. The guard patted him on the cheek and left.

Sarrin sat to his left. An extraordinarily tall, hook-nosed man leaned over her, whispering in her ear. She nodded once in response. After a few days working in engineering, he had no doubt she was smart as a whip, but she was weird as anything. He tried to take comfort from her seemingly relaxed posture, but his hands still trembled uncontrollably.

"What's going on?" he asked her.

Her eyes shut as she leaned her head back against the wall. Either she hadn't heard or she chose to ignore him.

A muffled shout drew his attention to the opposite side of the room where Gal and Halud sat side-by-side, hands tied. Halud had a binder tied over his mouth, and he looked wide-eyed-terrified.

The hook-nosed man bent down to untie Halud. "Don't scream," he said to the Poet, pulling off the gag. "I really hate that."

Halud lunged forwards. "What have you done?"

The man flicked him once in the neck, and Halud's eyes went wide, clutching at his throat as though he suddenly couldn't breathe at all.

Kieran gasped, throwing himself back against the wall, as though he could hide there. His training had not covered this situation. They weren't supposed to be involved, just watch, just observe.

"Where's Rayne?" shouted Gal.

Hook-nose turned, twisting another point on the Poet's neck, who gasped and panted. The man moved to Gal, reaching to untie him next. A single eyebrow arched as high and angular as the rest of his face. "Your friend panicked and was subject to a sedative gas — she is being cared for and will recover in a few hours."

He stood, brushing his hands over his crisp trousers. A vein bulged in his neck as he took a deep, calming breath. "My name is Hoepe. The Poet requested my assistance and that is what I intend to give. Had you not made such a foolish trespass into our warehouse, we would not have had to go through this charade. I am sorry this is the welcome you have received."

The man, Hoepe, moved to Kieran, and he tucked his hands in tight to his body. Gently, Hoepe pried the hands out and released the ties.

Blood stung painfully as the circulation returned to Kieran's hand. At the last minute, he remembered to look up and scan the man's face, noting it's intensely crystalline eyes, sharp features, and the shadow of pale blonde stubble.

"Relax," Hoepe whispered. He also patted Kieran on the cheek, quirking the corner of his mouth before he stood and turned away.

Kieran found himself frozen, breathing heavily. Definitely more than he'd bargained for. He wondered if there was a communication array he could access, or if he was going to die here without his family ever knowing what happened to him. Did *he* know what was happening to him?

Hoepe spoke again, hand on the door. "You are not in danger, I promise you. I would appreciate if you waited here until the boys bring your ship into the hangar. We tracked your entire approach and, while the soldiers at the outpost may not be bright, they're bound to notice sooner or later. You understand I can't take risks." The door sealed behind as he left.

"What's going on?" Kieran asked again. No one answered, and he glanced to his left, where Sarrin sat, her forearm rubbing across her opposite arm, fingers pinching periodically. Her hands were free — had they even been tied in the first place?

Her eyes opened a slit, and she glanced at him, tilting her head in an expressionless gesture. Wait, it seemed to say. So, he pressed his palms together, resigned. She had pushed him out of the way once, he had to hope she was doing it again.

Halud jumped to his feet. "I don't like this at all, Galiant." He crossed the room to Sarrin's side in an instant, reaching to brush away an errant strand of hair.

Sarrin pushed away from his touch, nearly bumping into Kieran.

Halud stared at her, leaning forward on his knees until he seemed to think better of it and bounced to his feet. He started to run his hands over every panel that made up the smooth wall. "We have to get out of here."

Gal made an odd noise, his body trembling. "Rayne?" he mumbled, rubbing his head in his shaking hands.

"What's going on?" Kieran tried again, louder.

The door to the room opened again. A man brought in a pitcher of water and set it on the floor. He raised an eyebrow at Halud, caught red-handed searching the wall, and grinned. "Boss must like you." He pointed to the water. "This stuff is hard to come by on Contyna."

Halud stared after the man, waiting until the door shut behind him. He took two strides to the centre of the room, and sent the pitcher flying, water crashing across the floor.

Sarrin leapt to her feet, water and shards of ceramic splashing over her and Kieran.

"Oh!" Halud scrambled, reaching for her arm. His other hand reached towards the smashed pitcher at the same time. "I didn't mean to frighten you. I just —."

"I told you this was a fool plan," Gal said, his voice straining as he stood.

Halud turned, staring at Gal. "Then you should have said from the beginning."

"I did." Gal looked past the Poet, pointing a finger at Kieran. "Where is Rayne?"

Kieran jumped, pulling this legs in close to his chest. "I don't know."

"If anything happens to her…." The captain turned his wrath on the Poet, scowling.

"You're not the only one with people to look after," Halud said.

"I was looking after my people just fine until you came along." Gal and Halud stood chest to chest, posturing for a fight.

Kieran felt dizzy — definitely more than he bargained for. He shut his eyes, and tried to envision the long, stretching and rusting corridors of his youth, the smile of his mother at his safe return home.

"This isn't something we can deny," said the Poet. "You know as well as anyone we have a duty to do what is right. No matter the risks."

"I'm not following your 'Path,'" Gal spit. "Rayne's not here, so let's call it like it is."

Kieran's ears perked up, and he told his internal freak-out to hush, just until he heard this.

"I thought you'd be happy to be here, working for this" — the Poet held out his hands — "for a mission you abandoned so many years ago."

Gal paused, then growled, "You don't know a thing about me. You're a cracked fool, Poet. If you'd asked me, I would have told you to leave it all alone. You don't know a thing about Hap Lansford and the other Speakers, you only think you do."

"For Gods'sake, she's my sister. What was I supposed to do?"

Gal went white. "Your sister?"

Kieran blinked, turning to the girl. Sarrin's hands dangled lamely by her sides, her face turned up to the ceiling, eyes darting back and forth, blissfully ignorant of the screaming fight beside her. There was an uncanny similarity between the raging Poet and the strange girl.

"Don't you understand?" pleaded Halud.

"You don't understand — you've sentenced everyone to death. Me, you, your cracked sister. Rayne." Gal buried his face in his hands. "We can't cross them. They're too powerful."

A tremor of fear shot through Kieran, good sense telling him to run far and fast, but he stayed listening. He'd been waiting for this, praying for something interesting to report home.

"You survived," said Halud. "You're still here."

Gal froze, eyes wide with terror.

Halud grabbed him by the shoulder. "What would John P have done? Not this. What happened to you?"

Spinning to action, Gal pushed Halud away from him, eyes gleaming. "You're a cracked fool to follow the rebel!"

Halud crashed into the wall so close Kieran had to dive out of the way. Sarrin's eyes shifted, meeting his for a millisecond.

Halud pushed himself back up. "I came for your help, Gal."

"Trust me, that's the last thing anybody wants." Gal swung his arms out blindly, as though he could physically push the entire situation away. He swung and swung, like a maniac, until he crouched down, pawing along the ground. "Where in the Deep is it?"

"Where's what?"

"Back off, Poet."

"Your flask?" Halud shouted. "It's hardly time for a drink, if that's what you're after."

"It spreading-well is!"

Sarrin caught Kieran's attention with a cough. She pointed at a fixture in the ceiling, then she shrugged and sat down. They had been looking for a way out, is that what she saw?

Kieran's pulse pounded in his ears. Bewilderment replaced fear, and he watched the scene in fascination, unable to react, unable to think.

"We need to get out of here," said the Poet.

"We need to never have been here," Gal said coldly, still searching on the floor. "You have no idea what happens to people who defy the Gods, who stray from the Gods' Path."

"I'm the Poet Laureate of the United Earth Central Army!"

"The most useless job I've ever heard of."

"I've written the words of the Gods!"

Gal climbed to his feet, pressing a finger into Halud's chest. "You've written whatever Hap Lansford told you to write. You're a dirty pawn."

"Sometimes you have to play in the system."

"Fool."

Halud grabbed Gal's wrist, voice dangerous, "At least I know what I believe in."

They stood toe-to-toe, huffing at each other.

Kieran pushed off the floor before he could think about what he was doing. If he stayed, if he tried to figure this whole thing out, it would be far easier if the main players didn't kill each other. "Knock it off. I'm sure we can agree that we need to find a way out. You can argue later."

Both men turned on him, chests heaving.

A deep baritone voice spoke behind them, and Kieran realized he hadn't even heard the door as Hoepe entered. "Wise words. Your ship is here. We took the liberty of removing the tracking device from your hull." He smiled grimly. "You're lucky the imbeciles at the outpost never bother to check their scanners, or we would have had more serious problems than whatever spat you're having." He turned to Halud, voice dropping even lower. "Master Poet, I trust we can get on amicably from here. I have a low tolerance for stupidity, and while I am keen to help, I had not expected such childish behaviour. I don't say this to be cruel, but because you have put my men in danger multiple times today, and I cannot allow that. Do we understand each other?"

Halud gritted his teeth, bristling, but his head dropped and he nodded mutely.

"Good. Sutherland will show you the facility."

The Poet swallowed noisily.

Hoepe gestured to Gal and Kieran, "You are free to return to your ship. Your friend is there, along with your effects. Sutherland can show you where to find tools for your repairs."

Kieran pushed himself to his feet, as Gal scurried out of the room followed hastily by Halud. Sarrin had already disappeared. Kieran found himself alone, standing alarmingly close to Hoepe

— maybe a captor, maybe a friend.

Hoepe twitched the corner of his mouth, in what Kieran presumed should have been a smile, except none of the man's facial features moved other than the lip, and even that was easy to miss.

He fell back on his training, as he stared into the much taller man's eyes, determined to figure it all out: *Be friendly. Don't be a threat.* Kieran forced a grin onto his face, teeth and all. He clapped the man on the back as he passed. "Thanks, buddy."

*   *   *

Hoepe Fallows — trauma surgeon turned smuggler — sat across the table from a silent Halud DeGazo, brother of Sarrin DeGazo, prodigy. The wide interior windows of his second floor office looked over the newly acquired freightship that sat in his hangar, and it was there that Halud kept turning his attention.

Hoepe cleared his throat. "How did you find her?"

Halud's pulse sped in the contours of his neck, pupils dilated — a fear-fuelled adrenaline surge. Perhaps Hoepe had been too harsh earlier. He filed the thought for future consideration.

"Where is she?" asked the Poet.

"I'm uncertain."

"What?"

Hoepe shrugged — an affable gesture the others indicated made them feel more comfortable. "The entire warehouse is safe, and I doubt she will leave, although the rest of the planet is not particularly dangerous either. We have business to discuss. I'm curious how you located her."

"What? I haven't seen her since you locked us up in that cell. We need to be out looking for her, not in here discussing business!"

Hoepe frowned. Somehow the Poet had done what he had

not been able to, but the way the Poet tried his patience might have been more trouble than he was worth. "You've already agreed to trust me. I've known Sarrin a long time, she can take care of herself. Besides, I would hardly consider a storage room with an unlocked door a cell," he said, feeling that should be the end of this inane conversation.

"You don't understand. They've done something to her, she can't even speak."

He dismissed the thought with a flick of his hand. "She's always been terse."

"You don't know her, she was always bubbly, quick to laugh. Quick to tease."

Hoepe pressed his lips together, drawing up an empathetic statement. "I understand it's been several years. I cannot imagine —."

"Where is she?"

He sighed. Unlike his crew who were all straight to work, the Poet was definitely more trouble that he was worth. "Probably in the walls, checking the wiring."

"What?"

"You asked where she was, and I have hazarded a guess that I think is most likely based on my experience."

Halud stared at him.

"Now, business." He hadn't intended to rush, but some of what he needed to discuss was time-sensitive. "I require your assistance to take advantage of a unique opportunity."

"What do you mean, 'unique opportunity'?"

"There is a mission I need your help with."

Halud stared at him, but remained silent.

"You have noticed some colonies do well and some do not," Hoepe continued.

The Poet held out a hand as though he were preaching. "It is the Will of the Gods."

"Hardly. One does not wait for success, one takes it. There are those that have what is given to them, and those who find ways to obtain what they need."

Halud frowned. "You want me to steal something."

"Yes."

"That was never part of the agreement. I won't be a part of it. To steal from our neighbours is against the Gods."

Hoepe raised a single eyebrow. "You have already stolen an entire person from the Gods."

"That's different."

"Not at all. The trouble with living out here in the Black is food: there is never enough. Just step outside, everyone is bone thin, bordering on malnutrition. We need food to feed the people of Contyna. That's the only way the colony survives. We steal so they can live. Surely, the Gods appreciate this."

"I want no part in it."

"You are certainly not ingratiating yourself to me, Poet."

Halud looked away, staring across the open hangar. "I'm a poet, not a thief. You've got your band of thugs to do that for you. What do you really want from me?"

Hoepe licked the corner of his lips. "You're correct, there is something else. An opportunity too good to waste."

"What is it, then?"

"I have word a ship will be passing through in a few days time, resupplying for training maneuvers. My crew will be going to steal the supplies and create a diversion. I want you and Sarrin to download the database core."

"A database?" Halud rocked back in his chair. "You want information."

"Correct. I am a smuggler — rations, clothes, water — but none of it interests me as much as information."

"I could give you information." Halud turned to him again. "We don't have to board a ship for that. I know all kinds of secrets."

Hoepe raised an eyebrow, "Very useful, indeed, Poet. But I am looking for something specific, something you would not know."

"There's very little I do not know."

"This you don't."

"Try me."

A spine! thought Hoepe, *the Poet did have one, even if it was quite flexible.* "I'm looking for others like your sister."

"Others? Why? It's a fools errand, they've been cursed by the Gods."

Hoepe raised an eyebrow. "And still here you are. My reasons are my own." He knew he'd been lucky so far, that one day they would come for him. But he had to keep looking. It would have been much easier to turn his head away from the whole thing, but some unnamed organ ached in him, a hole in his soul that couldn't be filled. And this was the only place he could think to look, his desperate longing bordering on obsession.

Halud bit his lip. "I will do whatever you ask of me, but leave Sarrin out of this, she doesn't have to go."

"I'm afraid we need her."

"You don't. She's not well, she can't go."

"We won't have another chance."

"Not Sarrin."

"My men will provide a distraction, but any database will be heavily fortified. Sarrin can get you there safely."

"What?"

"Through the walls."

"I don't understand."

"No, I see that," Hoepe said. He bit his lip before he laid down the threat: "If you want to stay here, you need to help me with this." Not that he meant it, not really, but time was critical.

"That wasn't part of the arrangement."

"This opportunity only made itself known recently. I didn't think you'd be so difficult."

"The only ship scheduled for maneuvers out here is the Aitor, a survey ship. It doesn't carry a database."

"My sources are well trusted. I'm sorry, Poet, I can't think how to explain the level of importance."

"I don't want Sarrin in danger."

"Properly executed, there is no danger. It's a survey ship. My men will work with the engineer to retrofit your ship."

"It's not my ship."

"You obviously hold say, I need you to speak with the captain."

"He won't agree."

"Then I will speak to him."

"There's no point. He's not who I thought; he won't agree."

"He will." Hoepe punched the communicator on his desk, shouting his orders into it. How had he let the Poet rile him up so much — more than exploded limbs or infected implants or open heart surgery ever had?

Still, his sources had never been wrong, and a database would be on the ship; he had to stay focussed on the mission at hand.

He closed his eyes until two of his men dragged the captain into the office and set out a chair for him.

"Trouble, Boss?" asked Sutherland, his unofficial right hand man. Sutherland glanced at Halud, his eyes scanning up and down. "Let us know whatever you need."

Hoepe sighed, smoothing over his emotions. "No, thank you." The Poet had brought him Sarrin and that was worth twice as much annoyance.

The captain fell into the chair by the desk. "What do you want? I was busy."

"Busy with what?"

"Busy." His pupils were unnecessarily dilated in the bright light and his jugular pulse beat at an erratically high rate; Hoepe made his diagnosis quickly.

"When I returned your effects, I didn't expect you would drink the flask all at once."

"None of your cracked business."

"It's not good for you. Highly addictive, mood altering."

"I said, none of your cracked business," the captain growled.

Hoepe glanced at Halud, who only shrugged. The man did seem rather difficult, but he would certainly have a price — they all did. "You weren't expecting this journey," said Hoepe, "I imagine you're undersupplied. Perhaps you've thought of rationing but are feeling the effects of withdrawal. I can get you more."

The captain's jaw worked side to side.

Beside the captain, the Poet's eyes flashed wide and horrified. "Don't enable him!"

Beyond caring, Hoepe saw himself as the kind of person who weighed the costs and benefits of each decision, the overall good more important than the warm-fuzzies of morality. Some of men called him ruthless, he preferred driven.

Twice before, his crew had tried to collect a database, and they'd lost men with nothing to show for the trouble. But this time, he could already see it, feel the data-tablet in his hands.

"Galiant, — may I call you Galiant?"

"Call me whatever you want," said the captain, his words slurring with intoxication.

The man was obviously in trouble, but it was hardly Hoepe's problem. He hadn't broken Galiant, the captain had already had the fractures of addiction written all over him when he walked into the facility. *The ends justified*, thought Hoepe, *the good of the many over the few*. The captain was expendable, the database was not. "I need your ship."

"I intend to fly it as far from here as possible as soon as possible." There was still some shrewdness left in his eyes. "I'd appreciate if you asked your men to stop tinkering with my ship."

Hoepe tried to reproduce an appropriately understanding smile. "Galiant, I —."

The captain heaved himself forward, markedly uncoordinated. "I don't know what kind of cracked situation we're in, and I don't want to know. The Poet's got my first officer convinced this is a mission for the Gods, but there's no way Hap Lansford sent you to me. I've lost enough friends to cracked do-good plans. As soon as she wakes up, we're out of here." He flopped back into the chair. "And another thing: don't you lay a hand on her. If my first officer doesn't wake up feeling one-hundred-percent, I'll throw you to the Demons of the Deep myself. Got it?"

Hoepe raised both eyebrows. "Captain, I am a highly trained medical doctor. Your first officer is in excellent health and will make a full recovery once the effects of the gas wear off. I imagine they have already started to do so."

"Good."

A new idea crawled into Hoepe's synapses, potentially terrible, potentially brilliant. "The first officer is a person of significance to you, yes?"

"This situation is cracked enough, I don't want her any further into it."

Halud began, "Gal, I think if you knew what was really going on, you would be more interested in helping us. The Path of the Gods is —."

"Don't give me that drivel about the Gods! What have they ever done for me?"

"Where would you go?" Hoepe asked.

Gal turned his head. "Away. Far away. Beyond the Deep."

"And what would your first officer say about that?"

Sighing, he shut his eyes. "She's not going to like it. No thanks to you, Poet. The military is her life, but what choice have you left me with?"

The Poet interrupted again, "If you go to the Army outpost and say you were following my orders, it won't be easy but you can —."

Gal laughed, loud and barking. "You're a fool. I'm already dead."

"My words are the words of the Gods, they can't punish you for following them."

"The worst part is you don't even know what you've pulled us all into." Gal shuddered, reaching around to pull his flask from his pocket. He took a long drink. "I had a life on that freightship, maybe not a good one, but something. Something safe. I'm as good as dead. Worse, Rayne is as good as dead. And you did that."

"If you —."

"I don't want to hear it. You've killed me for this fool dream of yours. Sister or not, you've damned us all."

Halud slumping against his chair.

Hoepe chose bluntness. "I need your ship, Captain."

"Didn't you hear me? I have to make my way to the deep Deep, before they put me there."

"You don't know me. You don't know the empire I control. I can make a person disappear, give them a new life. A person like your first officer."

"What?"

"Records are easy to falsify. Maybe she was transferred, maybe she never served aboard your ship. It won't be perfect, but she can be hidden. Retain a semblance of the life you value so much."

Gal leaned forwards again, but his voice softened, keen instead of defensive. "Are you saying you can keep her safe? Whatever cracked business the Poet has brought down on us, you can keep her out of all of it?"

Hoepe grinned, a real smile now that they were getting somewhere. "Yes. And for you as well, Captain."

"Not me," gal shook his head, "I'm too far gone. But the engineer? They're good people, they shouldn't have gotten caught up in this."

Hoepe nodded. Two wasn't any more difficult than one.

"What do you need from me?"

"Your ship."

"You can have the old tin can if you can make this unhappen for my officers."

Hoepe touched his fingers to his chest and reached across the desk to touch Gal in the same spot, the promise made. "Consider it done."

"No." Gal shook his head. "Not until it is. You can borrow the ship, but it's not yours until I see they're safe."

"Huh," said Hoepe. Even spread-drunk, the captain was no

fool. "I need to make modifications to your ship."

He took another drink. "For what?"

Hoepe considered, but bluntness won out again. "I intend to follow a survey ship through their FTL hole, board them, and take their food supplies. Consider it a downpayment, then I will start working on hiding your people."

Gal shrugged. "Believe it or not, that's not the dumbest thing I've heard today."

Hoepe raised an eyebrow while an uncertain fear settled in his gut.

"I assume you have a plan that won't get us all killed," said the captain.

SIX

SARRIN CLIMBED OUT OF AN access port, landing in a quiet corridor of the freightship. She tested the feel of the carpet, spreading her toes across the grey surface; worn fibres poking into her bare feet. She closed her eyes and grounded herself in the sensation, hoping that her mind would relax. It had been on high alert even though the danger had passed. She tracked every sound and shuffle in the warehouse, unable to cope with the sudden exposure to the real world after years in a sound-proofed white cell.

She walked, rapping her knuckles on the grey walls, beating out a coded pattern. Of course, no one answered, no one ever did, not anymore, but the habit comforted her. She thought back to the bunkhouse, to the girls who had been her squadron, her friends. They used to communicate with each other through their tapping — before Sarrin was selected and made to be alone.

The memory warmed her, only for a millisecond. Her mind travelled in time again, clippers buzzing as clumps of her hair fell away, someone screamed in her head. Involuntarily, her hands went up, bringing her back to the present.

Kieran had appeared somewhere during her blackout, and he was talking to her: "Do you know anything about it, Sarrin?"

Her mind scrambled, unsure how to answer, terrified he had snuck up so easily. He always asked questions, questions, questions.

"... There's six of 'em. They look like a cross between a ray-gun and an air-vent, pieced together from spare parts. I can't get one open, looks like they were put together and then sealed shut. All I can see is reams of wires and a massive solenoid." Kieran's hands flitted distractingly in front of his face. "Hoepe's man, Sutherland, told me it's a cloaking device. Have you ever seen anything like that?"

She frowned. "Yes." Once, she had built a cloak to cover small things, inanimate objects they wanted hidden.

"Really?" His eyes lit up. "Can we take a look? I need to know if you think it will actually hide the entire ship."

"Entire ship?" she gasped, shock rooting her in place.

"Yeah. Your buddy, Hoepe, seems to have a plan." Kieran didn't wait, already half-way down the corridor before she caught up to him. His excessive hand motions distracted her thoughts. He droned on about something excitedly, but her mind slipped out of focus. She slapped at the ghost of sensors probing her body.

Why was she remembering these things?

He led her to the cargo bay and down to the open main level, stopping in front of a collection of mid-sized welded boxes. One was split open a crack, wires bulging out. "So? Whaddya think?"

Across the bay, a familiar clicking caught her attention: Rayne stood by a table, laz-rifles spread across the surface. She disassembled a 450mV she held in her hands — click, click.

Sarrin gulped and turned her attention to the device in front of her, pushing back a flood of memories.

"He sent specific instructions on where to place them, equidistant on both sides of the hull," said Kieran.

She rocked the partly-open box, peering into the crack from different angles, assessing the large, compressed-transistor-solenoid. With the right amperage, it would bend the light around them and act like a cloak. A big one. Powerful enough to hide a ship.

The click-click drew her attention again. In her mind's ear, she heard the rapid echo of dozens of laz-guns being assembled and disassembled while little hands fumbled through the movement.

Kieran coughed, drawing her attention. His eyes met hers, a bemused grin on his face.

"Hoepe feels this will be safe?"

"Safe? Yeah. Why?"

She'd never been confident to test it on a living creature. But Hoepe was a doctor. If anyone would know about safety, he would.

"Wait, so *it is* a cloaking device. You think it'll work?"

It was bigger in scale, but the principle was the same. She nodded.

He stared at the boxes in awe. "How do you know?"

Her mind slipped in time again, explosions echoing around her. She shook her head to clear the noise. "Built ... before."

"Wow." He rubbed a hand over his jaw, studying the machine. "I thought it couldn't be done. How does it work?"

"It...," she started. She did know, schematics and force diagrams coming to her easily, but her mind was too wrecked to put it into words. The pressure of injections ghosted on her skin, laz-beams seared the air next to her body, all her senses turning cold as she touched the lifeless body of a friend. "Gravimetrics," she forced out. Sweat beaded on her back.

"Ah! Together these generators create a gravity field that bends photons and other particles around the ship." Kieran smiled with understanding. "Right?"

Sarrin heard the click-click across the cargo bay, and her feet moved towards it.

"Sarrin?" He jogged after her.

Her ears picked up an irregularity. Nothing specific, an indescribable change in pitch, and she bent her ear to it as she came closer. She took the laz-rifle from Rayne's hands, oblivious to the shout the commander made.

Rayne reached to get it back, but Sarrin easily stepped out of the way.

Kieran held up his hand, his words a distant echo in her mind. He whispered, "I want to see this."

Rayne whispered back, "It's against regulation."

"I think she knows what she's doing."

Sarrin studied the rifle, weighing it in her hands as a schematic drew itself in front of her, her focus narrowing down to a singular problem: an engineering problem.

"What if she hurts herself? What will the Poet say?"

"Give her some credit," said Kieran. "Besides, aren't you curious about this whole thing?"

"You're asking too many questions. If the Gods mean for us to know, they'll tell us."

"I'm not sure the Gods even know."

Sarrin spun the rifle around, twisted and popped open the refraction chamber. She adjusted the calibration, moving the lenses a fraction of a millimetre until the balance normalized. Then, she clicked it back together, rapidly, the way her hands had memorized so many years ago. The rifle was to her shoulder, her eye in the sight with the laz-rifle humming before she knew what she was doing.

She forced her hands to relax, finger sliding off the trigger. Breathing slowly, she neutralized the rifle's charge and set it on the table.

Rayne stared, and Sarrin waited, heart beating frantically. Kieran would have questions for sure, Rayne looked ready to unleash a string of reprimands. *I would be better if Rayne did reprimand her* — she had been careless to pick-up the rifle. Something had stopped her from firing it, but she could have just as easily lost control.

Hoepe shouted her name from the open cargo ramp, oblivious to the tense looks that passed between Kieran and Rayne. "There you are. I've been looking for you." His long, lanky stride carried him across the bay quickly, and he stood, dwarfing them all with his 7-foot frame. "You were supposed to report for a physical," he said to Sarrin.

His hand reached out and she flinched away. She had no interest in doctors, none whatsoever. "I'm fine." She glanced to her left, identifying six separate escape routes.

Hoepe opened his mouth to argue, but Kieran stepped forward, interrupting. "You know, Sarrin was just giving us a hand. We shouldn't be too much longer."

Unsmiling, Hoepe cast a skeptical gaze at the table. "Rifles? This is a stealth operation."

Rayne coughed nervously. "You can never be too careful."

"You're the tactician Gal seems so fond of." It was not a question.

"Er, yes."

Hoepe's attention turned back to Sarrin, intense blue gaze

impatient, and she shifted back preparing to run.

It wasn't that she didn't like or trust Hoepe — he'd been a friend in the short time they had travelled together — but she had tasted freedom, and part of that freedom included never submitting to another doctor or exam or experiment again.

Kieran interrupted again, his sidelong glance silently assessing her. "I just need her help for a few more minutes. Then she's all yours, okay?"

It occurred to Sarrin that he was trying to buy her time, or an escape — why?

A muscle in Hoepe's cheek twitched. "I see the cloak remains on your floor awaiting installation. I would like to leave you to complete your job. Please allow me to do my job."

"Look, I'm not trying to get in the way of anything here. If she wants to go, that's one thing, but she's just a girl and she looks right uncomfortable. If she was my sister…, well, you're a whole lot bigger, and the whole thing doesn't sit well with me."

Hoepe frowned, his eyes narrowing as he studied Kieran.

Sarrin studied Kieran too, her mind momentarily forgetting to run as it pulled apart and analyzed each of his words: '*Just a girl.*'

Sighing, Hoepe rubbed the spot between his eyebrows, releasing the crinkle that had set in. "I assure you there is no ill intent." He turned to Sarrin. "Come on. I know you don't like to be touched, but we have to do it. I'm sending you onto a UEC ship at some point in the next few days. You were in that prison for four years, I need to know that you're in good health."

"P-prison?" Rayne's voice squealed an octave higher than usual.

Sarrin cringed. She felt Kieran's gaze search her, calculating. He thought she was just a girl. A nice, normal, non-monster girl.

"Sarrin," Hoepe pressed.

Her heart hammered. He could say too much. Halud had kept her secret, but she had no idea if Hoepe would, or if he even knew it was a secret. Besides, normal people wanted to be healthy. Normal people probably liked to go to the doctor. She pressed her lips tight together, mimicking a smile. "Okay."

"Really?" He raised a single eyebrow. "That was uncharacteristically easy."

She nodded and stepped forward, encouraging him to follow so they would be away from the others as quickly as possible.

Hoepe caught up and took the lead as they descended the ship's cargo ramp into the large, open warehouse. Barren grey concrete with harsh fluorescent lighting. Cargo containers of every size lined the walls, and two men boxed in an area set aside for sparring, their comrades cheering them on. Escape routes: thirty-seven. Weapons: twenty-eight. Objects that could be used as deadly weapons: one-hundred-sixteen.

"Be careful with the engineer," Hoepe said quietly.

Surprised, she faltered in her step.

"He thinks you're something you're not."

"They all do. That's the point."

"Agreed." He paused, turning to her. "I have been observing my crew for the last several years. Some of them attempt to protect each other from perceived threats, the same as the engineer did for you today. This is what they call 'friendship'. I'm afraid I have no reference to understand it. But they spend time together, frequently discussing personal history. This would be an unwise discussion for someone like us." He spun on his heel, walking away without waiting for her to answer.

She followed him, uncertain what she would have said if he had given her the chance to speak.

A small room off the main warehouse held his makeshift lab. Several medical devices were crammed neatly in the space, lining every wall. In the centre stood a steel table, the only light in the room the overhead procedure lamp.

Her breath caught in her throat, and her hands slammed on the outside edge of the door frame, keeping her from going in. Blackness clouded in the edges of her vision while the remembered sound of an operating drill buzzed in her ears.

Hoepe glanced back from turning on his machines. "You're here now, might as well do it the easy way."

She had no doubt she could outrun him and seriously considered the option, but there were no escape routes unless she ran back into the warehouse. The men would see. And then there would be questions.

She placed one trepidatious foot inside the lab, reminding herself this was nothing like Selousa. Hoepe was nothing like Guitteriez. She slipped lightly onto the cold table, tucking her hands tightly against her torso.

Hoepe stepped behind her, his hands hovering over her back and arms. "It's good to see you again."

She nodded. It had been four years since she had seen a friendly face. Now both Halud and Hoepe were with her — there was hope after all, despite the haunting familiarity of the current medical. This moment, the exam, was short term, a few minutes maybe, she just had to remember to breathe. She wiggled her toes, bare feet swinging in the air, concentrating her mind on the action, pushing out the remembrance of steady beeping and the drip-drip of drugs pushing into her system.

"I'm going to scan your bio-electric field." He stepped away, and she sighed with relief.

The machine clicked as it took the picture, and she froze,

careful not to move for the full fifteen seconds it took to scan her.

"Standard physical palpation next." Hoepe stepped back, stretching his fingers. He stood in front, pressing into her.

She shut her eyes with each jab, his gentle touch on the exposed skin of her neck burning with the electrical energy from his fingertips.

"Breathe, Sarrin. I'm not going to hurt you. I've done this thousands of times."

Forcing her lungs to move, she nodded. Better to hold it all down, to keep everything as still as possible when the doctor came this close. Lest the monster rear its ugly head.

He traced down her arms, pressing through the fabric of her oversize coveralls.

"You've lost too much weight," he said.

She nodded.

"The boys are on rations, but I want you to take double. Even if you're not hungry."

She nodded again, although so far her stomach hadn't taken well to the change in diet.

He continued down to her elbows, tugging gently to pull her hands free from her sides, but she held them firmly out of view. He tried again, but she refused. "In all the years, you've never once let me look at your hands. Why not?"

She shook her head.

"I'm not blind. I know there are scars there. Do you have pain? Maybe I can help."

Pain was not the problem. Bile rose in her throat.

He sighed. "Fine." He stepped away, coming around to her spine. He pressed down each of the vertebrae, looking for reactivity, satisfied there wasn't. "Your axial skeleton and muscling are in excellent condition. Let me run some labs, but I'd say you're in fighting condition. Not that there was any doubt."

She pressed her lips together, debating silently with herself while he stepped away to retrieve a set of blood vials. "I don't want to hurt anyone," she said she he returned, voice small and quiet.

"I know." He frowned. "You won't. It's a simple mission. Data retrieval. I need you to help Halud; I need his access codes, but I don't know if he can handle himself."

She lifted her foot, gritting her teeth as he held the sensitive arch and centred the vein to draw his sample, bare skin sparking on bare skin.

"It'll be fine. I recall you and our old friend Grant going on similar missions all time. It'll be the same, just no hot head leaping into fights."

A quick smile, a real one, relaxed her features.

"You won't hurt anyone. There's no fighting. Get in, get the data, get out. Avoid fighting." He patted her on the leg.

She took a deep breath. It sounded simple, her brain wanted to believe it would be, but a feeling of dread had already settled deep into her core.

"Is there anything else I should know?"

"No."

* * *

Kieran swung across the hull of the ship, dangling from a suspended harness, his toes skimming lightly over the surface. Tools jangled on his harness while he found and confirmed the spot Hoepe indicated to install the drive.

Sutherland came much slower behind him, carrying the heavy and fragile solenoid.

Kieran took a minute to shut his eyes, centring himself. He hadn't felt confident to send a message to his parents, not certain if the warehouse might have a way to track and interpret the unique signals. Also, there hadn't been time. He'd been ordered to install the cloaking device, and a dozen other implements, ASAP. And if the altercation in the cargo bay was any indicator, Hoepe would not tolerate a delay for any reason.

"You okay, Sutherland?" He shouted over, as the shorter, muscly man rounded a corner of the ship into view. The solenoid dangled from his harness, and light gleamed off his bald head.

Sutherland grunted, working one foot over the other, carefully moving sideways.

While he waited, Kieran scuffed the hull with his boot. Engineers rarely got to work on their ship from the outside — not without a spacewalk anyway, and Lord knew he had no interest in that. The ship's outer layer was scuffed and burnt from hundreds of laz-bolts. They buffed out easily, but still — he frowned — they didn't have to mark it up. A ship was a thing of beauty, a thing of pride. He doubted Hoepe would allow the time to clean the old girl up.

Sutherland bumped into him. "Sorry, mate. Over judged it with all this extra weight."

Kieran grinned. "No worries." He helped the shorter, stockier man still the swinging contraption leashed to his belt. "Hey, do you think Hoepe will let me take a day to buff the hull?"

Sutherland barked out a single laugh. "Not a chance."

"What about check out that banged up thruster array?"

"Doubtful. Besides, it flew straight when I moved it from the landing platform, so that's good enough."

"Well at least the algorithms are holding." He pulled out his data-tablet, checking the installation schematics, confirming his position on the hull, and double-checking they were at the right access point. "Right here, then?"

"Looks like."

Kieran pulled up his pneumatic drill from where it dangled below him, gritting his teeth. "God, I hate drilling into the side of a ship."

"We have heat sealant."

"I know, I know. Just feels wrong."

Sutherland cracked a smile, and Kieran worked the drill up to speed before pressing it to the hull. "You been doing this long?"

"Long enough," Kieran answered.

Sutherland peered at him, while he moved the drill to make the next hole. "How old are you? You barely look like you could be in the academy, let alone graduated."

"Fast tracked."

"You seem to know a lot about ship's engineering."

"Guess so." He pressed in, making two more holes in the hull. "I learned it from my dad."

One of Sutherland's eyebrows rose. "Not the Academy?"

Kieran bit his tongue — he'd nearly said too much. Kids learned from their parents all the time, but ship's engineering had to be learned on a ship, and no one but Central Army engineers were allowed in the engineering bays.

"Well, Hoepe told me you could be trusted," Sutherland said with a smile. "I'm glad because those diagrams look complicated for me."

"Not too bad, really. The wiring for the power will be a bit tricky, but definitely doable." Kieran paused. "How does he know — Hoepe, I mean — that I'm a good engineer?"

"Said he had it on good authority."

"Oh really?"

Kieran finishing drilling the last of the hole, and checked the schematic one more time.

"Ready?"

"Yep."

Sutherland held up the mounting frame, aligning it to the pre-drilled holes.

"Tell me about Hoepe," said Kieran, starting to connect the frame to the hull, "he seems intense."

Sutherland laughed, free and easy, and for a minute, Kieran felt like he was home, working on his family's ship with his dad and brother.

"Nah, he's a big softie. Keeps to himself mostly, but always does whatever he needs to keep us safe, you know. And the folk here."

"Oh really?" Surprising for the very intimidating man.

"He was looking for a crew after the war and the loss of Earth, I didn't have many other prospects, so I joined up."

"What do you do?"

"Pilot. Almost-pilot technically; got kicked out of the Academy, or was pretty sure I was going to be so I disappeared. Now I do odd jobs, whatever we need."

"Ah." It was nearly impossible to get kicked out, but Sutherland kept going so Kieran kept the question to himself.

"The crew was in the Capital City on Etar for a little while — Boss kept looking for something — but it got a little too close even for him, so we moved out here."

"How long ago?"

"A standard year, maybe. It's tough to tell, there's no seasons on Contyna. Kind of a dull death-trap if you ask me."

"It wasn't terra-formed that long ago, right?"

"They started ten years ago. First couple colonies a few years ago didn't make it. Then they started mining the iron and there was a little more support. We've been working hard to build-it up.

Hoepe says it's important to build up the people around you."

"Who is Hoepe? How did he get here?"

Sutherland shrugged. "He used to be a doctor — good thing, we get beat up from time to time, you know. And he treats the miners when they need something."

"But if he's a doctor, why not stay on Etar, or one of the central planets? Surely the conditions would be nicer, easier."

"Dunno. Same reason as the rest of us, I suppose."

"What reason is that?"

Sutherland went silent, squinting at Kieran. Eventually, he said, "Come on, let's get this big box up. The harness is digging into my 'nads."

Kieran helped Sutherland pull up the heavy drive and lift it into place, grunting with effort. It slipped against the smooth hull. "This is harder than it looks," he puffed.

"I'll say."

"I don't know if I can hold it and put the bolts in. We need another hand." Kieran instantly thought of Sarrin, but she was with the doctor. He fumbled to hold the drive on his knee and fish around in his coveralls, pulling out a long bolt, but the drive slipped before he could get the mallet.

They hefted it back into place, sweating and panting.

"There," Sutherland said, "what about him?"

Below, the Poet strode across the hangar. It was no Sarrin, thought Kieran, but it was her brother—close enough, right? "Hey, Poet?" Kieran shouted.

He stopped short, momentarily confused before he looked up.

Kieran puffed again, the heavy drive shifting. "We could really use a hand."

The Poet's mouth dropped open. "No, I'm afraid I cannot."

"Please. It'll just take a sec."

Halud's hands twitched open and closed, face pale. "Have you seen Sarrin?" he asked after a minute.

"She went with Hoepe." He pointed towards the tiny corridor they had disappeared into.

The Poet started to walk away.

"Hey, wait!"

"Send some of the boys over," said Sutherland, pointing with his chin to the far side of the hangar where some of the men sparred in a circle with Rayne.

Halud bit his lip, following Sutherland's gaze. Without a word, he turned and walked away.

"Cracked useless Poet," Sutherland muttered.

The drive slipped.

"Jesus," gasped Kieran, catching the weight of it.

Sutherland helped him pick it back up. "Who?"

*   *   *

Halud picked his way down the narrow corridor, past the storage closet-cell, to last door that lead to Hoepe's — the doctor's — infirmary.

He grimaced at the dark corridor, the walls warped and the floor dirty — nothing like the hospitals in the Capital City on Etar. He told himself this was the new normal, and tried not to compare it to the life he had led. Besides, his sister was with him now, and for that there was no comparison.

He pushed the door open. "Sarrin?"

She sat on a steel table in the centre of the dim room, head jerking up, and he immediately felt ashamed for intruding. The light from the overhead surgical light cast dark shadows over her features: sharp cheekbones and hollowed out bags under the eyes, she looked part corpse and only part girl. A gasp escaped before he could stop himself.

Of course, it was only a trick of the light. She was obviously alive. Sitting in front of him. He chuckled at himself, smiling as he strode into the room to stand beside Sarrin.

Hoepe's back was turned as he worked at a machine, but he acknowledged Halud with a quick glance. His machine made a soft ding, and he turned his attention back to it. "The labs are finalizing now."

Halud pressed his lips tight, burying his concern. It didn't matter, Sarrin's gaze stayed firmly rooted to the floor. He swayed unsteadily on his feet as his mind started to run through a dozen different scenarios, and he became increasingly certain the doctor would tell him she was dying. She looked like she was dying, acted like she was dying. Had he come too late? Had he come all this way only to lose her again?

"Everything looks good, Sarrin," Hoepe announced.

Surprised, Halud turned. "She's fine?"

The doctor's mouth quirked. "Yes. Perfect health."

"Well that's good news!" He reached out, wrapping his sister in a hug, nearly jumping up and down.

She coiled into a tight, rigid board in his arms. Perhaps she hadn't heard. Pulling back, he patted her on the leg. "Sarrin, you're going to be fine."

She jumped, pulling back as far as she could while still seated. She flung her hands behind her back, and he remembered the soup bowl and the blisters that seared across her palms.

He turned to Hoepe. "What about the burns?"

The doctor tilted his head curiously. "Burns?"

"On her hands. A few days ago, I don't know what happened." Halud turned back to Sarrin, but she had somehow slipped off the table without his noticing. She stood on the floor, shifting her weight from bare foot to bare foot, her gaze still cast down and to the side.

The doctor became serious. "Do you need me to examine an injury, Sarrin?"

She shook her head.

"They were quite bad," Halud reminded her gently. "It would be good to have him take a look." He turned to Hoepe. "Did you see the burns?"

Hoepe's eyebrows furrowed, and he shook his head cautiously.

He turned to Sarrin. "Please, for me. I need to know you're okay."

She hesitated, glanced at the doctor, and then Halud. Slowly she stretched her hands out, flashing them open rapidly. Pale, perfectly smooth skin shone back, only a shadow where the worst of the burn had been in the centre of the palm.

"What?" He reached for the hands.

She snapped them out of his reach, eyes squeezing shut as though she'd been hurt.

"I don't...." He turned to Hoepe. "They're healed."

"Probably weren't that serious then." Hoepe shrugged.

Sarrin stepped back, pressing herself against the wall.

"And what about her not speaking?" Halud asked Hoepe.

The doctor blinked, his head tilting to the side. "There is no physical impediment to her speech." Shadows cast over his predatory, angular features, and Halud wondered if he did it on purpose or if the doctor really had no idea how terrifying he looked.

Gulping away his fear, he turned to his sister. "Then why won't you say anything?"

She bit her lip, still refusing to look at him. Her eyes lit with anguish and one shoulder started to tremble.

"Sarrin...?"

The doctor cleared his throat. "We're finished, Sarrin. You're free to go."

She bolted from the room. Halud stumbled, clutching his chest, as though his heart had whose out of the room with her as she fled.

The empty door leading to the dingy hallway stared back at him. His sister — the one thing he had sought out his entire life — had just run from him. But she wouldn't, he knew that, not normally. He growled low in his throat, turning on the doctor. "What are you doing?"

"Helping you."

"There's something wrong with her." He stomped his foot, even though he knew it was childish.

The doctor watched him with an infuriatingly neutral expression.

"Listen to me," Halud said, dropping his voice so the tones resonated deeply and clearly — a trick he had learned during the many long years he spent with Hap Lansford and the other Speakers if he needed to bent their will.

Both of Hoepe's eyebrows shot up.

"Sarrin hasn't spoken a word since I retrieved her from Selousa. Not 'good to see you,' not 'I've missed you,' not even 'thank you.'"

"Have you considered it has been several years since you last saw Sarrin? You can't expect her to be the same."

"Years I've worked at getting her back safely!"

"Halud" — the doctor rubbed his forehead, hesitating — "I appreciate it must be difficult to have your sister not be what you expect —."

"Something is wrong with her."

He sighed. "There is nothing wrong with her."

"She's my sister. I think I know when something is wrong."
He tried dropping his voice again: "You will help me figure out
what it is."

"That trick doesn't work on me, Poet," said Hoepe.

"Trick? No trick."

The doctor only shook his head. "You have no idea what's
happened in her life. What they did in that place."

"I—." A sweat broke out on his back. He'd seen her file, had
it in his possession, but he had never brought himself to read it.
And why not? Because he didn't want to know.

His mind played the scene that had haunted him for sixteen
years: *Her oversized child eyes pleaded with him, staring up into the foliage
where he hid. And then her eyes rolled back in her head, and she fell in a
seizure, taser wires protruding from her little body.* His fist squeezed, the
same as it had squeezed the branches high in the tree as they took
her away, and he did nothing, hiding like a coward.

"She's my sister," he whispered. "I have to help her."

"Then help me."

He nodded quietly.

"Only time will heal the wounds between you."

SEVEN

GAL LIFTED THE TIN MUG to his lips, eyeing the grey-brown, vaguely human-like apparitions on the opposite side of his room. "Go away," he muttered, and sipped his warm Jin-Jiu.

The demons followed him everywhere, copying his every move before cheering manically. They waited when he opened his eyes after sleep, bounced around the hallways where he walked, watched and jeered when he ate his rations…. He knew rationally that they were hallucinations, but wasn't sure if that was better or worse.

As the Jin-Jiu settled in his stomach, the demons started to blur, slowly disappearing. The drink was the only way to be rid of them, to gain some breathing space, but the bottle was running low.

He took a final sip and pushed himself up from his desk. They had summoned him to the bridge a half-hour ago — apparently the cracked doctor-thief intended to follow through on his plan — but he'd procrastinated long enough.

Briefly, he thought about staying in his room and ignoring the situation — how much worse could it get — but Rayne had refused to stay behind, and Hoepe hadn't even started finding her a place to hide.

The hallways were at least quiet as he stumbled through them.

Doors swooshed open as he climbed the steps to the bridge, and he tucked his flask in the pocket of his uniform. He hiccuped. Belatedly — several days belatedly — he glanced down wondering why he still wore the ugly, grey coveralls. At least they had good pockets.

Hoepe sat in the captain's chair, and Gal strode next to him, glaring down at the man.

"I'm reading chatter from the UEC station," said Rayne, standing behind the large Tactical console to one side of the room. "They're distracted."

"Good," said Hoepe, ignoring Gal even as the captain leaned down into his face. "Engage the cloak."

"Yes, sir," she answered. She frowned at her console. "The cloak didn't engage. Kieran says he's already working on it — wiring issues, he thinks."

In the chair, Hoepe grimaced.

Gal cleared his throat. "You're actually going ahead with this fool plan?" No one responded. "You and the Poet have some cracked ideas."

Finally the doctor acknowledged him, sighing. "Sit down, Gal. You're slurring your speech."

Gal shrugged. "You're in my chair."

"I am commanding the mission."

"It's still my ship, until you make good on your agreement with me." He glanced at Rayne.

Rayne frowned at him, but she waved her hand. "Gal, come over here. Sit with me."

His legs obeyed. He didn't mind — the Jin-Jiu made him abnormally calm. He'd take any excuse to be close to her. He took in the smell of her soap — clean, no fancy perfumes — shutting his eyes to commit it to memory.

"Kieran's got it. The cloak is coming online," she said, reporting to Hoepe. Her intense focus fixed on her console and Gal couldn't but help feel a pang of loneliness.

"Increase speed, Sutherland, take us up to the ship."

Gal pulled out his flask, thumbs rubbing the smooth surface. "Are you really okay with this, Raynie? Deceiving the Central Army, I mean."

She glanced him, her fingers pausing over the input panel in front of her. "We are working with the Poet, Gal. This is for the Gods."

He frowned, the drink making him light headed, possibly too calm. "You believe that?"

"Yes, of course. In the Gods we Trust."

"Rayne...."

"Is the cloak working?" Halud asked, his voice cracking. He paced nervously behind the pilot.

The man at the steering sphere shrugged. "No way to tell. We should be coming up on the ship's visual range shortly."

"There's no reason to think they've seen us so far," said Rayne. "They've maintained course and speed."

Gal glanced over at the rendered diagram in the middle of the Tactical console, currently in 2D mode. He frowned, the image not yet clear at this range. His head buzzed with a low hum.

"Thank you, Commander," Hoepe said.

"We don't know if it's working?" said Halud. "Shouldn't we be sure before we attempt a hostile approach? I'm not comfortable with this, Hoepe."

Gal shoved a finger in his ear, wiggling it around to pop the unusual pressure that built up. "Anyone else hear that buzzing?" He blinked at the display again, his thoughts seeming far away and sluggish.

"I don't hear anything," said Rayne.

Hoepe stared at the view screen. "I hear it too. The cloak is emitting an EM field — I hadn't anticipated how strong. That must be the sound."

"Then we should turn back," said Halud.

"Hardly. It means the cloak is working. More reason to push on." Hoepe pushed out of his chair, gazing intently at the viewscreen, which currently showed the planet below them and a vast expanse of stars. The ship was still too far away to be visible, but the tactical scanner's image was becoming clearer.

Gal's breath caught in his throat, and he blinked at the 2D display. "Five Gods, you're a bigger lunatic than the Poet!"

Hoepe spun around. "What?"

"Did you say we were boarding a survey ship?" Rayne asked warily.

"Yes. The Aitor is scheduled for maneuvers. Why?"

"My scanners are reading a warship."

Hoepe's eyes widened, the colour draining from his face.

"We have to abort," shouted Halud. "This is madness."

Hoepe gulped once, his eyes wide, then his expression grew stony. Gal's stomach sunk as he watched the doctor's jaw set as he came to his decision. "It doesn't matter," said Hoepe. "The mission is the same. The plan is the same."

Halud jumped. "A warship is a lot different than a survey ship!"

"It's not different at all." Hoepe strode forward, gripping the back of the pilot's chair as though he would not allow the pilot to turn. "My informant told me there would be a ship resupplying — not which ship. We made an assumption based on the ships with known missions in the area."

"We have to turn around," said Halud. "We can't afford to chance this!"

"On the contrary, we can't afford not to try. A warship will have a complete database — everything we're looking for."

"That's what you're looking for." Halud took the doctor by the shoulders, spinning him so they were face to face. "That's a warship; if your cloak doesn't work and they see us, they'll destroy us, no questions asked." He took a deep breath. "You told me you don't know what you're looking for. If all you want is information, try me. I'll tell you everything I know. No risk of death."

Hoepe opened his mouth once and closed it again. He pushed the Poet's hand off his shoulder. "I am surprised by your selfishness."

"Selfish? I risked everything to find Sarrin. And you want to throw that all away, for a reason you can't even name. For a feeling."

Rayne, watching the two intently, suddenly pressed her five fingers to her chest. "Faith allows us to trust as we follow the Path."

"Oh, Gods." Halud shut his eyes. "Commander, no. That's not...."

"This is our mission for the Gods, we must complete it," she said.

Gal watched the tactical display as what was now definitely a warship came closer and closer. There was no sign that the other ship had seen them, not yet, but they were moving between the

warship and the planet and dangerously close. "Hey," he said to
them. "I hope your pilot's got good luck."

"Luck?"

"We're about to enter that warship's alarm radius." He took
another drink. "I'd recommend an erratic flight path."

"What?" said Hoepe.

Gal took a sip from his flask. "You did do your research
before deciding on this cracked idea, right?"

"It was supposed to be a survey ship."

"Obviously it's not."

"How much have you had to drink?"

"Enough to let you sneak my freightship and my first officer
up next to a warship. Not enough to actually sit back and let you
lead us all to our doom. I still want to live." He stood up,
staggering to the now-empty captain's chair. He leaned sideways,
elbow braced on the armrest, legs dangling over the opposite side.
"You wanted my help. I'm giving it to you. The warships have
ping back. That's old tech, easily outmaneuvered, essentially
useless. But they keep it around in case some fool wearing an
invisibility cloak flies directly at them."

"Ping back?" said Hoepe.

"Photonic radar."

"We're in a gravimetric bubble, they won't be able to see
anything."

"Think." Gal tapped the side of his head with his flask.
"You're between a planet, a space station, and a couple moons —
they'll expect to see something. Only chance is to move around
randomly and hope they assume it's a sensor glitch."

"I've never heard of photonic radar," said Hoepe.

Gal took another drink, the lines on his face like deep
canyons. "Army doesn't tell you half of what they know."

"Then how do you know?"

Gal shrugged. A demon popped up, waving it's ugly hand of memory — it wore a warship Commandant's uniform. He squeezed his eyes shut, suppressing it while he waited for the Jin-Jiu to do its work. He'd been on a warship once. The mission was classified, and buried as deep as it could possibly get. "Are we going to do this? You want your database, I want to get back so you can finish your end of the bargain."

Hoepe studied him, blue eyes scanning him intensely. Gal took another sip from the flask. Hoepe pointed to his pilot. "Erratic path."

"We should turn around," Halud said, his voice dropping low, the words gliding over Gal's ear's strangely.

Hoepe growled, "I keep telling you that trick doesn't work on me, Poet."

"A warship is a lot different from a survey ship. Bigger ship, bigger crew, higher ranking crew, bigger weapons,…."

"It doesn't matter," Hoepe snapped. "We sneak on, we sneak off. Nobody sees us. Nobody dies."

"Dies!" Halud stumbled backwards in shock.

"No one is going to die." Hoepe pinched the bridge of his nose. "Let's just go."

Rayne sat behind her console, weary eyed and thin lipped. "Should we turn around?" She glanced from Halud to Gal to Hoepe.

"Yes," shouted Halud, at the same time as Hoepe ordered, "No."

She frowned. "I'm confused. You said you knew the Path of the Gods."

"We should turn back," Halud turned to Hoepe, ignoring Rayne. "I went to a lot of trouble to get my sister here and I will not send her back to the filthy hands of UEC soldiers."

"Sarrin wanted to come, you fool. She wants the database as much as I do."

Rayne frowned, staring blankly at a spot on the floor as her mouth moved — thinking or praying? Gal wasn't sure, but he regretted ever asking her to join his crew and every time he'd convinced her to stay since. He promised himself he would make up for it, no matter the cost.

The ship shook, a low thunk reverberating through the hull that nearly tossed him out of his chair.

"Sorry," said the pilot. "The cloak and the ship's modified thruster makes docking a little difficult to judge."

"Docking?" Halud gasped.

"We're here?" asked Hoepe.

"Yep," the pilot stood, rubbing his hands on his pants. "I put our auxiliary airlock as close to their auxiliary as I could manage. I'll let the others know and wait for your command." He jogged off the bridge, doors shutting behind him.

Hoepe turned, heading for the door as well, but Halud reached out and grabbed him by the shoulder. "I don't want Sarrin on that ship. A survey ship is one thing, but the warship is too dangerous."

Hoepe snapped his arm out of the Poet's grasp, expression dark. "Listen to me, Sarrin is the only way you're going to survive that warship." He marched away, followed by the few extra of men on the bridge.

Rayne stood to follow, but Gal rose to intercept her. His thoughts seemed far away, and the increasingly intense buzzing made his headache. "Rayne, please. Don't go on that ship."

She frowned. "I'm your tactitian. I've been working with the men, training them to form an attack team."

"This is dangerous. Too dangerous."

"If anything happens, you're going to want me there."

He shook his head. "If anything happens, I'm going to want you as far away from it as possible."

"I won't send the team in alone."

"Please stay behind."

"I can't do that." She stepped beside him as though to go around, but she paused, her expression softening. "When the Gods ask something of us, we must respond. This is our duty."

"You're willing to sneak onto a UEC warship and steal from them?"

She sighed. "I admit it feels wrong, but this is the mission laid out by the Gods. The Poet told us it was covert. That's why we had to leave Selousa even though all those guards were telling us to stop. Whatever the Poet and the girl are doing on that warship, the Gods say it's not for the soldiers to know. It's not for me to know either, but I've been thinking it through. The general told me the rebels were starting to rise up again, causing problems in the City. But what if some of the rebels are posing as Central Army soldiers? Or officers?"

"They're what?" All the air rushed out of his lungs, and a demon waved it's ugly grey arm from behind her head. "Don't talk like that," he whispered.

"The Poet collected that girl from a prison, Gal! Why would he do that? The Speakers don't even condone prisons — everyone follows the Path of the Gods." She pressed a finger to his lips, jumping in before he could speak, and her eyes lit up. "The girl wasn't supposed to be there in the first place. A rebel officer must have condemned her to a rebel prison. She's an agent, trying to stop the rebels from taking over, same as Hoepe and his men. Think about it, Gal: the Speakers don't know who is and is not loyal to the Gods. The Poet's mission is to find them and expose them, thus returning the Army to its divine intent. And we get to help."

Gal slowly closed his jaw. "You're spending too much time with Kieran."

"This is an opportunity to aid the Gods and ensure the righteousness of the Army. This is our duty."

How had she gotten it so wrong? And so right? "Please don't go on that warship."

"Gal!"

"What if the Poet isn't working with the Speakers? What if he's the rebel?" He licked his lips, stopping himself from saying more than he meant. "What if this mission doesn't go well and they catch us? I don't know what's happening, but I don't want you anywhere near it?"

"Gal?"

"Look. Hoepe says he can hide you, get you back into the Army, erase any evidence that you were on this ship or with me."

"What are you talking about?"

"It's a way out, a way for you to be safe. Please!"

She stepped back, crossing her arms over her chest. "I don't want a way out. I'm no coward. I will serve my Gods. The call has come, and I want to be someone who answers it. We will be safe, the Gods will protect us, so long as we stick to the Path."

She stormed away.

He reached his hand after her, but his legs were jelly and he collapsed to the ground.

* * *

Sarrin blinked twice. Bile licked at the back of her throat. It was hard to focus. The last place she remembered being was the shuttle bay, but she couldn't tell if she was still there now.

The electric field of the cloaking device thrummed around her. She'd used the device for things, not people.

She should have told them, told the engineer at least, but the words still were hard to come. The gamma gravitation field generated by the design needed to be offset with an inverse one, and the inverse wave would distort a bio-energetic field — the physical body was safe, but the etheric, the soul itself, would scatter.

She hadn't wanted to go, her instinct telling her to stay as far away as possible, despite Hoepe's assurances. If she'd told them about the inverse wave, maybe Hoepe could have found a solution. But the mission would still go ahead, and he would still send her in, the soldier she was. She had been trained for this, made for this.

Instead, she settled for disconnecting the wiring and disappearing. But the engineer was bright — brighter than she'd estimated. It had taken him almost no time to find the places deep in the wall where she had done her tampering.

The cloak, when it had turned on, had sent her to the ground, her soul exploding out from her in a million pieces. For this, the darkness had no solution. It threatened and clouded in, wanting to take control, but there it had no plan to offer. It was as scattered as she was.

Untold time passed while she pulled together enough of herself to form a rational thought. Her hand gripped the nearest bulkhead, steadying her against the dizzying waves. Her vision rolled black clouds over the grey haze that vaguely outlined the shuttle bay and the corridor beyond.

Her mind travelled in time, hearing the high pitched buzzing of clippers as clumps of her hair fell away.

But her hair hung there, in the present, long and matted in

clumps. It was long, like her mothers spread around her serene face on her deathbed.

Sarrin's hand fell away from her head, reaching for the next bulkhead before she let go of the first. The pulse in her veins trembled, thready and uncertain, like it had forgotten how to flow. All of her had forgotten how to work, her legs jerking as the electric field distorted her synapses, making her neurons fire disjointedly.

She rested, pushing the blackness away. She couldn't let it take her. She had to find the others. Explain. Turn the ship around and power down the cloak.

The wall made a dull thunk as Sarrin tapped her knuckles against it. She pressed her ear to the cold, grey surface, but no answer came. Her skin buzzed against the remembered pressure of injections. Laz-beams seared the air next to her body.

The ship jarred, and she nearly tumbled over again. There were shouts and running the corridor, and she staggered forward. She needed to explain. They had to turn away.

Her heart stopped, ice creeping up her arm as she remembered the cold body of a friend. Friends.

She forced the rapid clicking sound of laz-guns being assembled and disassembled over and over out of her head.

"Sarrin. There you are. We've reached the ship. It's time to go." She recognized the engineer by his voice, her vision still too hazy.

The ship? Already? It had felt like minutes.

"You okay?" he asked.

She blinked again, forcing the world back into focus.

"I think that cloaking device is giving me a splitting headache," he said, his pinched expression standing out against the foggy background behind him. "Others don't seem too bothered, but it's hard to think. You feel it too?"

So he understood, at least. She nodded.

"Come on. The others are already waiting at the airlock. Sooner we get in, sooner we get out and away from here and can turn this thing off."

Her feet slipped across the carpet of their own volition, following him down the corridor.

"Ugh," he groaned. "I feel like I'm falling apart, like half of me isn't here and is just floating away."

She nodded in agreement, even though he was ahead of her.

The door opened in front of them. The small auxiliary airlock had only a single-person-sized hatch set into the ceiling.

Hoepe's men repeatedly checked their laz-guns. The sound of their fast-beating hearts reached her ears, a cacophony of thumps and clunks mixed with nervous laughter. Weapons: twelve. Lethal objects: thirty-seven.

She gasped and pushed it out of her head. The darkness pulled a little stronger, trying to formulate a plan. Her muscles tensed and loosed repeatedly.

Kieran climbed a short ladder, sealing the hatch to the other ship. The door swung open and he started to work on bypassing the airlock on the opposite hull.

Beside her, Halud fidgeted nervously, emotions rolling off of him in waves, crashing into her.

Kieran stepped down from the controls, announcing everything was set. There was no turning back now.

An easy mission, stealth only, she reminded herself, forcing her mind to stay calm and her breathing even. Slip into the access tubes and walls, navigate to the mainframe terminal, download. They wouldn't even come close to the guards. As long as her mental map didn't fail; as long as it didn't scatter like the rest of her.

Kieran leaned over, speaking into her ear, "Are you okay? Your job is a lot harder than mine. You're about to go onto a warship. You shouldn't go if you're not feeling well."

A warship? She stared at him with eyes wide, his green ones meeting her own through the swirling background.

"Sarrin, are you ready?" Hoepe called her from next to the open airlock. "Time to go."

She stepped back.

Kieran said, "You don't have to go if you don't want to."

Could she truly say no? She looked from him to Hoepe. Kieran was trying to help her.

"Sarrin, we don't know how much time we have."

Halud stood next to Hoepe, fidgeting.

She stepped around Kieran.

"Be careful, yeah," he whispered as she passed. Hoepe noted friends often sought to protect each other from dangerous situations.

She stepped up the ladder, gripping the edge of the airlock and pulled herself through. Halud followed close behind.

*   *   *

Rayne double checked the weapons tucked into the holsters around her legs as Sarrin and the Poet disappeared up the ladder and through the hatch. Looking over her shoulder, she exchanged nods with each member of her team. "Ready?"

They gripped their rifles, and she tried to think of it as any other training drill. This wouldn't be any different. If all went according to plan, they wouldn't see another person — sneak on, sneak off, as Hoepe had said repeatedly. But a part of her — a shameful part — anticipated a fight.

Her father had pushed her into tactician training, and yet, she suspected, he'd arranged for any of her platoons to be as far from battle as possible. She suspected she would be good in combat; she wanted to be, at least. This was her chance to prove it.

She climbed the ladder, poking her head through the joined airlocks and into the warship. "Clear," she called down to the others and pulled herself through, adjusting to the perpendicular shift in artificial gravities from one ship to the next.

The men assembled themselves in the airlock, taking a haphazard formation behind her. Satisfied, she gripped her rifle and scanned the corridor. "Clear."

A loud thump sounded in the airlock followed by a groan. The men shifted to the side, and Gal staggered to his feet, finding his legs in the new gravity.

"Gal, what are you doing?" she hissed.

"Helping," he huffed.

"You're drunk. Go back."

"No." He slurred his speech, and she bit back her groan of disappointment. "If you won't stay where it's safe, then I'm coming with you."

She clenched her jaw. "You're a liability."

"And you don't understand what kind of danger you're in."

"Miss?" The men pointed to the corridor, others already setting up a defensive position. She knew what he meant: time ticked away.

She crept forward, rifle held at the ready. "Wait here," she told Gal before advancing into the corridor. Her eyes scanned the hall until they settled on an access screen several metres away. Having never served a warship, she had no idea where to find the store rooms or the supplies Hoepe sent them to retrieve. She moved towards the screen, hoping to find a map.

"It's this way," Gal slurred behind her. He stood in the

corridor with his thumb jerked over his shoulder, pointing in the opposite direction.

She glared at him. "What are you doing?"

He sighed, the flask in his hand reflecting the harsh overhead lighting. "The sooner you help these boys steal the supplies, the sooner you'll get off the ship."

"We don't know where the store room is." She pointed to the panel in the opposite direction.

"Don't touch the access panel. You'll set off a host of alarms. It's this way, trust me."

She frowned. "How do you know?"

He paused a minute, his belly sticking out as he leaned back and stared at the ceiling. She'd only seen him this drunk a few times. Assuming he had forgotten the question, she turned back to the access panel, about to tap on the screen when he answered quietly: "I was on one once."

"What? When?" He was a freightship captain. Before that he'd been in Exploration. And a ground forces captain before that. There would be no reason for him to be on a warship.

"Don't touch the panel, Rayne." He sighed again, turning to walk down the corridor in the opposite direction.

Uncertain and confused, she retracted her hand and followed him.

The men shuffled loudly behind them, but there was no sign of the warship's crew. A good thing, because Rayne had no idea what she would do. She carried the rifle, but her palms sweated uncontrollably and she had to keep readjusting her grip as the rifle slipped.

They were UEC soldiers on a UEC ship — they were all on the same side. But a warship patrol wouldn't know the difference between them and rogue invaders. They might shoot on sight,

UEC uniform or not.

"Gal, what's going on?"

He ignored her, his gaze fixed on the hallway ahead. She had never seen this expression in his eyes before: intense, calculating.

A shudder ran up her spine.

"This is it," he slurred, stopping at a door.

"Are you sure?"

"Yes." His voice came out cold and expressionless. He took a drink from his flask. "Who has the decryptor?"

One of the men stepped forward, pulling the panel off the door lock and attaching a small machine.

"Be careful. Their security algorithms are easy to trip, you'll have to use a rotating code instead of linear."

Rayne stared at Gal wide-eyed, a cold feeling starting to sink in her gut. "What's going on?" she asked. "Why are you here?"

He ignored this question too, watching the man with his device at the panel. He stepped forward just as the panel flashed red. "Five Gods," he muttered.

"Oh no," said the man. "The alarm's gone off." He started pressing buttons rapidly.

Gal pushed the man away from the device. "Set up a perimeter," he ordered the rest in the same cold, horribly unlike-Gal voice. "If I can't stop it before it relays to the bridge, they'll have a security team down here in under sixty seconds. Shoot on sight."

She gasped. "Gal, we can't —."

"Shoot on sight, Rayne."

"They're UEC soldiers, doing their jobs. I won't shoot them."

His hands flew over the controls on the machine and the door computer itself. "Then why bring the rifles?"

She stared at the rifle in her hands. Comfort. Habit.

"We're defectors, trespassing on the most fortified Army ship in existence," he said.

"We're not defectors. We're working for the Gods." But the uncomfortable feeling in her gut had turned to full on ice.

Gal grunted. The data on the screens in front of him whizzed by at a nearly unreadable speed. He pressed a final button, fingers pausing as he stared at the screen intently. The screen turned back to its standard grey-blue. He leaned his head on the wall. "The alarm's disabled. I don't know if I caught it in time. They might still be coming."

"Then we'll just explain why we're here," she decided. "I know the Poet wants it kept secret, but there's no reason not to tell another law-abiding citizen about our mission if we have to."

He glanced warily at the ceiling. "Set up a perimeter. Move the containers as fast as you can — one carrying, one defending. Shoot on sight; they're not going to listen long enough for us to explain."

"Gal, we won't kill UEC soldiers. We're on the same side!"

"We're not. You're going to have to decide, us or them."

"You're being ridiculous. This is the Path of the Gods. Surely they'll understand that."

Gal sighed. He didn't answer, his hands slowly disconnecting the device. "You don't deserve any of this. It will be okay, I promise."

She readjusted her laz-rifle, sweaty hands slick on the barrel. The men rushed by, already starting to retrieve cargo containers filled with supplies, but she couldn't pull her gaze away from Gal and the growing suspicion that something had gone very, very wrong.

* * *

The scattering energy field relieved its grip and Sarrin's senses came back to her as they moved down the corridor.

The ship she recognized immediately: UECAS Comrade.
Insignia Class warship, the Central Army's flagship. Class 8 laz-
cannons, electro- and photo- torpedoes, reinforced con-plas
construction, multiple sections able to be individually sealed.
Crew of 156, Lieutenant grade or higher. Crew roster: classified.
Missions: classified. It was a hunter, sleek and deadly as anything
Sarrin had ever known. This same ship had brought her to
Selousa four years ago. The same ship orbited over Selousa a
week ago.

Halud followed her to an access port, grunting as he pulled
himself into the narrow tube behind her.

Darkness crowded the edges of her vision, but she told herself
to keep moving. From the access tube, she pulled a panel from the
wall, slipping into the space behind it.

"So this is what Hoepe meant when he said you were likely
hiding in the walls," Halud said, but his attempt at humour was
marred by his shaking voice. Sarrin continued forward along the
twisting path up and around rooms and corridors.

The warship was nearly a kilometre in length, the mainframe
access buried deep in the beast. Twice on their journey she
paused, waiting for the blanks in her memory to fill in. Once, the
blackness clouded so far in she had to move by feel.

Almost by surprise, she emerged in a small room, lit only by
the eerie-red glow of a computer tower.

Halud fell out of the open wall panel behind her, whining and
groaning as he pushed himself to his feet.

Her eyes scanned the room automatically. Weapons: zero.
Objects that could be used as deadly weapons: zero. A thick
round column with dozens of lights blinking on and off at
random took up most of the 2-metre by 2-metre space. The

central nervous system for a ship this large was five times bigger than she was, and likely five times as intelligent.

Soldiers on the other side of the single door shifted on their feet — thirteen, she counted.

Halud stepped up to the single access screen, a glowing blue panel amidst the sea of red, and entered his personal code with shaking hands. If Halud's code didn't work, the alarm would sound and the guards would be through the door in an instant.

Time slowed, and the darkness reached it's gnarled tendrils around her. A movement diagram painted itself in her head, and the darkness showed her exactly how to hit and twist the men's necks to still them forever.

Halud swallowed dryly, the light from the screen casting an eerie-glow across his face. He pressed his lips tight and finalized the code.

Hoepe said it was an easy mission, that a ship running drills in the Deep wouldn't hear about the Poet's defection for weeks — communications taking weeks to get back to Etar. He promised the codes would still be good. But Hoepe waited safely on the freightship, not standing in the little, trapped chamber. He wasn't the one with a monster in his head, and Sarrin could do nothing but pray he was right.

Pain burst inside her head.

* * *

Gal sat on a cargo container and threw back another slug of Jin-Jiu. Shaking hands should have sloshed the liquid all over him, and probably would have if the flask wasn't already so close to empty.

The men moved the containers quickly, running back and forth, constantly on alert for signs of a UEC contingent. Rayne crouched in the corridor, watching.

It had been far more than sixty seconds, but instead of feeling relief he found it all left a bitter taste in his dry mouth.

"Where do you think they are?"

Startled, Gal looked up as Aaron sat down beside him. But it could not be Aaron; Aaron had died years before. This was a demon. He reached for more Jin-Jiu, taking the very last of the flask he had brought with him.

Aaron fuzzed, but did not disappear. "So, this is one of the great warships. Doesn't seem that different from the freightship. Newer, maybe. Less run down. But it's not as homey, you know. I like the freightship better. It reminds me of our old hideout on Earth — remember, where we met the hackers?"

"Shhh," Gal said without thinking.

Rayne glanced his way at the sudden noise, but she quickly turned back to her patrol.

"Relax." Aaron grinned. "You know she can't hear me." He stood, stretching. "Nice bit of hacking, you did there. Nice to see you haven't lost your touch."

Gal pressed his lips tight and stared at a spot on the floor, determined to ignore the apparition.

But Aaron leaned down, right in front of him, refusing to be dismissed. "Tell me about the warship — were you on this one before?"

"No." Gal shook his head. "The Valkas."

"Ah. Pity I wasn't around for that. I imagine you wish I was."

"Gal?" Rayne called out from the corridor. "What did you say?"

Gal froze. "Nothing. Talking to myself."

Aaron stared into the corridor and let out a long whistle. "She's pretty."

"Don't," whispered Gal.

Slapping his knee, Aaron laughed. "Come on, isn't this fun?"

Gal shook his head, wishing he could simply drop through the cargo container and away through the floor.

"It has to be at least a little gratifying."

"I just want the peaceful haul," he said. He'd made his decision when Hap Lansford had offered him his options.

"I know you, Galiant. This has to be the most exciting thing that's happened since you got demoted. Maybe even since the war."

"It's not exciting," muttered Gal. "It never was."

"A little exciting?"

"Try terrifying. Every second, I think about how she's going to die, how I'm going to die."

Aaron shrugged. "Everyone dies."

"I don't want to be here, Aaron. What do I do?"

"Sorry, old friend. You are here. And I don't see anything so wrong about it. It's a second chance. Remember, *Never give up the fight.*"

"There's no point in the fight. People kept dying, throwing their lives away. You died. For what? Nothing we did ever made a difference."

"Yes, it did!" Aaron laughed, pure and clear and vibrant. "Did you not see the girl?"

Gal's chest seized, and he clutched at his heart as he looked directly into Aaron's not-really-there eyes.

He laughed again. "You know what she is, I'm sure. You're not a fool."

"No," Gal whispered, but Aaron continued.

"Can you believe it? After all these years?" His eyes lit up, a huge grin spread across his face that made Gal think of the two of them playing together as kids. "They're alive. Because of you."

But Gal shut his eyes, refusing to acknowledge the one thing that scared him the most. The thing that would certainly get them all killed. Once and for all.

"Gal?" Rayne stood over him. Aaron was gone. "They've got everything. It's time to go."

* * *

Sarrin's hand flew to her temple and she staggered back, slamming into the wall.

Halud glanced over, concern sharp in his eyes. The screen flashed a normal grey, his code entered successfully. He let go of a heavy breath and reached for the storage device in his pocket, connecting it to the mainframe computer.

The flash of pain disappeared as quickly as it had come.

A progress bar ticked across the screen, the entire mainframe downloading onto the small memory chip. She willed its progress to be faster. The dark cloud on the edge of her vision crowded in tighter. Pain did not just happen, not like that, it had been created. How? Why?

Her mind raced through a list of possible explanations: blood clot: no; wound: no; concussion: no; infection: no. She'd spent years in a medical research facility, nothing had been missed. Hoepe himself had declared her to be in optimal health.

The list of acceptable, benign possibilities ran low. The darkness whispered to her, unhappy. The room closed in like a trap. Guards shifted beyond the door.

Some piece of the puzzle stayed hidden, something she didn't yet understand, buried behind a dark shroud. The monster willed her deeper into its dark abyss, promising an answer, telling her she could sense more than simply sounds, feel more than mere emotions; if she tried hard enough, she could see the ripples of space and time across the universe.

A presence — the feeling of standing next to an old friend — startled her, and she stepped back, but the darkness held her in it. Someone from very long ago, just a whisper, scarcely an imagination.

Surely, her mind was more wrecked than even she had suspected.

A sharp clack sounded in the hallway. A man shuffling irregularly: step-step-clack.

Guitteriez.

Her heart raced inside her chest and she snapped her attention back to her surroundings. *Trapped*, the monster whispered, and showed her the movement diagram, willing her to take the obvious choice and attack first, choose offence over defence.

She looked at Halud, who watched her with narrowed eyes. The progress bar crept across the screen, only part-complete.

The monster covered her vision in its dark tendrils. Guitteriez was here. But she could make him, and the thirteen guards, dead in eight moves. Then find the rest of the crew, commandeer the warship for herself. With the warship, she could fly to Etar, destroy every last minion in the capital city who had let her and the others suffer. And finally, the Speakers themselves would be destroyed. She would be victorious. She would be free.

But she hesitated.

"Sarrin," A voice whispered over her, dangerously close. "It's done."

In her own darkness, she stumbled, slamming into the wall. She pushed the dark curtain aside, straining with the effort. Halud stared at her.

Destroy them now, while you have a chance, the darkness commanded.

But she couldn't. She didn't want to hurt anyone. That's what she had told Hoepe; that's why she had been so afraid of the mission. What she wanted was to be a nice normal girl with no secrets, no experiments.

She ushered Halud into the open access panel ahead of her. She closed the panel on the still dark and quiet room and crawled after him.

Her mind reached out, but there was no presence nearby, no quiet shuffles, no clicking of laz-guns, no thumping hearts other than hers and Halud's. The darkness stayed in the periphery, pulsating, waiting for its opportunity.

At the nearest widening, she shot past him, clawing and dragging her way through the walls as fast possible.

Halud called out, begging her to wait.

Annoyed and impatient, the monster told her to leave him, and she nearly did. The darkness swirled so thick across her vision it left her nearly blind.

"Sarrin," Halud panted, and she waited for him to catch up, her muscles shaking and begging to go. "Slow down. What's going on?"

She leapt through the tiny crawlspace as soon as Halud came marginally close. She went as far in front of him as she dared, putting herself as far from Guitteriez as possible.

Her memory map took her to the freightship despite the encompassing haze. They are close now. A different empty sensation washed over her — the cloaking device — and her soul started to scatter. Her legs and arms flopped weakly, barely connected to the rest of her body. She focussed on her breathing, uneven and ragged. The freightship was her only option though, she just had to get there and hold on long enough for the others to clear the warship and turn the cloaking device off.

The monster offered her a different solution, but she could make it to the ship, she was sure.

Guitteriez stayed by the computer mainframe, she could still hear the echo of his cane on the deck far away. Was it possible he didn't know? That she had come and gone without his knowledge? And escaped? The halls near them were empty and completely quiet. The mission was easy. Stealth only.

She slipped out of the access tube, sprinting across the short stretch of empty hallway.

Kieran greeted them at the hatch, flashing a smile that shone through her spotty vision. His lips moved, but she couldn't hear the words, only see his teeth opening and closing, the image swimming in and out of focus against a backdrop of darkening black cloud.

The intense electromagnetic field swallowed her. She climbed down the ladder, holding on to her scattering self, stumbling as her feet hit the floor.

Hoepe's men stood at the far end of the airlock, stacking cargo containers. She breathed a sigh of relief knowing they had made it back safely. That both their missions had been successful. That they could go.

She just needed rest.

The ship disengaged. It wouldn't be long until they could power down the cloaking device. She could work on pulling herself back together. She would tell Hoepe she didn't want to go on any more missions, didn't want to join his crew. She would ask him to put her in a normal life, hide her like he was going to hide Rayne and Kieran. She would find the words to say to her brother and tell him everything that he meant to her.

She took a deep, relaxing breath. Nearly there. Nearly over. Relief flooded across her, a smile starting to creep its way across her lips.

A cargo container dropped to the ground, the sharp crack ricocheting around the small room like a bomb. Men shouted in surprise.

Her vision went black.

EIGHT

KIERAN SEALED THE AIRLOCK, SILENTLY singing an old song to keep his mind focussed. He would be glad when they were back at Contyna with the stupid cloaking device off.

Halud crouched on the ground, his chest heaving while he clutched the storage device to his chest. The men stacked their haul of foods and medicines. Sarrin looked nearly sick, weakly clutching the ladder to hold herself up.

Sarrin had not been herself — not that he knew what she was like normally — but he knew when he'd found her staggering in the corridor that she hadn't been right. Her eyes swam and her reactions were sluggish, sloppy. Far different from the usual clear gaze and quick, precise movements.

So, he was watching, studying, her when the container fell. He saw her hand grip the ladder so hard it bent. Saw her posture change, her body coil and then spring.

She flew across the room, landing where the container had fallen. The heel of her palm drove into the closest man's chest.

Halud pushed himself up. "Sarrin! No!"

Her head swivelled towards the noise. Without looking back,

she knocked three others to the ground, before leaping back across the room.

Men rushed in to subdue her. They went flying. Her movements sharp and efficient.

Kieran ran for the nearest comm panel. "Emergency in the rear airlock. Sarrin's gone bonkers."

Her feral gaze fixated on him, cold and set as stone. He was her the next target.

Jesus.

"Sarrin, relax, it's okay." He held his hands out instinctively to try to stop her. "It's me; it's Kieran."

Halud jumped up and reached for her. "Sarrin, stop."

Sarrin drove her elbow into his chest, throwing him away coughing and struggling to breathe.

She advanced as Kieran backed himself against the wall, both terrified and fascinated. Despite the pain and the scattering in his head, he knew there was only one thing she could be, one secret she had tried to keep.

There was only one reason she'd been held in a secret prison, why it had taken the Poet Laureate himself to rescue her. He knew because Kieran had done his dissertation on the Children of Evangecore. And Sarrin was an Augment, a child soldier.

They were supposed to all be dead, but here was one standing right in front of him!

He would have laughed with joy at his incredibly good luck if it weren't for the relatively small problem of her fixing to kill him.

He swallowed heavily; if he couldn't convince her he was a friend, he would be dead. They all would be.

Hoepe's men tackled her. Seven at once clinging to her tiny frame, and it slowed her down for mere seconds.

She pushed the last one off with a wild yell.

"Sarrin, Sarrin. It's me, it's Kieran," he tried. "I'm a friend."

Rayne fired her laz-rifle, but Sarrin dodged the beam and threw one of Hoepe's men in front of it, the smell of burning flesh filling the room.

Her advance continued. She jumped, knocking Kieran to the ground.

He landed, somehow, with his arms above his head, pinched tight and held down in her iron hands, totally immobilized. He couldn't fight back — it wouldn't be a good idea anyhow. He forced his body, against all sensible instinct, to relax.

She paused, her right hand squeezing his throat, and searched his face. Her pupils dilated in and out of focus.

"Kieran," he wheezed, chest crushed under her knee.

The men tackled her again. They struggled, and then Sarrin slumped and her hand relaxed.

Kieran pulled in a shaky breath. He could have been dead. He came inches from it. He should have been terrified.

Hoepe's men peeled themselves off the pile, slowly relieving the weight that crushed his chest. Sarrin lay unconscious and sprawled on top of him. One of the men pulled her off unceremoniously, and her body rolled to the floor.

Hoepe stood over them, his eyes wide as he clutched an injector.

"What's going on, Boss?" one of the men asked, rubbing an arm that had already started to bruise

"I've sedated her, she's not a threat," Hoepe's voice cracked. "No harm will come to her."

"What in the Deep is happening?" Gal shouted.

Kieran rubbed at his throat, finding it already difficult to breathe.

"What is she?" Gal shouted at the Poet, pointing to his sister.

"What did you bring to my ship?"

Halud still clutched his chest. "I — I didn't know this would happen," he choked out.

"I didn't want to believe it." Gal clutched his head in his hands and turned away. Then he faced Halud again. "You brought an Augment onto my ship. If you think any of us are going to get out of this alive, you're a fool."

Kieran tried to gasp but couldn't catch his breath. He tried to cough but nothing came out.

"She's my sister, Gal," said the Poet. "What was I supposed to do? Leave her to rot in that cell? It's not her fault what they've done to her."

"Yes!" Gal screamed, "Anywhere is better than here! She's too dangerous. Just look what happened here. Everyone was nearly killed."

"Why are you being like this?" shouted Halud.

Gal spun out of the room.

Kieran, still laying on the ground, tugged on the nearest man's leg, dark blotches appearing cross his vision.

"Oh Gods," said the man. "Hey, Boss."

Hoepe dropped down nearly on top of him, nimble hands pinching painfully around Kieran's neck, shifting quickly.

Sarrin laid on the ground beside him, arms flung out, unconscious. An Augment of Evangecore, a child soldier, an escapee who waged war with the Central Army for three years — they were said to all be dead, left behind on Earth when it imploded.

Kieran couldn't believe his good luck, a million questions bubbling up inside of him right before he passed out.

*   *   *

Rayne's legs thudded numbly with each step as she chased Gal down the corridor. The laz-rifle hung, bouncing at her side. The same rifle she'd shot at... at... that thing. And Sarrin had dodged it, simply ducked as though it were a ball on a playground.

The Poet, scrambling behind her, surged ahead. He reached his arm out, coming just short of grabbing Gal. "I thought you of all people would understand!" he cried. He lunged again, this time snagging the sleeve of Gal's uniform and spinning him around.

"Understand what?" Gal roared. "What a spread-mad idea this was."

"Why I had to help her."

"You can get in a lot of trouble helping people, Halud."

"She's just a girl —."

Gal shoved the Poet across the corridor. "You didn't fight in the war, you didn't see. But I've been there, I've seen exactly what these Augments can do. Sarrin's as dangerous as any other weapon created by the Army."

Rayne cried out as he said 'Augment'. An Augment on her ship. One she had helped protect. That the Poet Laureate was protecting.

"Gods," Gal huffed, running his hand through his hair. "I thought she was just a criminal, that they'd put her out on the planetary rehabilitation program. You know, 'disagree with the Gods, volunteer to make a new world, die trying'. Not a Gods-damned Augment."

"She's my sister."

"I don't care if she's Hap Lansford's sister! You brought an Augment on board a starship. You're going to get us all killed."

"Hap Lansford?" Wheels spun hopelessly in Rayne's head. "Isn't he the one that sent you out here?" Her own voice sounded far away.

The Poet gave her an odd look.

Gal sighed and started moving again. "No one sent him out here, Rayne. I told you, he defected. And we defected with him."

"What? But — but this is the Path of the Gods!"

"Come on, Rayne, use your head. He made that up."

Chest tightening, Rayne whipped around to Halud. "Did you?" An image of her father flared into her mind — frowning, eternally disappointed. There had to be a way out of this. Reason flew out the airlock, and years of combat training kicked in — she shoved the Poet, hard. He flattened on the opposite side of the hallway, arms out the sides. Advancing automatically, she pinned him and pulled back her right fist. "How could you? Betray the Gods like that?"

The Poet squeezed his eyes shut. "She's my sister, not a criminal."

She shut her eyes, suppressing her scream, and let her fist drop to her side. "'The Gods provide for us all,'" she said, "didn't you write that?"

"I — I did. And you listened, but you didn't hear the meaning."

Her eyes shut as she tried to reason through this situation that could not be happening. Not to her. "They offer us the Plan. The Augments are an abomination!"

The Poet cringed, ducking his head in anticipation. At the last moment, she let him go, stepping back. He slid to the floor.

When she turned, Gal had already disappeared, and she ran to the far end of the corridor. She caught up to him just as he turned into the hall where the officers had their quarters. "Gal, wait! What are we going to do?"

He slammed his hand into the mechanism for his door, keeping his gaze fixed straight ahead. "We'll go back to Contyna.

Hoepe can keep you safe."

"What?" Pieces started to fit into place. "The Poet defected and brought an Augment onto our ship." She took a deep breath. "My life is over. My career is over. If they think we defected… but we were just doing what the Poet said!"

The door opened, and Gal paused at the threshold. He sighed, his head dropping low, still refusing to look at her. "Hoepe can keep you safe. That's the deal we made."

"Deal?" She shouted. "Hoepe's not working the Central Army any more than we are." She gasped, realization dawning. "He knew she was an Augment. He's always talking about resources. He's going to sell her. And sell us!"

"I have to believe he'll keep you safe. What other option do we have."

"But you made this deal?" She stepped back. "You knew too!"

He sighed again. "No, I didn't know."

"Then why aren't you more upset?"

He stepped into his quarters. "I'm sorry, Raynie." The door shut behind him

"Galiant!" She slammed her fist into the control panel, but it was no use, he'd already locked it, already blocked her from overriding it. Panting, she fought to catch her breath. What was happening?

The Poet stood at the other end of the corridor.

Augments. What would her father say?

Storming up to the Poet, she searched his face, but found only pity — no fear, no disbelief. Her fist clenched in anger, but he was still the Poet Laureate, the mouthpiece of the Speakers of the Gods, the man whom she'd been taught to always respect and obey.

A false Poet. An enemy of the Gods.

She punched the wall instead.

Pain shot through her knuckles, and her hand recoiled, the grey wall totally unchanged. Her rage dissipated, replaced by an emptiness, a deep sucking hole that used to be her hope.

She took a shaking breath, fortifying herself. "Sometimes the Path is hard. Sometimes it feels as though we are lost, but it only means we can be found," she muttered. With start, she realized her mind had not remembered the words of the Gods. No, worse. With a groan she realized the quote came from the rebel, John P himself.

What *would* her father say?

Squeezing her eyes shut, she suppressed a scream, pulling at her hair instead. She could not give up, would not give in to her circumstances. She was a United Earth Central Army officer. She would make her father proud. She would uphold the Path of the Gods, even if no one else would. That was her duty, and she would rise to the call.

*　*　*

Gal slid down the back of the door, legs no longer able to support him. His brain ricocheted, spinning one memory flash to the next: a frozen battlefield, a girl climbing from ash, wailing cries, and the silent implosion of a planet through a viewport.

The past hounded him, twisting and turning and jumbling.

The Augment War destroyed the planet, that was fact. The rest? How was he supposed to remember the rest without cracking?

An icy hand wrapped around his finger, sending a chill through his body. Cold sweat broke out on his back. A demon, grey and hairless and rotting. It had followed him through the locked door as though it wasn't even there.

The demon tugged on his arm, pointing. When he looked up, Gal had been transported from his quarters, finding himself in another grey place, another Central Army outpost.

He shook his head, trying to clear the vision. He knew the corridor. His first year at the Academy, he had done a tour at the Army base at Evangecore. Before they knew what was happening at the facility below — he wasn't supposed to see that at all.

His supervising sergeant left him at his post. His first overnight watch. Not that anything would happen, Evangecore was in the middle of nowhere, the closest village over an hour away. The weather outside was freezing anyway, terrible and snowy.

A scream pierced the air.

He panted, looking for the source. There was no one.

The sergeant had said the night could play tricks on you, especially the first time. It was nothing, had to be nothing. A scared boy's nervous imagination.

Another scream, more distant.

Adolescent Gal gripped his laz-rifle.

Gal could already see what would happen next, the long chain of events that would change his life. He begged adolescent Gal to stop, to stay at his post as he'd been ordered. But adolescent Gal looked down the long corridor in front of him and the long corridor to his left, and then turned and headed to his right.

Another scream led him to a door. A locked door. There were places the cadets weren't supposed to go on every base. Normally, he left it alone. If it wasn't for him to see, it wasn't for him to know.

But another scream, and now a desperate wail called him through.

He fidgeted with the lock, overriding it like he had done countless times as a boy growing up in a small, dull, farming community with nothing else to do. He stepped through, leaving the grey corridors of the base, and entered clinical

white. His feet screeched on the polished floor, echoing around him.
Identical doors lined the hallway.

Gal tried to stop, willed the memory to change, but his feet carried him to the far end of the corridor, nearer and nearer to the wailing. His present and younger selves blended together, and he lived the memory first hand. He peered through one of the doors, through the window of fortified permaglass.

There, on the bed, lay a shrivelled demon. It's melted grey skin contrasted with the white walls. Blood smeared across the floor and up to the bed.

They locked eyes. Crystal clear, brilliant eyes that held Gal to a promise.

It started shrieking. They all started shrieking. Doors slammed open, and hundreds of them, millions of them poured into the hall.

He threw himself back into the corridor, stumbling over the little bodies. They were on his legs. And his arms. Screaming, screaming.

He pushed on, straining toward the door. His eyes burned, and he rubbed them furiously, trying to un-see what he had seen.

Screaming rang his ears, and then his gut and his chest and his soul. Louder and louder, more desperate with each raising decibel.

These horrid little creatures, tugging on him, asking everything from him.

"Stop!" he yelled. He pulled one off his arm, peeling back it's sticky, grey fingers, and slammed it as hard as he could against the wall.

It fell. Instantly dead.

And the others, as before, crumpled and died. Death radiated from Gal.

Gods, what had he done?

He yelled out, striking the air in front of him. And the whole thing shattered.

Pain shot through his knuckles as shards of glass exploded in a cloud around him. He found himself in his latrine on the old freightship. Pieces of mirror tinkled to the ground. Blood seeped from his hand. What was he doing?

He stumbled to his desk. Jin-Jiu. It wasn't warm, but who cared. He took a drink, and then another and another. The past was in the past, where he had buried it.

* * *

Halud tapped his fingers to his chest compulsively. The glaring lights of the mess hall and the odour of overcooked rations caused him to feel slightly nauseous.

Kieran watched him from across the long table made of several tables they'd pushed together, and that made him fidget even more. Kieran's neck had already coloured purple, and he wore a plastic brace around his throat. Bruised and partially collapsed trachea, the doctor had said.

His sister did that. His sister. Sarrin.

Discoloured tendrils crawled from the blooming blood pattern on the engineer's skin, the fingers wrapping across the flesh.

Kieran opened his mouth, but he started to cough, a horrible gasping sound.

Rayne sat beside him, straight and rigid as plasteel, nearly hovering out of her chair. She stared straight ahead, frozen and expressionless.

At the far end of the room, Hoepe stood between his men, hand placating as he shouting over them: "The situation is not so dire as it seems. Someone with such skill is a very valuable asset to our team." Two of the men had their arms in slings — one broken, the other shot.

His sister. A sweet young girl of four who had nursed him when he was sick with fever. What had happened to her? He gritted his teeth. Evangecore had happened.

The doors slid open, and the room turned silent. Gal stumbled into the empty chair beside him.

Rayne swivelled her head to look at Gal, the sound of flesh burning under her glare nearly audible. "You're drunk."

Gal sneered. "I'm not on duty." He seemed to shrug, but his head and arms just flopped lamely.

Halud's stomach ached. His one hope, plastered in the chair beside him. How could such a man fall so far?

Rayne hinged forward. "Gal, I am begging you. The Gods will have something to say about this. We should surrender her to the Army outpost."

Gal's head lolled to the side, his mouth flapping open. "The Gods always have something to say," he muttered, waving his hand in the air.

"We have to turn her over!" Rayne stood abruptly her chair.

"No!" said Halud.

Drool pooled at the side of Gal's open mouth.

"The Path I make for myself is the Path of the Gods," said Halud, "Isn't that right, Gal?"

Gal fell out of his chair.

Rayne gasped, "The rebel! Why would you quote the rebel? You're the Poet."

"John P said, 'embrace your fear and you will become brave'."

"John P?" she spat. "Do you know how long my father spent looking for that cracked heretic. He caused chaos, rebellions, riots…. He hijacked newsfeeds and distributed propaganda viruses. They say he started the war. I went to a rally once, and you know what he told us — he told us to do what we thought. Just whatever we thought."

Gal sat up from the floor, grasping the edge of the table. "You did what?"

"And do you know who spent the war reminding us of the True Path — you did, Poet. We need order, discipline, rules —."

Halud frowned. "I speak for the Speakers, they do not speak for me. Do not mistake the words I have said as High Poet as my own. They took my sister away sixteen years ago; they made her this way. My Path is to help her."

"You're the Poet Laureate," said Rayne.

"You're a mindless soldier," Halud growled in frustration.

Kieran started to cough. Rasps and rails grew louder, honking. It didn't stop. Hoepe ran up behind him and hit pressure points on his back in rapid succession. Kieran gasped for breath, his face as purple as his neck.

"She almost killed Kieran." Rayne pointed her finger at the struggling engineer. "There is an Augment aboard our ship — a deadly child soldier. We don't even know half of what she's capable of."

Hoepe pinched the bridge of his nose. "Sit down," he ordered, and wrapped a hand over both Kieran and Rayne's shoulders, pushing them into their chairs. "My offer to care for Sarrin still stands. And there is a place for all of you with my crew, if you'd like, where you will be looked after and protected."

"You're a Reaper!" Rayne accused.

"I prefer the term Privateer and Provider." Hoepe glared at her. "I knew of Sarrin's past when I agreed to help Halud. I admit —."

"You knew she was an Augment, Boss?"

Hoepe sighed and glanced at his men. "Her condition is a bit unexpected, but I suspect with treatment, a good diet, and some time, she will be functioning normally again."

There was hope, then, thought Halud, a fraction of the weight lifting itself from his chest. The doctor had been running tests, he must have found something. Sarrin was sick, not some deadly killing automaton. What happened in the airlock, that wasn't really her.

"Functioning normally? What does that mean — more deadly?" said one of the men. The others chuckled gloomily.

Gal snorted, laying back in his chair with a soppy smile.

Hoepe pressed his lips together, his gaze warning. "She is a person, just like any of us."

"A person?" Rayne scrunched up her nose and shook her head. "They destroyed the Earth. Maybe you don't understand how dangerous these Augments are, and why the Central Army worked so hard to eradicate them."

"I assure you I do understand what she is, better than you." Hoepe walked halfway around the table, clenching and unclenching his jaw. "When Sarrin is functioning normally again — that is to say calm and coherent — she will be looked after. You can all be here or somewhere else, but Sarrin will be looked after and protected. Is that clear?"

The men at the far end nodded quietly.

"This is spread-mad," cried Rayne, bolting out of her chair again. "She's an Augment. The enemy. They killed hundreds of soldiers, destroyed everything — the Earth, just gone. Now one of them is trying to kill us and you are talking about helping her." She leaned across the table, staring directly at Gal. "We need to march over to the Army outpost — preferably before that thing wakes up from the sedation so she can't kill us — and drop her off, into proper custody."

An uneasy feeling of dread settled in Halud's stomach.

Gal shut his eyes and turned away.

"I want no part in this. I want to go home," she said.

"You can't," mumbled Gal. "You know that."

"What?"

Hoepe answered, his words slow and direct, "Commander, if they discover any of us have knowledge of, or have come into contact with an Augment, they will kill you. Not Sarrin, but them, the Central Army. If you run to the outpost, not only will they torture you and hang you, but everyone else in this room will be dead by morning. Go to your room, get some rest — do as I say if you want to live. That's not a threat. That's advice."

Her jaw hung open. She lifted her head, turned abruptly, and left.

Hoepe made a subtle movement with his hand, and two of his men followed Rayne out. He turned to Kieran and then to Gal. "You both need rest. We'll figure the rest out in the morning."

The engineer and captain left quietly, each accompanied by their guard. Gal stumbled, one of Hoepe's men carrying him out.

Hoepe sighed heavily and slumped into one of the open chairs.

"I'd like to see her," Halud said.

Hoepe inclined his head, exhaustion plain in his eyes. "I don't know what condition she'll be in when she wakes."

"She's my sister."

"You've read her file. What did they do to her?"

Halud paled. He hadn't read it, hadn't wanted to know. Maybe it would have told him this was all a very bad idea.

Hoepe frowned. He leaned across the table. "You're lucky she didn't kill anyone. I don't know what my men would have done. I don't know what would have happened." He stood up, rapping his knuckles in a random pattern on the table between them. "The captain is your responsibility. And Rayne. The last thing we need is her running to the UECs. The situation is already too messy."

Hoepe stood and left the room, leaving Halud alone to contemplate what he had done.

*　*　*

Sarrin came back to herself slowly, her body abnormally heavy as she laid on the bed. It felt like she had been drugged, but she didn't remember how or when.

Something tight sat around her wrists, the pressure biting into the sensitive flesh. Her ankles were held down too. Someone beside her shifted in a chair: Halud — she knew it from his breathing.

She recalled him shouting at her, desperate and scared. Why? *The darkness. No, no, no, no.* Her breath caught, dragging her down. Legs jerked and flailed, but her body was too heavy to move. She had fallen into the trance, let it consume her.

Through slits in her eyelids, she glanced at Halud sitting in the middle of the cramped grey room. He stared blankly at something in his hands: an automatic syringe. Sedative. Pain seized her chest. Halud had given up everything for her, for his sister, but he got a monster instead. More than anyone, she had hoped to hide this from her brother. He deserved better. She had a chance to put away the past, but she cracked it. She was cracked. The whole thing was cracked.

Darkness prickled the edge of her vision.

Halud made no sign he knew she was awake. It was better that way. There wouldn't be any questions, any awkward silences. What could she possibly say to him now?

She closed her eyes and prayed. She would need all five Gods, Fortitude most of all.

Her mind ticked the time as four hours and thirty eight minutes passed. Halud shifted back and forth in his chair, the auto-syringe rattling softly as he spun it in his hands. Once she heard him sobbing softly.

The security pad in the corridor beeped, and the door opened. Hoepe entered, his long, smooth footfalls characteristic. "How is she doing?"

Halud rubbed his eyes quickly. "Still asleep." His rough voice sent a pang through her heart.

If only she wasn't so cracked.

Hoepe would know she wasn't truly asleep. But he didn't say anything. "Go get some rest. I can watch her."

Halud's voice shook, "No, I should be here when she wakes up."

"She'll sleep for several hours. You may as well do the same. Collect yourself."

Halud sniffed, and a minute later she heard him shuffle away and the door hiss open and closed.

"Sarrin, it's just me. Stop pretending." Hoepe's voice turned gruff and direct, nearly comforting in its familiarity. She opened her eyes and saw him staring down at her, dragging a hand through his hair. "Gods, you almost gave us away." He dropped into the chair with a sigh. "Well, no denying your talents now. They're all spread about it, planning the best way to get rid of you."

She tried to turn away, but the restraints cut across her wrists.

"The commons, they're so ignorant," he huffed. One of his long legs bounced erratically as he gazed into a distance that wasn't there. At least she wasn't the only one who got lost. She waited for him to refocus, and when he did it was with the cold, medical intensity she'd been expecting. "You had been on Selousa for years, yes?"

She nodded.

"I ran additional bloodwork —."

She inhaled sharply. If he had looked at her hands, he would know. There would be too many questions. Things she didn't like acknowledging, things she would have to hide if she wanted a normal life. Not that there was much chance of that now.

"You've got a chronic zinc deficiency. That artificial stuff they pedal is almost worthless. Your neural pathways are degrading."

Her breath left her.

"You look confused. See what I mean about the neural pathways," he smirked.

She stared at him. "You've never been very funny."

His grin spread. "You'll be fine. The ship has a stock of UEC rations from Etar with natural zinc. A couple weeks and you'll be right where you should be. I've already given you an injection to boost your blood levels."

Her head did feel clearer. "The gamma gravitation array?"

"Off. We're back on Contyna." He stood, stretching until his fingers almost brushed the ceiling. "Look, they figured those restraints would be enough. I couldn't tell them they weren't without telling them a whole lot more. If you want my advice, play nice, don't give them any reason to think you're more dangerous than they already do."

She never intended to let them think that at all. But a person could never hide their true colours: *Once a monster, always a monster.*

He shrugged, "The mission went well — I'm sure you're not surprised. Thank you for waiting until you got back to go psychotic. No sign the warship even knew we were there. We got a good haul of rations and medical supplies. We'll see about the data, I've just started going through it, but I'm excited."

Her hand caught on the restraint as she tried to reach up to the spot on the side of her head. It didn't hurt now, the whole thing seemed like a distant dream. Had it really happened at all?

Hoepe stretched once more and sat back down in the chair beside the bed. He pulled out a data pad. "Everyone felt better if there was someone keeping watch."

Her face fell. So that was it, strapped to the bed with a 24-hour guard. Same prison, different cage. She twisted her hand from the restraint like she'd learned to do at twelve, and rolled over to stare at the grey wall.

Hoepe scrolled through his data and talked idly, "I hid on Etar for a few months before falling in with a gang who needed a medic. That got a little too close, so I came out here and got these boys together. They're a good crew, know their job, don't ask questions. You shot one of them. They'll be alright though, won't hurt you, I talked to them. I want you to join us when you're better."

Pulling jobs, fighting, stealth missions, bombs…. A life fit for a monster. Her life. "Do you know where the others are?" she asked, the words surprising her.

"No. You're the first one I found. A couple of whispers here and there but nothing worth following up."

"That's what we were trying to find for you on the warship, wasn't it?"

He glanced over his data pad. "I'm surprised you didn't realize it sooner."

So was she, the damage must have been worse than either of them thought.

He sighed and turned back to his reading. "Don't get your hopes up though. They keep records of us sealed like plastiq-weld. Your brother found you on the mainframe in the central compound — friends in high places, I suppose."

Halud had given up a lot for her.

"Get some sleep, Sarrin, your neural pathways need it to regenerate."

It had been a long time since she'd slept deeply, but with Hoepe keeping watch, she felt she could risk it. She unclipped the other restraints from her legs and wrist. For now, she was safe. She dreamt about young girl and her brother playing in the orchards on their parents' farm.

NINE

ABOARD THE UECAS COMRADE, COMMANDANT Mallor gritted her teeth. The doctor had said they would come, and so they had, following the carefully laid out pieces like breadcrumbs.

Came and went.

"Relax, Amelia." The doctor's gnarled face frowned in her peripheral vision. They were alone in his darkened medical lab.

A growl escaped from deep in her throat, her hands clenching as she stared out of the small viewport to the empty expanse of space. "I find it difficult."

He scanned her head down to her toes, then pressed an auto-syringe into her shoulder. "Something to help you relax."

The medicine pushed through the fabric of her crisp, white uniform and raced through her veins. Her mind slowed, sluggish to the point she felt nearly asleep even as she stood, waiting for him.

"I am your master. You follow my commands," he said, his voice low and soothing.

She nodded, mumbling, "You are my master. I follow your commands."

"Good." His long scar turned up as he smiled. "Now, talk to me, Amelia dear."

A strange sensation of lost time passed quickly, and she blinked, returning to her usual hard self. "I admit to being impressed, Doctor. How did you know they would come?"

"Ah!" He waved his hand knowingly as he turned back to the long counter and started sorting through his instruments. "Psychology, my dear. Once you know what drives someone at their core, it is easy to predict their every move, often plan it."

An unknown thought, more like a heavy feeling, caught her before it fleeted away. "Still, the Augments can be unpredictable."

"I know these children better than anyone. Love them, in a way. I know all their secrets."

"May I ask, what is it that you want?"

"The same thing you want, my dear. To destroy them." His beady brown eyes twinkled. "Remember they killed your family."

She growled in agreement. "They killed my family."

"I know." He stepped closer to her, reaching a soothing, understanding hand to her shoulder. Most people kept their distance, but never the doctor. She revelled in the feeling of reassurance, just for a moment.

"What is our next move? When will we destroy them?" Releasing a captive Augment was foolish. As far as she was concerned, they should all be made dead. But this was the doctor's plan, and he was certain 005478F could be kept under control.

"We must flush her out first, and then follow her," said the doctor. "But this one is special, she is dangerous. We must keep track of her at all times, I want to know her movements before she makes them."

"Indeed."

"Are you ready?"

She frowned. "Ready?"

"To have your own chip activated."

"P-pardon?" A vision flashed of a cold, damp industrial laboratory, disappearing instantly.

He smiled, and a knot twisted itself in her stomach. "We brought her all this way to activate her chip. Now we need to switch on yours."

"I have an implant?"

"Of course. You were made as a soldier, weren't you?"

"Yes." The thought twitched again, far away and sluggish.

"Good." He gestured to the procedure table, inviting her to sit. As she did, he moved the head of a narrow beam generator — the same one they had set by the mainframe computer room — next to her skull. "There may be a small pressure."

Pain exploded against her temporal lobe. She clutched her head with her hand.

"This chip is powered by the human brain," shouted Guitteriez gleefully. "It will link with hers, connect you to her every thought. It works across galaxies, regardless of limits of distance and transmission speed."

"Connected?" Acid burned in the back of her throat, and a chill ran up her spine. Anger seized her and she gripped the edge of the table.

"My dear" — Guitteriez placed a calming hand once again on her shoulder — "it is perfectly safe. You will be in complete control."

"I do not want their vile thoughts in my head."

He smiled. "You feel her even now, don't you? Where is she?"

A strange doubled sensation came over her, and Amelia

concentrated a moment. "She is resting. She is on the planet." It was disconcerting that she could know that, could simply feel it as easily as she would know her own body.

"Good. We need her to move. It's time for hunting. Show her how dark the Deep can be."

At last. She grinned, clicking on her personal comm chip, ready to relay orders to her crew. "Prepare the drones."

* * *

Sarrin bolted upright, scrabbling with dead heads against the unfamiliar bedsheets. The walls closed in around her and she panted for breath. The dream had been too dark, too real. In it, she sat quietly, peacefully on a white bed, her hair being brushed smooth while the older girl hummed softly.

And then Guitteriez's ugly, grinning face had taken over everything.

Hoepe's eyes searched her intently over the top of his data pad. Rapidly, she unhooked the heavy-duty restraints from her legs, swinging off the bed and retreating to the latrine. Splashing cold water on her cheeks, she brought herself back to the present, back to the little cramped room. She let the water run, watching it twirl down the drain, hoping it would wash away the foreign DNA and training and experiments and surgeries.

But it never would.

Hoepe called to her from the other room, "Shift change is soon."

Started, she shook her head. How long had she been standing there? How long had she been asleep? She couldn't say. Her mind played tricks with time, remembering the past too clearly and none of the present.

She shut off the water. Hoepe may not care if she wandered around, but the others certainly would. She returned to the bed, clicking the restraints into place and shutting her eyes just as the door slid open.

Hoepe stood from the chair, the legs scraping as he pushed it back along the carpet. "I just gave her another dose," he told the new guard, "she should be sedated for a while. Comm me direct if you have any trouble."

Hoepe left and the man sat in the chair. He leaned back, his boots pressed against the edge of the bed. Dangerously close. "Pathetic scum," he snorted. And then he spit.

She forced her shaking body to be still, to ignore the angry emotions that rolled off of him and crashed into her. She was meant to be sedated; it was easier that way. Still, fear clawed at her chest and her mind told her to run. This wasn't her, wasn't who she was meant to be. But it was how she had been made.

His boot kicked her in the side, rocking her, stretching her arm out painfully against the restraint. "That's for Dyno's arm." Another kick. "And Troy."

The men she had injured. She forced her muscles to relax with a concentrated effort, and prepared to feign sleep. How cracked she had been to think she could live a normal life.

She waited two hours before his breathing evened into the deep rhythm of sleep. Unclipping her wrist and ankles, she flung herself across the room. Flying as though the bed would swallow her whole. She scrubbed her whole face with the freezing water from the latrine. Her eyes danced: eight different escapes and nineteen objects that could be used as deadly weapons.

No, she shook her head, she shouldn't be carrying weapons. She couldn't be trusted. And yet, the fool guard had brought his laz-gun with him. Had Hoepe told them nothing? The darkness called to her, reminding her she wasn't a bad person. These people hated her, would kill her if they had half a chance. She'd had a chance to live normally. But she'd cracked it.

The bolts unscrewed from the wall, and the panel ripped off easily. Her teeth gritted as she squeezed into the tight space. Wiggling and dragging her body, she escaped up the space behind the wall, finding an access tube. Her mind felt better, but it was far from clear. Flashes of laz-fire danced in the corners of her vision.

Only memories.

She dropped into a corridor and broke into a run. Feet struck the floor, a steady thump-thump-thump. The rhythm of it soothed her, let her mind lose itself. Pushed on by an undefined and desperate urge to flee, she ran, and ran, and ran.

Seventy-eight circuits of the ship — an estimated 12-kilometres. Usually the distance wouldn't have been a problem, but she had been incarcerated for three and a half years — she came to a sudden stop, bending over, legs aching.

A passage came to her: '*Though they will take me, they will not break me. I am a mind, independent of time. My trials shall pass, but I alone will last.*' Halud had written it the day after the Earth was lost. Sarrin had read it on a hacked newsfeed hidden between decks on a freightship not that different from this one. She had survived that, she would survive this, she told herself. A mineral deficiency — an illness, treatable — had done this. Not her. She would recover. She would find somewhere to go, somewhere she would just be another face in another crowd. Folk. Not Augment. Not soldier. Not monster.

The corridor was empty, the lights dimmed to 10-percent. The only sound was the gentle creaking of the ship's bulkheads and the grunt of the engines.

Her feet carried her to Engineering and through to the engine room.

The hum washed over her and took her away, as she rested her hands against the purring beast. She wanted to feel it, and pressed the whole of her arm against it, drinking in the vibration. She didn't hear the engineer come in, not until he tapped the wall with his spanner, the tinny sound echoing in the small room.

She stared at him wide-eyed, as he stared back. Her heart raced uncontrollably in her chest. He had gotten too close without her noticing.

"Hi." He lifted a cautious hand.

Sarrin retreated three steps, putting the engine between them.

He coughed involuntarily, turning away. He wore a thin plastic brace, and bruising crept from his slightly open coveralls to his jaw.

She stared at her hands — not her hands, tools, belonging to the Army. Slowly, they moved to wrap around her own throat, testing. She didn't remember what happened, but it must have been her, she must have crushed him. The bruising marks were a perfect match. What else could it have been?

Her eyes snapped up, looking at him, fearful of the answer.

"I'm okay," he croaked — his voice was terrible and raspy, no soft and irregular accent. He smiled, but he started to cough again.

She pointed a finger to him and then to herself, questioning.

His eyebrows knitted together, and Sarrin held her breath as he studied her, pressing his lips together seriously. Then, he nodded once.

The blow cascaded in her chest and left her gasping for air. Hoepe had told her there'd been injured but not who, not what. She'd attacked the engineer who she found both brilliant and, more importantly, kind. She had never wanted to hurt anybody, never — had worked her entire life to avoid it, but she couldn't escape what they had made her. No matter the treatment, Hoepe couldn't make the monster go away.

It had to stop. She pressed her hands to her head and clutched her hair.

"It's okay," he said again, reaching for her.

She threw herself backwards against the wall, putting as much space between them as possible. *Monster, monster, monster.*

He put his hands up in the air.

"Don't touch," she whispered. She didn't want to hurt anybody.

He frowned again, but nodded.

Sarrin catalogued the room: three escape routes and twelve deadly objects.

No! No weapons.

"Look" — he swallowed with effort and pressed on, speaking carefully — "I don't know what happened, but I don't think you meant for it to happen. Am I right?"

She nodded once. "A mineral imbalance."

He nodded with her. "Hoepe told us."

"It won't happen again."

He smiled weakly. "Is that what they trained you for in Evangecore?"

She felt behind her for the screws on the bulkhead.

"Is there something we should know, like a code-word to shut you off or something. You know, if… well, if it does happen again."

"It won't." One of the screws popped loose and fell into her hand.

He pressed his lips together. He knew it as well as she did: it could happen again, she would have no control. She was too cracked.

"Hoepe used 300mg of lorazepam combined with 150mg of telazol."

He stared. "I don't have any of that."

Another screw dropped, but her hand shook and it fell to the floor.

His eyes darted to it immediately, and then to her. "Sarrin, it's okay. I won't tell the others you were here."

She turned and pulled at the bulkhead, ripping the last of the screws off. A hand reached for her. She spun around, whipping the panel between her and him. "Don't touch me!"

He staggered back, clutching the panel in surprise. "Sarrin, wait! I just want to talk to you."

She slipped into the wall, pushing aside the heavy ropes of conduit and climbed up the wall and into the ceiling.

Below, she heard the engineer try to follow. "Come back. I'm not afraid of you. Sarrin!" A wave of coughing overtook him, and he staggered back.

She lay in the narrow space, panting to catch her breath. Inches separated her from the expanse of stars. She brought her hands up again and scratched at her neck, each dig stinging sharply against her flesh.

The walls pressed in, her chest heaving in the thing, stale air. It was safe here, far from the others.

She debated opening a hole and pressing her mouth into it before the hull's auto-seal could block her from the vacuum of space, but she recalled they were in Hoepe's hangar, on Contyna. The same oxygen outside as inside.

Why did she think she was in space?

Her poor neurons were wrecked.

She twisted herself around, sliding through the walls back to her cell. Sleep was what she needed. Her path would look clearer as her brain healed.

Her hands slipped easily into the restraints. She repeated, as she had done every night on Selousa, the litanies of the Gods: 'I follow the spirits of Faith the Brave, and Knowledge the Wise, and Fortitude the Strong, and Prudence the Thoughtful, and Strength the Powerful. In these I believe and I give to myself and I will persevere in my duty with them.'

* * *

Sarrin woke from her quasi-sleep. She'd had another dream, this one pleasant and familiar. She'd had it many times before: a lush, green planet, with beautiful birds in the sky and ungulates in the forest, hundreds of different species, more than she'd ever thought possible. In the dream, everyone knew everyone — even the animals — and they knew her. Warmth and comfort flooded her body, it felt like home.

No, not home. Another word echoed around her head as though it had been spoken to her. Roam? Dome?

An image flashed in her mind: a group of Central Army decoys, falling from the stars and ripping into the atmosphere.

Drone.

"I wondered when you'd wake up," said the guard, kicking at the edge of the bed again with his boot.

She turned her head away. Evangecore had put her through years of prescience training, and her instinct told her the vision was real, very real. Before she could stop it, the darkness pulled her into the space where she could feel the subtle ripples of space and time, and she saw them: tens of little spheroids dropping through the atmosphere. Drones.

It took a moment of searching, of useless tongue flapping, to find the words. "We are under attack. Release me."

The guard laughed, sharp and hard.

She flipped back, easily seeing the drone that were headed for them, their trajectory angled straight for the hangar. Darkness clouded at the edge of her vision.

"Come on, I wasn't born yesterday," he said.

She frowned. Hoepe had warned her to stay in the restraints; the men were terrified enough thinking they had her contained. But her mental clock had already calculated and started ticking down the time until impact.

"Boss brought you something to eat." He leaned down.

"Listen to me." Sweat beaded on her back, and she pushed away the darkness.

He lifted up a neat bowl of dehydrated rations. "He says you got to eat all of it. Regain your strength so you don't kill anybody." He sneered. "Me, I'd'a spaced you first chance I got, and you'd be dead just like the planet you destroyed, filthy demon."

Her eyes squeezed shut. If she waited any longer, they would all be dead. Or worse.

He dangled a piece of dehydrated meat in her direction, slapping it against her mouth. The auto-syringe was poised in his other hand.

With a smooth twist of her wrist, the restraint fell away. She grabbed the auto syringe and flung it across the room.

A shout escaped his lips, and he scrambled after it.

Quickly, she unlatched the rest of the restraints and sprung off the bed.

The second guard burst in from the corridor and fired his laz-rifle blindly.

Sarrin pushed the first guard out of the way and leapt back. Another pulse fired, close range this time, forcing her down. Darkness fogged at the edges of her vision, and she slipped for an instant.

She threw the laz-rifle, now in her hands it to the ground. Time slowed. She sprinted down the corridor and accessed a data panel, using it to start the ship's engines.

The guards rounded the corner with a yell, their auto-syringes outstretched, laz-bolts bouncing along the corridor. Too many things to track.

She shook her foggy head and ran. Her legs took her to the cargo bay, her vision swimming in and out of focus, black tendrils reaching across. She launched over the railing, landing on the lower cargo deck, and sprinted down the open loading ramp.

Her eyes adjusted quickly to the dark, quiet hangar, the only light shining from the under the second-story office door. She ran up the steps, pushing the door hard enough it bent off its lock before it opened. Hoepe sat up startled. "You're supposed to be under watch."

Her stomach churned and the vision of the sky flashed in her mind. "Drones," she said.

"What?" A single eyebrow quirked. "Are you sure?"

She nodded.

He reached for the hand-held on his desk, triggering an alarm that rang through the hangar. He turned back to her. "How many?"

Her guards stumbled into the office, finally catching up, panting and shouting.

"Stand down," Hoepe waved a warning hand. "How many?" he asked again.

Her heart raced, the darkness wrapping its tendrils around her. "Nearly a hundred."

"Time?"

The drones were well into the atmosphere by now. "Three

minutes."

His face paled. "Trigger the defence system," he ordered his men. "Then evacuate to the ship. Get everyone out."

"Sir?"

"Now."

She paused, waiting for Hoepe, but he waved her on from his desk. "I need to wipe the memory," he said, "I'll be along. Go."

"Two-twenty-three" she told him, and raced back down the stairs.

A forceshield flickered as it went up around the building.

She ran to the freightship and through its long corridors, sliding into the Pilot's chair. Tapping the thruster controls, the ship lifted off the floor, hovering there. A three degree twist of the steering sphere took the ship to the opposite edge of the hangar, ready to fly.

Her hand tapped absently against her chest. Her senses sharpened to deafening levels, each squeal and thud of the ship, the containers being blow around the hangar, thundering in her ears. Hoepe hadn't yet run onto the ship — she waited anxiously for the sound of his stride echoing through the ship. Halud was snoring in his quarters on the third deck. Hoepe's men shuffled around the cargo bay. A pair of boots — Kieran's? — ran along the central corridor to engineering.

The drones whistled down, close enough now to hear. The first impacts shook the walls of the hangar. The forceshield held most of it, but dust and pieces of debris started to fall, clattering across the hull.

Another impact rocked the hangar, this time loosing pieces of ceiling and sending cargo containers tumbling across the floor. A piece of con-plas fell onto the ship, jarring it.

They were out of time.

She took a deep, steadying breath and spun the steering sphere, pushing the thrusters to max. The ship punched out of the hangar, tearing a hole in the walls. Around them, dozens of drones rained from the sky, crashing into buildings. Not just the hangar, but tearing through everything for a two hundred yard radius.

Her heart crashed around, her vision nothing but a narrow spec, focussed solely on the path ahead of them. She threw the ship into a barrel roll, climbing erratically.

"What is this?" The captain's shriek, the only other person on the bridge, made her jump. He lurched forward. Anger poured off of him in waves, crashing into her like physical blows.

The ship rumbled as it pushed out of the atmosphere, going far faster than regulation. He swung at her. She kept a hand on the steering sphere, keeping them on course, even as she jumped. Darkness flashed, consuming her vision.

The ship shot into space, the rumbling ceased and the steering normalized. She threw herself across the room, as far from Gal as possible. She felt herself losing touch, losing the battle as the darkness called to her. Terrified of what he might do and what she might do the stop him, she started to undo the bolts on the panel behind her.

Her two guards stumbled onto the bridge. "What's she doing?" Their shouts were far away.

Flashing light caught her eye from the Pilot console. A proximity warning.

She looked to the large viewport. The warship loomed directly ahead. Bolts of electrically charged light shot from it's turrets.

The impact threw everyone back, though her instincts pulled her forwards. She spun the steering sphere wildly.

Gal recovered first. He came at her, his fist already clenched in a fist. He wasn't slow, he had training, but he was no Augment, no Evangecore simulator. She ducked, still twisting the sphere. His blow landed on the console beside her, and he stumbled, clutching his hand.

A laz-gun fired, and her own anger flared in her like fire, feeding the monster. The guards started to argue.

She reached for the Engineering console. The FTL had barely begun to spool. She forced it to bypass its checks. Once the ship was out of danger, when the guards and the captain stopped attacking her, she could push the darkness away.

Gal came at her with a shout. Her hand shot out of its own volition, her mind blank. He stumbled backwards, clutching at his throat.

A gasp sounded behind her: Halud.

Three laz-bolts narrowly missed her head as she automatically crouched to the ground. She fought the darkness off her as she pushed herself off the floor. Halud's horrified look burned into her vision, and she wished she had stayed restrained. This was too much. She was unwell, ready to lose control, again, at any moment.

Something landed on her legs, clinging to them. She screamed out.

The darkness pushed, but the memory of the engineer's bruised and battered neck kept her from giving in. If she gave into her fear, people would get hurt. And she couldn't let it happen. Not again. Never again.

She dragged herself until she could reach a hand up to the console, the guard still holding her legs, his touch burning with exchanging electricity. The FTL jump was instantaneous, no more than a few nanoseconds, yet it seemed to drag on forever.

Safely out of range of the warship, she sighed, dropping her head.

Another laz-bolt burned into the deck in front of her. Gal leaped and threw a punch that knocked her head against the wall. Her legs kicked out, throwing Gal. She leaped across the room with an in-human growl, taking the guard with her, twisting his arm mercilessly, the monster spurring her on.

Halud, standing just inside the door to the bridge with his trembling eyes and open mouth, stared at her.

One last ounce of self persevered against the darkness, reaching around the back of the guard and into his pocket. The auto-syringe hissed, releasing its contents into her neck, and she fell, unconscious, to the deck.

TEN

HALUD SAT STIFFLY IN THE uncomfortable, straight-backed dining chair. Ten hours ago, he had been woken from his bed when the ship suddenly flipped out from underneath him. On the bridge, his not-so-captive-as-thought sister attacked the captain and then injected herself with sedative.

It was not, he thought grimly, the absolute worst scenario he could have imagined, but it was close.

For a third time, they had pushed the tables in the mess hall together and convened to discuss disaster. One of Hoepe's men sat with his head in his hands, groaning, "I just don't understand what happened."

Hoepe, looking sour-faced and grim as he loomed over them, suddenly slammed his fists on the table. "I'll tell you what happened: someone told them where we were. I've been here two years and pulled dozens of missions that were far worse, and they've never found us. Never. Now the entire compound is destroyed — most of the city is gone." His glare pierced into each of them in turn, stopping at Rayne.

"It wasn't me," she squeaked.

"No?" he raised a challenging eyebrow. "What about your Path of the Gods? Do you even know what 'Gods' you serve?"

She whimpered, sinking into her chair. Her arms caught against the restraints, and she blinked in shock.

Beside Halud, Sarrin sat shackled to her own chair. She stared at the ceiling, her lips moving subtly, and Halud leaned away involuntarily.

"I told you not to go to them," shouted Hoepe, his deep voice shaking. "I told you! You didn't listen. Do you see what you've done?"

"I—I—," stammered Rayne.

"Don't talk to her like that," slurred Gal.

Halud shook his head, wrapping a hand over his own mouth. He'd spent his life reading between the lines — how could he have been so wrong? Galiant Idim was nothing but a washed up, drunk starship captain, and he was drunk now.

Rayne trembled, holding her shackled hands in front of her. "Please, I didn't tell them, I swear. You have to believe me. I was going to go — yes, that's true — but I — I didn't."

"What I want to know is, how did the girl escape? Who let her go?" Gal slumped back in his chair, lifting his flask up to the growing bruise on his temple. "She was on the bridge, alone. Doing Gods know what."

Hoepe frowned. "Gal, put down the flask, you have a subdural hematoma."

"Why?" The captain shrugged. "It's perfect — cold compress on the wound, isn't that what the Field Medic Handbook says, Rayne?" He patted her arm roughly, and Rayne tensed, face white. "Plus," Gal pointed to his head, "it warms up the drink. It's always cold in space."

Hoepe turned his hawk-stare to the Poet, making him retreat

against the chair back. The doctor gestured at Gal. "You couldn't have found anybody else? Literally any other ship? A drunk and a devout. I'm not even sure which is worse." He reached his long arm across the table and grabbed the flask from Gal's hand. He took a taste, and immediately spat it out, spraying across the room. "This is disgusting," he said and flung it away. "Methylamphetamine? Diacetylmorphine? Are you trying to kill yourself?"

Gal scurried after it. "Hey! There's not much left."

"Good," said Hoepe.

Gal resumed his chair. "I think you're forgetting there was an Augment loose on this ship. We could have all been killed!" He glanced warily at Sarrin as he took another drink. "Gods, don't let her look at me — they can read minds."

"This isn't Sarrin's fault," said Halud.

"She just jumped up and pushed me over," the guard said in disbelief, his voice still muffled by his head in his hands, "and grabbed the laz-rifle out of Vazquez's hands."

Gal's eyes grew very dark, expression dark. "She's a demon," he said plainly. "There's only one way out of this." He stood abruptly.

"Stop," warned Halud.

"I would push her out of an airlock, but I suspect she would survive that too. We have to destroy it." He reached for her.

Halud leapt to his feet, block Gal chest to chest. "Why do you think that? Do you hear the nonsense coming from your mouth? The hypocrisy?" He slapped him across the face.

Gal reached up, stunned, and took another drink. He shook his head. "I'm sorry, Halud. She's dangerous."

Halud looked at his sister, sitting perfectly still, relaxed, eyes closed. "We wouldn't be sitting here if it weren't for her. We'd be dead."

Gal took another drink. "Better off, maybe."

"Is that really what you want? It can be arranged," said Hoepe.

Rayne whimpered. "Please," she said, "I didn't do anything. I just want to go home."

Gal shut his eyes, turning away with a tired sigh. "Would you please just let her go."

"She's a traitor," answered Hoepe.

"I didn't tell them! What right do you have to accuse me?" She stood up, the chair scraping and dangling from the restraints awkwardly. "You're the one who's committing a crime, who's against the Gods. I never wanted to be here in the first place."

Hoepe gritted his teeth. "Which is why you told the UECs everything."

"Why would I have come back if I had? No, I was —." She looked at Gal. "I didn't tell them."

Beside Halud, Sarrin flicked her wrists, the restraints rattling softly. She stood up from her chair, and he saw the restraints were missing. She turned and took a step away from the table as the room fell silent.

Hoepe's men reacted first, the group of them leaping across the table and tackling her from all sides.

She shut her eyes, standing rigid even as one of them punched her in the head. Her expression stayed chillingly serene.

"Hey!" shouted Halud.

Kieran leapt across the table, tugging at one of the men. "Stop it," he rasped.

Hoepe pounded on the table, clearing his throat. The men froze in their places, and looked up like guilty children. "She escaped her restraints, Boss."

"She is not to be harmed," he said. Hoepe waved his hand, and the men backed away.

Kieran laid across the table and slowly started to pull himself back. "She saved our lives, you fools." His voice came out slow and thick, the bruising still prominent on his neck. "This is one of the Central Army's most highly trained soldiers, genetically enhanced, trained almost since birth. And you thought some chains were going to hold her." He frowned as he shifted back into his chair. "She's been cooperating, is all. And if she hadn't warned us, they'd be digging our bodies out of the rubble right now."

Sarrin stood in the same place, her eyes still closed, her fists clenching and unclenching rhythmically.

"Sarrin?" Hoepe asked.

Her eyes opened, glancing nervously around the room. Halud reached for her but she flinched away. She moved around the table silently, stopping with her hand outstretched, open palm inches away from Rayne. She reached down and unclipped the restraints. Rayne trembled, the chair falling away and clattering to the floor.

Sarrin glanced at Hoepe, the two exchanging a nod, and she turned padding silently out of the room.

"Boss?" said one of the men after the doors had shut behind her.

"Let her go," answered Hoepe.

"You can't be serious," said Gal.

"I am." He sighed. "The engineer is right, Galiant, Sarrin has been cooperating with us. If she wanted you dead, you would already be."

"What?" squeaked Rayne.

Gal grumbled, having retaken his chair, the flask coming

down from his lips. "We have to do something, she's an Augment. She can't just be running around the ship. It should be guarded at least."

"I'm sure that's not necessary." Hoepe fixed Gal with a stern look. "She helped your first officer, now be quiet."

"Rayne didn't do anything," he argued.

Hoepe sighed, and turned away. "I know."

"What?" Halud leaned forward over the table. "How?"

The doctor blinked back at him.

"Boss," said Vasquez, "you said yourself the Augment was dangerous. She took a laz-rifle out of my hand in the blink of an eye."

"There's no use in tying her down, but for the time being I want two men with her at all times."

"I could use Sarrin's help in Engineering," said Kieran. "The Kepheus Drive has been acting up, and that last jump was the last straw. I need to see if it's fixable."

Hoepe raised a single eyebrow. "Very well," nodded Hoepe. "But I do think an extra set of eyes is a good idea for the time being." He pulled two auto-syringes from his pocket, passing them out. "I need a detail on the first officer too."

"What?" Rayne said.

"You said yourself she didn't do anything," said Gal.

"There's nowhere for me to go."

"Be grateful. I was ready to push you out an airlock ten minutes ago."

Rayne gulped.

"Boss," asked one of the men, "what's going to happen to us now?"

Hoepe shook his head, "Contyna is destroyed. I didn't have time to erase the compound's hard drive fully, which means our hideouts at Perim and Nastalia could be compromised as well. We'll need to find a new place."

Gal took another drink, leaning back in his chair. "The deep Deep is the only place you've got to hide. I hope you like the cold, you fools."

Halud's chest grew tight — no where to hide, no one to call. With a pang, he longed for his apartments with his warm bed and his real-oak steady desk. But those were nothing but faraway dreams now; they were adrift in space.

* * *

"You okay?" Kieran rasped quietly from across the workbench in the main engineering bay, his bruised larynx still peppering his already unusual speech. Green eyes peered at her over the broken Kepheus Drive. "The one hit ya pretty hard, it looked like."

She turned her attention to the machinery, stripping it apart to see its insides.

"But really, are y'okay?" The second time he'd asked.

She frowned — how could she respond? How did normal people respond? She gave him a quick nod.

"D'ya need anything? Like t'eat? Drink?" His hand was unnecessarily close, reaching across the space between them. He pulled it back in response to her glare. "Jus' tryin' to be friendly." He turned away, racked with a small coughing fit.

The heavy hilt of a carving knife pressed against her leg as she shifted against the table. From her coverall pockets, she pulled out three food blades, a spanner, and a piece of electrical conduit. Weapons.

Kieran stared, his eyes going wide, the corners crinkling in confusion.

Somehow between the meeting in the Mess Hall and Engineering, she had gathered the arms. "Habit," she muttered, something she had done since she was ten years old. In Evangecore, you never knew when you would need a weapon. Of course, they never left anything lying around for the children to find.

Kieran let out a low whistle. His gaze swept quickly to her guard. Fortunately the man seemed preoccupied with the settings on his laz-rifle.

She handed Kieran the auto-syringe she had lifted from the same guard.

He stared at it. Then at her, question in his eyes. Not fear.

Shrugging her shoulders, she pressed it towards him again. He needed to take it. Kieran wasn't like the others, but he could keep them safe. That's why he needed to take it. "500 milligrams lorazepam."

Eyebrows rose in shock. Then he snorted, surprise melting into a carefree smile. "Yeah, alright." He shoved the injector into his coverall pocket, finding places to hide the other items too. "You shouldn't take things that don't belong to ya."

Her heart rate accelerated momentarily, until a cheeky grin and a wink told her he was plainly joking. Kieran Wood was not like the others at all. "Now what're we gonna do about this baby?" His hands turned to the dismantled Kepheus. The drive created the space-folding gravitational field they needed for long-distance jumps. Without it, the ship was limited to maneuvering thrusters. Sarrin estimated 115-years-standard to the nearest planet without it.

"Geez," he said, rubbing a hand over his frown. "Internal plasma chamber is cracked — that's bad. Ions have cooled back into their gaseous state." He tipped the device and maneuvered it around the table like it wasn't one of the most delicate pieces of technology under the stars. "Just too many jumps, too close

together. I shoulda been checking." He turned to her. "Not that
we coulda avoided that last jump, hey. Thank you, for, you know,
that. Seems no one else'll say it."

Sarrin couldn't help the puzzled look that spread across her
features.

"What I don't understand is we've aligned it three times since
leaving Etar. It just won't stay. But the fittings are all new,
replaced them after the first misalignment."

Odd indeed. She leaned forward, examining the machine
with new intrigue.

"I can repair the chamber, that's no big deal, but we don't
have a plasma charger. Without the plasma intact, we won't have
the superconductivity needed for making space-folds. No plasma,
no jumps. No jumps, we die out here in the deep." He rolled his
eyes, laughing. "If it's not one thing, it's another, right?" His eyes
glinted merrily as he gestured to his bruised and bandaged neck.

Could he be joking about his injury? About her attack?
Sarrin took a step back, thinking that she may not the least sane
person in the room. But her brain kept ticking away, sorting
through her inventory of knowledge while she wondered just
where Kieran Wood had come from. "Med Bay will have a
surgical laser. C-O-2 or free electron?"

First, Kieran's eyebrows drew down. Then raised in surprise
and the right corner of his lip twitched up. "Brilliant! Just
brilliant. Let's go look."

Sarrin jogged after him, turning to slip past the guard as he
ambled in front of her in surprise.

Rushing into the infirmary, Kieran pulled the surgical laser
out of its corner. They crouched down to check the specs. "Free
electron," he read breathlessly. "Do you think you can recalibrate
it to ignite the plasma?" An excited glint passed through his eyes.

His pupil dilated and contracted — the colour a brilliant, intricate green; it was not colour contacts as she'd originally assumed but his natural pigment. Startling, when nearly everyone had some variation of brown.

"Yes," answered the part of her brain that still focussed.

He pulled a tiny toolkit from his belt and started unscrewing the paneling. "What parts do you need?"

Sarrin shook her head, motioning for him to back away. The schematics drew themselves, an instructional diagram in the front of her brain.

"Okay. I'll try to salvage the gases from the broken chamber. Finding that much pure nitrogen and noble elements will be almost impossible on the ship." Kieran pointed to the comm console on the wall. "Let me know if you need anything." He smiled reassuringly, but his eyes glanced at the guards, his meaning clear.

Ignoring the brute, and his new friend who had come to accompany him, she reached for the machine. Hands rapidly disassembled the surgical device and adjusted the controls. But the hands in front of her were foreign. Senseless and limp, they weren't a part of her, they were a machine.

She had been good with machines once — no, great, the best. But those were their designs, machines for killing and destruction. The hands were never her own; they always belonged to someone else.

The scars were faint, she didn't like to look at them, but she knew they were there. Down the sides of each finger and onto the wrist. She pushed up the thick wrappings she had tied around the wrists, revealing the ugly, lumpy mess where all the scars met together.

"Sarrin, the engineer said I could find you here."

She gasped, throwing the hands behind her back and tugging down the wraps.

Halud carried a steaming bowl in his hands as he approached. "I came to check on you. Are you alright?"

Dumbly, she nodded.

He pushed the bowl towards her, hands shaking. "I — I brought you something to eat." He was scared of her. Just like the rest.

She opened her mouth, but no sound would form. He was her brother. She wouldn't hurt him, couldn't. Not if she'd had any choice. She had been sick. He knew that, didn't he?

Words got stuck or lost, spinning away into the deep of space. What was so wrong with her that she couldn't talk to her own brother?

But an idea came to her. She reached into her pocket — almost certainly she had taken the engineer's data tablet. She could use its screen to write or draw something for Halud. They had communicated in codes for years, that would be easier.

Instead, her hands gripped around the handle of something solid and she pulled it out, curious. A knife — where had she found a knife between Engineering and the infirmary? She set it on the floor beside her, and reached again for the tablet.

"Weapon!" shouted one of the guards. The other had his laz-rifle up in a heartbeat.

She pushed Halud to the side with a flick of her wrist, leaping at the same time into the guard, pushing him over, taking his laz-rifle, and spinning her leg into the other guard.

The guard landed hard against the wall. In panic, he reached into his jacket pocket, gripping around for something that wasn't there — the auto-syringe. Waves of his fear and hatred rolled off of him, making her nearly sick.

Her hands dismantled the laz-rifle and retrained the bio-sensor. The rifle pointed at the guards. Two shots; she never missed. Her mind painted them as targets from an Evangecore combat simulator.

A stifled cry from behind stopped her, and she turned her head mechanically to the sound. Halud pressed against the wall with his knees pulled to his chest.

The laz-rifle clattered to the ground.

He had every reason to fear her. They all did. *Monster*.

The guards leapt. They grabbed her wrists, the shock of the pressure on all the bundled nerve endings making her cry out. She let them push her into the ground, eyes riveted to Halud. Her brother's hands shook as he stared at the grey carpet beside him, refusing to look at her.

She opened her mouth but it wouldn't speak. Inside, she screamed as the guards dragged her away.

* * *

It didn't take Kieran much time to collect the gases and assess the inside of the Kepheus Drive: cracked, full thickness, a piece just dangling there. It had nearly punctured the secondary safety chamber — and if that had happened, there would be no fixing it.

He kept his hands busy, finding small tasks to fill the time he should have used to send a report home. But really, what would he say? 'Oh by the way, the terra forming research was a complete flop, but it turns out we picked up a girl who is also an Augment, still alive — she's pretty messed up and tried to kill everyone on the ship. Don't worry though, I'm perfectly fine except for a bruised larynx after she nearly strangled me to death. She's working with me in Engineering. I think it's going well — she unloaded an armful of weapons, which seemed like a good thing.'

Jesus, he was trying to gain the confidence of a killing
machine — they'd think he had lost all his marbles. He probably
had, but he could find them later. He pressed his thumb into the
keypad and waited for a response from the other side of the door.

Hoepe admitted him readily, looking up from a stack of
tablets on the desk of the quarters he had claimed as his own after
they left Contyna.

"Can I talk to you?" Kieran rubbed his palms on the legs of
his coveralls.

The doctor gave him an appraising scan which, from behind
the wicked nose and angular face, was positively terrifying. "How
are your crico-aretenoids?"

"My what?"

Hoepe pointed.

"Oh, my throat. It's fine. I can talk, so that's something."

The doctor's eyes narrowed. "Remarkable. I wasn't
anticipating such fast healing."

Kieran shrugged. "Always been a quick healer. Mama said it
was because I ate my vegetables."

"Indeed."

At the corner of the room, one of Hoepe's men shifted his
weight, ready to leap into action at the slightest sign. A shiver
trailed up Kieran's spine. *Note to parents:* 'There's a doctor here.
Scares me more than the Augment does.'

"Your business?" Hoepe asked.

"Right. The Kepheus is cracked. I can weld it, patch it, but I
don't know how long it will hold."

"That doesn't sound promising."

"I wondered if there was a way to get a replacement."

Hoepe leaned back, feet up on the desk. "We have an

Augment on board the ship. Contyna is destroyed. I'm afraid you'll have to patch it for now."

"I know. I can. But …. Look, whatever's going on, I don't think we want to be caught with our pants around our ankles."

Both of the doctor's eyebrows shot up. "Pardon?"

"I mean we need to be able to run. It'll take me a day to weld the jump drive. It'll jump, but it will be weak — any jump could tear it apart. When it cracks again, maybe it'll be fixable, maybe it won't. I don't wanna be adrift anymore than the rest of you. If there's anyway to get a replacement, we'll be a lot better off."

Hoepe fixed him with his stare, considering. Then, "There's a planet. A24-alpha. 'Junk'. Aptly named since the Central Army stores all their derelicts there. We may find something if the scavengers haven't gotten there first."

"Oh, that's simple."

"Relatively." The doctor's feet dropped down, and he returned to his data. "You're the acting navigator, you can plot the jumps?"

"Yeah, I guess."

"I'll send you the coordinates."

Kieran paused, wondering if there was a good way to ask the doctor what he knew about Sarrin, but the guard took a step forward before he could, effectively dismissing him. As he turned to leave, the doors sprung open. Two men shouted, shoving Sarrin in front of them. Halud hovered behind, and Gal stumbled along in the rear.

"Oh no." Kieran jumped out of the way as they rushed into the room.

Hoepe stood abruptly. "What's going on? Rye? Gunnar?"

"She tried to attack!" shouted the guard.

"She had a knife!" said the other.

How many knives could there be on one ship?

"She took my laz-rifle!"

"She threw me across the room!"

The girl in question stood still, staring at the ground. Her hand dug methodically in and out of her thin upper arm.

Halud hung back, dancing awkwardly between coming to his sister and keeping a wary distance.

"Sarrin?" Hoepe asked.

"Boss, what are we going to do?" asked the first guard.

The other put his hand on his hip. "I'm all for dangerous missions, but this is crazy. We should just get rid of her."

"Exactly!" shouted Gal, waving his flask through the air.

"Sarrin?" Hoepe said, louder.

Her whole body flinched, and she lifted her head. Hoepe's face changed, some message passed between them.

"Get rid of her!" shouted Gal. "Regulations be damned. Shove her out an airlock. She's what they want. We don't need this kind of trouble."

Hoepe turned to Gal, his expression darkened and his massive frame dominated the room. "You've got a faster ticket out of here right now than she does, Captain."

Drunk, Gal was not to be deterred. "Kieran, look at me. Between you and me, I don't trust these people. Not one bit. The Augments destroyed Earth. And these Reapers don't care about anybody but themselves."

Kieran looked away.

"She's dangerous." Gal patted him on the back. "It's not pleasant, but we have to get her out of here, any means necessary."

He was a soldier and Gal was his captain, he told himself. He had to act the same as any other person would in the situation.

That was the deal. He was there to observe, see how the people thought and felt, assess the non-tangibles you couldn't read from the facts of events. Not to change the course of them. His dissertation on the Augments included a study of the massive hate propaganda campaign put out by the Central Army. Maybe that's what he was here to see.

But he couldn't take his eyes away from Sarrin standing there, subdued to her fate. He hesitated. He had to know.

"Don't touch her!" He stepped forward, pulled the guard away. "She doesn't like it. What happened before she took your rifle? You must have scared her." He turned to Hoepe. "She was perfectly fine before, made a joke an' everything."

"A joke?"

Kieran shrugged. "Sorta." Was it a joke? He had laughed. "I thought it was funny, anyhow."

"What did happen?" Hoepe asked his men.

The first stepped up. "Nothing. She was fixing the engine, and all of a sudden she had a knife. And then my gun."

Kieran threw his hands up. "You put your gun on her? Are you nuts? Of course she was going to defend herself."

"She had a knife."

Kieran huffed. "She had it in her pocket. I carry a knife in my pocket." It was true, he had three clanging around in there right now, asking him why he was stepping way over the line for this girl right now. "For repairs."

The guards toed the ground, their mouths silent.

"She didn't hurt anyone. And she's standing here quietly." He turned to Hoepe. "I need her help."

"Kieran!" Gal shouted.

Kieran pressed his lips together, muscles tense. He'd have to find a way to rewrite this in his report. "The Kepheus is fried. I need her help to patch it, or we're dead in space. We'll fix it. And then I'll plot the jumps to Junk so we can find a replacement."

"Junk?" Gal cried. "A24-alpha? No." He paced, two steps this way, two steps back. "Absolutely not."

"We have to." Kieran looked at Hoepe, and Hoepe nodded.

"You are a lunatic," said Gal. "We need to stay off the grid."

"Galiant," Hoepe held up his hands.

"This is my ship. We're not going anywhere."

"Your engineer tells me we're going to be stranded soon with no way to return."

"We've got rations and recycled water for years. Off the grid is the safest we can be."

"Junk is *off the grid*!"

Gal growled, pushing his way to the front of the crowd at the desk. "This is my ship, or do you not remember the promise you made? A promise you knew you could never keep, not with an Augment on our ship."

Hoepe signalled, and his man in the corner came forward.

Gal picked dup his fists, preparing to fight, but Sarrin lifted a hand and flicked him hard three times in rapid succession. Gal slumped to the floor.

Hoepe breathed a sigh of relief, raising a hand to signal his advancing man to stop. "Thank you, Sarrin." He signalled again to the two guards behind Sarrin and directed them to Gal. "Take him to his room."

"Sir?"

He waved them away, making clear that his orders were final, and they picked up Gal's body unceremoniously and carried him from the room. Fixing his gaze on Kieran, Hoepe asked quietly, "You have something?" His deep set brow relayed his meaning.

Guilt washed over Kieran, and he refused to look at Sarrin as he pulled the auto-syringe out of his pocket, showing it to Hoepe.

"Good. Go fix the engine. Let's not sit out here any longer than we have to. We don't have time for this squabbling."

And Kieran found himself back in the corridor, alone with the Augment.

* * *

"Where are you from?" Kieran stood on a stool, leaning over the workbench in the engineering bay, his garbled drawl floating down around her.

Sarrin kept her gaze on the medical-laser plasma-igniter, ignoring Kieran. She was uncertain how many times he had helped her, uncertain how to respond.

His arm reached shoulder deep in the drive chamber, sanding smooth the welds he had made to seal the chamber again. "Okay. What about your parents, what were they like?"

She slipped the final lens into place, aligning it precisely, enjoying the feel of her mind falling into a singular focus.

"Right. Well, did you have other siblings? Besides Halud."

Biting the inside of her cheek, she checked the connections on the machine.

He sighed, exasperated. "Alright. Never mind. I'm just tryin' ta get to know ya. People do that sometimes."

Normal people? Perhaps. Hoepe had warned her about this, but now that they all knew it couldn't hurt. "Mariante. I don't remember. No."

"Pardon? Oh." He grinned.

She let the corners of her mouth tip up. The engineering bay was peaceful, nearly the freedom she had imagined. Hoepe's guards hadn't returned. It was Kieran she had to thank for it. Gods knew why he had helped her, or why he didn't say anything about the weapons.

She lifted a hand to her temple, pressing on the dull ache there.

"I think this chamber is as good as it's going to get. Hopefully it holds long enough."

She nodded, ready to bring the completed laser, but the pain in her head continued.

"Sarrin, you okay?"

She frowned. The eyes scanning her moved too slowly. But there was no reason for it. Darkness fuzzed at the edge of her vision. She shook her head as though it would clear. Why would the trance come on out of nowhere?

Warning lights flashed on the consoles — proximity alarm.

Kieran spun away, tapping at a console. "What?" All the colour drained from his face. "We have to get the FTL working."

A voice flowed through speakers overhead: "*Warship incoming.*"

Warship? They were floating in the black. In the middle of nowhere. Untraceable.

Kieran pushed their machines together.

There was no way for a warship to find them.

A stray thought came into her cracked mind. "The chamber isn't sterilized."

"It'll have to do." He jumped up. "Start loading the gas, I'll be there in a sec."

Forty-nine objects. Least of all the modified plasma ignition laser. They were coming for her, if she had to escape she could, the monster reminded her.

"Sarrin, you okay?" The engineer's bright green eyes startled her.

She clenched her teeth. "Yes."

"Good." His hands rushed, sealing the chamber and funnelling in the reserved gas. He looked at her again. "Help me get this to the engine room.

With the fortified chamber and all the heavy gases, it weighed as much as a person.

The comm chimed. *"Kieran, we need to get out of here now."*

"Steady," he said, locking eyes with her. "We can't drop this baby now."

Ten yards to the engine room.

"You're not gonna freak out are you?"

The ship rocked, and they went staggering. Cannon fire. Wide-eyed, he checked the drive. "I think it's okay."

His words crackled like electric shocks, shooting sparks through her nearly dark vision.

Eight yards from the engine. Twenty paces.

"Sarrin, look at me. We're fine. We just have to get it that far."

The engineer.

Three yards. Eight paces.

"Almost there," he said. "No big deal. We can do it."

Could they? What would happen if the trance took over? Would she destroy the entire ship? Or would they stop her? Would the warship take them?

The ship rocked again. Over the comm speakers, Hoepe shouted.

They set the drive on the floor. Kieran pulled at the insulated tubing, stretching it from the engine to the drive. She shook away the darkness and plunged into the engine, double checking the connections.

The ship shook violently. Her vision almost black by the time she came out. "Kieran?"

"Hold on, Sarrin."

"I can't." Not after tasting freedom, the monster wouldn't let it happen. It clawed its tendrils over her. She could sense the warship, sense the unwavering determination to find her and destroy her. The darkness dug in, preparing. She had to warn Kieran: "Go."

"We need to bypass the FTL checks."

"Leave."

"I'm not going to do that."

He had to go. Didn't he understand? The darkness drew schematics for his death.

"We're going to be fine. It's just one quick jump away and they'll be gone. Help me connect the drive."

She crushed her head between her hands. "Why are they here?"

"They just stumbled upon us. Bad luck, that's all."

"They're here for me."

"No, no. The odds are bad, but it could happen. Space isn't really that big."

A window in her vision cleared. Enough to see Kieran checking the auto-syringe.

He looked up, their eyes meeting, and he flinched. He spoke to her like a child: "One jump. I need your help. Is the drive charged? Can you check it's progress."

She blinked. Part of her wanted to be indignant, to tell him she wasn't a child. The other part understood, and her addled brain latched onto the simpleness of the request. Checking the jump drive was easy. She could do that. The console was two steps to the left, her hands moved over it automatically. "Fifty-eight."

"Good." His voice shook as he entered coordinates seemingly at random.

The ship rocked again, and she squeezed he eyes shut. They

had to jump away, he was right, but the monster dug in, asserting itself. She pulled a panel off the wall, not unscrewing it first.

He stared at her. The auto-syringe shifted in his hand.

The FTL flashed 100, and he sent the ship into a jump.

ELEVEN

KIERAN STEPPED OFF THE CARGO ramp and took a deep breath. Junk smelled oddly like his father: a combination of engine oil and rusting metal. A warm breeze rippled his hair, and he grinned up at the dark sky, stretching his arms so he could inhale as much non-recycled air as possible.

The planet surface was covered in scrap and spare parts. The ship itself perched at an angle, landing struts resting on swells of old metal. In the sky above, the orbital belt — also made of old space junk — could be seen shining in the dark blue sky.

"It's beautiful here," he said. He'd not had much opportunity in his life to step planetside, but the sun felt just right, warm and welcoming. "Too bad it was never colonized."

"Who says it's not?" Gal muttered inaudibly.

"What?" Kieran looked around, but no one else seemed to have heard. Gal hadn't moved, still sitting on the same set of packs with his flask of Jin-Jiu.

Hoepe stepped forward and organized the crew into pairs, sending them on different directions into the maze with a list of desperately needed parts. Rayne begrudgingly went along with

Gal, acquiescing to help only because, this far out in the deep black, their only option was to find a replacement Kepheus drive for the FTL.

Kieran's eyes roved hungrily over the piles as he walked away from the ship — transmitters, diodes, things that hadn't been used in centuries. He moved aside an old rubber wheel and found an intact hydrogen cell. He could use that.

"What are you doing?" Sarrin suddenly asked.

Of course she had been watching. He gulped, but her eyes showed only bright curiosity, none of the wildness she had slipped into before in the engine room. "Look at this — it's in perfect condition."

She raised one eyebrow. "What is it?"

He chided himself for the slip: hydrogen cell tech hadn't been used in three-hundred years. He'd already broken the rules once for her, and this was dangerously close to sharing outsider knowledge. "A hydrogen cell. Very old. I thought you knew a lot about engines."

"I do."

Quickly, he changed the subject before she could think on it too long. "How did you get to know so much about engines?"

"Reading."

Kieran followed her as they picked their way over and between piles. "Did they make you read a lot at Evangecore?"

She paused in her stride. She had started answering some of his questions, as long as they weren't too deep. He thought that one might have been too far, but, surprisingly, she answered: "Some things. When we were younger."

"Like what?"

Her eyes swivelled darkly — he was pushing his luck, but this was the most open she had been. "The Litanies, mostly."

"Oh." He had read the Litanies as part of his research, quotes from their Gods, reminding them to listen and keep faith and obey. "Then how did you get to know so much about engines?"

Sarrin stood with her hands held in front of her, studying a pile of scrap. "A nurse saw my interest and brought me books." She reached in, digging under old transmitters and canisters, grunted once, and pulled free a Kepheus Drive.

Kieran stared. "How did you do that?"

She passed it to him, carefully holding the heavy container at its extreme end.

"Incredible." He shook it lightly, listening for the rattle of broken pieces. The gas might need to be recharged, but it looked to be in good condition. "You just pulled this from a heap of junk. I never would have looked in a million years."

She shrugged, folding over her hands and turning away. Question period now evidently over.

Kieran lugged the heavy drive behind him. He followed her around a corner, finding her staring into another pile.

"Your list included an ion transmitter."

"What, did you find one?" This shopping trip was going far better than expected.

To answer, she reached forward. Halfway, she stopped. Her head turned, focus suddenly shifting to something in the distance. She murmured a single word: "Grant."

Squinting his eyes, Kieran strained to see what she might be seeing. There was nothing. Then, a round, grey spec flew through the air. A fireball erupted where it landed.

He jumped, hand automatically gripped the sedative in his coveralls pocket. His eyes darted to Sarrin. Her face had knitted into a frown, but otherwise she appeared relaxed.

Another bomb whistled overhead, wobbling like a football, and landed on the near side of them, close enough he could feel the heat. She dropped her shoulder and took off running back towards the ship. Kieran scrambled behind her. "Where are they coming from?" There shouldn't have been anyone else on the planet.

She pointed. A figure sprinted across the top of a ridge of crumbling junk — a creature with dark, mottled brown skin, no hair or facial features to mark it as human.

What was it?

Sarrin slid under an old panel, and Kieran took cover beside her. A series of bombs exploded making the ground shake — whatever it was, it was aiming right for them.

The auto-syringe slid into his grip. Sarrin's eyes wandered, her focus far away. He called her name.

She responded, turning slowly to look at him.

Poking his head out of their hiding space, he could see Rayne and Gal taking refuge under what looked like an old shuttle wing. Past them some of Hoepe and his men pressed their backs against a wide pile of scrap. They weren't far from the ship. He turned to tell Sarrin, but she already stood, her eyes darting across the junk yard.

"Sarrin —." He reached out to tug her back down into their hiding place.

She took off at a sprint, sure feet sprinting up the irregular side of a pile. Partway, she stopped dead. Her head swivelled from the fearsome alien to Gal and Rayne.

Even from this distance, he could read the change in her expression. He scrambled out of the hiding spot, injector in hand.

Another bomb launched from the grey-brown monster. As he

watched it, his eyes traced its path forwards, realizing its trajectory would land it somewhere very close to the captain and Rayne. He shouted out to warn them. Rayne must have seen it at the same time. She pulled on Gal's arm, but he wouldn't move. She tugged and shouted, but he only slumped forward.

Jesus.

Sarrin's arms and legs moved so fast they blurred. Down the crumbling mountain, across the ground. She jumped over Gal and Rayne, running along the broken shuttle wing that they hid under, and sprang into the air.

Not knowing what he would do when he got there, Kieran ran to meet them.

In mid-air, Sarrin snatched the bomb, clutching it to her chest. She landed fluidly, rolling to her feet and kept sprinting. She stuffed the bomb into an old scrap engine casing, pushing it down.

Rayne stood motionless, watching, mouth hung open.

The bomb exploded, fire coming up around Sarrin's arms and past her face.

Kieran's legs screamed, as he pushed them harder. "Sarrin!" He slid to his knees beside her.

She sat frozen, body perfectly tense. She didn't acknowledge him, her wide eyes staring into the casing.

"Sarrin?" Kieran tried. He gingerly shook her shoulder. "Sarrin."

Her eyes fixed on her hands as she pulled them into the light. Kieran gulped. Torn and charred flesh hung from her fingers. In between flashed a glint of silver.

"Jesus Christ," he said out loud, and quickly covered his mouth. She turned her hands over slowly. The smell of burning flesh churned his stomach. The metal fingers flexed gracefully.

Beautiful, if weren't so horrifying.

"It doesn't hurt," she said.

"Okay." He wiped a shaking hand across his thigh. He had to do something, anything. "Okay." They had to get back to the ship. The mottled brown figure was gone, but for how long? Kieran lifted Sarrin by her armpits. "Come on, Sarrin. Can you walk?"

She didn't respond. Her saucer eyes fixed on the glinting silver skeleton. He'd be in shock too. He was pretty sure he was. Clumsily, he draped his jacket over her hands so she wouldn't have to see. So he wouldn't have to see.

They just had to make it to the ship.

She tried to pull away. "Don't touch me."

He caught her before she fell. "It's okay, Hoepe is coming." He could see the tall doctor, long legs stretching across the ground as he ran. Her body trembled, so hard it nearly broke free from his hands. Her eyes swam, and she kept blinking and swallowing. Blinking and swallowing.

"You're not gonna… are you?" The auto-syringe lay somewhere behind him.

Her head jerked, a single shake he took to mean no.

"You're okay." He pulled her tighter to his side. "Stay with me, here."

Hoepe slid to a stop, reaching to tilt her chin, a penlight flashing into her eyes. "What happened?"

Kieran shook his head, glancing at the covered hands.

Hoepe pressed his lips grimly. "Bring her inside."

Make it to the ship. Kieran's breath came in short gasps as he half-led, half-carried Sarrin across the uneven ground. One foot in front of the other. He was here to observe, do what any normal person would do in this situation. He followed the doctor to the ship, up the cargo ramp, and through to the infirmary.

Together they maneuvered her onto the bed. Her eyes rolled to meet his, desperate and haunted. Vomit caught at the back of his throat.

Hoepe removed the jacket, revealing the charred and silvery ruined hands. "Sarrin?" Razor blue eyes danced over the injury as his hands took her pulse from her neck. "I'm going to sedate her," he concluded, and turned to the cabinets behind him.

Kieran nodded and took a deep breath. The edges of his vision were blurry.

"Kieran?" Hoepe's voice sounded strangely distant.

The world went dark, and Kieran fell to the floor.

* * *

Rayne blinked slowly, snapping her gaping mouth shut as her mind fought to catch up. The girl, the Augment, Sarrin — impossible. She watched as Kieran half-walked, half-dragged the limp killing machine to the ship. They must have been wrong, Sarrin was no Augment, just a girl.

The junkyard smoked from multiple explosions. Hoepe's men ran into the open cargo bay. Rayne's lifetime of military training clicked into place. They were at an extreme tactical disadvantage. Retreat was their best option.

Gal shook, clutching his knees to his chest. She reached for him, but her hand also trembled, and she clutched it against her side.

They could have died.

She tried again, reaching out to tap him.

His eyes lit up with recognition. "Rayne, you're here. I'm glad." His lips twitched into a smile, but it didn't last long. He glanced worriedly from side to side. "Get down, we have to hide."

She crouched without hesitation.

He reached out with his hand to cup her face. "It means everything to me that you're here, I didn't think you'd understand."

She flushed, her hand reaching up to cover his. His gentle embrace promised safety, and she pushed into it. "We have to get out of here."

"Has everyone gotten out?"

"Yes, Sarrin and Kieran got back to the ship. Hoepe's men just ran in. We're the last ones. We have to go."

He gave her his hand and she helped pull him to his feet. He stumbled once. "We have to hide, I don't want them to see us."

She frowned.

"No one can know we were here, Rayne. Ever." His voice was urgent. "The Speakers…. Get out of here. It's not safe, not at all. Who knows how long until they find us — I don't know what they'll do if they ever find out, if anyone ever finds out."

He pulled her to the ship, slamming his fist on the control to close the cargo bay door as they ran by and through the cargo bay to the main ship.

"What was that thing?" she asked breathlessly, still clutching his other hand.

He stopped suddenly in the middle of the corridor. "What thing?"

"Didn't you see? The bombs…."

"Five Gods, the bombs." He turned his head away, looking into an unseen distance. She thought she heard him mutter a name under his breath: "Aaron?"

"Who?" Her heart leapt into her throat. Gal's hand went limp in hers

He turned back to her, his expression far away. "We have to get out of here."

She pulled her hand out of his, the moment of closeness and safety fleeting as she remembered the situation, and all of the choices — Gal's choices — that got them here. Still, some thing on the planet had tried to kill them. She turned in the direction of the engineering bay. "Come on. We have to figure out how to turn on the thruster engines."

She stomped down the corridor, determined not going to die on some scrapyard in the deep black, and definitely not going to die a traitor. She expected Gal to follow, but when she looked back, he was no where in sight.

*　*　*

Gal tumbled into his ready room, arms raised to protect his head from the falling explosions. He hid in the trees, in the vision that had overtaken him. No one could ever know he was here — they would kill him for sure.

Horrible demons ran back and forth, screaming. They paid no attention to him, their haggard grey mouth open in silent screams. He kept his head down. They were on their own now. He had done all he could.

He took his clothes from the bag he had hidden and changed, burning the rest.

The demons threw themselves against the walls over and over.

Bombs fell. Bright flashes of fire and crashing thunder.

He threw himself to the floor.

It wasn't real. It wasn't happening.

He groped around, crawling on all fours, searching for his flask. Glass dug into his palm, drawing blood. He held the piece of broken bathroom mirror, his reflection obscured by red.

Fitting. A vision of who he had been.

He crawled instead to the desk, finding the secret drawer and the bottle within.

Suckling, he waited for the visions to end. For the memories to fade.

The thunder grew distant, the demons silent and still. He breathed a sigh of relief.

He stood, steadying himself until he could fall into the chair. He took another draw of the Jin-Jiu and shook his head, laughing.

What a cracked individual he was, the bloody mirror still in his hand. He laughed and laughed and laughed. And he stopped.

Aaron stood in the corner, his arms crossed, his face drawn with real anger.

Gal needed another drink. Blinking, he waited for the apparition to fade with the others.

"Galiant John Peroneus Idim." In all the years, Aaron had called him by his full name only once, and Gal cringed. The mirror dropped to the floor.

"So this is who you are now." Aaron stepped forward, wiping a hand across the desk sending the Jin-Jiu flying across the room. The hand-drawn picture of Aaron slammed into the wall, tearing.

Gal scrambled to pick it up, clutching the photo to his chest.

Around him, the explosions started anew. Children screaming. Laz-cannons blazing. Hover transports dropping platoons of soldiers. Bodies piling up across the field.

Aaron pulled the picture from his hand, snapping the wooden frame. "I died for this. Did you forget? My life gone. Did it mean nothing to you?"

Gal let out a whimper.

"They caught me and burned me and still I didn't get up the fight. I bought your freedom with my life. And you're cowering."

Gal reached across the room, aiming for his small flask that lay on the floor, contents dripping into the grey carpet. Aaron blocked him. "Please!" he shouted. "I need to forget."

"You can't forget! This is who you are."

"No, no! I can't."

Aaron snarled. "Embrace your fear and you will become brave. What have you become?"

"There's nothing left."

Aaron pushed him, Gal's head slamming into the wall. "I know."

Gal found himself alone, picking through bodies on the charred remains of a battlefield. The first real battle he had seen as a young cadet. Not the last and not the worst catastrophe he had seen. Far from the worst disaster he had ever had a hand in creating.

As he crawled on his hands and his knees, blood seeping from his head and down his arm, his quarters and the freightship slipped far away and the memory swallowed him whole.

* * *

Rayne rammed her finger into the controls. Wasn't it enough that they'd taken her, held her, and brought an Augment on board? Now there was a… a thing out there, trying to blow them all up.

The communication panel flashed, and she shouted into it, "Kieran to Engineering."

The creature was out there — how long until it returned with more explosives and it destroyed them? Without the engine generator running, they couldn't even power the shields.

Halud appeared. "Where's Sarrin?"

"You!" she narrowed her eyes. The false prophet who had brought her into this mess.

The comm sounded: "*This is Hoepe, Kieran is indisposed.*"

"What?" she cried. "We need him to start the engines."

"*I'm afraid he's unconscious.*"

Her blood ran cold, and she stared at the pale Poet willing him to undo the entire situation.

"*Sutherland is knowledgeable about shuttle engines. I'll send him.*"

She tapped frantically on a console. Years ago, she'd been trained how to start the complex thrusters, but she couldn't remember the steps.

"I have to go find her," said Halud.

"You and your stupid sister." She stabbed a menacing finger at him. "I don't like you, but we need to get these engines running. If that thing comes back, who knows what it will do."

He shrank away, trembling.

"Gods! This is your mess," she screamed. She found the instruction manual on the computer terminal and read out loud: "Ensure all switches are in 'off' position. Engage hyper-coolant system to sixty-percent capacity. Connect run-off re-return." She shook her head. "What does this mean?"

She stared blankly at the console, hoping for some inspiration or flash of memory, when four of Hoepe's men appeared at the door. "We heard you could use some help," said the first.

Rayne hesitated. But they were all in the same danger. She was a tactician, not an engineer, what choice did she have? "Yeah, okay." She showed them the instruction manual.

The first one — Sutherland — nodded as he read. "We need to find the hyper-coolant system," he said, disappearing into the engine room.

She stood frozen, next to Halud, and watched them dart back and forth. She hated these reapers, wanted nothing to do with them, and yet, it warred with her that she needed them now.

Sutherland shouted from the engine room, "What's he done to the FTL?"

She sprinted to the engine room, seeing the mess of wires and conduits scattered around the normally bare space. The main panel hung open, revealing the engine's innards. Wires spilled from inside, connecting it to a messy looking object she could only guess was the repaired Kepheus Drive.

Sutherland held up a several loose wires in his hands. "What if we need the FTL?"

She tapped her fingers to her chest reflexively. "We only need to get off the planet."

"Okay." He flipped a set of switches and ran back to the console. He tapped the controls again, and the engines hummed to life. "Quincy, get to the bridge, fly us out of here," he ordered. He turned to Rayne. "You too, miss."

"Yes, sir." She nodded and ran. Her eyes closed briefly. How did it come to this? A reaper in the engine room and a reaper on the bridge — which was worse? Needs must, she told herself. She had to return them to the Path, but first she had to get off the stupid planet.

TWELVE

GRANT PARKER WOKE IN HIS cell, staring up at the harsh fluorescent lighting that buzzed in the distance. Four thick, permaglass walls surrounded him, monitoring stations at every corner. Before, they had kept him with the others in the dark cells below, but the experiments were becoming too drastic and his last escape attempt too dramatic.

The grey-brown suit of second skin had retreated to its resting place under the skin in his mid back, leaving an oozing wound. A deep feeling of loss choked him, as it always did after one of their sessions. Memories started to come to him, flashing before his eyes, things he had seen without any recollection of how he got there or why. Their experiments controlled him, but his vision recorded events all the same.

During their test, he had stumbled across a ship. Scavengers who were too close to the compound and needed to be sent away. He rigged the bombs from scraps and threw them. In the past, scavengers and trespassers had fled at the first sight of him, but these people were different. Some girl snatched one of his bombs from the air. Some girl....

Sarrin. Grant jolted. Sarrin was the girl; alive; here.

His eyes sought out the ceiling and light fixtures therein, seriously this time. The walls were over ten metres high, but he could see his escape above.

He steadied his breathing. As soon as he sat up, as soon as he jumped, they would gas him. And then they would take control, and his escape would turn into a hunt. His pressed his palms into his legs to steady them. He had to take the chance.

Faster than he had moved in a long time, Grant sprung up onto his bed and then leaped straight up into the air.

Alarms and flashing lights flared. Gas hissed as it filled the cell.

His feet met the slick surface of the permaglass, but he pressed off quickly, leaping from side to side, climbing. Thee guards wearing respiratory masks rushed in, aiming their sedative darts. They clanked off the wall, passing behind him as he jumped.

His lungs screamed for lack of oxygen, but he forced himself to stay calm, keep his heart rate level and even.

Another volley of darts came his way, and he leapt, nearly at the top, grasping the narrow edge of the vent on the ceiling.   The gas whispered past his body, it's slightly sweet odour invading his nose.

He pushed up on the ceiling panel, hearing it pop open, and climbed through the hole.

The guards below called to the others, shouting frantically.

Ducking in the narrow space between floors, he gasped for air and started scooting himself through the ceiling, up and over walls. He climbed through a refuse hatch and reached the outside of the building, just in time to see the freightship leave the atmosphere.

He sagged. It couldn't be too late. No, Sarrin would wait for him. But did she see him, or just some thing?

He needed a shuttle. Now or never.

The shuttle hangar was on the upper floor of the compound — he had mapped the facility top to bottom in his years of captivity. Klaxons shrieked as he made his way through the walls in the building.

There were twenty guards in the shuttle hangar. He wiped sweaty palms on his jumpsuit. Not a problem. Dropping down, he took out two guards as he landed. A third let out a yell and raised his laz-rifle. Grant dispatched him with a swift kick and grabbed the rifle. He used the rifle to take out three more guards before running for the nearest shuttle.

He pressed the manual door release hidden to the bottom left, and thanked the UECs for being so wholly uncreative in their new designs.

A laz-bolt seared across his shoulder, causing him to grunt in surprise. He spun away and lifted his rifle to aim. Soon, an additional four guards lay prone on the ground.

Grant climbed into the shuttle and sealed the door behind him. Laz-bolts pinged off the titanium hull. He set himself to bypassing the security codes and initiating the start-up sequence.

The door opened behind him — one of the idiot guards must have managed to override the lock-out. Grant jumped to the entrance and shot him point-blank. Rapidly, he fired on the two guards flanking the first, who seemed frozen where they stood. He rolled his shoulders; it felt good to move again.

He locked the door and blocked it shut.

The engines cycled through their warm-up automatically. Grant let out a small relieved laugh. Angling the shuttle towards the open hangar door, he left the compound and accelerated through the atmosphere, the shuttle rumbling as it passed into space.

He scanned the stars around him, looking for the ship. For Sarrin's ship.

Warmth radiated in his body, spreading into a huge smile. From the moment he'd met her, they had been a team — he was the fight, the muscle, and she was the engineer. Together they were unstoppable. He would see her again, and they'd blast the UECs from the sky for all eternity.

* * *

Hoepe bent over the meticulous work that lay on the table before him. Here he truly felt at peace, doing the actions that had become so rote. With professional detachment, he ignored the girl the hands were attached to and focussed on piecing the jigsaw of burned flesh back together.

The microscars of fine suturing were evident, would have been evident to someone with his training and keen eye — no wonder she'd never wanted him to look. The 'bones' and 'joints' were an incredible feat of engineering, if nothing else. They were perfectly smooth and moved effortlessly, designed for precision and strength. But why had she never told him?

On the bench, Kieran started to stir. He sat up and rubbed his head, clutching at the cold pack resting over his swollen cranium.

"What happened?" he asked groggily.

"You suffered acute cerebral hypotension likely attributed to shock." Then, in response to the blank stare, he said, "You fainted and hit your head on the table."

"Ah, that's why it hurts so much."

Hoepe's instruments clinked softly as he manipulated the charred tissue.

Kieran looked away over his shoulder, his cheeks turning a pale green.

"Never seen a scratch before, Lieutenant?"

Kieran made no response. Few people appreciated Hoepe's humour. Possibly it was the timing.

"How is she?"

The monitor beeped steadily beside her head. "Stable," Hoepe concluded. "Her hands will heal once the tissue is sutured."

Kieran gulped audibly and looked at the exposed hand. His face turned as grey as the walls of the infirmary.

"Can you push point-two cc's?" Hoepe asked quickly, nodding to the syringe stuck in the IV that ran into her leg. "It's sedation — midazolam — we don't have anything stronger, and she metabolizes it so fast."

Stoically, the engineer nodded and fumbled with the syringe. Hoepe watched him work — confident and careful at the same time. Kieran had proved nothing but useful, a pleasant surprise in the rest of the chaos.

"Is that… normal?" Kieran asked, slumping down on the bench. "The hands, like that."

Hoepe raised a single eyebrow, debating how much to tell him. Something had happened to Sarrin to necessitate replacing all the bones in her hands with prosthetics. It must have been in Evangecore, before he knew her — he hadn't done the work, but someone else equally skilled had. "No," he answered.

"Then, why? It seems… barbaric."

Hoepe shook his head. Sarrin had never mentioned it, never in the three years they had spent running and fighting together — not that she ever talked about anything that happened in that place. No one really talked about it, Hoepe was just there to patch them up.

The hole in his sole flared. It hadn't been easy, putting back together kid after kid, pulling them from the brink of death. Sometimes they slipped over and he couldn't resuscitate them. The others didn't understand how similar they were, didn't think he understood them, just because he'd been trained as a doctor and they as soldiers.

He snipped the last piece of suture, examining his work. There were a few places where the skin wouldn't pull together, which he'd had to leave open, but the skin would scab and granulate together. The scars would fade just like the others.

"Can I ask you something?" Kieran said quietly.

Hoepe glanced up from bandaging Sarrin's hand.

The engineer studied him intently. "Are you one too? An Augment, I mean. You knew Sarrin — that's why you took her in, and you knew what she could do."

Hoepe's heart paused for a second, then resumed its usually steady beat. The engineer was a peculiar character. But in him, Hoepe saw someone that perhaps could understand it. Still, secrets were unpredictably dangerous.

"Did you do this to her?"

His eyes snapped up. "Of course not."

"Okay," he nodded. "Just someone did, someone who knew what they were doing. Someone with a very enhanced skill set and an ability for detailed work."

"It wasn't me," he said softly.

They stared at each other for a long time.

"What else happened there?"

"Why do you want to know?"

"I had no idea," he stated boldly. "Not a clue they would do anything like this in Evangecore. I want to know what else."

Hoepe blinked, torn with indecision. In the end, Hoepe trusted Sarrin, and Sarrin seemed to trust Kieran more than anyone else. "Help me roll her over."

"What?"

"Help me roll her over. I'll show you." He pushed more of the sedative into her IV line.

"She doesn't like being touched." Kieran rubbed his arm uncomfortably. "Why not?"

"I don't know," Hoepe said honestly. "She's asleep though."

Hesitating, Kieran came to the table and they flipped her on her side.

Gently, Hoepe pulled her matted hair to the side, revealing the barcode stamped into the back of her neck.

Kieran reached his hand out, slowly tracing its edges.

"We all have them." Hoepe told him. "Neck and each arm. To help with identification."

"I assumed something like that."

Hoepe considered a moment. Sarrin certainly would never have condoned this, but there no hatred, no evil crossed Kieran's eyes, only curiosity. And if he had a chance to make an ally, he would take it. He's already told Kieran more than he'd told anyone in four years. Hoepe unzipped the top of Sarrin's jumpsuit and pulled on the collar, revealing the first set of marks.

Kieran's hand traced the first one: a black circle with a thick cross in it. The three below it were visible too, a code of hashmarks and geometric shapes.

"Procedure marks," Hoepe explained. "Some people have more or less, depending how many experiments they were part of."

"Experiments, huh." Kieran tugged, peering under her collar. "How many does she have?"

Hoepe frowned. "I don't know, I've never seen them all. Most people have ten or fifteen, but they used to call her twenty-seven in the war — I assume that's why."

Kieran's eyes flared open and his mouth dropped. "Twenty seven? Experiments? It can't be that many."

Curiosity got the best of him, and Hoepe pulled down the jumpsuit as though he were going to expose a wound, and lifted the thin undershirt.

Kieran stuck his hand out to stop him. "What are you doing?"

"I'm her doctor, Kieran."

He spoke quietly again, "How many do you have, Hoepe?"

Hoepe pulled back his hands. For years, he put these kids — his friends — back together after the experiments broke them down, over and over again. But in truth he had been lucky. "Three — but I'm different. I wasn't trained to fight, I was trained to heal. I had to learn what they could take after each of those marks. And what they couldn't. Do you understand?"

Kieran turned his head and nodded.

The thing Hoepe had always searched for, the unfilled hole in his heart, it felt like the answer was right here, somehow, on Sarrin's back with Kieran standing next to him. "I have to know." Desperately, he pulled the rest of the covering off.

A long line of marks trailed down the left side of her spine, all the way down. A second line started on the right, beside her scapula and continued half-way down again. There were nine marks beside that row.

Kieran counted under his breath.

"Forty-two." Hoepe told him.

Gasping, Kieran turns to look up. "I thought you said twenty-seven."

Hoepe shook his head, "I must have been wrong."

"Or they're more recent."

"Possibly. Only Grant would know how many she had during the war."

"Why would — wait, did you say Grant?"

"Yes, why?"

"She muttered 'Grant' when the bombs started falling."

Hoepe's heart slammed in his chest. "That was Grant? Grant's alive? By the Gods, what are they doing to him?"

"I thought Junk was uninhabited. I don't understand."

"If Sarrin saw him…."

"Why would he throw bombs at us?"

Hoepe shook his head. "An experiment."

"An experiment?"

"The war may be over, but nothing's changed."

* * *

The warship arrived without warning. Rayne's eyes snapped to the 3-D display as the proximity alarms blared. The warship sent a volley of laz-cannon fire.

"Shields! Evasive action!" she screamed.

In the pilot's chair, the man named Quincy gripped and spun the steering sphere. The Ishash'tor shook from the shear forces, and Rayne gritted her teeth. Beside her, Halud clutched the Tactical console.

The ship dipped and rolled. "Should we return fire, Ma'am?" asked one of the men.

Fire on a UEC ship? Her instinct warred with her duty. "Absolutely not!"

The warship fired again. She didn't need to look at the ship ID, but she did anyway: UECAS Comrade.

"We need to make an FTL jump," said the Poet.

Jump away? The whole situation didn't make any sense. The warship should be helping them.

"Rayne. The FTL is our only option," shouted Halud.

"We don't have the FTL," Rayne snarled. "Quincy, easier on the oversteer, or you'll pull us apart."

"Yes, Ma'am."

Sweat beaded out on her back. They were going to be blown apart.

She called down to Engineering. "Any luck with that FTL? We need it now."

Sutherland responded, "*Not yet. I don't know what he's done down here.*"

Where was Kieran? Why was the warship attacking? More importantly, how had she gotten here? This was insane. They were truly going to be blown apart. By an Army warship.

She had to uphold the Path.

Rayne turned to the communications console. She opened up a mayday on all frequencies and spoke into the com's microphone: "This is Lieutenant Commander Rayne Nairu of the U.E.C.A.S. Ishash'tor. We surrender."

"Rayne!" the Poet shouted. He lurched towards her, but stumbled and caught himself on the console between them.

"What?" Her laz-gun slipped from it's hidden holster and she held it in his direction instantly. "You're a traitor to the Central Army. This is a Central Army ship and I am taking control"

He paused. "You don't understand."

She reached for the communications microphone again. "Repeat, this is Commander Rayne Nairu. I have taken control of the ship and am surrendering. Please cease fire."

A voice transmission came through. "*Commander Nairu, this is Commandant Mallor of the U.E.C.A.S. Comrade. Your surrender is*

*accepted. Please shut down all weapons systems and prepare for boarding.
We are engaging magne-grav lock."*

The ship jolted under their feet as the magnetic field caught
them. The lights dimmed to ten percent.

The Poet gripped the console unit this knuckles turned white.
"Quincy, get us out of here."

"It's not responding, sir, we can't move."

"I'm sorry, Poet," said Rayne. "This is the Path of the Gods."
She turned to the pilot. "Power down the engines. I'm going to
prepare the shuttle bay."

*   *   *

"What's going on?" Kieran gripped the edge of the surgical table
as the ship shook underneath him. Vials of medicine and rolls of
cotton tumbled from their tidy shelves.

He scrambled for the tiny console screen set into the wall
above the bench. "The warship," he said, his eyes going wide,
"it's here."

"Impossible," said Hoepe. "That's the third time they've
found us."

"I haveta get the FTL going." Kieran shouted, lunging for the
door. Another rumble sent him flying down the corridor.

He found several of Hoepe's men arguing when he arrived in
Engineering:

"I think it goes there."

"No, the duality will be reversed. It goes there, and you
connect this wire to that bit."

"I thought the wire went to that other thing."

"Get out of my way," called Kieran, running to the engine
room.

The group parted readily. "Oh, thank the Gods," muttered
one.

"I admit it's not the most elegant solution," said Kieran, his fingers already flying over the connectors, "but it works. As long as the welds hold."

The ship jerked, and then felt unnaturally still. "What was that?" The lighting dropped to an emergency glow.

"I don't know, sir."

Frowning, Kieran made the connections on the damaged FTL. He stifled a groan realizing he had dropped the spare, and sent a silent prayer that this one would make it.

He bypassed the safety relays, and the FTL spooled almost instantly. He clicked the comm. "Wood to Command, FTL is a go."

He waited, expecting the pull of a gravity well, but none came.

A transmission came through from the bridge. He recognized Quincy's voice: "*Kieran, we're stuck here.*"

Kieran frowned, "What do you mean 'stuck'?"

"Immobilized, sir. The warship has a magne-grav on us. I have no control over the ship whatsoever."

Well, that explained the lighting.

"*What do we do?*" asked Quincy.

"Sit tight," ordered Kieran. There wasn't much they could do short of disassembling and jettisoning everything magnetic on the ship, including the engine.

All of their systems were shut down, the magnets wrecking the electronics. The only thing operational was life support. And the FTL.

For a minute, Kieran wondered what would happen if he managed to engage the gravity drives and open a jump hole while the magne-grav held the two ships together. The phrase 'utter catastrophe' rang a bell.

"Hold on," he shouted in to the comm. There had to be a way to disengage it. "I'm coming to you."

* * *

Grant urged the shuttle forward, but the engines were already at max. Through the window, he saw the warship overtake the small freightship and lock onto it with their magne-grav traction beam. Sarrin's ship froze in place, caught by the same hunters that had caught him. He gritted his teeth.

The shuttle had no weapons, only welding torches, short-range laz-drills and laz-saws. Still, he could work with that. He engaged the maneuvering thrusters to adjust his course, angling towards the warship.

Grant pushed the shuttle into a vertical roll, aiming the laz-saw as he shot past the magne-grav generator on the front of the warship's hull. He spun for another pass, this time seeing sparks fly as the heavy-duty laser made contact.

Laz-cannons fired from the warship, narrowly missing him.

Grant pushed the engines into a tighter turn, testing their limits. A warning flashed on the screen, but he swiped it away, targeting the traction beam once more. He attacked with drill and torches.

He would save Sarrin, even if it was the last thing he did. Always a team, no matter how she had left him after their last meeting.

The warship started to move, pushing dangerously close. Grant twirled the steering sphere forward, driving engines that whined in protest. The warning flashed on the screen again, and the shuttle slipped into the pull of the magnetic beam.

A sharp shot of pain flashed in the back of his head. He could feel them trying to take control.

Grant spun the sphere wildly. The warning flashed again, this time bright amber: engine overload. He angled for another attack. The beam flickered once, but didn't go out. Grant set his teeth, he needed more.

The engine warning flashed red, accompanied by alarm bells. He glanced at it quickly: Engine Failure Imminent. One more attack run. Direct this time. He had to help her, to make up for his mistakes if nothing else.

He rolled the steering forward, throttle at full speed. He lived for battle, he would die in battle and would he would die of his own accord, helping his friend. The pain in his head flared, and the mottled grey-brown skin ripped through the scar on his back, sliding its tendrils over his arms and legs until it covered his entire body.

The shuttle exploded, engulfing him in flames and rocketing shrapnel in all directions. The suit protected him completely. Even the cold of space didn't touch him. The oxygen sucked out of his lungs into the vacuum of space, and Grant could do nothing but wait, ticking off the seconds until his body could no longer survive without air.

The explosion pushed him away from the ship, sending him tumbling through space. In the distance, the wrecked shuttle crushed the magne-grav, and the freightship shot from its grasp.

* * *

Rayne clapped her hands behind her back and waited in the shuttle bay. Through the thick viewing window, she looked into the empty shuttle bay and through the open doors to the stars beyond. The Comrade would send a boarding shuttle to take the Augment and the ship, and then they could all go home.

She repeated it to herself — "We can all go home, we can all go home." — to keep the sinking terror from overtaking her.

In the Gods she Trusted, but she couldn't help thinking of

Hoepe's repeated warnings, the terrible look in the Poet's eyes, of Gal — what if she had made a mistake?

The Gods were merciful. It wasn't her fault, she had been following orders. And now she was correcting the mistake, surely that was what was important.

Something flew into the bay, crashing and bouncing along the landing platform. Shaking, it stood up. A creature, distinctly humanoid, but its skin mottled brown and almost rubbery. Its face held no eyes or mouth, no distinguishing features at all.

She screamed.

It staggered toward her, arm reaching as though through the permaglass. It took step after step, coming for her.

Where was the shuttle?

"Rayne, you okay?" Kieran ran into the bay behind her. "I was on my way to the bridge when I heard you screaming."

Rayne pointed to the viewport. "It's here. It's coming for us."

"Holy shit." Kieran punched the controls, shutting and re-pressurizing the shuttle bay.

The demon-man in the shuttle bay collapsed, gasping frantically.

Kieran reached for the microphone, "Are you Grant?"

The man nodded, still gasping.

"Don't worry, buddy. We gotcha."

Rayne stared at Kieran, ice shooting down her spine. "What are you doing?"

He ignored her, tapping on the controls.

The ship condensed around them — the uncomfortable feeling of making a jump, of falling into a gravity well. Her eyes flared wide.

In the airlocks shuttle bay, the rubbery brown man hunched

over. Incredibly, the mottled skin retracted from his limbs and into his upper back, revealing a young man no more than twenty. He smiled, and then started laughing. And laughing and laughing.

Rayne stared, horrified.

Kieran started laughing too. He pressed the comm. "Good job, Quincy. How the heck did we make it out of that one?"

"*The FTL was ready, and all of a sudden, the magne-grav let go. So I jumped, sir.*"

Kieran turned to the man in the airlock. "Did you do that? Get us out of that magne-grav problem? I thought we were toast."

The man grinned as he tousled his sandy hair and bowed.

Kieran laughed again. "Well, thank you. Welcome aboard."

Rayne's eyes shot open with surprise. "Lieutenant, " she hissed, "what are you doing?"

Kieran waved her off. Instead, he opened the inner door and invited the demon into the hangar.

"What if he's a" — she dropped her voice — "an Augment?"

"I am," said the man. His eyes narrowed. "And you're not."

She gripped her laz-rifle.

"Thanks for getting us out of that bind." Kieran smiled, ushering the man in. "There's a few people I'm sure will be excited to see ya."

Blocking his path, she pushed her laz-rifle right into the Augment's chest. She could not allow him to board her ship.

Grant lifted a single eyebrow and glanced down at her rifle, grinning.

She took a step back.

"I'm not so violent as I seem." He pushed the tip of the rifle away from his chest. "I have no reason to attack you. As far as what happened planet-side, I was under a mind-control device."

Kieran reached out, pressing her shoulder so she spun away
from the Augment. He shook his head, asking her to be quiet.
He turned to Grant. "Are we in any danger now?"

Rayne glared at Kieran, her voice trembling. "Lieutenant,
this goes against every regulation —."

"Danger? No," answered the Augment, ignoring her. "Not
so long as we are out of range."

"Okay." Kieran rubbed his hand through his short hair.
"Anything else we need to know?"

The Augment's narrow gaze scanned Kieran, and Rayne felt
the urge to press between them, lifting her laz-rifle once again to
his chest. He didn't flinch. "I'm a friend of Sarrin. I believe she's
aboard this ship."

"Uh." Kieran glanced at Rayne.

With Kieran's one worried look, her trembling finger
squeezed the trigger. A killing blow at this range, for an Augment
or human alike. But she was shaken off her feet, the ship jolting
out from under them. The laz-beam fell wide, and the Augment
jumped. Her heart hammered in her chest.

Kieran scrambled to the console. "Report?"

A panicked voice came through the speakers: "*The warship
followed us through.*"

Her started look met Kieran's. "That isn't possible."

Grant reached out, eyes wide with fear. "We have to get
away; they can control me."

Kieran nodded. "Okay. Get back in the bay." He pushed
the Augment back into the shuttle bay, and hit the controls to
close the door.

"Kieran?" Rayne held out a hand, alarmed at her own
shaking. "What's going on?" Her voice bordered on hysteria, but

she didn't care anymore.

"Keep an eye on him," he shouted, already running out the door. "I gotta reset the FTL."

Rayne stared, arms hanging limp by her sides. She had been so close to going home.

* * *

Kieran rushed to Engineering. The FTL was too hot, but they didn't have any other choice — even with weapons modifications, they didn't have a chance against the warship for more than a couple minutes.

He shouted orders to the men clustered around console displays.

How had the Comrade followed them through? The ship should have been too big to fit through their FTL hole. And jumps were impossible to track. Was it just bad luck? There had to be a way to get the warship to go away.

Sutherland came up beside him. "Tell me you've got a demon on our side for once."

"Get those guys to stop touching the shield controls," he pointed across the engineering bay.

Sutherland shouted, and the men moved away.

"Think, think, think." Kieran pressed his head into his hands. "I don't know how many jumps the engine can take. And if they just keep following us through…." His mind went blank with despair.

Sutherland growled, "I just want to punt these guys to the next dimension."

"Wait, that's it!"

"What?"

Kieran laughed. It was crazy enough to work. "We're gonna put a rabbit in a hat."

"A what?" Sutherland took a step back, eyes wide.

"Bad joke," he waved it off. Of course no one here had ever even heard of a rabbit.

Sparks flew as Kieran modified the FTL. They would need a bigger hole for this to work. His mind raced as he thought through the modifications and rough calculations and odd of success. "Vazquez, can you prepare to reverse the polarity of the shields?"

A wide-eyed stare.

Kieran rushed over and keyed in the codes himself. He grabbed the stunned man's hand. "When I say 'go,' press this button," he told the man, "this one right here."

He closed his eyes, vaguely wishing Sarrin could help — there was too much to do, too many permutations to think through by himself.

He pulled another of Hoepe's men to the life systems support console. "When I say 'now,' you need to push this button and then this one. Got it? This one and this one." Another, he brought to the controls for their modified cloaking device.

The men nodded. At least they were good at taking orders.

"Quincy," he called into the comm, "ready for this?"

"*Uh, sure.*"

Sutherland stood beside him. "Kieran, what are you planning?"

"This is gonna work, ok," he shouted into the comm.

"*Sure. What do you want me to do?*"

"Get close, get them on our tail." If they followed through once, maybe they would try it again.

"*Yes, sir.*"

Kieran felt the shift of the ship as it made a hard turn. He took a deep breath — even his dad, the crazy wildcard who taught him everything he knew, would have thought this was too much. Kieran estimated a 67-percent chance of success. But hey, two out of three ain't bad.

"*They're on us, sir,*" Quincy's harried voice carried over the comm.

"Good, when I say 'go,' turn hard left."

He took a deep breath, subtly made the sign of the cross over himself and said a little prayer. "Ok, ready?" He threw the FTL switch, shouting, "Go! Now!"

The ship veered. Consoles sparked. The shields reversed polarity, combined with the gamma gravitation in the cloak, and repelled them from the gaping FTL hole.

"Full power!" Kieran shouted into the comm. He could hear the thruster engines straining, could feel the ship fighting the pull of gravity, the drag causing the whole ship to go sideways.

Please, God, he prayed, let the ship hold together. Let the warship slide through that open wormhole. He really didn't want to die here.

The strain eased, the FTL closing, and the ship released, slingshotting them across the deck. Kieran scrambled to check the hologram.

Sutherland, white-faced, picked himself up, shaking. "Are they gone? I can't believe it worked."

Together, they clutched the edge of the display, watching for five standard minutes, then ten. No sign of the warship, no grav-hole re-opening. Kieran let out a laugh, slumping to the floor on his weak knees.

Beside him, Sutherland breathed a sigh of relief. "Just one thing, Kieran. What's a rabbit?"

THIRTEEN

RAYNE SAT AT A DARK table in the empty mess hall. It was well into the ship's night cycle. She wrapped her hands around a warmed ration container, hoping it would stop the shaking. It didn't.

Over and over she played the scene from the shuttle bay in her head, trying to determine if it was real or not. First, the man arriving in the shuttle bay from nowhere — the same man that had attacked them on the planet. Then, Kieran telling her to help him before running off. She had been so shocked by it all, she had missed her opportunity to re-open the external airlock — something she hadn't realized until the third playback, some tactical officer she turned out to be. At the end of it, Hoepe arrived in the shuttle hangar, and she watched dumbfounded while Hoepe released the man, they embraced, and then Hoepe had nodded appreciatively at her as the two men left.

The rations in front of her grew cold, her fingers tapping anxiously on the side of the flimsy container. Now, there were two Augments on board — Sarrin and this new Grant. Either one of them could destroy the ship in an instant. Did no one else see that?

The doors to the mess hall opened. Familiar grey, regulation coveralls strode in, and she smiled in recognition: Kieran. He whistled as he opened two ration packs and put them in the warmer.

She called his name.

Pausing, he glanced over. "Hey, Commander." A polite smile spread over his otherwise exhausted features. "I didn't see you there. What's up?"

Rayne let out a breath, letting the tension roll out of her shoulders. Everything had been so upside down lately, but Kieran... Kieran was dependable. She had watched him go with the flow, his head up, shoulders back, confident. She motioned for him to come to her small table, and waited for him to settle into the chair opposite her. "Kieran, maybe you can tell me what's going on with these Augments?"

He frowned. "What do you mean?"

She leaned forward on her elbows, whispering even though they were alone. Hoepe and his men had already shackled her and put her on trial once, and she had no interest in repeating the scenario. "First Sarrin. And now Grant. The ship is taken over by Reapers, and Gal isn't doing a thing about it. And then there's the Poet — are we with him or against him?" She lifted her hands up to cover her face, leaning heavily on the table, suddenly exhausted by the gravity of their situation. She squeezed her eyes shut and groaned in an effort to pretend it wasn't happening. "Ugh. We need to do something. We're soldiers in the United Earth Central Army. We serve the Gods."

Kieran nodded, his gaze shifting to the floor while he chewed the inside of his lip. "Well, Raynie," — he picked his words slowly — "I think we've found ourselves in a very complicated situation."

"I almost saved us," she said. "I contacted the warship —
they were going to help us. But then we broke away."

Kieran's eyes grew dark and he leaned back in his chair.
Surely, Kieran understood — there had to be someone on this
ship still loyal to the Gods besides her. But the typically
unflappable lieutenant clenched his jaw, ropey muscles along the
side of his cheek twitching angrily under his skin. "You did what?
I don't think they're exaggerating when they say the UECs will kill
us all. Like it or not, we're all trying to survive together."

Her breath caught in her throat as she jerked back. Her
stomach rolled, her mouth suddenly too dry to speak. Her voice
came out as a whisper: "I just wanted to reunite us with the Path."
She was trying to work for the Gods, surely it was right. "I don't
know what else to do. This is our duty."

He sighed, his shoulders relaxing, and a sad smile crossed his
face. "I dunno what to do."

For the first time, she noted the bags under his eyes, the
rumpled and stained uniform that was only partly done up, the
stoop in his upper back. She'd been neglecting her duties as First
Officer, failing to take care of her crew. "You're tired," she said.
"You're not getting enough rest."

"Yeah." He chuckled. "There's been a lot to do. You know, I
lost my whole staff and this old freightship's been falling apart for
years."

Immediately, her mind fell to the familiar task of determining
which crew, which resources could be re-assigned to help with the
extra workload in Engineering. But there was no one. Just her
and Gal and Kieran.

"It's been a huge help to have Sarrin — do you know she
reprogrammed the shields to be more effective? She's the one

that figured out how to fix the FTL. But now she's hurt, so it's just me and I'm doing what I can to keep this old boat in the sky."

Rayne's breath caught, the memory of the girl catching the bomb and the explosion that engulfed her playing across her mind. She hadn't even asked about the injuries. It wasn't important, she reminded herself, the girl was an Augment. An enemy. She turned her gaze back to Kieran. "I didn't think about all the work you've been doing. I'm going to recommend you for a commendation when we get back."

Instead of the smile she expected, he frowned. "Maybe I shouldn't be saying this, but have you ever considered that this whole thing, finding Sarrin and Grant and Hoepe, that this might be the right thing to do — the Path of the Gods?"

"Careful, Kieran!" She ducked her head as though it could keep the ever-watchful Gods from noticing his blasphemy. "The Speakers tell us the Will of the Gods."

He stuck his tongue in the corner of his mouth, biting on it while he looked straight into her eyes. "Grant flew through space into our airlock from an exploding shuttle. What are the odds? A billion to one?

"What are you implying?"

"Finding Sarrin, Halud choosing this ship, boarding a warship — the odds are all unbelievable. Like there's something bigger going on, some unseen force."

Bile rose in her throat. "You think the Gods are protecting us, them?"

"I don't know what I believe."

"The Augments are monsters. The virus changed them to be hyper-aggressive and dangerous. They don't think the way we do. They don't connect with or see other people the way we do. They killed our soldiers without blinking an eye, destroyed a planet without hesitation."

The muscles running the angle of Kieran's jaw twitched again. "Sarrin saved your life. She ran across the yard and grabbed that bomb out of the air. She carried it far away enough no one else got hurt. Seems she does think differently than the rest of us."

The air rushed out of her lungs, and Rayne suddenly felt no more than a foot tall. But still… surely… Augments were enemies. The Gods said it was so. Her father said it was so.

Kieran stood, leaning across the table. "Don't forget, she released you when everyone else thought you were behind the attack on Contyna." He stepped back, scrubbing a hand across his tired eyes. "Maybe…. Look, maybe the Gods and the Speakers are not the same; we haven't been told the whole story. Sarrin isn't a monster. If you would open your eyes, you would see. It's not her fault, the UECs trained her, made her what she is, and she fights it every day. We've just met Grant, but I doubt he's a psychotic killing machine either."

Rayne's mouth went dry.

"I'm too tired. I said some things I shouldn't have." He walked away, calling behind him, "Keep an open mind is all. Don't let someone else do your thinking for you."

She turned, watching him pass through the kitchenette on his way to the door. "Where are you going?"

He sighed, scooping two steaming dishes from the warmer into his hands. "Sarrin should be waking up soon, and I think she'll need some help. I owe her, after all."

* * *

Hoepe kicked a path across the floor of the infirmary, pushing aside fallen medicine and bandages. He led Grant to the table and made him sit.

"What happened here?" Grant asked, raising an eyebrow.

"Turbulence."

Grant snorted. "The whole ship went sideways for a little while. I got tossed around that airlock like a practice dummy."

Hoepe raised an eyebrow. "Not the worse you've had."

A familiar impish grin lit up his old friend's face. "No, not by far."

"Let me take a look at you?"

Grant pulled off his shirt and turned around.

Hoepe noted the large oozing hole in the middle of his back, already healing. There were more of the geometric procedural marks running down the side of his spine than he had four years ago.

"The implant is biologic, I think," said Grant. "Strong, flexible. Protective, no problem with fire or explosives."

"You always did favour incendiaries. Probably too much."

Grant turned his head and smirked. But his bravado failed, and his expression grew sombre. He hung his head. Quietly, he said, "They can control my mind. With the suit I think. That's what happened on the planet. I didn't know what I was doing; it was all them. But, I woke up and remembered and realized I had to go."

Hoepe put a hand on his shoulder, happier than he could say to be with him again. A little warmth inside of him had been filled, and maybe he could fill some of Grant's. "It's good to see you."

"Yeah, you too." But all of the muscles in his shoulders rippled with tension. Grant asked, "How's Sarrin? That was her, right?"

Hoepe pulled out a stethoscope, running it over Grant's chest. "She'll be okay. Some burns. Nothing that won't heal in a few days." His hands moved through a long-familiar physical pressure point scan, checking for areas of injury or weakness.

Grant sighed, "There's something you're not telling me. I've known you too long."

There was no way to explain what he had been thinking, that she would be okay physically but the new procedural marks and the episodes where she lost control made him think there was far more to deal with than the superficial wounds. She needed something he couldn't offer, healing in an area he had no understanding of.

"I want to see her," Grant said.

Hoepe pushed and twisted a few active points, boosting the body's ability to heal. "Not now. She needs to rest."

"Things didn't end well. The last time I saw her was a confused mess." Grant looked up at him. "Has she said anything?"

"You know she's always been quiet."

Grant winced as Hoepe released a tight point.

"You never told me what happened."

"It was stupid. We disagreed on how to handle a situation. And I did what I thought best."

"I'm sure it's in the past."

He snorted. "I'm sure it is; not like she has an eidetic memory or anything."

Hoepe chuckled. "That's the spirit." He twisted another point. "How did you end up on Junk?"

Pausing a moment, Grant shrugged as though trying to brush it off. "Typical story. I fell into one of their traps. How did you end up out here? You and Sarrin must have a pretty good operation going."

Hoepe shook his head. "Sarrin was on Selousa until a couple

weeks ago."

"How did she get caught? If anyone was going to avoid it, you think she would have."

"I don't know. Her brother found her actually."

"The Poet?"

"Yes. He's here as well. I've got a crew, we were based on Contyna, doing food and supply smuggling, but that's over. I haven't found anyone else."

Grant raised an eyebrow. "Omblepharon, Maisie, the Pauls — they're all on Junk. Thirty-three total, I think, but I haven't seen all of them. There are facilities on Jade and Porter as well, if I heard right."

Hoepe's mouth dropped open, his hands falling to his sides. "What?"

"Yeah," Grant twisted around to look at him, his eyebrows knitting together. "Isn't that why you came to Junk in the first place?"

Hoepe's soul soared. "N-No," he stammered. "We needed a spare part."

Grant jumped off the table. "Then, we have to go back. It's spread what Guitteriez is doing now, worse than before."

Hoepe nodded. "You said there's thirty-three Augments?"

Grant grinned his eyes sparking with excitement. "It's just you, me, and Sarrin. It will be a bit tricky, but we can do it. I've got a plan."

"Yes." Hoepe felt his own, usually reserved, excitement starting to rise. "We've got my crew as well."

Grant paused. "But they're not —. They're commons, aren't they?"

"They're good men," Hoepe assured him. "They're tough, strong, know their work."

"Still, Hoepe. This is a UEC facility."

"We can't infiltrate the facility just the three of us. I'm no fighter, you know that. And Sarrin… you haven't seen…. What if there's trouble, what if something goes wrong? We could use the men for leg power if nothing else."

"You know how I feel about the commons. Especially if they're all like those lunatics in the shuttle bay. I thought for sure that woman was going to shoot me out the airlock."

"Ah. Be glad Rayne didn't." He triggered another point, Grant grunting as his body adjusted. "My men are useful. Loyal. Trust me."

Grant eyed him warily. "I never took you for such a lover of commons, not after what they did to us in the war, and what they let happen to us for all those years in Evangecore."

They all bore a resentment of commons — normal people not infected with the Red Fever virus — for their complacency when they turned their backs on all those children held in the UEC facility, and for their mindless fear during the war when the Augments only wanted to escape and protect themselves. But Hoepe had been forced to make peace with it; he needed his crew, he had even come to appreciate their company from time to time. "You need rest," he told Grant, hoping to steer away from the topic. Grant's anger ran deep, and Hoepe doubted spending years in another research facility had helped.

"We should head to Junk right away." Grant's eyes lit up with a familiar wildness. "They're still in there."

"We can't afford to be reckless. We need to plan," said Hoepe. "Besides, it will be a few hours before the jump coils are ready. The engineer tells me the FTL is 'on thin ice' — his words, not mine."

"What does that mean?"

"I don't know, honestly, but I think we should heed his warning."

"You trust him, even though he's a common wearing a UEC uniform?"

Hoepe shrugged, avoiding a direct answer. He had enough trouble explaining it to himself.

"Fine, we'll wait. No more than a day." Grant pulled his stained, torn shirt back on as he headed to the door. "I'm going to go find Sarrin. We'll make a plan."

"No, don't," Hoepe called after him. "I told you she needs rest. We all do. I'll set up a meeting with my men for tomorrow."

"But, she's —."

Hoepe crossed his arms over his chest, putting on his sternest physician's scowl. "Let her rest."

"I have to see her. You don't understand what happened that day she left. I have to talk to her. I've been killing myself over it for four years."

"No."

"Why not?"

Hoepe bit his lip. "She got hurt." He held up his hands before Grant could get too upset and start flinging himself around the room. "But she's okay. She's resting and being looked after."

Both Grant's hands raked through his hair. "By who? Her brother?"

He'd known it was the right decision when he'd asked Kieran to look after her, but he wasn't looking forward to explaining it. Hoepe looked directly into Grant's eyes, hoping to convey an expression of certainty, of his superior ranking when it came to medical decisions. "By the engineer."

Grant's upper lip twitched. "What?"

Hoepe shrugged again. "He was the best option."

"What about me? What about her brother?"

He gave a quick shake of his head. "Don't go looking for her, Grant. Doctor's orders."

Grant scowled, turning on his heel he marched out of the infirmary.

* * *

Sarrin dreamed: *An invisible force held her to the table, gravity crushing her. Bright lights shone down, dazzling her eyes. She should scream, but she was too tired.*

A man with a jagged, curving scar running down the side of his face appeared above her, silhouetted in the light: Luis Guitteriez. He grinned behind his surgical mask, long scar warping into something wicked.

A scar she had put there with her own hands — her real hands. That was when she had had small freedom, enough freedom to rebel. That was the day they started whispering her name through the barracks, 'Twenty-seven'. The day Guitteriez had started watching her every movement.

The whirring sound of a saw brought her attention. Her arms were shackled, the muscles frozen so she couldn't move them. The skin peeled from her hands. Guitteriez pulled the bones out one-by-one, a terrible popping sound with each joint he tore apart. He replaced hem with prosthetics offered from a steel tray.

Her hand flexed, bright skeleton glimmering. "You're mine now," said Guitteriez.

She woke in an unfamiliar place, panting. It took a full minute to bring her heart rate under control. Her mind quickly calculated the thirteen escape routes and twenty-six deadly objects in the room.

Standard layout for officer's quarters: bed, desk, cabinet, latrine. On the nightstand sat a framed picture of Kieran and a girl, roughly his age — they were smiling, their arms wrapped around each other. With a start, she realized this was his room.

The smell of engine oil assaulted her nostrils.

The desk held a neat row of engineering texts stacked under the computer access console. On the wall hung a schematic of the Comrade, its engine systems highlighted, and neat little notes printed by the corner. The floor was clear and the sheets on the bed were tightly turned in.

Rolling from the bed, she automatically pressed her hands into the corner of the mattress to push off. Her hands were more numb than usual. She looked down and saw they were wrapped in think cotton, turning them into almost comical clubs at the ends of her arms. She blinked, trying to compute the incongruence of the harsh mechanical structure buried underneath to the soft coverings.

Above the computer console, an unusual knick-knack caught her eye. Its use as a weapon was limited, being only a small soft-plastic cube, each side faced with nine squares of differing colours. She picked it up clumsily, twisting it between her clubs.

The door slid open without warning, surprising her.

"Oh, you're up." Kieran smiled, a steaming container in each hand. "Uh, Hoepe suggested you hide out here until you're feelin' better."

She reached to put the cube back in its place, somehow embarrassed to be caught. It slid out of her bulky hands and tumbled across the floor.

Kieran laughed, stopping her from bending to retrieve it. "Here, I'll get it. No worries." Quickly, he set his containers on the desk and squatted down. He popped back up, smiling. "It's a puzzle," he told her. "You want to make it so each side has just one colour." He spun it around a few times to show her.

Her eyes tracked the movements of the device.

"I brought you something to eat." He pulled a trunk next to

the desk, offering her the single chair and the ration bowl placed closest to the edge. "I don't know about you, but I'm starvin'."

She stared at the bowl.

"Oh." He rubbed his leg anxiously. "I, uh, didn't think about how you would use that spoon. Do you, um, want me to, uh, feed you?"

A growl caught in her throat and she took a step back.

He snorted, "Yeah, sorry, bad idea."

The room felt incongruent, a peculiarity she couldn't name. A star chart she didn't recognize from the government's database hung on the wall beside her. Mostly, though, her attention fixated on the picture on the nightstand. She pointed at it grunting.

"Huh?" Kieran's gaze followed her club. "Oh, that's my sister, Lauren."

She tilted her head, marvelling at the normal sibling relationship, studying it. "Where is she?"

"Um, well" — Kieran's face darkened — "she died." He tried to brush away the sadness with a laugh.

A twinge of regret twisted in her stomach. Her brother was down the hall — she could hear him fussing in his room if she listened for it — but she couldn't find the words to say to him. What if he was dead? "I'm sorry." Normal people said that to one another, didn't they?

Kieran's expression relaxed. He suddenly looked very different — older, wearier — his carefree mask slipping off and revealing a glimpse of his true self. "Thanks."

"How?"

The mask replaced instantly. He changed the subject instead: "How are your hands?"

Sarrin felt her own walls go up. "There is no discomfort."

He nodded and took another sip of his ration. His gaze

stayed fixed to the floor between them, one leg bouncing erratically.

She watched him curiously, the furrow in his brow, the set of his shoulders, the greyness in his skin. "Are you not going to ask more questions? Hoepe suggests we are 'friends'."

She expected him to laugh — he had never missed a joke before — but he didn't. After a minute, he said, "Oh, I guess I should." But his gaze strained into the distance. He rubbed his hands over his face, the mask crumbling. His normally bright complexion paled, eyes dull. Finally he sighed, his gaze dropping to her bandaged hands. "It's just enough to wrap my head around for one day. Maybe tomorrow."

So he had seen. Knew she was a monster. He no longer held interested in friendship, if he had in the first place. Her heart panged, and the darkness whispered to her. Had Halud seen?

"We didn't tell anybody, Hoepe and I, just so you know. No one else saw."

She stared at her hands, the pristine bandages bringing another flood of memory: *Rubble poured down over her, the lighting overhead flickered and went out. The faintest glow seeped through the spaces in the crumbled con-plas stone.*

Unfamiliar and invigorating air hit her nostrils: outside.

Evangecore had been bombed.

Her bandaged hands fumbled on the rocks as she dug and climbed her way out. The fingers and palm were numb, no feeling in them whatsoever.

Sarrin could see others, hundreds of them pop up out of the ruined building, look around, and start to run. They were running for the trees beyond the fence. The drone of an aerial hovercraft warned her before it began raining laz-fire across the field.

She unwrapped the bandages, skin not yet healed from a procedure done a day ago. But the bandages would make it impossible to climb the fence, and speed was paramount.

In the distance she saw something out of place: a man running into the rubble, a duffel in hand. He pulled at his outer clothes exposing a UEC soldier uniform. The bomber. Familiarity tugged at her, although she did not see his face.

"Too bad those bandages are so bulky," said Kieran.

"What?" The laz-beams and fire receded, her hands still wrapped.

"Hoepe said you would need them for three or four days, and I'm supposed to make sure you keep 'em on." His eyes glinted warmly, a trace of laughter in his voice. Perhaps he sought friendship after all.

Sarrin raised an eyebrow. "I would not risk going against the doctor's orders. His bedside manner is … unpredictable."

Kieran laughed, full and true, music warming her soul.

"One of your friends came on board," he told her, "someone named Grant."

Her good mood dissipated, sucked out an open airlock. So, it was him, the skin-who-was-not-Grant, throwing bombs on Junk. "How?"

Kieran scratched his back idly. "I'm not sure exactly, fell into the ship somewhere between Junk and our first grav-hole. Is he a friend of yours? Do you want to see him?"

She shook her head no. Grant who had found her in the woods, her bleeding hands ripped open, and helped her. Grant who had been the closest thing to a friend for years. Grant whom she had left in the forest after he had killed commons and Augments alike, proving she hadn't truly known him at all. She certainly didn't want to see him.

FOURTEEN

KIERAN SAT DOWN AT THE console in his office in Engineering to write a letter home. His fingers hovered over the keypad, but the words didn't come. Where could he even start, at this point, too much had happened to sum it up quickly.

Three living Augments. Sarrin had metal in her hands and forty-two procedural marks. Grant had something else entirely. They were being chased by a warship. Gal was an addict. Rayne had tried to surrender them. How could he report it all? The feelings? The excitement? The fear? How could he say all that and make his parents not worry, not come and retrieve him immediately for his safety? Heck, he was worried, but he wanted to see it through until the end.

But would it be so bad if he called for an extraction? He didn't want to die out here, and the likelihood seemed particularly high. Regardless of how he felt, this was their fight, not his. He had to remind himself of that. His tour would be officially over in three months, whenever his parents' ship came close enough to this region of space. Then he would go home. There would be a big celebration, a graduation of sorts, from child-apprentice to full-fledged contributing adult. He'd take a position in research or engine maintenance, wherever they wanted him.

A knock at the partition wall that separated his office from the rest of the bay startled him, and he punched the console to turn the display off.

Hoepe stepped into the office space. "Am I interrupting?"

Kieran swallowed, forcing a smile. "No, sir. What's up?"

"Shouldn't you be sleeping?" The doctor's hand came up to examine him.

"Oh, ah, no room. Plus, still trying to catch up on work." He waved his hand vaguely.

"Right." Hoepe nodded. "How is Sarrin?"

"Sleeping, I think. She ate a little earlier. Seemed okay." He handed Hoepe a tablet from his desk. "I am worried about the FTL though, and the Kepheus Drive."

"I thought you'd found a spare."

"We did, but I — ah — dropped it in all the commotion. I can fortify the chamber, but I don't know how long it will hold. We almost cooked 'er with the two jumps back to back. It's the strangest thing, it keeps shifting out of alignment, no matter what I do."

Hoepe nodded, frowning at the tablet.

"We need to get a replacement part. There's no way around it. Maybe now that Grant is on our side, we could go back."

Hoepe's frown deepened. "That's actually what I came here to talk to you about. I need you to plot the jumps to Junk. There are more Augments there."

"What?"

"Grant has seen them. Thirty-three more, he says."

Kieran's mouth hung open.

The doctor's face was grim. "It will be a technically

challenging mission."

Thirty-three Augments, plus three. His mind boggled at the possibility. Could they rescue them all? Grant had done most of the work when he escaped, and still they had almost been caught. A whole group would be that much harder.

Another thought occurred to him: what would happen if the UECs caught him and found out who he was? He had a cover, sure, but if anyone looked closely they would see it was just a flimsy story. The last time someone had been found, it had altered history. Forever. He glanced at the dark console screen, perhaps an extraction wouldn't be so bad.

And yet, he had signed on to the crew. If Hoepe ordered him to join the mission, he would — observe and participate. Plus, thirty-six Augments. Incredible. "Count me in, Doc."

Hoepe searched his face for a minute. "We are going to have a briefing in the cargo bay in half an hour."

"Sure."

"One more thing." The doctor pressed his lips together. "Would you mind telling Sarrin?"

Kieran raised an eyebrow.

"It will be better coming from you."

"Me? Why not you or Grant, if it's his idea?"

Hoepe shook his head. "She seems to like you, more than the rest of us anyhow. Maybe you can talk her into it. Grant mentioned their last parting was not entirely amicable."

Kieran faltered. "Yeah, I guess, I can ask."

"Good. Do you have a syringe still?"

He tried to chuckle, although he still found the weight and bulk of the auto-injector in his pocket uncomfortable. "Always do, now."

Hoepe reached out and squeezed his shoulder. "Thank you

for taking care of her earlier. I hope you don't have to use the sedative, but her neural pathways haven't fully regenerated and I don't want to take any chances. Anywhere you can make contact, press the injector to her skin and it will do the rest."

"Was she always like that?"

"No."

Kieran stared after the doctor as he left, and the injector pinched as he shifted his leg. How had going to his quarters become a possibly lethal situation?

* * *

Stars twinkled in unusual constellations as she stared at the star chart on the wall. Absently, she bounced her bandaged hands together, the dull, repetitive thunk soothing her mind into blankness. It was a welcome change from the constant thought stream that flooded her with images of Grant and Halud, Kieran and Evangecore, the freightship and explosive fireballs.

The door opened, the hiss shaking her from her lost thoughts. She hadn't heard the footsteps. Or the keypad.

She breathed a sigh of relief when Kieran entered. His face was drawn, his hand buried in his pocket, the silhouette of an auto-injector apparent through the grey fabric of his coveralls. She flinched.

The tendons in his arm strained as his grip tightened. His eyes narrowed, calculating, preparing. Her heart rate sped up. The rapid movement of his arm brought up all of her defences.

But his hand came out empty, customary grin painted back across his features. "Sorry, sorry," he said. "I just came from talking with Hoepe, and he had me thinking the worst."

She frowned, but her breathing normalized.

"Just…." He ran his hand through his hair, tousling the short strands so they stood up in fat spikes. "Sorry." He turned, tossing the auto-syringe carelessly on top of the short dresser. His skin sagged, dark smudging under his eyes.

"You didn't sleep last night," she noted. He hadn't returned to the room in nearly thirty-six hours.

An easy grin slipped over his face again, part of the mask. "No, ah, no room. Besides, I had work to do."

It was his bed she sat on. A place she had occupied for two days. She had meant to leave, but Grant's footsteps continually prowled the corridors. A meeting she would avoid as long as possible.

Besides, the engineer had been absent, too busy making repairs. She would have helped, but her hands, wrapped as they were, were too clumsy to be of any use. And unwrapping them meant facing what lay underneath, another meeting she desperately wanted to avoid.

The bed shifted, Kieran flopping so he lay across the far end. She watched him, eyes wide, as he sighed and stretched his arms over his head, bringing them back to rub his eyes.

She swallowed heavily. "It's careless to leave the sedative out of reach."

"I'm not afraid of you."

"Why?" She pulled her legs up tight to her chest.

He chuckled, the light playing across his features where he lay face-up. "Hoepe seems to think you're starting to like me."

Her eyebrow quirked.

"He said you don't usually talk to people at all, so I should count myself lucky." He made an exaggerated yawn, stretching and rolling himself off the bed, landing awkwardly on his knees.

She realized her mouth hung open. A warm buzz had overtaken her entire body. It was so unusual, her mind stopped, curious only about the feeling.

"You knew Hoepe before. In the war?" Kieran said, picking himself up and striding casually across the room.

The feeling crashed around her, like so many buildings and bombs and laz-bolts. She folded her arms across her chest.

"Sarrin?"

"What did Hoepe ask you to say?"

He picked up the puzzle cube and spun it idly in his hands. "Uh."

"The message is unpleasant, no doubt."

"It's not unpleasant, I don't think." His voice fell flat, his eyes darted to the auto-syringe sitting on the dresser. "They found more Augments. Grant has a plan to help them. Your presence is requested in the cargo bay for a briefing."

"When?" Her heart leapt into her throat.

He glanced at the chronometer. "Six minutes."

Her muscles coiled instantly. "No."

"He said you'd say that." The corner of his lip quirked up. "But, there are more Augments. More of your friends."

It wasn't safe. Didn't they see that? Didn't they know? She turned away, making herself small in the corner where the bed pressed into the wall.

"Sarrin." The bed shifted under his weight. "It's just a briefing. Trying to decide what to do." A warning twinged in her head, and she gasped, his hand stretched toward her.

"Don't!" She pressed as hard as she could into the corner.

"Sarrin." He inched closer.

Eyes squeezed shut, she clamped down on the monster the same way she did when Hoepe insisted on examining her. But Kieran was no doctor, he had no practiced distant touch. His fingers barely grazed her leg, as she pushed off the wall and sent herself flying across the room.

His pulse bounced erratically in his neck, fear rolling off of him into her. Ragged breathing tore through her throat. "Don't touch me."

"I'm sorry." He folded his hands between his legs, tucking them away. "You just looked so sad."

Sad equalled dead in Evangecore. "You don't understand."

He swallowed several times, preparing himself. "Then, tell me."

She stared at him, blinking. A vision of a cold corpse in a dark room flashed before her eyes. The edges of it were fuzzy.

"Sarrin?" He moved off the bed, gaze shifting between her and the syringe that lay on top of the dresser. "Your eyes have gone funny. I didn't mean to upset you."

Of course he didn't, but she had overreacted. Again. Because to touch her could spell death, she had no control over what the monster would do. She was tired of fighting; fighting herself, fighting them. She longed to escape into the deep Deep, and run and run and run until her feet stopped and she left her body behind, running through the stars. But that was not her life, not what she was made for.

The bandages fell away as she tugged the edge of the cotton with her teeth.

"Whoa, what are you doing?" said Kieran. "Hoepe said you need those for a few days." He reached out as though he wanted to come closer, but his feet were fixed to the floor.

It didn't really matter though, did it? She shook her head. "Grant will want to spar." The suture lines running jagged across her hands were bright pink, scabs in the places the flesh had burned too far back. But the skin had healed. Enough, anyway.

He gasped, leaning forward where he stood. "That's incredible."

She tucked her hands to her sides so he couldn't see. Another gift of the monster.

"But you don't have to…." His gazed lingered on her, she could feel it burning into her with an intense curiosity. But then the smile folded back onto his features when she lifted her eyes to meet his. "It's only a meeting," he said. "To try to figure out how to help your friends."

"It's not a meeting."

"What do you mean?"

How could she explain that Grant would want to start a war, and no one had been made more for war than she.

"You don't have to go," he said. "But if you want me to, I'll go with you. No one can make you do anything you don't want to do."

If only her life were so simple. She had tried resisting their demands once. "If there are weapons, I… I don't want to lose myself."

He smiled from across the room. "I'll go with you."

* * *

Grant cleared a space between the cargo boxes on the large main floor of the bay. A few training mats that he'd found lay in a neat square at one side of the room.

Hoepe came down the stairs, carrying a heavy kit with him. "Did you find what you needed?"

"It's enough."

"I found the shooting simulator," said Hoepe. "The men should be bringing it along."

"Never did like to get your hands dirty," smirked Grant.

The doctor gave him a look over his hook nose, and Grant instantly thought of Hoepe working at his makeshift hospitals in the middle of the battlefield. Blood and screams pooled in the air and on the floor, the doctor often covered in spatters of it. Including, usually, Grant's own blood — a price he gladly paid in the fight for freedom.

The men arrived shortly and not at all quietly, clacking down the stairs. Eight of them. Big and strong, or wiry and quick. According to Hoepe, many of them had seen actual combat in the war — although how they had survived with foot falls like that was a total mystery.

Hoepe directed them to set up the holographic projector and targeting simulator.

Familiar movement caught he eye on the upper level: Sarrin. Purposeful, efficient, calculating. Her eyes rapidly catalogued the room, and his heart lifted, she was exactly as he remembered her. When she had left that night, it broken him in two. "Sarrin!"

She stiffened, her body perfectly still. Behind her stood the engineer — the one who had admitted him to the shuttle hangar — he whispered something in her ear, leaning close. Too close. Grant's eyes narrowed, waiting for her reaction. She didn't like to be touched.

And yet, she descended the stairs. Muscles tense with anticipation, expression neutral. Kieran followed behind, and Grant found himself hoping the engineer would trip and tumble over the side.

But he made it safely to the bottom and stretched his hand out. "Good to see you."

"What happened to your neck?" asked Grant.

Kieran's hand withdrew quickly, reaching to cover the faint bruising surrounding his trachea.

Grant guided Sarrin across the cargo bay, hovering this hand inches from her back where he knew she could feel him but not be overwhelmed. "I've missed you. I want to talk about what happened."

Her big blue eyes stared up at him, wide.

Suddenly, the engineer was there. "Hey, Grant." He slid, somehow, into the little space between him and Sarrin, arm draped across Grant's shoulders. "I've been meaning to ask ya how you made your way into the shuttle bay. Must've been quite a maneuver."

Grant pulled away.

An idiotic grin met him.

"Grant" — Hoepe's call distracted him from across the bay — "give us your opinion on this set up."

Kieran still stood before him, grinning. Weak, out of shape, out of balance. Common. Pathetic. He would have to talk to Sarrin later.

The engineer shuffled after him. "What's this?" He pointed to the simulator and the mats. His voice edged with panic. "I thought this was a briefing, a discussion, ya know."

"It is," said Grant. "But I need to know what I'm working with before I finalize the plan." He stalked to where Hoepe held up a holographic projector lens.

On the upper platform, the wild eyed woman who had tried to shoot him in the shuttle hangar entered. "What are you doing?" she called down. "That equipment is Central Army property."

Grant glanced at Hoepe with a smirk. "Well, until not so long ago, so was I. I think it'll be okay if I use it."

Her feet rushed down the stairs one at a time.

"Hey, Rayne," the engineer shouted, "glad you could join us."

"What are you doing?" She paused at the bottom, glancing from Grant to Kieran.

"Training," said Grant.

"Training!" her voice shrilled with surprise.

The oblivious engineer kept the ridiculous smile on his face. "Join us. You're always saying we need more tactical drills."

Grant felt the tiny muscle in his cheek twitch.

She clenched her jaw, glancing warily around the room, then nodded.

"Really?" said Kieran.

"Keep an open mind, you said. We're all surviving together, for now anyway."

"Yeah."

"Wait," said Grant, "sorry to interrupt, but neither of you was invited to the party."

Hoepe coughed. "Actually, I invited Kieran."

"And Rayne is the best shot under the stars." Kieran gestured to the training machine. "If you're gonna want us to shoot something, you're gonna want Rayne to do it."

Hoepe caught his eye and shrugged. "It's not live bolts."

Rayne stripped her jacket down, revealing a tactical tee underneath. She at least had reasonable body composition and balance. Grant shrugged. "Alright, let's see."

The first officer followed him hesitantly. She took the simulator's light-beam rifle and stood on the little platform. Good stance, defensive grip, acceptable. She might be helpful.

Hoepe started the simulator, and projections danced in the air. She watched for a minute, eyes tracking. The rifle came up to her shoulder, and harmless beams of light shot out of it in controlled bursts. Target after target flashed out, even as the simulator sped up.

Grant had to admit she had reasonable skill, for a common. Hoepe's men each took their turn through the simulation. Even the Poet wasn't too bad, better than his poetry anyhow.

"Sarrin?"

She took a halting step, her gaze fixed to the floor.

"Actually, I think it's my turn." Kieran brushed past her, shooting a look behind. Something about his voice made every muscle in Grant's body tense.

Grant's teeth ground together. "No, it's —." But the engineer already stood on the mark. Reluctantly, he handed him the rifle.

"Go easy on me, yeah? I'm an engineer, not a tactician. Never was any good at this in school."

Grant saw Sarrin watching the engineer, eyes alight with intense interest. For whatever motivation came over him, Grant seized the controls and increased the difficulty by two points.

Projections sped through the air. The engineer missed every single target, badly. Grant powered down the simulator, growling. "Don't waste my time."

"Hey," he shouted, "I was just getting warmed up."

Grant turned his back. "Sarrin."

"Nah, let me have another go." Grant glared at him, but the engineer stepped right up to him. "She's hurt, she can't today."

His head started to throb, the stupid common trying his patience. He pinched the bridge of his nose. "Sarrin, come on."

* * *

Sarrin watched as Kieran gripped the rifle, stance unbalanced, rifle held at an impossible angle, and fire glow after glow of pulsated light into the empty air. The simulator flashed targets at three times the standard speed. Had Kieran been in Evangecore, he would have been disposed of.

Too soon, the projectors shut down, the simulation whirring to a close. Kieran objected, Grant said something, and suddenly all eyes were on her.

Grant held out the rifle. The words that accompanied it were lost to the indistinct buzzing in her head, but she stepped forward all the same.

Kieran's green eyes locked onto hers. She caught the last of his words: "... Just a sim. A game."

Sarrin was good at games. Evangecore had many games.

The monster didn't flare up when she held the simulated rifle, but her body itched with recognition. Pulse pounding, she took her stance, body locking in like a familiar friend. The light-rifle in her hands could be rewired in a matter of seconds becoming a catastrophic heat ray. Had anyone thought of that? Had Hoepe told Grant about her imbalance?

The holograms sprung to life. Targets danced in the air. The light-pulse hit one, and it was the same game as always — *ding.* It flashed out — *omega.* Another — *ding, omega.* And another and another — *ding, ding.*

She had trained in the simulator at Evangecore. Hours and hours. Too much. The movements were automatic, even as the simulator sped up to 4, 5, 7, 10 times standard.

Her finger pulled the trigger repeatedly. *Ding, ding, ding.* She didn't see the targets anymore, simply knew where they would appear. *Ding, Ding-ding-ding-DING-DING.* The world around her disappeared, leaving nothing but targets and omegas.

The sim shut off and she slammed back into herself with a gasp. Her chest heaved, the laz-rifle clattered to the ground. She had been slipping and not even realized it.

Vaguely, she heard the men cheering. Grant came towards her, smiling. She ducked before he could rest his hand on her shoulder, and scooted away.

Crouched in the corner, she forced the air in and out, as Grant led the others to a set of practice mats.

A shadow stood over her: Kieran. Of course he was watching, of course he saw what happened. "I didn't think it would be like this. Go back to the room. I'll tell them you're sick, your hands still hurt and that shooting was too much."

She stared.

"It's not a big deal." His expression held no trace of its usual casual smile. "Your hands were in an explosion and you had surgery yesterday. Hoepe knows that. I don't know why he wanted me to ask you to come."

Behind him, grunts echoed across the cargo bay as Rayne sparred with one of Hoepe's men, grappling across the mats. She flipped and pinned him. Not efficient, but effective.

"Sarrin," he said, "I saw your eyes go funny. Get out of here."

She nodded, pushing herself up at his beckoning. He led her to the stairs, which she took three at a time.

Grant called out and stopped her. "Where are you going?"

Caught, she looked at Kieran.

"She doesn't feel good," he shouted back.

"She's fine, you saw her shoot. Same old Sarrin."

"No, really —."

"Let's show them how it's done." He waved an incessant arm.

Automatically, her feet backed down a step.

Kieran looked from her to Grant. He stiffened, his back straight, and stalked forward. "I'll spar with ya."

Grant's eyes narrowed. "I think Sarrin —."

"Nah," said Kieran, his accent extra thick, "I think I can take ya."

Sarrin's heart thumped painfully, her eyes wide as Grant accepted and invited Kieran onto the mats. Kieran climbed up, setting his feet and fists like a child. If he'd had any training, he'd forgotten it to make room for engine schematics.

Grant pulled back. "You're just a common. This isn't —."

"A common?" Kieran's head jerked in surprise. "What does that mean?"

Grant growled. "A common. Not an Augment. Don't think you're the same as me? You're not."

Kieran's cheery grin disappeared. "So?"

"So, this is a very bad idea for you."

Kieran glanced back at Sarrin, jutting his chin in the direction of the stairs, urging her to take them, but she stood rooted to the spot. He turned back to Grant. "I think this is good. You wanted to spar with someone, show off a little. Here I am."

Suicide.

"Have you ever fought before?"

"Sure. My brother and I used to roughhouse all the time."

Grant's nostrils flared. "Okay, then." He spun, and hooked him, hard and fast and dirty. But Kieran ducked down, avoiding the hit entirely.

The edge of Sarrin's vision started to fuzz. Her feet took a few more steps down the stairs.

Grant threw a cross-jab directly into Kieran's face, landing full force with a sickening snap. Stumbling back, Kieran fell from the edge. He spat blood, smearing it from his mouth and nose. Still, he stood, clambering back onto the mat. Ducking low, he rushed Grant, clutching him around the abdomen.

Grant let loose a harsh, jarring laugh.

Kieran landed a single punch, throwing the whole of his weight into Grant's abdomen. Grant didn't flinch. Surprised, Kieran looked up and Grant came in hard, timing his punch so Kieran couldn't possibly have time to see it.

Hoepe's men tried to help him up, but Kieran slumped where he fell. The doctor pressed an auto-syringe into his neck and frantically triggered a series of pressure points.

Grant turned to her. "Come on, Sar. I was in that cell too long, help me get the kinks out."

She stared at Kieran, only starting to breathe again when she saw him stir. There was no avoiding it, Grant was determined. Stepping to the mat, she knew she would do this the same as she had always done with Grant when he got like this: stay slow, focussed, stumble, concede defeat and let Grant win.

He stretched, the pop-pop of muscles sliding over vertebrae sounding from his neck, too much like mini explosions lighting up behind her eyes. He pulled his shirt over his head, his back a mass of scar tissue, fresh and raw.

Stay focussed. Stay slow. She took a shuddering breath. Kieran had been moved to the side where he sat up, conscious if not a little dazed. His blood still stained the mat. She dug her toes into the slightly padded surface, grounding herself.

She shuffled her feet, staying opposite Grant as he circled around her. Grant used to say it was a wasted step between them — they had sparred so much, they already knew how the other moved, already knew the rhythm — but it had been five years since she'd left him. She noted an injury in his right knee, and a favouring of the left elbow.

He threw a lazy jab that was easily blocked. Sarrin replied with the customary cross, letting him dodge.

And so it started, give and take, punch and block. Grant threw a kick at her side, she returned an elbow strike. He grinned, speeding up.

Still, they were moving slowly, upper cuts and spin kicks hovering in the air.

The next gear was a familiar one, the speed that Evangecore demanded. Grant started to miss his targets fractionally, not enough that anyone but her would noticed. He pushed faster. Fists flew at her like hologram targets. And each of them sounded a quiet *ding* against her arm.

A ragged breath.

Arms and legs faster and faster, time started to slow.

Fear blinked in his eyes. Grant's movements became stiff, reactive. Sloppy.

Time to stumble, she thought. But she was a machine hunting a machine, and the monster danced with joy. Where Grant faltered, she was sure. Her core hummed with the sheer glow of power.

Grant clutched his head, suddenly thrashing in pain. The second skin erupted from his back in slow motion, pouring like a river over his body.

A final jab, Sarrin reached out and grabbed, ripping a piece from his head. Fury, hot and blind. The monster would not be denied. She smashed his head-target to the floor. Through the suit, no way to know if he was alive or *omega*. Her lip curled, baring her teeth.

"Sarrin! Sarrin!" She turned slowly to the noise, to the familiar set of syllables. A voice pulled her from her carnal instincts. Who was she if not a machine? On the floor, Kieran gripped the edge of the mat, begging her, "Sarrin! Calm down. You're gonna kill him."

Why was he looking at her like that? With fear?

Confused, she looked behind. Grant lay on the ground, deathly still. His mottled brown suit covered his body, except for a jagged hole over his left eye.

A chunk of flabby brown skin wobbled in her own hand.

She stared at Kieran, at his green eyes. What had she done? She threw the skin away and dropped to her knees. She gasped and fought for breath that wouldn't come.

Kieran reached for her, his face distorted and bloody. "It's okay," he said.

Behind him, a raucous cheer sounded, men clapping and yelling. Grant wobbled, rising on unsteady legs as his suit retracted with a wet slurp. "She's still got it," he wheezed, grinning, laughing with the crowd. "We're going to go to Junk. We're going to get everyone else out. With you there, it's going to be a breeze."

Kieran's gaze met hers, his eyes reflecting the same fear and worry she felt pound through her soul.

FIFTEEN

A NERVOUS HUM BUZZED THROUGH the small shuttle. Sarrin shut
her eyes against the anxious shuffling of men, their heartbeats
clattering around in side of their fleshy bone boxes. The memory
of Kieran's departing words echoed in her head, mixing with the
din: *"Is this smart? You and I both know what almost happened in the cargo
bay. What happens if… if…?"* He left the last unsaid, the silence
ringing more loudly than anything else.

What if? What if?

She pulled up a mental image of his eyes, green orbs that
danced and left her with an entirely different jittery sensation.

From the pilot's seat, Grant's gaze shifted from the route
ahead to her. He warily tracked her every move, the feel of his
gaze making her fidget. He had been the one to find her after the
near-calamity at the training session, mistaking his own near-miss
for a controllable unstoppable power they could use to their
advantage. He reminded her there were others who needed help,
insisting she come. But he didn't look at her the same.

Rayne sat on the other side of the shuttle. Kieran's voice
echoed around her again: *"Keeping an open mind, I guess."* Face to

face, the first officer had been nothing but professional, intent on the logistics of the mission and the tactical points related to the layout of the building. But her devotion to the Speakers rooted deep, and Rayne's wide eyes scanned her while practiced fingers worked over her laz-rifle.

Still, Sarrin wanted to believe Rayne could overcome her upbringing. After all, the UECs had pounded her into their mould, the same as they had done Sarrin. If not quite the same, not that different either. If Rayne could be something other than what she had been made, maybe Sarrin could do. But a dark cloud niggled at her, reminding her that she would never escape it.

Three of Hoepe's men sat quietly, nervously, occupying the remaining seats in the shuttle. Not Kieran. She shut her eyes and tried to pretend he sat beside her, that someone who understood the monster was there. But she felt glad too that Kieran and Halud were on the freightship, safe. Kieran's combat skills were abysmal, and she couldn't help but feel that none of them were coming back from this trip.

Ahead of them loomed a dark cloud, a black hole that sucked, drawing in everything. A trap unwilling to relent, impossible to escape. The zing of charging laz-rifles in the shuttle around her brought her back from the event horizon.

Grant set the shuttle down in the empty hangar. They braced for attack, but it didn't come.

Gingerly, Sarrin reached for the two laz-pistols holstered against her thigh. They zinged to life at the feel of her pulse, and her vision crowded in a little around the edges. Grant had insisted she take them — infinitely more deadly with two weapons than none.

"It's been a long time since we've done this, hey, Sarrin?"

Grant flashed her a smile, false bravado painting over his fear.

The shuttle door opened, and they filed out into the empty shuttle bay. Still no guards. They crossed the bay quietly, pulling a panel off the wall and sliding into the space in the ceiling. Danger crowded at the back of her brain. Why was the hangar unmanned? Why did alarms not sound the instant their shuttle crossed into the base?

Grant led as they crawled across, then slipped down the walls until they were three floors underground. "Nothing to it," he whispered, coming too close to her ear in the small space. He lead them through the maze. Over walls, under floors, across internal support beams. Finally, he stopped and motioned for one of the men to help him lift a panel beneath their feet.

The room below was small, only an anteroom. Two guards stood at attention — Sarrin could hear them breathing. Silently, Grant slipped down. Two flashes of laz-fire, and he came to the hatch and motioned them all through.

The guards were slumped behind the control panel. A heavily fortified door sat beside the control panel — the entrance to the cells. Grant handed her the toolkit.

She assessed the door, mechanical schematic drawing itself quickly in her mind: Magnetic lock. Retinal scanner. Failsafe wire.

The men pulled the panelling off the walls at her instruction. Grant cleared the bodies from the console, while Sarrin accessed its programming, preparing to deliver an appropriate positive pulse.

"What's taking so long?"

Sarrin looked up from the console, frowning at Grant. To answer, she pulled two more panels from the wall. The failsafe wire, now fully exposed, ran to the door, but also to the walls where it rigged into a series of explosives.

Stepping back, Grant muttered, "Oh." Then, "Hepta-nitrate. Enough to blow us all to the next circle of stars. Take your time."

Splicing the wire, she resected it from the main console, disarming the explosive trigger. With steady hands, she plugged her hand held into the retina scanner and delivered the override signal.

The door opened with a pleasant chime.

She frowned. Too easy.

A quiet hiss started in the room, gas being pushed through the air vents. Hoepe's men and Rayne fell to the ground instantly. Grant's eyes met hers, big and wide and scared.

* * *

Halud watched large viewscreen on the freightship's bridge for far too long, staring at the spot where the little shuttle had disappeared into the dull grey planetary background.

The soft chimes of consoles murmured in the background, and Kieran shifted uneasily beside him.

"She'll be okay. She's trained for this. A simple mission," said Halud, but his voice came out too loud, too firm.

Kieran lips turned up, an attempt at a smile. "Yeah."

Halud took stock of all his jittering limbs and tight drawn expression. Sarrin spent more time with him than anyone else. "Will she be?" he asked suddenly, "Okay, I mean."

The half-smile faded. "You know how she is."

That was the problem, wasn't it? "I'm afraid I don't."

Kieran tore his eyes from the screen, concern woven across them. "Whaddya mean? She's your sister."

It gripped him, squeezing all the air out of his lungs. "I don't know her, not anymore." It was hard to admit the truth, even harder out loud. "I saw what happened in the cargo bay. She

only stopped because you were there. I couldn't do anything."
He waved his hands wildly. "She talks to you. Why? No offence,
but you're a stranger. I'm her brother. She should be talking to
me."

After a silent minute, Kieran shrugged. "I dunno. Maybe it's
easier."

"Easier than her brother? Sarrin was always this chatty,
charming, cute little girl. I don't understand what happened."

The engineer dragged a hand over his stubble-covered jaw.
"Maybe that's the problem. I'm a blank slate. No expectations.
She doesn't care about me or what I think. Not like she cares
about you. That has to be easier."

"What happened to her in there? What happened to my little
sister?" His voice cracked.

"I don't know." Kieran turned away, giving him the decency
of privacy while tears started to pool in Halud's eyes. "A lot, I
think."

"What should I do?"

"Maybe, wait for her. Give her space. Support her. Let her
figure it out. She will, I'm sure."

A hiccough caught in Halud's throat.

"She cares about you. Of course she does. But everyone
changes. And she changed in a way she didn't have any say over.
That has to be hard."

"None of this has gone the way it was supposed to."

A sharp laugh rang out. "Things never do. Sometimes that's
a good thing. Look at me, I was supposed to be transferred when
we got back to Etar — to the Comrade, believe it or not. Instead,
I'm out here with you guys."

"I am sorry for that, Lieutenant." Another life ruined by his
mission. "You were never supposed to be on the ship. You or

Rayne."

Kieran laughed again, grinning. "Call me Kieran. I don't think Lieutenant quite fits anymore. And I'm glad I'm here." He turned to Halud, eyes bright. "Can I ask you one thing?

"Certainly."

"Why in the stars would you choose this ship — choose Gal for this? You had to know he would be stubborn as hell."

"I thought Gal was someone else. Someone I used to know."

Both of Kieran's eyebrows shot up. "What do you mean?"

Halud laughed in spite of himself. The idea was ludicrous when he thought about it now. "I thought he was John P."

But Kieran didn't laugh. His gaze bored into Halud so intensely it made him draw back. "The rebel? Why?"

Why *had* he thought it? Why could he not stop thinking it? How could the captain — so drunk, he hadn't been seen in days — be the same man that rallied thousands, that forced the Speakers into late-night damage-control meetings, the same man that nearly won a revolution?

Am urgent ping sounded from a console on the opposite side of the bridge.

"What was that?"

"I don't know." Kieran vaulted over the console they were sitting on, jogging to see the warning coming from Tactical. His face grew dark, disbelieving. "It's the warship."

"I thought there was no one around."

Kieran slammed his fist down as he studied the read out in front of him. "We only did a quick scan — Grant was so anxious to get down there, and we figured the sooner they went down, the less likely someone would find us."

"Have they seen us?"

"I don't know."

"Is Sarrin safe?"

"Safer than us, probably."

* * *

Sarrin exhaled completely, the gas misting around her. With pre-oxygenation, she could hold her breath for eight minutes. Surprised like this, it was more like four and only for low-exertion.

Grant glanced her way, the only ally still standing.

It took her eyes a second to adjust to the dimly lit room beyond the door. A huge, open space, ten times the freightship's cargo hold. Along the centre ran neat rows of individual cells. More like cages, the walls were made of criss-crossing black metal-alloy bars. A low humming told her they were electrified. The people inside didn't spare them a glance. They hung their heads in their sorry cells, or lay down in sleep. Augments all — what happened to their fight?

She flinched when Grant took a step toward her. He pointed to the nearest corner where low light shone out the windows of a raised observation room. There were guards inside, laz-rifles in hand, pulling breathing masks over their faces. The first came out of the station, aiming his rifle from the top of the stairs. Sarrin slipped the laz-guns into her hands, forgetting for a moment what it would do to her.

Ding, omega. *Ding*, omega on the second one who appeared half a second later. The two guards fell, tumbling down the full flight of stairs.

"Don't lose yourself," the engineer's voice rang in her head, and she tucked the laz-guns back into their holsters.

Grant ran to the guards and pulled the respiratory filters from their heads, tossing one to her. Her starving lungs sucked in the stale, filtered air. The thrumming pulse in her head eased.

The few Augments who were still awake in their cages

watched them with hesitantly curious expressions. They would be running out of oxygen too. As if on cue, one of them slumped to the ground.

"The commons. The gas," she said to Grant, words muffled through the ventilator as she pointed behind them. "They'll die." The caged Augments had dropped incredibly fast to the sedative gas, even Grant stumbled slightly. She couldn't imagine what it would do to the others who didn't have the benefit of the heightened Augment systems and rapid metabolism. Hoepe once told her he estimated normal Augments needed at least fifty times more drug compared to a common human. She needed one-hundred-and-fifty times.

Grant shrugged, slapping his legs and arms as though trying to get feeling back in them. "They knew the dangers."

Her breath caught, and she stared at him. He would abandon them the same as he had abandoned their friends in the war. Ruthless, reckless, uncaring.

"What?" he said. "They're just commons, Sarrin. Let's get our friends out."

"They're helping us," she said coldly.

His stare locked onto hers, but she wouldn't back down, not this time. Finally, he huffed and left.

More Augments dropped to the floor; they were wasting valuable time. Seconds ticked away. She ran up the stairs into the guard tower, hands flying immediately to the controls. In the far corner, lights came on, outlining windows from another guard tower.

Footsteps climbed the stairs to the sealed room, the sound clanging around her. She tapped commands, the computer lagging slowly. Or she was speeding up?

The first guard pushed through the door.

She grabbed her laz-gun, fear slamming her into the trance.

Ding, ding, ding. A laz-bolt burned across her shoulder, barely notable. A hit on the target: *ding.*

It fell back, stunned, but it kept moving. A familiar voice, pained, reached her ears: "-rrin, Sarrin, Sarrin. Stop."

Her laz-gun clattered to the floor, and she pushed the monster away with a grunt.

Grant crouched in front of her, mottled grey-brown skin covering his body. His suit retracted from his body as he stared at her. "What in the Deep, Sarrin?"

She stared at him. What a pair — him with his suit and her with her monster.

He bent, his hands on his knees, grimacing as the last trails of the suit disappeared into his own flesh. He held up a small device that she had seen Kieran give him earlier. "I don't know if this single jammer works or not." He batted it a few times, as though foolishly trying to knock a circuit back into place, the looked at her. "Why did you shoot at me?"

Gulping, she struggling to find the words to explain and warred with the idea of telling him she hadn't wanted to come in the first place.

But he continued, stepping next to her as though nothing had happened. "Did you think I was a guard or something? Gods, this place makes my skin crawl too."

Silently, she pointed to the other towers.

"More guards? How many?" He pressed his five fingers into his chest, praying. "Have they seen us?"

Her head shook in answer. There were too many people in the cell block to identify, and she didn't want to risk trying to go deeper, ask the monster for help, in order to find out.

"I put the men back in the ceiling and closed the panel. That should at least slow their exposure. Let's turn the gas off."

Sarrin focussed back to the console. Guards moved through the main room, but it would be a few minutes before they crossed the huge cell block.

"Oh no," Grant muttered. He stared out the window, Sarrin followed his gaze.

Beams of laz-fire shot lit up the dark room below. Not a fight, the guards fired through the bars of the cells one-by-one, the sedated Augments inside defenceless.

Grant took off at a dead run, his own laz-rifle in hand.

* * *

Halud clutched desperately to the console in front of him. The warship released a flash of laz-cannon fire that streaked through space, landing on the freightship's hull. The viewscreen flared with the impact as the floor rocked under them.

"That answers whether they've seen us or not," grunted Kieran.

Hoepe and two men charged onto the bridge. "Shields at maximum," he ordered.

"They're powering up," replied Kieran. "I don't understand how the warship keeps finding us."

"I want to know why our scan didn't see them. We never would have sent the shuttle down if we knew they were out here."

Halud felt his chest stutter. "But Sarrin will okay, right?"

"Evasive maneuvers," Hoepe shouted, one of the men already sliding into the Pilot's chair.

"I'm bringing the cannons online," replied Kieran. He pointed at Halud.

With a start, Halud realized he was steadying himself on the Tactical station. The controls were foreign. He'd never had need to drive a ground vehicle, let alone a starship or weapons system.

The pilot swung the ship around. Everyone stumbled.

He gripped the targeting control. He'd done this — arcade simulators anyway — as a boy. The warship headed straight for them, coming closer at an alarming rate. Laz-fire flashed repeatedly across the view-screen.

"Cannons," shouted Hoepe, pointing to him.

Halud's fist clenched on the trigger, feeling the powerful weapons shake the ship. He heard Kieran swear.

Hoepe rushed over pushed him away from the console. "You hit us," he growled.

"Just grazed the side," reported Kieran, but his face was pale and he pressed his lips into a thin line. "No significant damage."

"You could have blown a hole in the hull!"

One of Hoepe's men took over the Tactical console as Halud stepped back. Had he actually hit them, his own ship?

The ship rocked again, the lights flashing as Halud stumbled to the floor.

"That was a direct hit, knocked out most of our shielding," yelled Kieran.

"They're hitting us hard," Hoepe said. "Any word from the ground?"

"No, not yet," said Kieran.

Halud felt all his blood drain into his toes, leaving a solid rock in the pit of his stomach.

"Can you get the shield's back up, Kieran?"

"Working on it."

"We'll have to jump away."

"No!" Halud's stomach turned. "We can't strand them here."

Hoepe grimaced. "We can't hold up in this firefight much longer."

"He's right," said Kieran. "If that Kepheus Drive explodes, we won't be able to jump back. We'd leave the shuttle defenceless."

Five fingers tapped Hoepe's chest, and he closed his eyes. "Rye, keep us close to the planet. Between them and the warship. I want to be ready as soon as they come back. We might have to go, but we'll wait as long as we can." He tapped his chest repeatedly, and Halud, too, felt the need to pray.

The lights flickered continuously, the floor unsteady, and Halud sat against the wall. A violent shake knocked him sprawling to the side.

"Shit, that last one surged," shouted Kieran.

Hoepe spun. "Damage?"

"The shields overloaded and spiked the power. I'm checking the systems now." Sweat glistened on the engineer's forehead as he typed rapidly into the console. "Shields are still operational at twenty-two percent."

Halud blinked rapidly, suddenly dizzy. The ship rocked again. A dark pit ate away his insides.

"We can't take much more of this," said Hoepe. "We have to go. Draw them away. We'll come back."

Kieran shook his head. "The FTL got hit with the surge. It's offline."

Hoepe paused, suddenly still amid the chaos. "Without that FTL, we're dead."

Another jolt sent Kieran stumbling. "I'm on my way already."

SIXTEEN

SARRIN RAN DOWN THE STAIRS as the sedative was still being sucked from the room.

There were only three Augments still standing, but they each gasped hungrily.

"Twenty-seven, is that you? All grown up?" The Augment smiled when he saw her. "I should have known it would be you to come save us."

She hated the nick-name. "Sarrin," she corrected him.

"Thomas," he said.

She nodded. He had been with them in the war for the catastrophe in the North. "I know."

"The bars are electrified."

She nodded — she knew that too, but hadn't been able to find the controls in the console in the guard station.

"The generator is over there. And the locking mechanisms are biometric — combination scan of retina, palm, and pulse."

She studied the small box, identical boxes on each of the cells. Conduits running between them and overhead.

Grant ran up. "No more guards," he smiled.

Sarrin stared at the puzzle in front of her. "Rigged with explosives," she said quietly.

Grant looked at it. "We'll just pull off the connecting wires, rewire the thing."

"No." She held up a hand to stop his reaching arm. "Find the generator to turn off the electric current."

Thomas pointed. "It's over there, somewhere."

Grant nodded and went to search.

"Annika tried to rewire it," said Thomas. "She and four others ended up dead."

The panel was rigged, judging by the shape and thickness. Taking it off could trigger the explosive, could self-destruct the whole cell block if she was reading the wires right.

She heard the electric buzz relax. Grant sprinted back to them.

"Who can unlock the scanner?" she asked.

"I don't know their names. A handful of researchers."

"Maybe the guards out front," Grant muttered.

"No." Thomas shook his head.

"Then we'll find the researchers."

She bit her lip and looked at Thomas. And at the tens of other Augments, some of them starting to stir. It would take hours to locate the researchers, if they were here at all. They would have to be captured and brought back alive without raising alarm.

Augments all around them were starting to wake, to raise their heads up and stagger to the edge of their cells. Still no alarm, no warning klaxon. Something didn't feel right and she found her legs shaking, preparing to flee.

"Don't lose yourself." An image of Kieran's easy smile broke into her thoughts. He had a way of seeing things differently. He

could probably engineer a solution around the whole thing and not even worry about the explosive hand scanner.

"What do we do?" Grant said, shaking the bars with his fists.

"We should have brought Kieran." she said, but it would do no good to get angry with Grant now. There had to be a solution to get them all out alive.

Around the whole thing.

Of course.

She pulled her remaining laz-pistol from its holster. The idea unfolded clearly in her head, wrapping her in a steady rush. She popped the side panel off and stripped the connections — her hands barely keeping up with her mind.

"What are you doing, Sar?"

She needed something to reorient the laz-stream, focus its energy nearer to the outlet. Pulling at her pockets, she emptied the contents on the ground.

"Sarrin?"

Two knives, spanner set, power cell. How could she collect all this and still not have anything useful? Auto-sealing gasket, spice packet, length of string. Her hands landed on a riveting gun, and she smiled.

Pulling it apart, she wedged the components into the laz-pistol. Rapidly she pressed the connections into place and lifted the modified pistol to the cage. She squeezed the trigger and the bar snapped with a loud pop. A second pop shot it across the cell. And then the next bar and the next until she had cut a hole big enough for Thomas to climb through.

Shaking, he broke into a grin. "I thought I was going to die in that cell."

She handed the bar cutter to Grant. They still had to release the others, the long line of cages stretching out of sight. Time

ticked by relentlessly in her head. A deep sense of foreboding
tightened around her like smog. The little anteroom shone like a
bright beacon in the dark dungeon, and she moved towards it,
towards escape.

* * *

Rayne blinked, lids heavy with unnatural sleep. She coughed
twice, something pressing sharply into her back. Her
surroundings came into the focus, all the beams and structural
supports crisscrossing in the dark. Around her, more sleeping
bodies started to stir. She recognized Hoepe's men. They were in
the ceiling. Above an anteroom. In a UEC facility. On Junk.

She sat up. Where were Sarrin and Grant?

Grant had insisted she come along. For no reason other than
her combat skills were adequate, the best they had to offer
anyway. She hadn't argued. The Path of the Gods was true, and
opportunities always presented themselves. It was her duty to
warn the UECs before it was too late.

Sluggishly, she rolled herself to her knees, and then onto her
feet. The space in the ceiling was low, but enough for her to run
if she crouched.

With a final glance, she wondered if she should bring the men
with her. They were just as caught up in all of this as she was.
But they were still asleep. She would come back for them.

Light shone up from the anteroom, quickly dimming as she
moved farther away. The facility didn't follow a standard
schematic, certainly not with its three subterranean floors, but she
had spent their mission briefings memorizing its layout.

She pulled up a panel and dropped down into what should
have been a research laboratory. The smell of combat armour
wafted heavy into her senses, and the sounds of shuffling boots
and settling laz-guns. A platoon of soldiers spread out in front of

her.

A dozen rifle barrels aimed at her.

* * *

Sarrin climbed in to the ceiling where Grant had tucked the others to keep them safe. Sutherland sat up, resting against a support. Two others laid beside him. "Where's Rayne?"

Sutherland shrugged sleepily. "She muttered something about the Gods and stumbled away."

The worry at the back of Sarrin's mind slammed into her full force. She sprinted through the narrow space, following the commander instinctively. It wasn't far. A gleaming square of light shone where the panel had been removed.

Voices drifted from below:

"What a surprise." A familiar, icy voice shot shivers down her spine.

"My name is Commander Ray—."

Sarrin leapt, time moving slowly.

She pushed Rayne to the ground, landing on her. She gritted her teeth as Rayne's energy passed into her like an electric shock, and a laz-bolt seared across her back.

Dr. Guitteriez stared, his wicked scar curling up as he grinned.

She pulled Rayne up by the back of her coveralls, straining to push her up through the open panel in one fluid movement. Laz-beams blurred across the room towards them, grazing Sarrin's arm, leg, and cheek as she launched herself through the hole after Rayne.

She hit Rayne, slapping her across the arm, not as hard as she could but hard enough.

The other woman squeaked.

"Stop being so stupid," Sarrin growled. The darkness crept

across her vision, close to taking over, and she stumbled.

"I… I just. I don't understand what's happening."

Nearly blind, Sarrin staggered away. "Guitteriez is here." She clutched the bulkhead, looking for something to ground herself. She tapped at her chest repeatedly. "Sarrin DeGazo. Female. 005478F."

Kieran's green eyes peered at her through the darkness. *Don't lose yourself.*

The soldiers came, their hands grasping the edge around the open panel.

Rayne stood and reached a hand towards her. But Sarrin could not see the commander or anything else in the ceiling space. Her vision, her fear, latched onto Guitteriez, seeing him even though he stood, watching the soldiers, a floor below. His maniacial grin spread.

Rayne reached her. "Sarrin?"

"…005478F. Sarrin DeGazo. Female. 005478F…." Her vision went completely black.

*   *   *

Halud stumbled to the shuttle hangar. Sarrin and the others still hadn't returned from the surface. And the ship wouldn't last much longer. He had to buy them time, if he could. The whole mess was his fault.

"What're you doing, Poet?"

Surprised, Halud turned. Gal sat on the bench behind him, nursing his flask.

He had done his best to keep her safe, to rescue her and protect her. But nothing worked the way it was supposed to. How had he been so wrong? She was worse off than when he found her.

Gal cleared his throat. "I said, what are you doing?"

He took a deep breath. He absolutely could not afford to let anger rattle him, not with the desperate plan he had concocted.

"Poet?"

"I'm no good at this fighting and attacking and plotting," he sighed. "Politics is my game. Give me a room full of Hap Lansfords and I can dance my way out of any trap."

"Except this one."

"I'm no good to Sarrin here. I don't belong. There are plenty of people here who can keep her safe. People she likes more and trusts more than me." He didn't owe Gal an explanation, but he still wanted to give him one. Let him know how badly he'd cracked it. "You know she hasn't said a word to me. I thought maybe she couldn't, but she talks to Kieran all the time."

Gal's lips quirked into a sort of smile. "Oaf," he muttered.

Teeth clenched together, Halud growled, "He's not the only one."

The flask tipped up, Gal's eyes glinting with acknowledgement.

"Sarrin doesn't need me here."

"She's your sister."

"I can do more for her over there."

Gal sighed. He gave a half laugh, lifting his flask as though he was going to toast the Poet. Instead, he quoted the rebel, tongue in cheek: "Embrace your fears, and you will become brave."

Halud opened the door to shuttle bay. "You know, I really thought you could help me."

"Why would you ever think that?" Gal winced. "Everyone I've ever helped is dead. Or will be." He hung over himself, sloppy and drunk.

"What happened to 'never give up the fight,' Galiant? You wrote that, didn't you?"

He stared at the floor. "You wrote it too."

"You wrote it first."

"John P is dead, Halud."

"Fine." He opened the shuttle, climbing through the door.

Gal called after him, "There's a firefight out there."

"I have to try." The shuttle powered up around him. He could be brave, he had to, for her.

"It's suicide," Gal said plainly.

From the pilot's chair, he could see Gal take another sorry drink. He pulled up the autopilot, and the shuttle took over. The airlock sealed and vented atmosphere, the shuttle launching into space.

Laz-beams seared around him. Somehow, the little shuttle continued on its course, adjusting side-to-side, casually dodging the weapons fire that blazed through the dark space.

He squeezed his eyes shut, touching his five fingers to his chest and then his forehead. "Faith, guide me."

When he opened them again, the shuttle hovered in front of the big bay doors of the warship. The doors opened, and the shuttle landed on the deck. Halud blinked. He had made it.

On the other side of the viewport stood a squadron of soldiers. He swallowed the lump in his throat. "Fortitude, don't leave me now."

* * *

The darkness rolled over Sarrin in waves, deadly directions flooding her mind. Save yourself, it said, there's too much danger. Forget about anything else and save yourself.

She groped in the dark, hands moving one steel beam to the next as she navigated through the ceiling.

"Sarrin, come on." Rayne's shrill voice nearly pushed her beyond panic.

The guards hadn't pursued through the open panel. With Rayne's urging, they made it back to the others, Sutherland and the others already stirring. Augments paced uneasily in the anteroom below, the last running in as they were freed. Three lay dead in their cells, their cold death burning in her mind and making her hands shake.

"We have to get out of here," Rayne said.

The darkness stabbed into her mind, and she gasped. *Don't lose yourself.*

Grant leapt into the ceiling, pushing past her through the tight space. "This way. Follow me." He grinned. "See, nothing to it."

She didn't have the breath to tell him about Guitteriez or the platoon of class A combat soldiers.

They moved, all thirty-five of them, inching through the ceiling toward the hangar.

Without warning, the Augments ahead started to wince and groan. Some of them stumbled. It passed through their line in a wave.

Sarrin lit on fire. Her hands screamed. In her mind, electric blue flame licked up and down her body. When it cleared, she was on the floor, uninjured, unburnt.

Rayne stared at her, eyes wild.

"What was that?" Grant asked.

One of the others answered, "Bio-energetic pulse. They've been testing them recently. Nothing serious."

Sarrin struggled to get her body moving. The pounding in her head crescendoed, battering her insides. She fell, stifling a scream.

Beside her, Thomas glanced down. "Twenty-seven?"

Without warning, laz-bolts tore up the ceiling beneath their feet. Grant cut left, everyone sprinting behind him. Again, laz-bolts erupted. Funnelling them. Herding them.

Guitteriez.

Sarrin ran as flashes pinged off the metal support structure. The dark crawlspace transformed into a chaotic show of lasers and wide, panicking eyes. Deadly fire surrounded them on all sides. Trapped. A flash of memory played in her mind, unbidden: *Kids, dirty and bloody from the fight, screaming and running in the training arena. More kids hammering them with 50V laz-rifles. With a shout, a young boy fell as he ran, trampled by those behind him.*

Gasping, Sarrin threw herself out of the way of an errant bolt. Her mind turned all the moving objects into targets — laz-fire and Augments alike.

Don't lose yourself. She nodded, agreeing with the ghost of Kieran, making his voice louder than the monster's.

A laz-saw cut through the ceiling. Pieces fell away, exposing them. Someone stepped back, surprised, and fell through the hole. The girl clutched at the scaffold, clinging for only an instant until laz-fire from below tore across her. The crawlspace filled with the putrid stench of burning flesh and her short lived scream.

Again, fire raced through Sarrin's veins, suddenly adding pulsating blue and red to the rolling blackness. Despair washed over her — they would never get out alive. She dropped to her knees, and though the torn-apart ceiling she caught sight of the soldiers below and a pulsing blue orb.

Thomas took a laz-rifle from one of Hoepe's men, lifting it to his shoulder and shooting. Two others joined him, spraying laz-fire through the hole. The bolts hit their targets, only the guards didn't fall. Laz-beams landed on their chests, and they barely flinched. The crawlspace came alive with shooting light once more as the guards returned fire.

Grant fashioned a pulse bomb out of one of the rifles and threw it down. Heat from the explosion melted the edges of the steel-plastique, but the guards were unrelenting. "Limpets," he said. The same flesh-material that made up Grant's suit — they had turned it into armour for their soldiers.

"We'll have to fight our way out," Grant shouted. "Their armour is impervious to energy weapons, but it's not immune." She remembered the piece of suit she ripped apart with her hands, shuddering. They would have to do the same. "How many, Sarrin?"

She shook her head. They could see ten through the hole, but there were more. So many more. Her mind was too jumbled to count them all, it was all she could do to hold onto herself.

Grant crouched by the edge, others assembling behind him with the few rifles they had. He signalled, and they jumped as one. Laz-fire shot at him from behind, even as he spun and took out the two nearest guards. Without warning, he collapsed, the second skin exploding from his back.

He laid still, fingers twitching. The other three Augments fell to the ground.

Sarrin took a ragged breath. If Grant lost himself to their mind control….

He turned his head toward her, his one eye visible through the jagged tear in the mottled skin. The look in his eyes was foreign: fear, raw and unfettered. He winked at her in code, a number: one-hundred-fifty-six.

Another group prepared, launching through the ceiling unarmed. Someone landed a shattering hook, but the guard only staggered back before lifting his laz-rifle and shooting her point blank in the chest. The Augment fell and did not move again.

"Gods," muttered a girl still in the tiny island of ceiling beside Sarrin.

"We have to run, all together," Thomas said in a panic.

They were trapped, beyond a doubt, no weapons besides themselves. No other option. They had strength in numbers, some of them would die, but some would pass.

Only once before had they found themselves facing such desperate odds — when reprogrammed Augments had been sent to seek and destroy their hideouts during the war. Sarrin clung to the steel truss, bending it with her grip. *Don't lose yourself.*

Thomas leapt through the laz-fire, the others following closely.

She pressed her head into the truss, desperate for something solid as the trance crowded in.

Augments fell. Many kept running. Thomas stooped to pick up Grant and pushed him ahead.

A guard shouted, and the UEC laz-fire stopped. She knew it would.

She crouched alone in the ceiling. In a second, Grant turned, his eye meeting hers. She shook her head slowly, and his one visible eye widened slightly as he understood her meaning.

The guards turned their laz-fire upwards, circling, slowly chipping away at what remained of the platform.

She closed her eyes, pulling up the image of Kieran and Halud. There would be no saving her, but, the others, if they were smart, would run. A strange calm came over her. No more fighting. The trance dissipated and her body felt light.

It was always inevitable, wasn't it, in the end?

She held the truss, even as the ceiling under her fell away. Even as laz-fire grazed her side. It didn't matter now, the black hole that had always been sucking her in pulled inescapably, a finish line, the event horizon. Maybe she could have a night's rest without dreams.

She waited for the final laz-bolt. It would be a close shot aimed mid-back, between the eighth and ninth rips, slightly to the left. A killing blow.

She had strangled Kieran, shot Grant. She was a monster, she couldn't help it, it was in her DNA. Such aberrations deserved to be omega. A smile cracked across her face, imaging Kieran there to crack some absurd joke. Knowing peace would come.

Her muscles faltered, her hand slipping from her hold. She closed her eyes as she fell. She landed with a hard thud. Pain ripped through her body. Five of the glowing blue orbs surrounded her, their power thrumming loudly in her ears. A hundred-odd laz-rifles pointed down.

She laid on the ground, too tired to fight back.

A man limped toward her, his silver cane clunking on the ground, *step-step-clack*, hideous scar running from above his right eye all the way to his jawline.

Panic tore through her. She yelled at her body to get up, to flee, but it couldn't. Even the monster was quiet. She heard herself scream.

He signalled with his hand, and the energy field intensified, filling her with despair. Guitteriez's sadistic grin filled her vision as the flames consumed her.

SEVENTEEN

SPARKS EXPLODED ACROSS THE ENGINE room, and Kieran swore under his breath. The Kepheus Drive swung dangerously back and forth where part of its makeshift supports had given way. Lifting his arm up to protect his face, he ran in and shook the drive — no rattle. Only disconnected then, not cracked. Thank God.

The ship rocked, nearly knocking his feet out from under him as he secured the drive and re-attached the conduits. His fingers punched the console so hard they hurt.

The FTL failed to power up. He tried again, by-passing safety checks. Nothing.

He crawled inside the engine, wishing for Sarrin — she at least fit inside the thing. He lifted a panel, smoke billowing around him. "Jesus," he swore. Heaving himself back out, he checked the conduit under the floor. The relays were on fire, smoking from the inside.

Bad. Very, very bad.

Reaching for the nearest console, he called the bridge. "The relays are fried," he said, trying to keep his voice steady. Even his wildcard of a father wouldn't have had a solution for this.

On the other end of the comm call, Hoepe hesitated. *"What does that mean?"*

"It means they can't carry the energy from the engine to the graviton emitters. No FTL."

"So, you're saying?"

"I have replacements. Some anyway. But it will take me a few hours."

"We can't jump out of here." Silence hung between them. *"Get started, Kieran."*

Short of a better idea, he ran to the storage room. They kept two replacement relays, even though the ship needed eight. Huge long, heavy things. The lines weaved through the ship, almost impossible to damage, but the surge coming through the modified shields had hit them in just the wrong way.

He squeezed his eyes shut, trying to remember to breathe. He'd never written that letter home. The ship jerked out from under him again.

Kieran dripped with sweat, chest straining as he heaved the conduit across the deck. He had to work faster.

"Kieran!" Hoepe called him again. *"We can see the shuttles."*

"What?" He dropped the conduit and glanced up at the console. The shuttles carrying the Augments from Junk — carrying Sarrin — were docking. They were still alive. He called out, "I need Sarrin's help right away, and anyone else."

"I'll send her," replied Hoepe.

Pulling the conduit into the engine room, he lifted up the floor panels and dropped down on top of the burnt relays. He grunted, detaching the first conduit from the engine. He strained with the second, the valve sealed from years of FTL jumps.

As he strained, a stream of people — Augments presumably

— came into Engineering. They automatically moved to display consoles lining the main engineering bay, talking quickly and quietly to each other.

"Hey," he called out. A burst of sparks from the engine punctuated his shout, making him duck.

Several of the men and women ran into the engine room, stopping at the doorway. Their eyes went wide at the sight of so much smoke.

"I need help replacing these relays," he said, pointing at the stuck valve in front of him and the coiled conduit on the floor. Twelve sets of bright blue eyes stared at him, but none that he knew. "Where's Sarrin?"

They looked between each other, hesitant. Grant appeared in the doorway, his face haunted.

A terrible feeling washed over Kieran. "Where's Sarrin?"

Grant turned away without answering, the back of his shirt torn and bloody.

Blindly, Kieran jumped up. His body shook as he pushed through the crowd. "Sarrin? Sarrin?" he called, surging forward.

Grant put a hand on his arm, stopping him. "She fell."

Kieran spun around and shoved him. Hard. "Did you kill her?" He felt sick, his thoughts firing in so many different directions he felt numb.

"No — no, she fell." Grant swallowed. "She was captured."

She fell. She was captured. The words echoed, the only thoughts he could discern in the jumble.

"How?" Sarrin who could run a kilometre in three minutes and count her enemies through a solid wall. His hands clenched at his sides. It didn't make sense.

"It was a trap. I didn't realize it. One of the UECs filthy, elaborate traps. They were waiting for us."

He stared, pulse pounding in his ears, trying to make sense of it. Something inside of him snapped. He punched Grant as hard as he could. "You said it would be simple!"

Grant put his hands up. "I didn't know."

"She didn't want to go, but you made her." He threw another blind punch. Augments crowded around, but Kieran no longer cared what he said or kind of a scene he made. "You and your stupid plan. You didn't listen. None of us did."

"There are always casualties in battle."

Kieran pulled back, blinking. "Is she —?" Somehow, he couldn't picture her dead.

Grant looked away.

"You just left her there." Kieran's vision went white with rage. Grant could kill him with one blow, but it didn't even matter. All sense had flown out the viewport. All worry of keeping a low profile, of not interfering, went with it.

"She'll be okay," Grant said.

"They're gonna kill her," he screamed. "She said so herself, it's her they want. They want to destroy her." He lunged forward, but three sets of hands clamped onto his back, holding him.

Grant took a step forward. "Don't make the mistake of thinking you're the only one who cared. If I thought I could have saved her, I would have. Now, I have to live watching her fall over and over and over."

Kieran staggered back, cold regret suddenly pulling all the air from his lungs. "I shouldn't have gotten so upset." But it was his fault too. He could have told Grant or Hoepe what he had seen in the cargo bay. He could have pushed harder when he saw the worry plain on her face. But he'd let her go. He'd wanted the Augments on board and wanted to believe she could get them there, so when she stepped onto that shuttle, blue eyes pleading with him, he'd done nothing.

And now she was gone.

He drew in a deep breath, forcing his emotions down. He couldn't afford to let this become personal, not now. *Don't interfere. Observation only.*

He missed home so badly. He wanted to see his mom and brother again, to run through the engine banks with his dad. But he was here too, part of the crew, whether he'd planned to be or not. Somehow, he had let it happen.

The ship rocked violently, sending them all staggering.

"That burned into Deck 3," someone cried, reading off a console.

"*Kieran,*" called Hoepe over the comm, "*we can't survive another direct hit like that.*"

Kieran gave Grant a warning look. "We'll figure this out later."

* * *

The ship rocked violently as Rayne climbed the last step to the bridge. She gripped the doorframe to keep from tumbling over on weak legs. She had watched Sarrin fall. Seen her disappear into the grip of over a hundred heavily armed UEC soldiers. And she had turned her back and run.

A dark-haired girl pushed past her and into the pilots seat. She took the steering sphere in her hands and the ship levelled out. There were Augments all around, manning multiple consoles. They talked in urgent voices, trying to survive the warship attack the same as anyone.

"Shields are down," reported a short, muscular man at Tactical.

Rayne leapt up beside him, elbowing him out of the way so

she could spread her hands over the console. This was her ship, after all; no one knew its systems better than she did. She coaxed a little more out of the shields. "Shields back to twenty-percent."

The pilot spun the sphere casually, a laz-cannon burst flying harmlessly past them.

Hoepe hit the comm. "Kieran, where's that FTL?"

Kieran's reply sounded strained, far away. "*Sarrin is still down there.*"

Rayne shut her eyes. She had left Sarrin helpless, moments after the girl had lifted her from certain death. Death. At the hands of the UECs.

"What?" Hoepe stared at the console.

Grant shouted, "*It was a trap, Hoepe.*"

"Keep working on the FTL."

"*We can't leave her here.*"

"We have to lose this warship."

"*I'm worried if we jump, we might not make it back.*"

"Kieran, the FTL."

"*Even if we jump, there's no predictin' how many jumps the Kepheus has left in 'er. Or what the warship will do when we leave.*"

"We're going to be blown apart. Then we won't be able to help anybody."

"*I won't leave her.*" Kieran's quiet voice hung in the room.

Hoepe scrubbed a hand over his face. "Lieutenant," he chided.

"We can't leave her there," said Rayne. Even if she was an Augment, even if it went against the Gods. "We have to go back."

Hoepe turned to her, both eyebrows drawn with a deep furrow etched between them.

"She went down and got all your friends," Rayne explained.

"You have to get her out too."

His head tilted in a nearly imperceptible nod. But he closed his eyes and shook his head. "It's too dangerous. We have to escape before the warship destroys us."

Rayne slammed her open palms on the console, voice raising an octave. "Too dangerous?"

He frowned again. "Do you want to go back out there in a shuttle? Go back to the base and find her?"

"Yes, I do," shouted Rayne. She looked at the men and women around her. "Sarrin is our friend. She saved our lives. I would have died if it weren't for her. You can't think we're going to just leave her there."

Hoepe's head tilted again, angling to the side, and his eyes narrow, this time in confusion.

"That place was no work of the Gods," she said, more to herself than to him. She suppressed a shudder thinking of her brief glimpse at rows and rows of cells, the armed platoon in what should have been a research lab, at the unrelenting attack as they all cowered in the ceiling. She saw the injuries and the deep seated horror painted on the faces around her. "I don't know who those people are, but Sarrin is not safe there."

"She's right," said an Augment to her left. "We can't leave Twenty-seven. You saw how she was affected by their new weapon." Others nodded.

"New weapon?" Hoepe's eyebrows shot up.

"A bioenergetic pulse," said the Augment. "She just crumpled."

Hoepe rubbed a hand across his temples.

"That was Twenty-seven?" said another Augment. A murmur passed through the crowd. "After everything she's done for us, we have to help her."

Hoepe shook his head. "She's probably already dead. And we will be soon." As though to accentuate his point, the ship shook with another blow from the warship's laz-cannons.

Rayne gripped the edge of the console. "I refuse to believe that."

Pointing his arm at the viewscreen where supercharged laser beams criss-crossed the darkness, Hoepe growled, "We can't fight our way out."

"We don't have to," said Rayne. "Those are UEC ships, they serve the Gods."

All eyes on the bridge turned to her.

"They're trying to kill us," said Hoepe.

"They're following orders."

"Rayne," — he rubbed his temples again — "that's no righteous UEC ship. They're hunting us. They know what's going on in that facility and they're a part of it."

She shook her head. "You don't know that."

"They're all the same," said Hoepe, "filthy, rotten, soulless."

Rayne stuck out her lower jaw, working it back and forth. Somebody had to follow the Path and do the right thing. She pushed in the command codes before Hoepe could take the two long strides to her station. "Warship Comrade, this is UECAS Ishash'tor," she sent her hail. "Please acknowledge. We are not your enemy."

The bridge went silent, the viewscreen dark. "They've stopped firing," breathed an Augment.

Rayne pressed the controls again. They may have stopped firing, but they hadn't responded. She needed to tell them about Sarrin. "Please, acknowledge. Comrade, this is Ishash'tor. We request assistance with a rescue operation."

More silence. "Comrade. This is Commander Rayne Nairu

of UECAS Ishash'tor, daughter of Oleander Nairu, First General to the Speakers of the Gods. You are in violation. Please acknowledge. Acknowledge." Why weren't they responding? She clenched her hands to stop them from shaking.

The Augment beside her tapped in a series of commands, peering at the console. "It looks like they're standing down."

Rayne let out a sigh. "See, we're not all bad." She smiled at the Augment beside her.

Hoepe raised a single eyebrow, a twitch of a smile turning up on his lips. "I can't believe it."

Rayne shrugged, suppressing her grin. Now they could go home. And better yet, they could reveal the truth about the Augments: they were alive and they weren't ruthless killing machines. They were people following the Path of the Gods just like everyone else.

The Tactical console beeped in alarm. She looked down at the screen as two rocket torpedoes launched from the warship.

"Evasive!' screamed Hoepe.

Rayne clung to the console as the ship lurched. Why was the warship firing? Why hadn't they acknowledged her hails? Maybe Hoepe was right. They didn't want to know the truth. They had already chosen their side.

"Rayne!" Hoepe turned around.

She roared, her fingers flying across the controls. The Pilot took them on a dizzying series of rolls, as laz-fire arced across the space between the ships. Rayne moved with the shifts, her hands and eyes fixed to her console. She was a tactician and a cracked good one at that; there was no way she was going to let the ship, her ship, be destroyed.

Despite it all, the warship landed another hit. The lighting flickered and her console blinked out. The Augment beside her swore. A second later, the console blinked back on. "Shields at five-percent."

"Kieran," shouted Hoepe, "What about those shields?"

A minute later, the engineer's frantic voice responded: "*Their cannons are too powerful, the energy is getting caught up. It's frying the shield generators themselves. I don't know what we're gonna do. If it overloads....*"

"If it overloads, it will be just like The North," said the man beside her.

"The shield will implode. We'll be destroyed, just like Earth," finished one of the other Augments.

Rayne gasped. If the Augment designed shields overloaded, the energy would tear the ship apart. If the shield integrity went down to 0%, they were all going to die.

"*I have an idea,*" said the engineer. "*Yer not gonna like it.*"

"Tell me," said Hoepe.

"*We can wire that energy into the weapons array — supercharge the laz-cannons.*"

"Is that possible?"

"*Might be,*" said Kieran. "*I can't fix the FTL in time. I don't see any other options.*"

"Do you think it will work?"

He paused. "*One of two things is gonna happen: we're gonna fry all the circuits, and I mean all of 'em. Or we're gonna whoop this puppy's butt.*"

Hoepe furrowed his eyebrows together. "Pardon?"

Kieran coughed, "*Er, destroy that UEC ship.*"

"Do it." Hoepe turned to Rayne, his voice quiet. "Remind me to do a brain scan of that boy if we ever get the chance."

If she ever got the chance, Rayne would recommend him for every type of commendation she could.

She looked down at her console again. It was impossible to keep the panic out of her voice. "Shields at three percent."

Hoepe nodded. "Keep firing. Hold them off long enough for Kieran to make his modifications."

She fired again and again, the Pilot twisting the ship mercilessly, but it was no use. The Comrade was the pinnacle of Army ship design, the flagship of strength. Twelve 3,000mV Class 8 laz-cannons, polarized hull plating that reflected light weapons, a spread of over a hundred rocket torpedoes. What chance did they have? More startling, what reason could the Central Army have ever had to build such a warship?

*　*　*

Kieran stripped the wires that controlled the shield generator, squinting against the bright sparks that flew into his face. The idea was too crazy. But his dad had always said, 'if it's crazy enough, it just might work.'

"You need to have a ground," one of the Augments reminded him, hovering over his shoulder.

"Yeah, I know," he shrugged, "but there ain't no ground here big enough for this."

Another of the Augments passed him the end of the cable that ran into the laz-cannons. "Who are you?" questioned a gravelly voice.

He didn't bother to answer, as he spliced the thick cable into the wires and three hands reached in to solder it together. He wrapped the splice in insulating foam, calling out a set of instructions before he'd even finished.

"Got it, redirecting power," replied one of the Augment's working at the main console.

Kieran glanced at the central display, a new red light on the 3D diagram of the ship catching his attention. "Thrusters are running hot. I need a team on the fore-starboard thruster coolant," he shouted.

Someone replied, "On it!"

"Sir." An Augment ran up, waving a tablet. "I can boost the steering controls, we've checked the calculations twice."

"In real-time?" he asked.

"I'd need the system offline for a few minutes."

"Then no go. No steering system leaves us sitting ducks."

"Sitting what?"

"Maybe once we get out of this mess, yeah?" he clapped her on the shoulder.

One of the ion scrubbers clogged. He grabbed the woman and two others, dragging them to the engine. "Do you know how to bypass this, pull the scrubber, clean it out, and recharge it?"

They nodded.

"Good. As fast as you can. Then see if any of the others need to be done." At least he had a crew again even if they were battered and bruised. And a few of them knew about engines. He stopped himself from thinking about Sarrin.

The overhead comm stopped him in him tracks: "*Kieran,*" said Rayne, "*I've lost three laz-cannons.*"

What else could go wrong? He mopped the sweat from his short hair, wiped his hand on his coveralls. He needed to start his recording device.

"On it!" he replied, and started tapping into the diagnostics. The results flashed on the screen. Damn. Kieran hit the comm: "Looks like the crystals are fried. Too much energy passing through them. Keep firin' 'em, though, to dissipate the energy from the shields. Maybe we can make the others last a little longer."

Kieran's eyes drifted to his office, where the recording chip sat in his desk drawer. There were no immediate crises, so he took the chance. It might be a little selfish, but he needed to capture this to report home — if they made it out alive, which was not at all guaranteed.

At least if they didn't, maybe someone would find the recording and piece together what happened, for better or for worse.

"*I've lost another one, Kieran,*" Rayne shrieked over the comm.

Jesus, that was four. Out of five.

"We need options," said one of the Augments.

He huffed, "I'm fresh out. The FTL is fried. The shields are dangerously close to catastrophic failure. We're down to one laz-cannon. At this rate, our only option is going to be destroy the ship before someone else does…," he joked darkly. But the thought started an idea. "Wait. That's it!"

A man nearby looked up. "What?"

"Crash the ship," he said.

Movement in the engine room stopped.

He held his hands out, asking for the chance to explain. "They're hunting us, they want us dead, right? Make it look like we've been destroyed and their mission will be complete."

The faces around him contorted into a weird sort of dismay followed by realization.

"Engineer," someone called him from a console on the wall. Kieran did a double take: Hoepe — but he couldn't be on the bridge and in engineering. The doctor zoomed out and pointed to one of the moons. "This body has a high concentration of magnetic ore — the distortion field will mask our bio-signs and heat signatures."

"Perfect." Kieran smiled. Pressing the comm control, he signalled directly to the Pilot's console. "I need us to land on body alpha-8. Give me ten minutes. Make it dramatic."

"Acknowledged," came the reply.

Hoepe nodded. "The pilot's name is Isuma, she's capable."

Kieran's mind ran through the possibilities. "Thanks, Hoepe." He clapped him on the arm as he rushed away.

Hoepe gave him a funny look. "Yes, I hope it works too."

Kieran dashed across the bay. Part of always looking forward to recording some kind of historic event or disaster was always being prepared. He was almost out of tricks, but he had been stockpiling potentially useful equipment since he'd arrived. "Where's Grant?" he asked no one in particular.

A girl paused, silently pointing to the door at the back of the engineering bay that led to the storage lockers. Hurriedly, Kieran pushed through the door.

Grant sat with his back against the wall, his head in his hands. His limpet suit covered his body.

Kieran rushed over. "You're a pyrotechnic expert, right? I need your help."

Grant turned his head slowly — God, the piece hadn't grown back where Sarrin ripped it apart, exposing one regret-filled eye. "No."

"What?" Kieran gritted his jaw.

"I can't. I tried. Look what happened."

"Get up." Kieran grabbed his rubbery arm, heaving him to his feet. "We don't have time for this. Stuff happens, things don't go according to plan — happens to me all the time. Pick yourself up and help me."

Grant towered over him, his one visible eye narrowed.

"I don't know what happened down there. I'm sorry for what I said. But right now, there's a very good chance that what happened to Sarrin is going to happen to the rest of us. I have an idea, but it's only going to work if you rig me a great big bomb."

* * *

"Take us into the debris cloud," Hoepe ordered. The pilot didn't hesitate, already zipping around the moons, grinning wildly. Hoepe worried he might be the only sane one left.

The pilot drove the ship towards the ring of space junk. Pieces of scrap floated across the view screen. Among them were huge, torn chunks of starship with multiple decks exposed along jagged edges, interspersed with free-floating I-beams or sheets of hull. The freightship would end up looking the same if they hit any of it. Still she pushed in.

The warship stopped at the edge of the debris field, firing a volley of torpedoes.

This far into the cloud, the torpedoes couldn't weave through all the debris. Indirect implosions sent a wave of free floating pieces flying wildly in their direction.

The pilot rolled the ship's steering sphere violently. "Impact," she shouted. A vicious shudder ran through the ship.

"We lost part of the aft-port wing," Rayne reported.

"Switching to manual," shouted the Pilot. "Aft-port thrusters went with the wing, and the computer algorithms can't compensate."

Another Augment ran to the helm and started analyzing the debris field on the positional display.

Their weakened shields flashed constantly as they deflected micro-debris.

Hoepe's mental timer reached ten minutes, and he hit the comm. "Ten minutes are up, Kieran. What's your plan?"

"*Nearly in position,*" his panted. "*What are you doing on the bridge?*"

"Trying not to get torn apart."

"*It's just…. I swore you were here a second ago. Or someone who looks a heck of a lot like you.*"

The pilot grunted, "We have to go soon, or that crash is going to be more real than we want."

"*We're ready,*" shouted Kieran. "*Keep the comm open.*"

She took the ship into a steep dive, conferring with her co-pilot. The ship shook and rolled, klaxons screaming. The co-pilot zoomed in on the tactical display, studying the moon. They exchanged a few terse words and a nod.

The moon spun on the view screen, growing larger at an alarming pace.

"Crash in minus one minute. Brace for impact," yelled the co-pilot.

Debris knocked the dorsal section, sending them spinning stern-over-bow. The force pushed Hoepe into his chair. He would vomit, he thought, if the Gs weren't pushing everything down.

The ship bounced off another clump of metal, throwing the spin sideways.

"Top deck sections 3 and 4 are crushed," called Rayne.

"Fifty seconds," said the co-pilot. The Pilot deftly tapped on the controls, maneuvering slightly, just before they made contact with another piece of space junk. Sparks flew across the viewport as they grazed off an old section of hull, and the Pilot triggered the thrusters hard, pushing them into an eccentric roll.

Horrified, Hoepe realized she was doing it on purpose.

"Forty-five."

They pinged against two more space objects before flinging out of the debris field.

"Engineering," the pilot hit the comm, "vent ion debris." The ship jerked forward, and Hoepe could imagine the glowing trail streaming from the ship's thruster vents.

The klaxons raged. Every computer console flashed with incessant red warnings. Someone in the back retched.

"Thirty seconds," informed the co-pilot.

They tumbled down, aiming straight for the moon. It rotated in and out of view on the viewscreen. Hoepe's body forced him to take a breath.

"Fifteen seconds."

He tapped his five fingers to his chest and closed his eyes.

"Ten. Nine. Eight…."

He forced his eyes open. The view screen still showed a spinning view, rapidly alternating between moon and planet and debris and space. His eyes caught on a huge canyon on the surface of the moon.

The pilot exhaled and hit the thrusters. The force bounced Hoepe out of his chair, sprawling him across the deck. "Impact!" she shouted. Lunar dust billowed around them, the viewscreen turning dusty grey-brown and then black. A terrible grinding noise shook the entire ship.

Warnings on the display showed the cargo bay doors opening, and half the atmosphere venting. Behind them raged an unreasonable pyrotechnical show — some of the plumes were twenty kilometres high.

Hoepe gulped. The engineer was a lunatic.

The ship decelerated, the deck tipping forward as the bow buried itself in the dust.

The co-pilot murmured, staring at her screen: "Ten thousand. Nine thousand."

Hoepe looked up and inhaled sharply. Dust had fallen from the viewscreen and he could see again. On either side of the ship, grey walls towered above them. They were in the canyon, but the walls narrowed, the end of the trench directly ahead, the solid wall rapidly approaching.

The pilot nodded, somehow satisfied. She turned off the

power to the engines and the thrusters and the view screen.

"Four thousand. Three thousand," murmured the co-pilot.

Hoepe's breath rattled as it left his lungs.

"Five hundred. Three hundred. Two hundred."

He shut his eyes tight.

The ship stopped, coming to a grinding, tilting halt. On the viewscreen, an intimate close-up of the canyon wall. The displayed showed they had stopped less than a hundred metres from being crumpled and crushed.

Hoepe grunted, picking himself up from the floor. Kieran did say he wanted dramatic, hopefully that would suffice. Hopefully that would be enough to keep the warship at bay.

EIGHTEEN

HALUD DROPPED TO HIS KNEES on the deck of the shuttle hangar of the UECAS Comrade, his arms raised above his head. A full squadron of heavily armed soldiers surrounded him, rifles trained on his head, but he swallowed his fear and announced himself in a clear, booming voice, "Halud DeGazo. Poet Laureate of the United Earth Central Army. Mouthpiece to the Right and Honourable Hap Lansford. *Tau Sigma Omega thirty-nine Bravo*."

The squadron leader tapped a comm device on his wrist and spoke into it, requesting instructions.

He didn't hear the reply, but the leader made an abrupt hand motion. Two soldiers let their rifles swing to their sides and came towards him. They grabbed him firmly by the shoulders and pulled his hands down, securing them behind his back before lifting him to his feet.

"I wish to speak to the commandant," he said.

The leader gave him a side-long look. "My orders are to remove you to the brig."

"The brig?" Halud held his shoulders square. "Need I repeat my designation?"

"I had no trouble hearing it the first time."

"Then you will bring me to your commandant." He modified his voice, deep, controlling tones rolling from his lips. "This is an urgent matter. I insist."

The man frowned and spoke again into his wrist-comm. At the reply, he nodded. "Bring him to the bridge."

Halud breathed a sigh of relief, even as the two guards shoved him forward. They steered him roughly through the corridors, letting him stumble through the doors that led to the bridge. Pristine white uniforms with white consoles, chairs, and floors startled him, burning his eyes in the harsh light.

The commandant stood at the centre of the deck, hands clasped tightly behind her back. A new commandant, one he had not seen before. Tall, slender, hair tied up in a high tail. Her features were sharp and angular. She turned, eyes scanning him rapidly. "Master Poet," she intoned, voice fully devoid of emotion, "I hear you have been insistent."

His guards stepped back.

The view screen wrapped around the whole bridge instead of a ceiling or walls, making him feel as though they were exposed to space. The fore section caught this attention where the tiny freightship twisted and dove, a show of electric light flashing across the space between them.

"Direct hit, sir," announced the tactical officer. "Minimal damage."

The commandant dipped her head once, her order reverberating darkly in Halud's heart: "Fire at will."

"Leave the ship alone," Halud said, putting as much authority into his voice as he could manage. "The crew are not part of this. I commandeered the ship, it was me and me alone. I am who you want."

A sadistic grin spread across the commandant's face. "You're not what we want."

Halud recoiled. "Spare the crew. They're good officers. They took my orders without hesitation."

"These are my orders."

"I'm giving you new orders."

She snorted.

One of the bridge crew put a hand to his ear. "Ma'am, surface has confirmed they have captured the target. The rest have fled."

"Destroy them."

"Wait!" he cried — their deaths would be on his hands. "There are Augments on the ship, government assets."

The guards behind him gasped, causing the commandant to give them a side-long look. "I am aware," she said.

"I've seen the facilities," said Halud, "The Speakers want them alive."

The commandant turned away. "We have what we want." She gave a discreet nod to one of the officers. "Augment 005478F is your sister. She was the primary target, you are a nice bonus. The rest are unimportant, nothing more than bait in a trap, and will be destroyed along with your crew."

The bridge officer walked towards them, his footfalls measured and even. He passed Halud and shot the two guards. They fell unceremoniously to the floor, smouldering wounds in the centre of their foreheads.

An involuntary gasp escaped. Halud's heart thrashed, encouraging him to flee. But he forced his feet to stay steady, staring at the commandant for explanation.

She licked the corner of her mouth. "Unfortunately for the lieutenants, information pertaining to the Augments is heavily classified."

No one on the bridge seemed alarmed or upset.

His jaw clenched. He would have to be strong, for her. But that's what the disease did, it made you stronger. "Kill me then."

The commandant smirked. "Sadly, no. Believe me, Poet, that was my recommendation, but unfortunately, it seems you are too great an asset to lose."

"What will happen to me then?"

"You'll be returned to your rightful, Gods-given position. Speaker Lansford has been worried about you."

In the view screen, the little freightship spiraled out of control, bouncing off debris, spinning erratically. They plummeted, straight for one of the moons, lighting up an explosion of flame and dust.

"Gods," he gasped.

"Life signs?" barked the commandant.

"I'm not reading any," reported the Lieutenant controlling the scanners. "But a heavy magnetic field is distorting our sensors."

"No one could have survived that, Ma'am," said the pilot. "They impacted going over 345,000kph."

The commandant growled, deep and ferocious.

Halud said a prayer in his head, not daring to move his hands in the normal supplication. The ship, the crew, the Augments were gone. He was Sarrin's only hope now, really he had been all along. He managed to crack that up, but he could be stronger, smarter. It would be more difficult, for sure, but he would save his sister.

"Very well," said the commandant. "Plot the jumps for Etar 1."

"Wait," said Halud. "I want to see my sister."

Her lip curled, and she turned to him with cold, hard eyes.

"You will never see your sister again."

* * *

Kieran let out a gleeful whoop. He bounced wildly, suspended in a body harness, staring out the open cargo bay doors as giant dust clouds slowly settled.

Grant turned. "We did it!"

"Holy cow. I can't believe that worked."

When the ship impacted on the moon, they opened the doors and blew out six barrels of deuterium, twelve torpedoes, and twenty-eight pounds of explosive.

"Of course it worked," Grant smirked. "You asked for a massive explosion."

"That was crazy," breathed Kieran, only now becoming aware of his heart beating painfully fast. He sucked air from his O2 tank, greedily taking breaths. "I'm glad you were here to trigger the bombs."

Grant nodded, lifting his laz-rifle in acknowledgement. He hung, similarly suspended, but he had only a breathing mask over his mottled brown suit. "I saw you hit a couple, too."

"I think I might have shot up the inside of the ship more than anything," laughed Kieran, gesturing to the rifle strapped across his own chest.

Grant's singular exposed eye twinkled. "You are a pretty bad shot." They laughed, far longer and louder than normal. Grant sobered first. "You sure did a lot of other good things today, yeah."

Kieran unclipped himself from the harness, slowly floating down to the floor with the moon's low gravity. He caught himself, nearly tumbling over as his feet touched down on the very tilted floor. Artificial gravity generators were offline and the ship stuck sideways in the dirt. "You too, Grant. I'm sorry about before."

Grant landed beside him, grinned, and jumped into a triple flip. "Do you think we're in the clear?"

"Too early to tell." Kieran shrugged. Immediately, his mind started to worry. They were in a very bad position if the warship decided to investigate closely.

First problem: the lower cargo bay door ripped off when they opened it. If he couldn't seal the doors, he couldn't re-pressurize the bay. If they couldn't pressurize the bay, they couldn't open the doors to get back into the ship.

Second problem: they were ass-over-tea-kettle and half-buried on a moon. At least one thruster had ripped off completely. Who knew what else they lost pin-balling around the debris field. Somehow, they had to get space-borne again.

Third problem: low G and space-walks made Kieran nauseous. Always. Without exception.

"Hey, Kieran," said Grant. "I'm sorry too. You should have come with us."

Kieran shrugged. "You don't have to say that."

"Sarrin wanted you there. She told me I was a fool for not bringing you. You know, before she fell."

Bile floated up the back of Kieran's throat. He couldn't let himself think about Sarrin right now. They had to repair the ship before anything else.

It only took two leaps to reach the edge of the cargo bay, where the tilted floor met open space over a jagged edge of torn metal and wires. The door was missing entirely, probably floating somewhere or incinerated in the explosion — absolutely no chance of fixing it and depressurizing the cargo bay. The nearest airlock was the shuttle bay, four decks up.

Grant landed beside him. "So, we're good?"

"Huh?"

"You and me. You're sorry, I'm sorry. Everything is good?"

"As soon as we get Sarrin back."

Grant nodded. "Then let's go." He looked up, aimed himself, and jumped, seemingly headed for the vast empty field of stars.

Sweat beaded on Kieran's back. He hated spacewalks. When he was a boy, one of the engineers performing an extra-vehicular repair fell off going near the speed of light. Every effort to get him back just pushed him farther away. Who knew how long it took him to die.

At least there was a bit of gravity here, he told himself, at least he would land somewhere. Cautiously, he maneuvered to the edge of the doorway, careful of his suit on the sharp edges. That was a whole other set of problems with space. He pressed hard into the hall panelling, shaking.

"You okay, Kieran?" Grant called from above, his voice laced with actual concern.

Kieran forced himself to nod. "Yeah, 'm okay."

Grant jumped down smoothly to a ledge just above Kieran, offering his hand.

Kieran tried to crawl, desperately clinging to the slick paneling with even slicker boots.

"You have to jump," Grant said awkwardly. "The hull is tilted and you're just going to slide down."

Kieran's feet slipped. He glanced down, seeing the end of the ship and a long drop to the lunar surface below. Even with the low gravity, that fall would still cripple a person for a long time.

And he needed to go get Sarrin.

"Come on, I'll catch you."

He gritted his teeth, terrified but more terrified of falling, and jumped as hard as he could, feet slipping as he took off. The

uneven pressure sent him into a slow spin, already shooting way
too far. A vision of the engineer floating off into the abyss flashed
in his mind.

Grant's hand snapped around his leg. Both floated up into
the air a little, until Grant tugged him and they came back down.

"I don't like spacewalks," admitted Kieran.

Grant nodded, then cast his gaze up to the shuttle hangar.
"One of the shuttles is missing."

"What?"

"Yeah, one of the bays is open and the shuttle is gone. Come
on, it's not far. Go slow but keep moving."

Kieran nodded, despite the acrid taste burning in his mouth.
He had to do it. He started to crawl up the tilted side of the ship,
Grant behind him. Once, his foot pushed too hard and he started
to lift up, but Grant pressed him back down.

They reached the open shuttle bay, Kieran clinging to the
ledge, gasping for breath he didn't know he'd been holding.

"How long has it been?" Kieran asked.

"Twenty minutes-standard."

"The warship hasn't attacked yet." Maybe, just maybe, they
did believe they had imploded on the rock.

They climbed into the open shuttle bay, letting gravity slowly
pull them down the tilted tunnel to the airlock. Grant accessed
the controls and shut the external door. The bay re-pressurized.

The internal door slid open, and gravity pulled them to the
sideways wall. Grant's suit slipped back to it's hiding spot in his
upper back, and they both pulled off their masks.

"Does that hurt?" Kieran asked, gesturing to his bleeding
back.

Grant shrugged.

Gal moaned from where he lay crumpled in the corner. He

reached around, looking for something. "We're cracked," he said matter-of-factly.

Grant frowned, bouncing over to toe the captain in the side. "What happened to the other shuttle?"

"Huh? What?"

"There's a shuttle missing."

"Oh, yeah. Poet took it. Have you seen my —."

"Halud took it?" Kieran said. "When? Where did he go?"

Gal shrugged. "Don't know." Suddenly his eyes focussed, and he sat up and smiled.

Kieran followed his gaze to the flask, caught on the bench by his feet. He grabbed it, clenching his fist. "Is this what you're looking for?" The cruelness in his voice surprising him.

Gal nodded, like a puppet.

"Where did he go?" Kieran asked sweetly.

Gal squirmed and started to sweat. "I don't know."

"You can remember, if you want this back."

He scratched his arms violently, grumbling to himself. "Coward went to save his sister."

Grant and Kieran looked at each other. "Where did he go?" Kieran asked slowly. "To the planet, or…?"

"The ship."

"The warship?" Grant ran a hand over his head. "He's more cracked than I thought."

Kieran threw the flask at Gal, a bone to the old dog. They made their way to the bridge, his stomach starting to settle the slightest bit as they crawled through the sideways corridors.

The bridge smelled a bit like vomit, but everyone looked okay. They held onto consoles or braced themselves between the floor and wall, sitting quietly, waiting.

"Halud took a shuttle," Grant said without pre-amble, "he

went to the warship."

Hoepe's eyes opened wide, where he sat perched on the arm of the captain's chair.

Grant reached to turn on a console, bracing himself against another station to access it. "Worth a scan, right?" But the console didn't turn on.

"All non-essential systems are offline," Hoepe said, "to avoid detection."

"Maybe we can still help him," said Kieran, eyeing the navigation console and its scanner.

Hoepe shook his head. "He was probably blown apart in the firefight. He had no experience piloting a shuttle."

Grant sighed. "He's Sarrin's brother. We have to look."

"Even if he made it through, he would have been shot on sight for being a traitor," said Hoepe.

"She'll be devastated," said Grant.

"She might not be alive."

Kieran's legs finally gave out, and he clutched a console behind him.

"She is," said Grant. "I have to believe that. They set a trap, they want her alive."

Hoepe shook his head. "If we're caught here, we'll all be dead and then no one will be able to help Sarrin. No scans. No gravity. No nothing."

All the energy left Kieran with a whoosh, his hand barely rubbing over his shock-tired face as he clung to the console just to keep himself upright.

"We can't just leave him," said Grant. "Sure, he's caused some problems, but he's Sarrin's brother."

Hoepe pressed his lips together. "How do you propose we go and help him?"

"There's a way." But Grant shook his head, his voice dropping to a whisper. "We'll get him. We'll get Sarrin."

"This is war. There are casualties," Hoepe said, his voice flat. "He knew that as well as anyone. We have to look after ourselves."

Grant's head bowed in acquiescence. "You're right."

"Wait. No, he's not." Kieran pulled himself to his feet. He shouldn't interfere, but his nerves were already past the point of frayed. "'Look after ourselves'? An hour ago, you wanted to save everybody. We infiltrated an UEC facility to rescue Augments. Sarrin's going to be crushed if he's not here. Why can't we infiltrate a warship to rescue Halud? We've been on that warship before."

"We can't —."

Kieran's fists clenched irrationally. "Is this because he's just a — what do you call us — a common?"

"That's not it at all," said Grant.

A sudden coldness drained his core, but Kieran set his jaw. "Are you telling me that if Rayne or I were trapped in the facility, you would come for us? Because I'm starting to think you wouldn't. I've given you the benefit of the doubt, I've helped you. I know you've said some not nice things about me, about 'commons', but this is too far. Just because Halud's not like you doesn't mean we can let him rot."

"Kieran." Hoepe held up a hand.

"No! How is that fair? You can't choose like that. We're all in this mess together."

Grant and Hoepe shared a look. "We're not choosing." Grant stepped forward. "I know I said some not-nice things. I was angry. I was wrong. I'm sorry. But you're got the wrong idea."

"Halud's not a common," said Hoepe. "He's an Augment."

Kieran's eyes narrowed. "What?"

"Halud is an Augment, and somehow he hid that for twenty years while he worked directly with the Speakers. He saved us in the war, and he rescued Sarrin. Halud was incredibly capable, and — if by some grace of the Gods he is not dead already — he may very well survive."

Kieran took a step back, shaking his head in disbelief. "What? How do you know?"

Grant shrugged. "His eyes."

"The virus, the genes it encodes, changes the eye colour."

The crystal blue irises — of course Kieran had noticed the striking, inhuman colour, but he hadn't put together what it meant. Around the room, identical sets of eyes stared at him. Only Rayne's were a dark, dull brown. "But that's worse isn't it — if he's an Augment? We have to save him from the warship."

"We would if we could, but I don't see how," said Grant.

"The same way we snuck onto the warship before."

Raising a single eyebrow, Hoepe said, "With our ship that can't fly, and our cloaking device that emits dangerous levels of inverse gamma radiation? We only got on that warship before because they wanted us there."

Kieran gasped. "You don't know that."

The doctor shut his eyes. "But I do, I'm sure of it. I should have known it then too. Sarrin didn't escape from Selousa. They let her go. And I wanted her to be free so badly, I refused to see it."

Grant whispered, "They were controlling us, controlling her."

"They've controlled every aspect of our lives," said another Augment.

Hoepe sighed. "We've fallen right into their trap. Each and

every one of us."

A heaviness settled over the bridge, Kieran felt it crushing his chest. "Hardly," he said into the silence. He looked around the room, meeting each set of bright, blue, genetically-enhanced eyes. "They've controlled your lives, but right now, they think you're all dead. You're unpredictable. Which, I think, is probably a huge advantage. We're going to find Sarrin. We're going to find Halud. And we're all going to do it together."

* * *

Gravity pressed down on Sarrin's chest, holding her to the cold, hard table. She struggled, knowing it was futile but wanting to thrash all the same. The short gravitational field emitted close to thirty-eight times standard. Even if she could stand, her bones would shatter under the weight. The darkness crowded in, convincing her it could set her free.

Don't lose yourself. Kieran's voice pulled her back from the edge. She panted wildly, pushing the monster away. Her eyes cast around for a solution, for any hope that could stop the rising panic.

"You know better than that, Sarrin," Guitteriez's disembodied voice scratched across the room from behind her. "You know there is no escape from a gravity well." Footsteps echoing in the sterile room — soft, soft, thunk, his walking stick hitting the hard floor as he came forward stopping directly in front. "Do you like our new machines, Sarrin?" he said, dangerously close to touching. Bloody serum seeped from his jagged scar. "We designed them just for you."

She followed his gaze to one of the blue orb towers. The guard beside it pressed a switch, and instantly fire lit inside her hands, pouring into the rest of her body. Her muscles collapsed underneath her, and for a minute, she was sure the gravity well would suck her in and crush her.

"Interesting, yes? I thought perhaps this might capture more of your attention, since our previous experiments failed to elicit much reaction."

Never had she felt anything like it, nothing like the pain the machines emitted. And yet, the doctor and the soldiers in the room barely blinked.

"I know what you did to the nurse."

Her eyes flared open.

He grinned at her wickedly. "Do you even know what you did to the nurse?"

The memory assaulted her: *Sarrin lay in her tiny, dark and damp cell, completely empty following a round of experiments. She hadn't even had the energy to lift her head when the researchers entered the room and carried her back for more.*

The nurse — Rebecca, who had brought her books as a little girl — reached out to her, holding her hand. It was warm and loving, and Sarrin drank in the sensation hungrily. And the nurse had fallen, before Sarrin could even realize what was happening, or why she had felt so suddenly so much more alive.

"You pulled all of the life-energy out of her," said Guitteriez, watching her closely. "You drained hers to feed your own. Absolutely fascinating." He clicked his tongue as he walked around the far side of the bed. "It was then we learned about your extreme sensitive to energetic fields, especially those of others. And yet you never showed any of us that ability again, not even after we changed your hands. But I started thinking about you, and about energy and emotion and this fabric plane we call reality. And I think there's more you can do." He whacked the table with his walking stick, the clang making her jump. He snarled, "You're going to show me everything, no matter what it takes. You'll have no choice. I can make you feel such pain that your body will take over and try to save itself."

She kept her eyes firmly shut. *Don't lose yourself.*

He waited, watching for a full minute.

The fire engulfed her body again, making her cry out.

"This device emits concentrated negative energy. For the rest of us, it's nothing more than an annoying little buzz, but for you… I can't even imagine what that must feel like, but you must want it to stop. I can stop it, if you want."

She clenched her hands, futilely trying to hide them. They had not been changed for strength or precision, no. The alloy was a superconductor, designed to transfer energy, uninhibited. And they had designed a weapon that her super-conducting hands were unable to resist. She felt it all, bare to the desperation and misery the weapon emitted.

"Show me what you can do." The doctor grinned, made sinister by his scar.

She shook her head.

The table jerked and lifted her up. Suddenly, the gravity-well turned off, and she collapsed on to the floor. The fire-pain started anew, and she curled into a quivering-heap. A circle of pulsating blue-orbs surrounded her.

She threw an arm out, desperately dragging herself away.

Two guards approached, unfazed by the ring of devices. They lifted her with gloved hands — muscles too limp to resist, her body too exhausted to even try — and tied her arms to a hook that dangled from the ceiling. The restraints dug into the bundle of nerves that had been stripped from her hands and bunched carelessly at her wrists. The physical pain was welcome relief.

Guitteriez approached again, stopping to look in her eyes. He laughed. "You know, in all the years, this is the most docile you've ever been." A sick and twisted emotion rolled off him: glee. Lifting his hand, he showed her his thick, black gloves. He threw a fake punch, stopping short of her nose, then a few playful jabs, and laughed again. He placed his hand on her face, and caressed her cheek

With what little strength she had, Sarrin rolled her head and chomped.

She missed his hand entirely, but it still made him jump, and he pulled his hand back, checking for damage. Anger creased his forehead, the scar knitting into a ferocious hook. He motioned and two assistants came forward. A new machine carried between them, long wires spilling off the back.

They attached sensors to her fingers and an imaging halo to her skull with their gloved hands.

"Level 1," instructed Guitteriez. The others stepped back, but he stayed.

A white hot current of energy seared through her. Images and charts flashed on the screens. Guitteriez nodded, motioning for it to be done again. Over and over.

Lights and colours danced in her eyes. The edges of her vision clouded. *Don't lose yourself.* But what was she — what was herself — to lose? Nothing was concrete, somewhere between awake and unconscious, alive and dead. A vast emptiness opened deep in her abdomen, horrible and hollow.

She clenched her jaw, fighting against the monster inside herself even more than she fought Guitteriez. What secrets were buried there? What was inside her? What if she showed him? What would he do to her then?

The machine stopped. A reprieve. Everything collapsed until only the ties around her wrists held her up. The physical pain grounded her, and she blinked, seeing her surroundings once again.

"Stand up." Guitteriez hit her with his stick. "Stand up!"

She managed to look up at him, hopefully feigning a look of defiance or hate. Anything to cover the utter desperation.

He scowled. "Level 2."

New found pain arced through her body, pulsing again and again. Strong muscles went into violent spasms, threatening to tear her apart from the inside.

"Oh, I wish it wasn't you." Guitteriez grabbed her between shocks, yanking on her jaw, forcing her to face him. "You made me look foolish, Sarrin. All those years I spent working on you, and you're so stubborn. But you were always special, always the one. I've tried pushing the others, but no one can do the things you do. We're stuck with each other." He shook her, hard. A sliver of his exposed skin touched her, and she felt cold tendrils crawl into her skin. "The way you fight. They way you think," he continued, cold tendrils growing more and more desperate. "There is more, I know it," he shouted. "Show it to me!"

Another jolt ran through her, blinding her. Her mind went far away, walling itself off from the pain.

NINETEEN

KIERAN SWALLOWED DOWN THE BILE that crept up the back of his throat. He was staring to get used to the low gravity — point-two-one g's, he's been told — but he still clutched the edge of the engine room's doorway to steady himself.

It was a good thing the gravity was so weak, or he would have fallen, his knees buckling at the sight of his beloved engine. Everything had melted together, all the wires and computer chips ending up in one solid chunk. The relays in the exposed floor were still smoking. The ion chambers were empty. And the FTL laid in three scattered pieces. The damn Kepheus Drive had come loose, and he couldn't even see where it had gone in all the mess.

He kicked the stupid engine out of sheer frustration. The impact sent him flying back in the low gravity, floating through the air and bouncing down on his rump.

"That bad?" Rayne stood in the doorway looking him, a data tablet in her hands.

He sighed, carefully maneuvering back onto his feet. "Yep," he said, forcing a smile.

"You'll fix it. I know you will."

He could only grunt in response. He had to fix it, there was no other option. But all he wanted was to scream and smash everything on the stupid ship with his stupid hands.

"Hoepe wants you to drink this," she said, holding out a small cup. "For the nausea."

He eyed the thick, green liquid, plugged his nose, and downed it in one gulp. Apparently, his stomach hated low-gravity even more than it did during zero-g training at the academy. The sticky, foul medicine smeared down his throat, making him gag, but at least it stopped his stomach rolling. "Thanks," he said.

She nodded once. "How does it look?"

"Bad." He rested his hand on the engine casing, taking in as much of the damage as he could. Something about the action made him think of Sarrin, of the way she ran her wrist across the smooth surface, leaning her ear down to hear its vibrations. His breath caught and he coughed, sputtering up some of the green liquid. Leaning on the engine, he gasped, "What are you doing here, Rayne?"

"Facilitating." Her hands clenched on her tablet. "I don't know what else to do." They stared at each other for a moment, until Rayne cleared her throat primly, expression molding into well-practiced, professional attention. "I'm trying to assign work crews — what do you need help with?"

"Everything." Earlier, he had gone for another spacewalk, assessing the damage to the hull. Magnetic lunar dust buried half the ship. The entire port-aft wing complex had been torn off, including the thrusters and landing struts. What hull plating he could see had ripped off in huge patches, making atmospheric entry dangerous if not impossible. "Two of the Augments are trying to figure out how to fix some thrusters to replace the ones we lost. Someone else is figuring out how to unbury us from the dust." He had no idea how they were doing — they'd sent him in when he vomited in his spacesuit for the second time, and Hoepe had forbidden the use of communication devices, lest the warship pick up any of their signals.

It had been three hours since they had crashed the ship, faking their deaths on the moon. So far, the warship hadn't arrived to finish the job, but they had no way of knowing where it was or what it was doing. For all he knew, it hovered over them, watching and having a good laugh.

A rough knock sounded at the doorway, and one of the Augments leaned, back from assessing the thrusters. She rubbed her arm through her spacesuit. There were some pretty significant looking laz-wounds on her arms, but Hoepe had bandaged them and cleared her for duty. Kieran hated to think how the others looked, considering most of them were still being assessed and treated in the infirmary. She beckoned him into the main engineering bay. "We have an idea."

Kieran followed her to the central console, Rayne close behind. Three others moved around slowly, cleaning up the debris from the deck. One of them limped visibly, another had their arm in a sling. "How are your burns?" he asked.

"Minor," she said. She triggered the basic display, touring him around a schematic of the ship as she explained. "We're planning to move some of the thruster banks from the other arms and tie them in on what remains of the post-aft wing. We'll be able to balance the thrust then."

Kieran frowned at the schematic. "Is this all that's left?"

"We haven't seen the starboard thrusters, but we were able to access and assess the other wings. It looks like a little less than half survived the impact."

"Half!" His legs wobbled again. He slammed his hands on the console. "There has to be more than this!"

She leaned back, eyeing him warily.

"Sorry." Suppressing the urge to scream, he reached for the console's controls, elbowing the Augment out of the way. His quick calculations confirmed what he suspected. "We're not going to have enough lift to get off the moon."

"It's all we've got."

"We need more." He looked to Rayne, silently pleading she had an answer, but she could only shrug. He tried another calculation, and another, slamming his hand on the console when they kept returning the same answer. They were stuck on the planet.

Rayne laid a light hand on his shoulder. "We'll get her back," she said softly.

His chest crumpled, and he leaned agains the console, no longer able to support his own weight.

"What if we salvaged some thrusters from the debris field?" Rayne asked hopefully.

Kieran shook his head.

The other Augment added, "Hoepe won't let us take a shuttle out, the warship would see us for sure."

His breath started to come back to him. He pressed his palms against his eyes, wiping away moisture that collected there. "We don't have days to wait around for the warship to leave."

"Well, what do we have?" asked Rayne, her tablet poised. "You're the best engineer I've ever met. You'll think of something."

Kieran frowned. He was not the best engineer he'd ever met. No, that honour went to a girl currently captured on the planet, terrible things happening to her. And he had let her go, even when she didn't want to. He'd just let it happen.

And their ship was buried on some unknown moon. That was his idea. He'd gotten everyone into this mess. Sarrin was going to die, just like the rest of them. Some observer he turned out to be.

"The Gods always have a Plan," said Rayne. "Faith, and Strength, and Prudence, Fortitude, and Knowledge." She listed the Gods, bringing her fingers together one by one and then tapping them on her chest in supplication. "There must be something we can use. Some spare part, some connection, some obscure piece of machinery…. Anything? Something about the moon, itself? I don't know. Think, Kieran!"

But he couldn't. Instead, his mind flashed pictures of Sarrin: Sarrin crawling through the engine, Sarrin freezing and escaping into the wall, Sarrin smirking as she handed him the weapons she had collected.

He shook his head, trying to pull it together.

He needed to write a letter home.

He needed to sort through this mess.

He needed to rescue Sarrin.

* * *

Hoepe sighed and looked down the line of Augments. He'd worked hard to find them, but he had never imagined it would be like this. They braced themselves in the still-sideways corridor outside of the infirmary. Many clutched arms or legs. Some lay unconscious on the deck, worn out after the adrenalin of escape in their weakened states. He'd already treated or discharged half, but the line remained long.

He beckoned the next one into the infirmary, rubbing a hand over his exhausted eyes. The fight with the warship and the worry of rescuing everyone had weighed more heavily than he thought.

And while he should be excited at seeing so many of the Augments safe, he felt nothing but an open pit of longing and a desperate urge to run screaming. As though he had been looking for something his entire life, and it seemed so close but never found.

The short and stocky Augment entered and climbed onto the examining table. A deep laz-bolt wound seeped across his upper arm, cutting through the deltoid muscle, the arm hanging limp by his side.

"It's not that bad," he said through gritted teeth, "but you told me to wait. I suppose I'm not that useful with only an arm and a half." The man shuffled back and forth where he sat.

Hoepe nodded, injecting local anesthetic as he held the arm to keep it still. He opened the skin with a 10-blade steel scalpel, extending the wound so he could visualize the muscle fully. The wound was deep, and the man flinched when Hoepe probed it. "Sorry. I need you to hold still."

The man gave an apologetic smile, which did nothing to reassure Hoepe that he would actually sit quietly.

He sprayed a numbing agent into the wound and proceeded to dissect the burnt bits of muscle from the healthy tissue, testing and stretching it across the gap. He frowned, "It will be tight, but I can appose the edges — I don't have any artificial mesh."

"Sure, Doc, whatever you say."

"It's going to hurt for a few days until the muscle stretches."

The man shrugged.

"Don't move."

"Yeah, I heard you the first time."

Hoepe took a heavy suture and pulled the edges together, working the muscle until it connected across the missing chunk. Satisfied with the apposition, he used a smaller gauge and sewed it together.

The Augment fidgeted, shimmying his entire body but thankfully leaving the arm in one place. He let out a pain-filled sigh. "Hey, you remember that time that we broke into that training facility in Northcott?"

"Pardon?" Hoepe's hand stilled as he looked at the man, wondering if he had forgotten some key event or person in his life, but he remembered everything — they all did.

The Augment looked at Hoepe, flailing his good arm expressively. "Yeah, you remember. You, me, and Donovan. You wanted to try the combat plexus, and nearly shot Donovan's foot off."

The suture snapped in his hand. "I did no such thing."

The man gave him a hard look. "Come on, Leove."

"Love what?"

Hoepe felt himself under intense scrutiny as the man stared at him. His heart leapt irrationally.

A smile quirked on the edges of his lips. "I thought you were someone else."

Hoepe continued his suturing, but the man wouldn't stop staring at him. He wiped a liquid adhesive over the skin wound, tapping the man lightly on the back. "That's finished. Any other injuries?"

The man shook his head.

"Good." Hoepe ushered him off the table, calling out instructions to rest at the same time as he beckoned the next patient in.

Hurried footsteps and anxious voices caught his ear, and he paused in the doorway. Three men rushed down the corridor, a fourth carried between them unconscious, his breathing shallow. Boiling blisters covered half his face, and his sleeve had melted into his arm. "What happened?" shouted Hoepe.

"He was decompressing the ion overload," Kieran said. "Forgot to open the pressure valve."

"Ion burns," said another voice, deep and tauntingly familiar. Hoepe looked up.

Kieran continued, but Hoepe had stopped. He and the other man stared at each other. Both unnaturally tall, both with long, hooked noses and dark features. Each a perfect mirror of the other.

The other man grinned, and then hurried to catch up. Hoepe followed as Kieran and the other man laid the injured on the table, and his twin started a rapid medical examination.

"I shoulda been paying attention," said Kieran. "I'm sorry. I didn't see what he was doing." He pressed his hands against his jaw, stepping back. He looked between Hoepe and the identical stranger. "Oh yeah, there's two of you. Hoepe meet Leove."

The stranger looked up at him. A brother. A twin brother. Another half of himself. "Do you have a low-frequency electron lamp?"

The fast moving hands of his brother snapped Hoepe back to attention, and he stepped forward, starting his own medical palpation. "No. I'll start colloids for the shock. We can fashion a cold poultice. The bandage material is" — he kicked the floor, still strewn with medical supplies —"on the floor."

A wry grin twisted his brother's features. "I see." Hoepe's soul sung.

Kieran and the other man returned to Engineering, leaving the brothers to work in the tiny infirmary. Together they healed, side by side, each action anticipating the other's. With their patient stable, they moved him to the low bench to recover.

"It's too bad he was injured on the ship," said Leove. "It is unlike Ramirez to miss a simple step."

Hoepe frowned. "They are exhausted and malnourished."

"Yes." His brother paled, rubbing his face in the same way Hoepe did only when he felt the worst defeat. "Doctor Guitteriez continues his experiments. I'm afraid what he did in Evangecore would be considered gentle."

"You are safe now." Hoepe reached out and, not knowing what else to do, started to examine his brother.

Leove stopped him. "I'm alright. There's much to do."

"You were in that facility too."

"Yes, and I worry about your friend. Guitteriez is unstable. Many were submitted to experiments and never returned. He has no inhibition now, no remorse for killing any of us. If he was willing to let us all go to capture her, I hate to think what he has planned."

"Then this is very bad indeed."

* * *

Sarrin slammed back into reality with a gasp. Cold water drenched her bones where she hung, still suspended from the machine.

"No time for sleep." Guitteriez thumped his cane on the ground.

The machine shocked her. Level three.

A vein across his forehead pulsed, his eyes as black as demons. "Why won't you show it to me?"

She fought a wail. Another shock, and this time she did cry out. She'd had it all, everything she wanted.

"I can make it stop, Sarrin."

Blindly, she shook her head. "I don't know what you want." Spittle dribbled down her chin.

Another shock. "You do know."

Pain shot across her temple, and she whimpered. Her training in Evagecore, the experiments on Selousa, nothing had been like this. The blue-orb machines pulsated around her. Despair withered her bones.

She pictured Kieran — a friend. Pictured his easy smile and laugh. Remembered the way he tossed around his mis-matched puzzle cube and chatted with her about engine repairs. The way he hadn't once asked her about fighting, and his easy acceptance — almost nonchalance — about what had happened when she attacked him after leaving the warship. She had liked it. She felt good and whole.

Guitteriez sauntered forward, leaning on his cane. His face contorted into a taunting pout. "Poor, Sarrin. So trusting. So happy to toodle around the stars, tra-la-la. You didn't think we would really let you walk away from Selousa." He tapped her skull. "We've been following you, my dear."

Everything — Halud, Hoepe, Kieran — was not meant to be. Guitteriez had orchestrated it. A cruel temptation to loosen her mental barriers.

"It was necessary to move you. They thought it wasn't safe, but I explained. Explained what it is you truly want Sarrin, and then it was easy to manipulate you. You and your little friends skitter away enough times, your engine breaks, and you arrive at Junk. You see a long-lost friend, and you can't help yourself. You have to help. Isn't that what got you caught in the first place, helping your friends? The only risk was tying you to that wretched commandant."

Foolishly, Sarrin reached for her temple, hand catching on the restraints. Energy pulsed there, loud and clear. How had she not seen it before? Because she hadn't wanted to. The signs had been obvious: the burst of pain when they infiltrated the warship, the ache each time the warship emerged; they were tracking her.

"They say that the commandant is my greatest achievement, but you are, Sarrin. Did you know that?" He reached for her, tilting her chin, forcing her to look into his hideous scowl. "Your friend, the nurse, she begged me. Said you were just a little girl. But we both know better. You're the answer, and I'm going to have it one way or another."

He pulled his hand away and the pulse tore into her, shrieking up her veins.

"Show me! Tell me!" he growled.

Another shriek, this time hers.

He grabbed her throat, squeezing. "I chased you halfway across the galaxy. Dozens of my experiments set free, right into the arms of the hunter. I gave up everything." His cane flew up, catching her lip and driving it across her teeth. He stared at her, panting. "Why did I do that? Because you're it, Sarrin. You've always been it, from the moment you climbed that observation tower and cut my face wide open. You're not leaving this room until I get what I want."

The pulse slammed into her full force. Bright hues of green and pink and blue glazed her vision. When she surfaced again, the echo of her own screaming and wailing slammed her in the gut.

He loomed over her. "A war is coming. And you're the weapon we need. I told the nurse, I'm not cruel. I did what had to be done. She understood it, now tell me she didn't die in vain."

"You don't understand," croaked Sarrin. But it was her that didn't understand.

"Level four," ordered Guitteriez.

* * *

Hoepe studied his brother surreptitiously. There were minor

differences: an extra fold in the lines by Leove's mouth, darker circles under his eyes, a few days of stubble on his chin. But otherwise, entirely the same. Even the movements of his hands as he studied a data tablet, and the set of his brow furrowed in concentration.

A knock sounded at the door to the infirmary.

They had finished clearing the injured Augments from the corridor an hour ago, only the burned man still laying unconscious on the bench. But Hoepe's heart jumped to his throat, fearing a new casualty.

His brother must have had the same thought and also jumped to his feet, addressing the girl who stood in the doorway. "What can we do for you?"

"Um." She hesitated and looked between the two of them. "The engineer — the common you said we could trust, he's —."

Hoepe shot to his feet. "What's happened to Kieran?" If Kieran couldn't fix the ship, they might all end up dead on this moon after all.

"He's okay," she started, "But he's acting strange. Seems kind of cracked."

"He is a bit odd," Hoepe reassured her.

"Well, he hasn't slept. He keeps talking to himself. He's asking for all these things we've never heard of, crazy things that don't make sense."

Leove glanced at him. "Mental overwhelm, acute psychiatric break."

Hoepe shook his head. "No, not Kieran." He turned to the woman. "Has he said anything dangerous? I'm sure it all makes sense."

"Perhaps we should go and examine him," suggested Leove.

The woman led the way to engineering. The gravity

generators had been fixed, so at least they could walk on the floor normally, even if they still tilted slightly.

The doors opened, and immediately Hoepe's eyes landed on Kieran. His face was red, and he shouted loudly, firing order in multiple directions, walking up and down the engineering bay and reaching his hands in and out of different projects.

"After Rami — Ramirez — got hurt, he came back and sat in his office. We were scrubbing the ion manifold when he suddenly came out and grabbed me. He said 'the moon is magnetic', and then he started all of this."

Hoepe raised a single eyebrow.

Kieran leaned over an Augment's shoulder, peering down at the data tablet they were working on. "Naw," he said, taking the tablet, "it'll work better if we counteract the ion thrust. I want you to spin it around."

"But that's —."

"I don't care what the protocol says, it's gonna work better if it's spun around." He pushed the tablet back to her and strode away.

The Augment stood stunned, then took the tablet to confer with another group. They too looked over the drawings and shook their heads.

Hoepe glanced quickly at Leove and took a deep breath, marching forward. "Kieran," he called out.

The engineer turned, a manic and likely over-medicated smile spreading on his features. "Hey, Hoepe!" He did a double take. "And Leove. Who's who?" Kieran started moving again, and Hoepe followed. "To what do I owe the pleasure. I thought you would have been up to your eyeballs in work."

"Well," started Hoepe, glancing back. But his brother only shook his head and hung back. "I wanted to talk to you, actually."

"Oh? What's up?"

"I came to see if you needed help."

"Super. There's a lot to do. Annika could probably use some help scrubbing the ion manifolds." He gestured to the woman who still hung by the door with Leove.

"That's not quite what I had in mind." He steeled himself. "I need minute of your time."

"I'm a little busy, Doc."

His long legs kept stride easily beside Kieran's frantic pace. He clenched his hands behind his back. "People have asked me to talk to you because they're worried."

Kieran glanced at him. "Worried? I'm fine."

"I don't know if that's true." He reached his hand out to feel his pressure nodes, but Kieran spun away too fast.

"Yer right. I am a little stressed."

Hoepe nodded. "When was the last time you slept?"

Kieran looked away.

Hoepe sighed. "I know; we're worried too. But you have to look out for yourself. You're not built for days without sleep."

Kieran tensed, snarling, "Because I'm a 'common'."

"That's not what this is about," Hoepe said.

Leove stepped up beside him. "We're trying to look out for you. People are upset about the things you're asking them to do. I know these are all good engineers who know what they're doing, and they're telling us they're confused."

"I'm fine. I know what I'm doing." Kieran waved his hands in the air. "But I don't have time to explain every little thing. I've been in an engine room my entire life, seen more than you could dream of." He turned away, pulling out an auto syringe and injecting it into his arm.

Hoepe frowned. "How many stims have you taken, Kieran?"

"I'm fine."

"Let me see." He took it from the engineer's hands, turning the syringe. The cartridge was nearly out of doses. "Kieran, this is dangerous. You're going to make a mistake. You're going to hurt yourself or someone else."

He held a hand to his forehead, eyelids drooping shut for just a minute. But he inhaled sharply, eyes snapping open again. "We have to get her back."

A noise came from the engine room, and Kieran spun away, disappearing into the other room.

The woman who had come to find them sighed. "At least you tried. For what it's worth, I like Kieran. He does always have an explanation for what he's asking, and it's usually brilliant. But he's cracked. This can't continue."

Hoepe clenched the cartridge in his palm. "I know. Keep an eye on him. I switched his stim cartridge for a sedative. When he falls asleep, tuck him away somewhere quiet."

Her mouth hung open, but she closed it and nodded.

Hoepe bent his head and retreated, Leove close behind him. "He's a good engineer," he said once they were in the corridor, feeling the need to justify himself.

"I can tell you have a great deal of respect for him. Annika as well."

Hoepe stopped, his legs suddenly too heavy to carry on. He pressed his forehead into the wall.

Leove waited patiently.

"I'm afraid I just sedated our best chance at survival."

An understanding hum came from Leove.

"This is far more than I anticipated. When the Poet told me he had found Sarrin and could get her out, I didn't look at it. I didn't think there would still be facilities or experiments. I just thought about seeing someone I knew again." Leove maneuvered him gently, pushing him down the corridor with his arm wrapped around Hoepe's shoulders. "I'm glad we were able to rescue you, but there are thirty badly injured Augments, a dozen commons, a wrecked ship, and Guitteriez and his warship wanting us dead."

"At least we are in it together."

TWENTY

"READY, KIERAN?"

KIERAN CLENCHED HIS jaw. "You don't hafta treat me with kid gloves." Immediately, he sighed and rubbed his jaw in his hands. Three days of digging in the lunar dirt, transposing thrusters from one section to another, re-routing conduits, and the ship was maybe ready to try to push off the rock. The FTL still hadn't been repaired, but it could wait — Sarrin couldn't.

Anger roiled in his gut when he thought of Hoepe switching his stims for seds and the hours he'd lost, but there were far better uses of his time now. He turned back to the obviously-annoyed pilot, asking her to go over the heavily modified engine controls one last time, and she indulged him. Satisfied, he nodded to Hoepe. "Ready as we'll ever be."

"Take a rest."

He gritted his teeth. "I'm fine."

"You've earned some sleep, I think."

"I did sleep." For three hours. Kieran clenched his fists and bit his tongue.

"Not enough."

Realistically, he knew Hoepe was right. His body sagged and his vision had gone a bit funny, begging for sleep. But he couldn't rest. Every time he closed his eyes, his imagination ran wild — what were they doing to her? "Let's just get this goddam boat off this goddam rock."

It had taken him longer than he wanted to admit to realize that the moon was magnetic, and their shield, the pieces that were left of it anyway, could be rigged to generate a matching, repulsive magnetic field. At his order, the pilot fired each of the thruster groups independently, shaking the last bits of dust off the wings. He flicked a finger over the controls, and the magnetic field engaged, giving them enough boost to break away from the moon's surface.

He slumped down to the floor, the adrenaline that had been supporting him now completely spent. "Think she's still alive?"

No one responded. Hoepe approached, features as angular and horrifying and grim as ever. "You should sleep, your adrenal glands are depleted."

"I can't."

"Let me help you."

"I don't want to sleep!"

"Shut up, Kieran." Hoepe pushed him over, laying Kieran on the deck, and dug his long fingers into the tight knots across his back, twisting trigger points. Kieran cried out in pain for an instant, until the tiredness and Hoepe's ministrations overtook him, sending him floating in a warm, quasi-sleep.

* * *

Dried blood streaked her nose and ears. Three days of this, and still Sarrin had not died. She groaned inwardly at the realization, laying where they had left her, crumpled in a pile on the floor. Her skin crawled where new procedural marks had been branded into her.

In the last session, they had turned the machine up to five, and she had started hallucinating.

Her dreams were of unusual ungulate creatures, taller than a man with four legs and single hooves. They had flowing hair on their necks and a long tail. Their eyes were kind and understanding. She sat atop one while it ran — across fields, though forest, through the surf on a sandy beach. It was flying, it was freedom. She was in the place of the Gods.

She had assumed she had died. Finally. But cruelly, she woke up. Cold and naked and alone.

The machines glowed around her, the weight of their negative emotion stream crushing her soul. She forced her body to be still, even as its muscles shook from hunger. Her hands she braced slightly in the air, keeping them from resting against the manacles, which now ran a constant electric current.

A door slid open and Guitteriez entered. *Step-step-thunk.* The soldiers, fussing at their machines and outputs, snapped to attention.

The shuffles came closed, and he poked her with his walking stick. Sarrin let her body roll, too weak to fight it, and he pushed until she flopped over, sending a shock through her wrists.

"So, you are awake," he snorted, wicked glee dancing across his eyes. "Good."

Her wrist shackles tightened and lifted her by her arms. The researchers attached their electrodes.

"Do you have anything to show me?" Guitteriez said.

If she could have lifted her head, she would have spit on him. Maybe vomit. It didn't matter though, it would be over soon enough. Her body had already gone long past its point of resistance. Her heart beat irregularly and she had no feeling in the lower part of her body — in most of her body.

The monster had retreated far to the back corners of the room, where it watched her so she both saw through her eyes and saw herself through its eyes.

"I didn't think so," he sneered, stepping back. "Let us resume."

Pain was a distant, corporeal sensation, far from the place she sent her mind. Soon, she would pass out and return to the dream world forever. She was satisfied. This was always how it was going to end. How it should end. Such a vicious monster could not be allowed to live.

But the dream didn't come. She phased in and out, but always came back to the same dark room, the same screams, the same pain.

Guitteriez leaned back on his stool, studying her EEG, his hand gently manipulating dials. He played with her, keeping her teetering on the edge of torture and release. He would not kill her, it would not be so easy. He took great pains to make sure she stayed alive and conscious.

He was a monster.

Something stirred in her, dark and dense and angry. The monster lifted its head, snarling. Dark tendrils wrapped around her. It whispered until a growl left her own throat.

She had tried for years to keep it in, while they fought to bring it out, never understanding exactly what it was. She had tolerated it, even welcomed the pain, ashamed and fearful for herself of what lay buried inside. But she feared she could not hold it much longer.

The monster reminded her of all she had to lose. *I am me and mine alone* — words from one of the Halud's poems jumped into her head. More words, the writings of John P this time: *To fight is to live and to cede is to die.* And Kieran, *Don't lose yourself.*

But if she stayed here, she had already lost.

The monster shook, calling, promising. It vibrated until she could not control it anymore. Sagging, she closed her eyes and let it in.

Bottled inside for decades, it could finally have its revenge. The scream built inside her, rocketing off every neuron and synapse. She was Sarrin, the girl who defied Evangecore. The girl who attacked and killed twenty-seven guards during a training exercise. Sarrin, when they isolated her and brutalized her and turned her into a thing.

A small part of her retreated, curling in the corner, and let out a terrified peep.

Thirty-two objects that could be used as weapons. Seven targets. One escape.

I cannot be controlled by things external, the monster recited. *I am me and mine alone. I am me and mine alone. I am ME and MINE ALONE.* Her muscles coiled.

Guitteriez studied the read-outs mildly, flicking a lazy finger to order the machine's intensity increased.

Fool.

They had delved too deep in Evangecore, opening her mind, releasing secrets no human should know. He begged, but she never let him see.

For a minute, she was back in her isolated cell, waking from an experiment. Her hands trembled, objects in the room tumbling through the air. Hands sensitive enough to pull energy out of objects could shape it too.

She hid it, always. Wanted to believe it wasn't true.

But not now.

Time slowed. Her pulse flowed, heart shaking with the force

of each beat. Thump — thump — thump. Muscles spasmed and released, neurons fired electric current through their axons. Billions of her pieces and parts moved as one, held together by will alone.

Sarrin flicked her hand.

The lights went out. The guards shouted. The large, centre display screen ripped from the wall and flew across the room. Guitteriez fell to the ground.

She willed the restraints on her arms to release, and they did.

With a grunt, she made a clawing motion with her hands, and pulled.

Guitteriez screamed.

Everything in the world, every piece of matter, was made of energy. Energy that came from each living soul, giving rise to the physical world around them. She had been sensitized, could see it plain in front of her, and now that energy acted at her will. She dug in to Guitteriez, pulling him apart. Pulled until his molecules no longer felt their bonds and he scattered, dead.

The soldiers started to move. They rose from their chairs and hoisted their laz-rifles, beams of light buzzing across the room. They were far too slow to hit her, and Sarrin slipped casually out of the way.

With a flip of her hand, she sent the guards backwards into the wall.

Almost an afterthought, pain flared in her temple. She drove her fingers through the flesh, blood catching in her fingernails. She pulled out the small tracking chip — less than a centimetre square — it pulsed twice and went out, crushed between her fingers.

Anger coursed through her — no way to distinguish how much was the monster's and how much was hers. They would all burn. The room lit on fire, flames springing up spontaneously from the walls and floor. The door lock melted away at her request, and she strode into the hall.

The monster sketched a schematic of the compound, showing her the forty-six guards as blinking target blips on her map.

A fire alarm rang out, distantly.

The targets stopped their patrol, and she could feel their confusion as they stared at each other.

Her iron hand ripped the door off a nearby weapons locker, and she stowed away three laz-rifles, two pistols, and a throwing knife. This was what she was trained for, after all.

Two target-blips raced toward her, and the knife embedded in the guard's skull before he had finished turning the corner. The second, stopped short behind him — an easy target for her laz-rifle.

Ding-omega.

Reinforcements arrived. Sarrin ran straight into them. In one swift leap, she snapped one's neck and knocked another two unconscious. The fourth, she drove her elbow into his eye, crushing the socket and sending splinters into his brain.

Ding, ding, d-ding, ding.

The quiet voice tucked away in the back of her brain, nearly out of sight, whimpered, *Brutal.*

More guard-blips shuffled through the building. Sarrin viewed the building beyond herself, she was only a piece in the puzzle, a character in a vid-arcade. The girl-weapon ran, igniting the corridor behind her.

Fire climbed the walls and burst from electrical panels, consuming the compound. The flames licked up into the chemical storage tanks, and the powerful explosion tore the fortified construction apart at the seams.

Sarrin ran for the door, leaping as the flames licked around her ankles. She hit the tarmac, rolling with the impact. Heat seared over her in waves. Finding her feet, she started to run.

And run and run and run.

Run! screamed the small voice.

Her exhausted legs wobbled, her foot missed, and she fell. The impact crashed her back into herself, and she suddenly saw out of her own eyes. Blood filled her nostrils. Her hands too were covered, and she felt the sticky drops all over her face.

Vomit sprayed across the ground. Breath escaped, impossible to catch. Each brutal moment came crashing over her, remembered in excruciating detail. Tears streamed, blurring her eyes so she could see nothing but memories. She had killed fifty-seven men. Brutal, brutal.

She fell to her side against the cold tarmac.

Monster.

She should have died in there. But they wouldn't give her that peace, not even after all this time.

Legs pulled tight to her chest, she waited. Death would come for her. Sooner or later.

TWENTY-ONE

KIERAN LAID ON THE DECK, in a half-dream state — relaxed, not asleep. He should send word to his parents or they would start worrying and come rescue him. Maybe his sister Lauren would like to see them. He frowned, that didn't make sense.

Hoepe nudged him with the toe of his boot, and he gasped, fully awake again. "What?"

"Come on, we're approaching orbit."

Kieran sat up and realized the bridge had nearly emptied. The rescue team would already be assembling in the shuttle hangar. Hoepe pushed an auto syringe to his neck. The stim surged through his body instantly, making his heart beat faster than it should and his hands tremble. The doctor pressed something else in that made his heart stabilize so it wasn't so painful.

"Be careful, Kieran," Hoepe clapped him on the shoulder. "And bring her back."

Kieran nodded and ran to the Hangar. Rayne handed him a laz-rifle and gave him a grim nod. He climbed into the shuttle, taking his place beside Grant.

The door closed and the airlock decompressed. They started moving into space. Tension filled the air, and Kieran's knee wouldn't stop shaking.

"Engineer, you shouldn't be here," said one of the Augments. "This will be dangerous, your seat should have been saved for someone useful."

Grant put a hand on his leg, forcing it to be still. "Kieran's the most useful person here. I made the mistake of not bringing him before, and it nearly cost all our lives. I hope it hasn't cost Sarrin's."

Kieran's eyes went wide.

He whispered for just Kieran to hear. "I was wrong before. I've gotten so used to being against everyone, it was hard for me to accept help. But you've proven your worth to me, again and again."

As the shuttle flew, the Augments started supplicating, touching their fingers to their chests and then foreheads, repeating the motion over and over. Strange, that people who had suffered so much at the hands of the Speakers could still believe so devoutly in their Gods, but they must figure they could use all the help they could get. Glancing around to be sure no one was looking, Kieran moved his hand, making the sign of the cross, and prayed.

Into the silence, Grant said, "We walk the Path of the Gods, my friends." Around them, the Augments beat their fists to their chests, right over their hearts, and cheered. Then Grant held out a small data tablet. "I brought a poem," he announced. Then he turned to Kieran and explained: "In the war, we used to always read something from Sarrin's brother before a mission or a battle or anything like that. We used to get messages from him in the poems sometimes, about the UECs plans or traps. But this one is just encouragement — I think."

Someone chuckled.

Grant read:

> *Fiercely battle, for what you believe*
> *Fear has no tract, that I can see*
> *Nothing to hold you, nothing to win*
> *But, fear can be brave,*
> *If you let it come in.*

> *Take what you need from this fear that you see*
> *Take its courage, its wisdom, take what you need*
> *But the fear cannot control you, cannot make you bleed.*
> *Its fight is what guides you, what makes you proceed.*

> *Take it to heart, this strength in the fear*
> *Believe in it always, we will be near.*
> *You have everything to fear, everything to fight.*
> *Belief in yourself,*
> *It's for you that I write.*

* * *

The shuttle bounced through the thin atmosphere.

"Uh, you're going to want to come look at this," the shuttle pilot said, turning in his seat.

Grant and Kieran surged forward, pushing anyone else aside. They peered out the viewport. Ahead, where the facility should have been, laid only rubble and smouldering ash.

"UECs must have bombed it," commented the co-pilot.

Kieran's stomach dropped — after everything, she couldn't be dead. She just couldn't.

"We'll check it out anyway," said Grant. "Maybe we can find

some information."

The pilot nodded and angled the shuttle down.

Kieran waited by the door, every muscle in his body trembling, waiting to spring into action. The adrenalin and stims mixed in his body, and he started to feel woozy. His knees buckled with the impact as the shuttle landed, but Grant caught him without a word.

The rear door barely opened before Kieran leapt out, stumbling on unsteady legs.

"Kieran!" Grant shouted from far behind.

Smoke clouded the landscape. Burning piles of con-plas littered the ground, leaving an acrid stench. Kieran had long since abandoned any notion of a plan or a search pattern, and he pulled his sleeve over his mouth, running into the wreckage.

"Kieran, slow down." Grant caught his shoulder and spun him around.

Kieran blinked. His eyes caught on something fleshy. A charred arm lay across the ground, the rest of the body nowhere to be seen. He dropped to his knees. The arm was red and black, bubbled and disfigured. Where the flesh had melted away shone bright white bone. "It's bone," panted Kieran. Not alloy.

"What?"

Kieran stumbled ahead. His eyes darted from jagged, torn supports to scattered, flaming cargo containers. Chemical's in the air stung, but he blinked back tears and pushed on.

"Look!" Grant shouted and pushed past. He couldn't see what Grant saw, but he followed him running into the haze.

Something small and pale lay in a clear patch.

"Sarrin!" He pushed his legs even faster, screaming, "Sarrin! Sarrin!"

She lay curled into a ball, smeared with dirt and completely naked. They stood stock still, three paces from her. Kieran's eye caught on the new brand over her ribs. "Is she…?"

"I don't know," answered Grant.

Her body jerked with a sharp inhale. Kieran threw himself to the ground next to her. Her shoulder trembled, cold under his hand. Her eyes stared at ahead, unblinking and unseeing. "Sarrin?"

Another jolt wracked her tiny frame. Her crystal blue eyes went wide, searching back and forth. Startlingly, they focussed on Kieran. "Don't touch me," she whispered, too weak to move away.

"Gods," muttered Grant. "Come on, we have to get her out of here."

Kieran threw his jacket over her and lifted her into his arms. So much for observation only. He knew he'd lost himself in this, but it didn't matter.

Her hand fumbled, groping for the side of her head. Blood streaked through her hair and across her face.

Kieran gasped. "Jesus."

Grant pulled back her hair. "It's not that bad."

She reached for her head again. "We have tracking chips."

Grant reached for his own temple.

"I killed them all," she said, her voice gravely and quiet. Her hands dug into Kieran's shirt, dried blood flaking from them. "Don't touch me."

He pulled her closer.

"Pretend you're asleep, Sar." Grant rubbed ash onto her cheeks, blotting away the moisture that tore bright streaks through the dirt there. "No one cries in Evangecore," he explained.

Kieran felt her slump even further into his arms, her eyes closed, arm hanging limp. Only the desperate grip on his shirt told him she was still awake, still alive.

He brought her back to the shuttled, the others crowding around. Some reached out to touch her, murmuring with a both awe and dread.

In his arms, she didn't react, a perfect mimic of unconsciousness, her head rolling unnaturally to the side.

Grant pushed Kieran onto the shuttle, forcing him all the way to the front and into the co-pilot seat with Sarrin on his lap. He barely waited for the others to board before he closed the hatch and engaged the thrusters, taking them away from the planet.

He pulled her tight to him, even as her grip relented and she slipped away.

TWENTY-TWO

SARRIN LAID STILL A LONG time, her back to the room, pretending to be asleep. She stared at the starchart on the wall, studying every detail. It held a dramatic appeal, something she couldn't quite name, but it captured her attention completely. Another mystery she couldn't solve.

Kieran watched her from across the room. He slumped tiredly. He had slept a little earlier, but not much.

Her body felt dead. A constant sensation of falling held her down. Even if she wanted to turn around, she wasn't sure if she could. She was caught in the grav-well all over again. Her heart beat at a steady forty beats-per-minute, the pulse shaking her body with every push of blood, reminding her that she was very much, in fact, alive.

The door chimed, and Kieran rose to answer it. Hoepe's voice carried into the room: "How is she?"

Kieran grunted once, rubbing a tired hand sloppily over his face. "Still asleep."

"Do you need anything? You should try to get some rest."

"No, I'm alright. Everything going okay in Engineering?"

"Yes, I was just there."

"Any luck with the FTL?"

A pause. "No, not yet."

"Warship?"

"No sign. We're taking out everyone's tracking chips. So far, Sarrin's is the only one that was active."

Another pause, and the muffled sound of something exchanging hands. "Rayne found her these."

"Thanks."

The door closed and sealed. Kieran shuffled back, leaving the parcel on the table before dropping himself into the chair.

"How did your sister die?" The question surprised Sarrin as it came past her lips.

"Huh?"

Her mind had latched onto something in Kieran's incongruous room, and she needed to know why. She repeated herself.

He paused a long time. "It's been a long couple days," he said.

"I want to know." It felt different to be asking the questions, but maybe some small part of her had earned it.

He finally admitted, "Old age."

Surprised, Sarrin rolled over to study the picture on the nightstand, even though its image had been perfectly etched in her memory. "She's younger than you," she observed.

"Yeah." He scratched the back of his neck, staring at a spot on the floor. "That's the problem with time, isn't it? It's always relative."

Indeed. Some days were long. Others were short. "How old are you?"

He laughed, once quick and sad. "Twenty-three."

"How old was your sister?"

His lips pressed together, twisting to the side in thought. "I'm not quite sure. I got word that she had died a few weeks before I went to the academy."

"I'm sorry."

Kieran quirked a smile, but it didn't reach the rest of his features.

Sarrin studied the picture again. "You loved her?"

He nodded. "I'd give anything to see her again. I miss her everyday." His voice cracked and he dropped his head in his two hands.

Sarrin turned away, his grief slamming into her full force. She pushed down a sob. What a fool she had been, with her brother just down the hall. She hadn't said two words to him.

But Kieran's sister dying of old age made no sense. Relativity didn't apply unless travelling at sub-luminal speeds — grav-hole FTL jumps were instantaneous. "I don't understand," she said.

"Don't understand what?"

"How your sister died when you're so young."

A strange expression passed across his face. "Sarrin, try to get some sleep."

A thought occurred. "Unless you've been travelling near the speed of light and she wasn't." Her eyes locked on his.

"I shouldn't have told you any of that."

"Why did you?"

"I don't know." He sighed, slumping back in his chair again. "Maybe… maybe because you remind me of her."

Thoughts started to combine: his strange expressions, unexpected solutions, the unknown quality about him and his room. "You come from a place that exists outside standard time?"

"Yes." He gauged her, staring intently into her eyes. "I grew up on a ship travelling nine-tenths the speed of light. We —."

Her heart raced, and the last three days were forgotten. "An Observer? I remember my — my friend told me stories." Observers lived for centuries, seeing everything from their ship in the stars. "I think she was encouraging me to behave."

The corners of his lips eased up. "I can't imagine how much trouble you were as a child."

"But I can see you?" she whispered.

He laughed out loud, the melodious sound stirring her chest. "I don't know what your stories say, but I'm still just human."

Human — the thing that she wasn't. She swallowed, mouth suddenly dry. "What are you doing here?"

"Learning," he said. "I don't know why I'm telling you this. Maybe it's just good to see a smile on your face. Maybe because I've broken more rules than I can count." His hand rubbed across his temples. "I'm just glad you're alright. When they told me you were gone, I…."

She pulled away as his hand reached out.

"Sorry," he stammered.

But it was her that was sorry. She turned away and stared at the starchart — some distant galaxy his ship passed through, that's why she couldn't recognize it. Maybe that was her escape, to go somewhere that no one knew existed.

The sutures on her hands had faded to invisible fine lines, but the healing was superficial.

"The good news is," Kieran said, "we saved all of the Augments from Junk. Everyone is safe now, including you."

She would never be safe. Guitteriez was gone, but others would continue. There had been cameras in the room she didn't disable.

"Sarrin?"

She should tell him what happened on Junk. He was a friend. He could help. But what would he say? Would he see her for the monster she was truly? She tested the words on her tongue, but each combination felt worse than the last.

"I have bad news too." He shifted uncomfortably. "Your brother, Halud, he's missing."

"Missing?" She didn't want to believe, but she couldn't sense any part of him on the ship. "What happened? Where is he?" She struggled out of the bed, numb legs folding as they hit the ground.

"Sarrin!" He reached to help her.

"Don't touch me!" she screamed. If he died, if she killed him….

"I know, I know. Just, please — sit back down. Hoepe says you need to rest. Whatever happened on Junk nearly killed you."

She pulled herself up with her arms, failing body collapsing onto the mattress.

"Halud left the ship while we were attacked by the warship. We think he tried to stop them. No one had any idea he'd left until after."

Sarrin crawled to the pillow. Halud gone, and she hadn't said a single word to him.

"I'm so sorry. Hoepe wanted me to tell you."

She shook her head, voice pleading, "What if they've taken him. I don't know what they'll do."

"Probably, his shuttle blew apart in the firefight."

"He can't be dead."

"We'll find him," he placated her. "As soon as the ship isn't falling apart."

"There's a war coming, Kieran. That's what Guitteriez said. They'll use him. Against me." She paused. How to make him understand something she barely understood herself? "Halud thought Gal could help us."

"Gal doesn't know up from down, right now."

"He's our only chance."

* * *

Gal swirled the warm liquid around his cup, letting the sweet, spicy aroma wash over him. It was comfort, it was peace — if only for a minute. The empty bottle stood on the desk in front of him, the very last of it in his hand. Tiny grey hands reached from all sides, threatening to pull him down.

He breathed deep, savouring the Jin-Jiu, relishing in every minute of the experience.

The demons, stronger now, closer, clawed at his skin, leaving it cracked and bleeding. They pulled at his hair and swiped at his eyes. A fist reached in and pulled at his spinal cord, making his chest dance like a puppet.

One of the demons leaned close, it's slimy breath chilling across his cheek. *It's your fault.*

He blinked — it couldn't be. At the back of the room stood Rayne. He willed it to stop, but everything was inevitable. The demons fell around him, dying out in a wave. Rayne fell.

"No," he gasped. Scrambling from his chair, he rushed over to grab her. Demon Rayne disappeared in his arms.

"You killed her," said a voice.

Gal spun around, panting.

Aaron sat on his desk, his head tilted with a silly smile. "You killed them all."

His heart pounded in his chest. "I didn't kill anybody."

The apparition flipped his head back and forth, weighing, deciding. "Nobody?"

"Not me. They — they all wanted to."

"What about me? You brought me there. Try to drink me away all you'd like, but I'm still here. I'll always be here."

"That's not fair!" he screamed.

"Death for John P." Aaron gave him a pointed stare. "You drowned him, Gal."

"He was drowning me." His voice nothing more than a whisper in the freightship, but it echoed around in his head like a storm of flash smoke and ash.

"More than now?"

On his knees, Gal clutched at his scalp, squeezing his brain to make it all stop.

The demon voice whispered to him, *You knew they were dangerous.*

Yes. All the warning signs had been there, the writing on every single wall — literally.

You disobeyed the Gods, and now look at you.

Their orders were clear: report them, destroy them, fear them. For Gods' sake, don't help them!

Who were you to do what you did?

A fool. If, if, if — too many wrong turns on the road. How did he end up on this path?

In the Gods we Trust.

A flash of red jolted across his vision. "There's no such thing as Gods!" he shouted out loud. "You don't know what they were doing, what they're trying to destroy!"

Aaron arched an eyebrow. "Why did you give up?"

He shook his head, the voices quiet, for now. "This fight is too big. No way to win." The liquid sloshed dangerously close to the edge of the trembling cup. He brought it to his lips and drank.

"So that's it? You're out. Now what happens? How will you

forget all the people you abandoned. They didn't have anyone else to fight for them, Johnny."

He threw back the rest of the Jin-Jiu. The last of it, gone.

The warm liquid ran down his throat and coated his insides, drowning the demons.

It was always cold in space.

The Story Continues....

Traitor by C R MacFarlane
Red Fever Book 2
Coming August 2018

Pre-Order available on Amazon

Stranded above Junk, the crew rushes to repair the wrecked freightship. Tempers flare between the Augments and former UEC officers. Time ticks down before the expected reappearance of the warship Comrade and her Commander, bent on the merciless destruction of every last Augment.

A mysterious planet may be the safe haven they have been hoping for, but Gal refuses, adamant they must not go but unable to offer an explanation why. Determined to keep them from reaching the demon planet, Gal will stop short of nothing, including destroying his own ship to keep them from discovering the secrets of his past he has buried so deep.

Meanwhile, Halud is transported back to Etar, where he continues his dangerous game with Hap Lansford and the Central Army Speakers.

Traitor is a story of sabotage, desperation, and the limits of human endurance.

About the Author...

C R MacFarlane is an award winning author of short stories and poetry. Fascinated by the human experience, her fiction strives to explore deep and meaningful themes in exciting ways. She lives in Alberta with her ever-patient husband, three cats, dog, and horse.

Augment is her debut novel.

More of her work can be found at

www.thewritable.com

@CRMacFarlane

CRMacFarlane